WHAT ARE
THE CHANCES

WHAT ARE
THE CHANCES

KENNY ROGERS

with MIKE BLAKELY

A TOM DOHERTY ASSOCIATES BOOK

NEW YORK

This is a work of fiction. All of the characters, organizations, and events portrayed in this novel are either products of the authors' imaginations or are used fictitiously.

WHAT ARE THE CHANCES

A Forge Book
Published by Tom Doherty Associates, LLC
175 Fifth Avenue
New York, NY 10010

www.tor-forge.com

Forge® is a registered trademark of Tom Doherty Associates, LLC.

Library of Congress Cataloging-in-Publication Data

Rogers, Kenny.
    What are the chances / Kenny Rogers, Mike Blakely. — First Edition.
        p. cm.
    ISBN 978-0-7653-2385-9 (hardcover)
    ISBN 978-1-4668-2485-0 (e-book)
    1. Musicians—Fiction. 2. Gambling—Fiction. I. Blakely, Mike. II. Title.
    PS3568.O444W57 2013
    813'.54—dc23

                                                            2013018349

Forge books may be purchased for educational, business, or promotional use. For information on bulk purchases, please contact Macmillan Corporate and Premium Sales Department at 1-800-221-7945, extension 5442, or write specialmarkets@macmillan.com.

First Edition: September 2013

Printed in the United States of America

0 9 8 7 6 5 4 3 2 1

To all of those who have ever played Texas hold 'em
and know what decisions have to be made,
how quickly they must be made,
and the consequences for making them . . .

ACKNOWLEDGMENTS

Writing an autobiography is one thing, but writing a book that has peaks and valleys and maintains a person's interest all the way to the end is something altogether different. So I called on my cowriter, Mike Blakely, who obviously has spent a lot of time in Texas and knows the people and the lifestyle well. I gave him an idea that was originally considered for an episode of *The Gambler* series, but it felt more current than the Old West. Mike did some amazing things with these ideas, and took them to a level I could have never achieved. The book itself is written in true Texas style—a fast-paced story with plenty of excitement, twists, and turns . . . the ending is awesome. My thanks to Mike for developing this book and allowing my input. I truly hope we can do more together.

I would also like to thank our editor, Bob Gleason, who must be a poker player himself. His enthusiasm for this project was never ending.

WHAT ARE
THE CHANCES

PROLOGUE

I PROMISED my cousin Dan that I would not tell the tale of what we had gotten away with in the summer of 1975 until Archie Zeller had died and gone on to his reward, which may well have been a flaming eternity in hell. I promised I would wait until Zeller's death to set this story down in ink because Zeller—Archie "Whipstock" Zeller, also known as Archie "Wildcat" Zeller—was the only soul alive who might have pressed charges against us for our crime.

"And, Dan," I added, "if you're really worried about the story messing up your reputation, I'll wait until you pass on, too. I mean, assuming that I outlive you."

Dan had laughed himself teary-eyed when I told him that. "Cuz," he finally said—he always called me Cuz—"I don't give a hoot who you tell. Reputation? That's a laugh. Anyway, you *know* you're gonna outlive me. I'll be lucky to see the ripe old age of thirty-five, the way I've been livin'."

He had a point. Dan was a wild one. He liked motorcycles and broncs, barrooms and dangerous women. For a while he flew a crop duster for a living, and he didn't even have a pilot's license. He was the nicest guy in the world, and funny as hell, but if you crossed him, he'd just as soon whip your ass as look at you. He was not afraid of anything that walked, flew, or swam.

Ever since we were kids, growing up together in the countryside outside of Houston, Texas, he had been the poster boy for moronic fearlessness. On the football field, in a rodeo arena, or wading among gators and water moccasins in the bayous, he would just shrug at things that could hurt or kill him, the way most people would brush away a mosquito. I think he lived for the chance to cheat death, to tell you the truth. He liked to jump off bridges and run drag races on those long, straight roads between the corn and cotton fields outside of town. He was just born to hunt down danger of the most perilous stripe—look it in the eye, spit in its face, and laugh as he tangled with it.

The summer before we graduated from high school, he became a rodeo clown—a bullfighter as they call themselves these days. He invented this stunt where he'd get the bull facing him—snortin', slobberin', and pawin' the dirt—then he'd sprint right at the bull, step on his head, and run down his back before that bull even knew what had happened. You see a lot of rodeo bullfighters using that trick today, but Dan invented it. He was crazy. Wild. Fearless. And good as gold.

Dan was the drummer in my first band. He had good rhythm, and he hit the skins hard. We started out as a four-piece garage band—just a bunch of high school kids playing the hit rock and country songs of the day. When I started making up my own songs, Dan was the first to encourage me. My songs were sort of a blend of country and rock. These days, I'm sometimes credited with helping to start the "progressive country" movement, along with the Eagles, the Flying Burrito Brothers, Pure Prairie League, Gram Parsons, and some others.

I don't know about all that, but I do know that Dan started promoting the hell out of the band, and my original tunes, and got us some great shows for a bunch of high school boys. He used his country-boy charisma to BS our band into a showcase outside the Astrodome during the Houston Livestock Show and Rodeo.

The Houston Rodeo always featured a huge country music act in the middle of all the rodeo events. I forget who the headliner was inside the dome the day we got to play outside it for the folks waiting in line to get in, but apparently the headliner must have been a Walnut Records recording artist, because an A&R guy from Walnut's L.A. office discovered me there and offered me a staff songwriter

deal in la-la land. (Excuse my industry jargon; A&R stands for Artists and Repertoire; the A&R guy is the label exec in charge of
finding new talent.) The monthly pay Walnut Records offered me
as a tunesmith would barely amount to enough for rent and gro-
ceries, but held the promise of royalties should one of my songs get
recorded.

The day after I graduated from high school, I left for California,
and things really started to happen with my music. Within a year, I
had started a new band—Ronnie Breed and the Half Breeds—and
we landed a recording contract with Walnut. You might remember
that we had half a dozen hit songs on the pop charts in the late sixties and early seventies. We were marketed as a rock band, and we
could rock and roll with the best of them, but my songs had country
themes and influences, even though we produced them as rockers.
Our last hit, called "If Love Was a Pawnshop," which included a
steel guitar and a fiddle, actually crossed over to the country charts.

Because I was in L.A., I would run into some Hollywood types at
celebrity events and plain old bars. Some movie-studio talent scout
liked my "look" for a supporting role in a Western film, and so began my side career as an actor. One of the films I appeared in had
me sitting at a poker table in a high-stakes game, and because of
that, I earned a reputation as a gambler. I liked that rep, so I milked
it, writing a couple of tunes about games of chance, and playing in
celebrity poker events in Vegas.

One crapshoot I did not win was the draft lottery. My number
never came up, so I did not have to interrupt my burgeoning music
career for an all-expense-paid trip to Vietnam. Cousin Dan, on the
other hand, volunteered for the Marine Corps. He was on a six-
man recon team that they'd drop behind enemy lines from a Huey
helicopter. His team got into an all-night firefight in the jungle one
night and Dan got all shot up and punctured with shrapnel, but
through pure guts and orneriness he stayed conscious until dawn
and fought off the enemy until a chopper could shoot its way in
there and extract the dead and wounded. They gave Dan the Silver
Star for that mission.

"They would have given me the Medal of Honor," he told me years later, "but you have to have two witnesses to get the Medal of Honor, and only one ol' boy other than me lived to see breakfast."

I've recorded some gold records, but Dan wore a Silver Star on his chest. Nobody ever shot at me in a recording studio.

After he recovered from his wounds, Dan got recruited into some sort of top secret military intelligence outfit. After that, I didn't hear from him as often. God only knows what he was doing, and where, during those days.

So, anyway, I promised Dan I wouldn't tell this story until he was dead and gone, should I manage to outlive him. That's when he told me he didn't expect to see the age of thirty-five.

"What makes you so sure I'm gonna outlive you?" I replied.

He laughed and punched me on the shoulder and said, "You're the smart, careful one, remember? You're gonna die rich and famous with platinum records all over your walls—an old man in some mansion. We all have our own date with destiny."

It turns out Dan was something of a prophet, although he did live beyond thirty-five. Made it all the way to fifty-six, as a matter of fact. He died on September 15, 2001—just four days after 9/11. Folks have pretty much forgotten this, but that was the date that a barge hit the Queen Isabella Causeway leading to South Padre Island, Texas, in the middle of the night. Two sections of the causeway collapsed.

Before the police could get there and close the road, five vehicles drove off that broken bridge and plunged eighty-five feet into the bay. Nine people died, including my cousin Dan Campbell. At first, some folks thought it was another terrorist attack related to 9/11, but it was just a tragic accident.

Anyway, Dan was driving his vintage Thunderbird convertible alone over the causeway that night. They found the T-Bird sunk quite a distance beyond the other cars that plummeted into the fifty-foot-deep waters of the Laguna Madre. That meant that he had been driving faster than the other vehicles. Well, of course he was driving faster. He was Dan Campbell.

I've got this image in my head. Somehow I know—I just know—that when Dan spotted that void in the causeway in his headlights, and knew he was too close and driving too fast even to attempt hitting the brakes and saving his life—he gunned it. He stomped on it, pedal to the metal. I just *know* he did. He sailed out into that void, yelling for pure joy. I know what he was thinking: *What a way to end it all!* I bet he wished he could somehow ignite the T-Bird right then and go out in a blazing fireball.

So, the Prophet Dan was right about not outliving me. He also predicted my future with a fair degree of accuracy. Here I sit, looking out over the hills from my mansion outside of Nashville, Tennessee, twenty-some-odd gold and platinum records on the wall. I lose count.

It's August 2005 as I set this down on paper. I am, as Dan predicted, wealthier than I ever dreamed. A songwriter, singer, musician, record producer, and reluctant movie star. (Making movies is boring as all get-out.) Dan is gone, and I've mourned him longer than he would have liked, so I'm going to tell the story of what we did in the summer of '75. It doesn't seem like that long ago.

I'm a pretty successful composer of three-minute songs, but I never thought of myself as a storybook author. Still, that's what I am attempting here. I'm going to change some names to protect the guilty, and I'm going to set this down as if it were fiction, but I'm here to tell you that this really happened.

I'm not sure what the authorities would have indicted us on if Archie Zeller had pressed charges. Grand larceny maybe? It was a two-million-dollar crime. Like a couple of modern-day Robin Hoods, we got away with it in the summer of '75—my cousin Dan and I.

1

I KNEW it was time to break up the band when that two-thousand-dollar Neumann microphone bounced off the side of my head, leaving a gash just behind my right ear. If you're up on your Ronnie Breed trivia from my rock-and-roll years, you may be familiar with the incident.

The members of my band, Ronnie Breed and the Half Breeds, had gathered at my bungalow in L.A. to learn some new songs I had written, and to make some demos that we could use to land another recording contract with Walnut Records. I had a decent demo studio in my bungalow.

Unfortunately, there had been some bad blood between me and the Half Breeds for years. Musicians—especially the good ones—usually come equipped with egos slightly larger than their talents might warrant. I include myself and my ego in that analysis.

"I'm not making another damn record with you getting top billing!" shouted Joe McLeod, my bass player, even before we could get started on the demos. He was drunk, and I think a little high on something. Probably coke, and I don't mean the cola.

"Well, Joe, I put this band together," I explained. "I hired all y'all, remember? I write the songs and produce the records. I front the band and make the deals. I'm the lead singer. I play guitar, keyboards, banjo, and mandolin. I can even play bass for you, if you want me to."

"You don't know squat," Joe replied, an angry sneer twisting his face. "You'd be nowhere without us."

"Well, maybe so, but you know the label won't let us change the band name. We've been through this. There's no need to confuse our fans after six chart hits. We're Ronnie Breed and the Half Breeds, and that's just all there is to it."

"So, you're a whole Breed, and we're just Half Breeds," Joe said, seething. I vaguely noticed when he picked up the vintage Neumann U 47 microphone, which was about the size, shape, and weight of a full, sixteen-ounce, tallboy beer can.

"How do the rest of you feel?" I asked the other band members.

After a silence, my drummer spoke up. "We're with Joe on this."

"Well, I thought y'all came over to hear some new songs, but that's obviously not going to happen today." I turned to put my favorite vintage Gibson guitar back on the rack.

When I did, Joe threw that Neumann like a pitcher hurling a fastball and hit me just behind my right ear. It hurt, and it made my ears ring. Plus, it made me mad. We were in my home! Nobody throws my own stuff at me in my own house! I turned slowly, looking at the blood on my hand from where I had felt the impact to my head.

"Joe, you've got ten seconds to clear out of here before I start kicking your ass."

Now Joe had to make a stand if he really wanted to try to take over my band. "Try it," he said.

I counted to ten out loud, then put my fists up and stalked toward Joe. That rascal grabbed my brand-new Martin D-28 guitar from a floor rack and started swinging it like a baseball bat. But, being stoned, he swung wild, exposing himself to my jabs, which staggered him. He tried to collect himself to backhand me with the guitar, but I ducked when I saw the six strings and the sunburst coming. The D-28 slipped from his grip, sailed across the studio, and crashed into the cymbals on the drum kit. About then I got him in the jaw with a right cross that dropped him to his knees.

In those days, you didn't want to mess with a Texas country boy from the Gulf Coast. We had all grown up fistfighting for fun, glory, and survival.

"Get him out of here," I said, backing away from Joe so that I wouldn't be tempted to kick him while he was down. I glanced at the Martin he had chunked across the room. The neck had broken, and the back was bashed in.

"You didn't have to do that!" the drummer said.

"He drew first blood," I replied, feeling the warm trickle down the right side of my neck. "If you guys want to start your own band with your own name, this is your chance. I'm done with the Half Breeds. Get out. All of you. I'm *done!*"

And I *was* done. This had been a long time coming. Years of jealousy and backstabbing had led to this. I felt a great relief as the Half Breeds left my bungalow, a groggy Joe McLeod waving good-bye by flashing half a peace sign at me. I took a deep breath and exhaled the tension brought on by years of ill feelings. It was like being on the bottom of a dog pile in a football game, and then everybody gets up off you, and you find yourself still holding the ball. I had been flirting with the notion of going solo for a long time. This moment had opportunity written all over it.

(As for that Martin guitar, I had it braced up and glued back together and I still own it. It looks pretty rough but it sounds great—not unlike me. And Joe? He would soon go to rehab, get straight, find Jesus, and start one of the most successful gospel bands in the country. I still see him and the other Half Breeds occasionally. They're all still in the music business in one way or another. The bad blood has dried up and blown away. There's even some talk of a Half Breeds reunion tour, though the name is not politically correct anymore.)

So, I was going solo! Along with the relief and the opportunity, however, came a measure of fear. Panic, actually. The Half Breeds contract had been a sure thing. A solo deal represented uncharted waters.

I held a paper towel to the back of my head to stop the blood and sat down to have a beer. What now? I needed to call my agent, my manager, and my record label. I realized they would all be in a tizzy over this. Any kind of change always shakes those people up. I didn't care. I was free.

That day was among the most pivotal in my life. The timing was crucial. Had the Half Breeds heard the songs I wanted to demo, I think they would have suffered through another album. It was the best batch of songs I had ever written. If you're a music fan, you probably know most of them. They all became mega hits later on. I might have never gotten clear of that unhappy band, had Joe not chunked that Neumann microphone at me.

The other thing about the timing was that I needed a break from the grind. The music machine had been pushing me way too hard, and I needed a dose of reality. And then there was my cousin Dan.

At this point, because of his military intelligence career, I had lost touch with my cousin, who was really more like a brother. Our mothers were sisters. Dan's mother had married a soldier who had survived World War II only to die in a military plane crash shortly after Dan was conceived. Dan never even knew his own dad. My father was killed in an offshore oil rig accident before I was old enough to remember him.

So Dan and I, both born in 1946, were raised by our single moms. But we did have a male role model—our moms' brother, whom we knew as Uncle Bubba. In those days, a firstborn son in Texas often acquired the nickname of Bubba, which was baby talk for "brother." Our mothers called their brother Bubba, so we called him Uncle Bubba. A bachelor, and a bit of a rounder, Uncle Bubba took his responsibility of raising Dan and me very seriously. We spent hours with him almost every day after school at his little stock farm just outside of town.

Uncle Bubba was tough, kind, funny, and scary all rolled into one, which was just what Dan and I needed. He was the disciplinarian who took a belt to our hind ends if our mothers deemed it necessary. But he taught us everything we needed to know, from manners to boxing techniques, cowboying to horse-trading skills. (Once you learn to horse-trade, you can trade anything.) He could weld, hunt and fish, bust a bronc, plow a field, build a house or a barn, dance the two-step, fix trucks and tractors and outboard motors, act proper in church, and fight his way out of a honky-tonk. By the time we left home, Dan I had learned to do all of the above and more, thanks to our uncle Bubba.

Like I said, I had lost touch with Dan after he got back from Vietnam. Dan was a restless adventurer his whole life, and I never knew where he was half the time. But he was good about checking in whenever he could with a phone call, a postcard, or a surprise visit.

I had, in fact, received a call from him not long before Joe McLeod threw that Neumann mic at me. The conversation went something like this:

"Where the hell have you been?" I had demanded.

"Abroad," he answered vaguely.

"Where?"

"I'd tell you, but I'd have to kill you," he said.

The phone connection was so poor that I could barely hear him over the static at times. "Where are you calling from?"

"You don't want to know. Listen, Cuz, I've cooked up this deal, and I want to let you in on it. In fact, it won't work unless you're in on it."

"Uh-oh," I replied. I had gotten this kind of offer from Dan before. Like the time he recruited me to steal that goat. Not just any goat, but the mascot of a rival football team we were about to play for the state title—the Battlin' Billies, of Fredericksburg, Texas. He had to have me in on that deal because we used my band's PA equipment trailer to hide the stolen goat, which we dyed pink and tied to the flagpole in front of Fredericksburg High School. We never got caught, because Dan had planned the whole enterprise with military precision, and this was before he even went to boot camp. He just had a knack for organized mayhem.

(The plan backfired, however. The Battlin' Billies were so mad about the dye job to their mascot that they beat the snot out of us at the state championship.)

"Dan, what the hell have you cooked up now, and why do you need me in on it?" I said into the phone.

"It has to do with Uncle Bubba's heart."

This got my attention. I had heard from my mom that Uncle Bubba was staring death in the face because of some kind of heart disease I had never heard of before. His only hope was a heart transplant, and this was back in the day when the long-term survival rate of transplant recipients was only about fifty–fifty. Still,

Dan and I loved Uncle Bubba and would do anything we could to give him a chance at a few more good years.

The problem was that transplants were expensive and Uncle Bubba would not take charity. He wouldn't let his family members spend their savings on him. He wouldn't sell his farm to pay for the procedure, either, for he had promised to will the land to Dan and me, and Uncle Bubba never, ever failed to keep a promise. Nor would he agree to burdening taxpayers with his health problems.

"You know I'll do anything to get Uncle Bubba a new ticker," I had said to Dan. "What's your plan?"

Dan had then gone on for several minutes about this wild scheme he had concocted, involving the filming of a pilot show for broadcast television. This didn't surprise me. Dan had an affinity for pipe dreams and high-risk ventures. After describing the television idea, he asked me if I'd help him.

"Dan, you don't know diddly about showbiz. It'll never work."

"There's more to it that I can't talk about over the phone," he replied. "I guarantee it will work, but I need your celebrity status."

"Dan, I can't get involved in something like that without more details," I had admitted. Refusing Dan anything always racked me with guilt, but I knew the label wanted those demos, and a new album, and I did have bills to pay and people on the payroll. Generating a lot of record sales does not always make a guy rich—especially a guy who had not learned how to manage money yet.

"I tell you what, Cuz," he had replied after a well-timed silence and a hurt sigh, "I'll give you some time to think about it, then I'll fly to L.A. and lay the whole plan out for you. I'll call you in a couple of weeks."

At that point, Dan had either hung up or gotten disconnected.

So, here I was, a couple of weeks later, with a paper towel blood-stuck to the side of my head, drinking a cold Corona with a slice of lime and enjoying my newfound feeling of creative freedom, when the phone rang.

"Hello."

"Cuz, you thought any more about that idea of mine?"

As Dan had always reminded me, I'm usually the smart, careful one. But over the years I have experienced lapses. "Count me in!" I sang.

"I thought you wanted to hear the details first."

"It's for Uncle Bubba's heart, right?"

"Right."

"Then I'll do it, whatever it is. I just cleared my calendar for the summer."

"I knew you'd come around! I'll be there this weekend to lay the whole thing out for you in detail."

2

DAN CAME to L.A. and took a couple of days explaining his plan. It took that long to absorb it all, for it was quite complex, as you will find out if you stick with my story. Dan also introduced me to a friend of his named Mona, who almost immediately became my very public girlfriend.

I guess this would be a good time to try to explain my tabloid girlfriend, Mona. If you're a die-hard Ronnie Breed fan, you may have seen some pictures of us together after the Half Breeds broke up. She would follow me from L.A. to Houston even though I had just met her through Dan, and we didn't know each other very well. Still, it was fun to have her hanging on my arm, and we each had our reasons for flaunting our relationship in front of the paparazzi cameras.

Mona was a looker and a live wire. She weighed about ninety-nine pounds soaking wet, and she had a dark, dangerous rocker edge to her. She dressed skimpily and wore gobs of makeup. I grew to like her a lot, but I was never in love with her. Nor did she love me. I guess you could say we were using each other.

I'll tell you one thing: She was trouble, but sometimes trouble is fun. I wonder where she is now. I hope she's alive and well. I can't say I don't occasionally miss her, but I'm glad I didn't have to spend the rest of my life with her. Our very public breakup has become a celebrity legend, complete with a barroom brawl in the world's biggest honky-tonk. But I'm getting way ahead of my story now, so just let me back up.

Less than a month after Dan explained his plan and introduced me to Mona, I had sold all my property in L.A. to settle my debts, and I was on my way home to Houston in my personal tour bus. Most rock stars had drivers for their touring coaches, and I did, too, when I was touring, but I also loved driving the bus myself. I wrote a lot of songs in my head while driving alone. On the way to Houston, I saw some beautiful wild desert and mountain country between the Pacific and the Gulf Coast and took in a trucker's view of Hank's "lost highway."

Arriving in Houston, I drove to the blue-collar suburb of Pasadena, where Dan had made arrangements for me to park my bus out behind a famous honky-tonk called Gilley's. Having driven all night, I arrived on a Thursday morning and slept all day. I awoke at dark and walked to a burger joint for some grub. Then I went back to my bus and got ready for the poker game, for Dan had informed me that we would be playing stud in some warehouse downtown.

Leaving the bus, I strolled toward Gilley's, where I was to meet Dan. I paid my cover charge and entered the huge honky-tonk. I was a few minutes early, so I ordered a beer. Waiting at one of the several bars in the huge dance hall, I sipped my brew and reabsorbed the Texas Gulf Coast lifestyle I had left behind for L.A.: country music, two-stepping dancers, beer, and barroom smoke. It was good to be home.

As I took a pull from the ice-cold bottle, I saw Dan coming across the dance floor through the dense cigarette smoke. Dan had always been tough, but these days he looked like some bare-knuckle fighter, lean and chiseled, with a burr haircut and new tattoos on his arms. His stride across the near-empty dance floor looked like the stalking prowl of a mountain lion. He wore a tight white undershirt to flaunt his physique, with an unbuttoned short-sleeve paisley pearl-snap over it. He looked like the one guy in the bar you didn't want to mess with.

Then he saw me and smiled, and his charisma kicked in, and he looked like the one guy in the bar you wanted to befriend—especially if you had to fight your way out of it. When I shook his hand and gave him a brotherly hug, I got the same impression that had struck me in L.A., when I greeted Dan there after not seeing him in years. I felt the most solidly built human being I could imagine. It was as if he were made of concrete or chiseled out of marble. He had not even been this stout when he came back from Nam. I had to wonder where he had ventured following his discharge from the Corps, and why he refused to talk about it.

"You ready for this?" he said.

I finished my beer and banged the bottle down on the bar like a gavel. "I'm ready."

"This is your last chance to back out."

"I ain't backin' out. This is the only way to get Uncle Bubba a heart."

"Right, and don't you forget it. I've conducted a lot of clandestine operations around the world, but they were all for a good cause. Same with this one. It may seem shady to some people, but we know it's only fair, and it's the right thing to do."

"You don't have to convince me anymore, Cuz."

He winced. "Don't call me 'Cuz' in public."

"I *know* that!" I said. "Nobody's listening to us right now."

"All right, let's go."

We left Gilley's and got into Dan's vintage T-Bird. We drove toward downtown Houston and pulled into a small parking lot hidden down an alley between some old industrial buildings. Dan parked his T-Bird between a Harley motorcycle and a Mercedes sedan. Next to the Mercedes, I noticed Mexican license plates on an older-model Cadillac. We entered the back door of an empty warehouse. Way across the warehouse, I saw the glow of an electric light coming from an office area. This, I realized, was a light that would never be seen from the outside. This was a great place for a little illegal gambling.

Dan and I walked into the office to find three sketchy-looking characters sitting around a makeshift poker table, drinking whiskey, and smoking. One of them was aimlessly shuffling a deck of cards. He looked up when we entered.

"Howdy, Ralph. Where's Zeller?" Dan asked.

"He just went to the pisser," Ralph said in a thick Texas drawl.

Dan patted me on the back. "This is Ronnie. He's a rock star."

The three men gawked at me, unimpressed.

"This is Benny and this is Ramón," Ralph said.

I reached over the table to shake the hands of the gamblers. Benny looked like a car salesman or an ambulance-chasing lawyer. Ramón struck me as a wealthy businessman from south of the border, and I thought of the Mexican plates on the Caddy outside.

"What are we waiting on?" Dan asked. "Deal me and Ronnie in. I'll pour us a drink."

So we sat down and started playing seven-card stud. Ralph gave me a cheap cigar. The whiskey was rough, and there was no ice. The tiny air conditioner mounted in a hole cut in the wall did not quite put out enough cool air to make the place comfortable. Even so, I started to have fun playing cards and trading barbs with these strangers. I even won the hand. For a while, I almost forgot why we were there.

Then Dan glanced through the crack in the door and said, "Here he comes. Tally ho the fox."

The door opened wide and in stepped Archie Zeller. He wore a short-brimmed felt hat, known in Texas as a "cocksucker." You had to be someone who invited conflict to wear one of those things because sooner or later somebody was going to use that term. Zeller also had a short cigar stuck in his mouth, unlit. In those days, some guys liked to chew their tobacco that way. They'd carry a cigar around in their mouth all day, and never light it. By the end of the day, the cigar would be chewed, swallowed, and spit away to nothing. Zeller was of that school of tobacco use. He had a brown stain around his mouth, and black flakes of the cigar stuck to his lips.

"Hey, Wildcat, the last two yahoos just showed up," Ralph said, pointing his chin at me and Dan while he dealt.

"Looks like y'all spudded this one in without me," Zeller said, throwing around some oil-patch jargon for getting started on a new well.

"Sit down. Hundred-dollar ante."

Archie "Wildcat" Zeller smiled slyly. His teeth were yellow. I knew already that he was filthy rich, but he dressed like a common, working-class, oil-patch roughneck. Except for his boots. He had tucked his khakis into the fancy-stitched tops of those fresh-shined gators with roach-killer toes. His khaki button-up work shirt was faded, sweat-stained at the armpits, the cuffs rolled up a turn or two. The shirttail was tucked into his pants, which were held up by a tooled leather belt and a rodeo buckle that I was almost certain he had not won in an arena.

Archie Zeller was famous for something less glorious than rodeo.

The truth was that Zeller was more infamous than famous. The son of a two-bit con man father and a gypsy fortune-teller mother, he had been brought up in the grifter's life, drifting from town to town, pulling penny-ante swindles on unsuspecting rubes. But Archie had bigger profits in mind and went out on his own to orchestrate some more ambitious flimflams. Usually, he was successful, but he did get busted a time or two, trying to swindle someone who caught on. He did a few years in the state pen.

When he got out, Zeller seemed to go straight. He entered into a partnership with a former cell mate who knew how to drill oil wells. Together, they became wildcat drillers. Wildcatters were independent contractors who drilled more for sport than for profit. They were hit-or-miss gamblers, hoping that if they poked enough holes in the ground, they'd eventually strike oil.

Early on, Zeller and his partner got lucky and located a promising oil field near Houston. They made a pretty good bundle of money and hired more crews to drill. Then his partner disappeared and was never heard from again. Zeller always maintained that he had won his partner's share of the business in a poker game, and that the ex-partner had moved to Mexico. At any rate, he found himself the sole owner of a small drilling empire.

Archie "Wildcat" Zeller, as he liked to call himself, started making good money, but only wanted more. He became a notorious cheapskate, paying low wages, working his men long hours, constantly withholding overtime pay and bonuses. By the time he was a self-made millionaire, he had become notorious as a non-tipper at cafés and bars.

He also got sued repeatedly for underpaying property owners who had leased land to him for drilling purposes. You can't just go

onto anybody's land and start drilling, of course. You have to pay
the landowner a lease fee just to drill a test well. If your test well
hits oil, you have to pay that landowner a prenegotiated percentage
of the profits from the crude oil pumped from that tract of acreage.
This is where Archie Zeller got too greedy.

Zeller started using a thing called a whipstock. His erstwhile cell
mate probably told him about this particular piece of equipment,
which was likely why Zeller went into the oil business in the first
place. With the whipstock, he melded wildcatting with the confidence scams he had grown up learning from his parents.

The whipstock was nothing more than a long steel wedge that
was used to deflect the drill bit from the original vertical direction.
It would angle the direction of the wellbore to one side. There
were legitimate uses for the whipstock, like when drillers needed
to straighten a crooked hole, or angle around some pipe that had
twisted off and hung up in the shaft and couldn't be fished out.

However, Archie "Whipstock" Zeller, as he would later become
known, used the whipstock for illegal gain. By using the wedge, he
could set up his drilling rig near (but not on) your property and
angle the shaft underground to pump your oil out from under your
land without having to pay you. The practice became known as
slant-drilling. It was stealing, pure and simple. And he got away
with it for years.

Here's what he'd do: He'd buy a small piece of land—maybe as
small as ten or twenty acres—in an area he was pretty sure would
yield crude. He'd drill his first test well smack dab in the middle of
his small acreage. If he hit oil with his test well, he'd start slant-
drilling other wells around the perimeter of his little piece of property, using the whipstock to angle the bore under the bordering
properties, thus cheating neighbors out of royalties that amounted
to hundreds of thousands or even millions of dollars. And this was
back in the fifties and sixties, when a million was worth something.

No oil well lasts forever. When the crude started to play out on
Zeller's little piece of oil patch, he'd close the slant wells around the
perimeter, and hide the evidence of their illegality by pouring con-

crete down the shafts. This left one legal well in the middle of the property, which Zeller knew would soon play out. Then, he'd sell the acreage as a working oil field at a ridiculously inflated price to some greenhorn who just wanted to own a piece of the oil patch. Usually, the production would play out within months, or even weeks, after the sale. The new owners were left with a worthless pumpjack and a patch of coastal prairie.

Zeller had a pretty good run at slant-drilling all over East Texas for several years, until one of his tool pushers got drunk in a bar somewhere and talked. Word got around. Authorities were alerted. The tool pusher was questioned and started to sing like a mockingbird. Zeller got wind of all this and had his work crews close all the slant wells overnight. They were ordered to fill the shafts with whatever they had on hand—concrete, dirt, rocks, oyster shells, bowling balls, kitchen sinks. . . .

By the time Zeller was subpoenaed and hauled into court, all the evidence had been covered up. Two other factors got him off the hook: One, he hired the best lawyers money could buy. Two, the star witness for the prosecution—the hard-drinking tool pusher who had blown the whistle—mysteriously disappeared and was never heard from again.

Zeller walked free, but everyone in the oil field industry knew he had gotten away with many counts of grand larceny, and probably murder. After the trial, Zeller didn't drill much. Maybe a little hobby well now and then. Mostly, he laid low and enjoyed his millions, occasionally surfacing to flaunt his ill-gotten wealth and infamy. Having evolved into a notorious miser, he lived well enough off the interest of his bank holdings, cultivating his image as a high-stakes gambler. In truth, Zeller was never better than a break-even cardsharp, but he ran with the big dogs, for he had money to lose.

Now here he was—this legendary card cheat and crude thief, right in front of me. I could not help recalling that people who associated with Zeller sometimes disappeared from the face of the earth. He sat down across from me in the empty chair he had vacated to visit the men's room.

"This is Wildcat," Ralph said, introducing us to the old slant driller. "Wildcat, this is Dan and—" He snapped his fingers at me absentmindedly.

"Ronnie," I said.

Zeller gave us a slashing glance and threw a hundred into the pot. "Who's dealing?"

"I am," Benny said, raking the cards together.

"We pass the deal to the left with each hand," Ralph explained for the benefit of me and Dan.

"You back in?" Benny asked Zeller.

"Let's hook 'em to the right," Wildcat said. This was another oil field term that meant to "get on with it."

We began playing cards at a hundred dollars a pop just to ante up. The game went on for an hour or more with all the players seeming to be pretty well matched. The pots increased into the thousands. Then Zeller began to build his pile of winnings. The rest of us gradually lost more and more. Especially the guy called Ramón, whose body language showed the frustration any poker player would feel on a losing streak.

"Can't win 'em all," Dan said, throwing in his cards as Zeller took another pot.

I grunted my reply as I shoved the cards to Dan, for I had just dealt my own losing hand, and it was Dan's turn to deal. Dan shuffled the cards like a pro and flipped them across the table with a familiar ease. Zeller, poker-faced, began to raise bets immediately on the hand Dan dealt us.

I glanced across Dan to get a look at Ramón's face when he called the last bet. Ramón looked agitated, and a little drunk, but confident in his current hand. Zeller raised Ramón's bet. That was enough for me on the hand. I dropped out, and so did Dan and Ralph, leaving only Zeller and Ramón in the hunt.

When the bet fell to Ramón, he raised Zeller with everything he had on the table. Zeller called, then flipped his cards. Three aces and some change. Ramón stared at them a moment with glassy eyes, leaned back in his chair, and let his hands drop from the table in defeat. Zeller read the sign of resignation with a grin and began raking in cash.

"Come to Daddy," he purred at the pot as he gathered it in.

Ramón suddenly sprang to his feet and brandished a small revolver that he had pulled from somewhere. Like everyone else at the table, I sprang to my feet in shock, ready to dodge bullets if I had to.

Ramón waved the muzzle around the room. "Everybody be still! Don't move!"

"All right, take it easy," Dan said.

Angling the gun back toward Zeller, Ramón said, "You're marking cards!" His English was perfect, colored with a Mexican accent. He swayed a little as he glared crazily at Zeller over the gun sight.

"Whoa, hoss," Zeller said, his eyes widening in alarm.

"Settle down, Ramón," Dan suggested.

"I don't like being cheated!" Ramón seethed. He cocked the pistol.

Zeller's hands were trembling over the table. "Take it easy, stud. This is just a friendly game."

"I *kill* cheaters!" Ramón barked.

Dan's fist swung up in a blur to Ramón's face, backhanding the Mexican in the nose. Ramón's head flew back and his pistol fired toward the ceiling. Blood spewed from Ramón's mouth and he staggered backwards into the wall, then slid to the floor and fell over, facedown.

In the next instant, Dan had everyone covered with a .357 Magnum. "Everybody relax," he ordered.

"I'm out of here, Dan," said Ralph.

"Me, too," Benny said. "That's enough for me."

I just stood there, truly stunned at the instant change of mood. I realized I had been holding my breath since Ramón pulled the weapon. I gasped, and began breathing again.

"Go ahead and pick up your winnings, then," Dan said. "We should all get out of here, in case somebody heard that gunshot."

Ralph and Benny stuffed bills into their pockets and cleared out, leaving Ramón unconscious on the floor.

"Looks like you're the big winner," Dan said to Zeller. "Let's leave this asshole here and get the hell out of Dodge."

"Did you see the crazy look in that bastard's eyes?" Zeller said, gathering his winnings from the table. "He was fixin' to shoot me in the head with that popgun, sure as shit."

"Why do you think I knocked his teeth in?"

"How'd you know I wasn't cheatin'?" Zeller quizzed.

Dan chuckled. "I never said you weren't cheatin', but I knew you weren't marking cards."

"Well, I owe you a favor," Zeller said. "I was a split second away from gittin' shot in the head full of bad luck."

I picked up the small pile of cash I had left on the table and crammed it into my pocket.

As we walked out through the warehouse, Dan put his pistol away under his shirttail. "I have a good idea on how I can collect on that favor," he said to Zeller. "I think you'll like this idea, Wildcat. You and I can make a shitload of money together, and you can get square on that favor you owe me."

"Oh, yeah?" Zeller sounded skeptically intrigued.

By the time we got to the parking lot, Dan had talked Zeller into meeting us the next day at Gilley's Club. "Ronnie will be there, too."

Zeller looked at me and said, "Who are you, anyway? You look familiar."

Dan laughed. "This is Ronnie Breed, the rock star. He's my biggest investor."

I saw the realization in Zeller's eyes. "In what?"

"We'll tell you tomorrow, Wildcat. Right now, it's time to clear out of this dive."

3

DAN HAD instructed Mona and me to join him at Gilley's for Friday afternoon happy hour. Mona had flown in from L.A. to help us schmooze Archie Zeller into funding Dan's television pilot. Because of Dan's scheme, I would get better acquainted with Zeller than I ever really cared to, and I would gather what made him tick. Mostly it was greed.

As Mona and I waited at the bar for Dan and Zeller, I ordered a Lone Star beer for myself, and a Cuba Libre for Mona. Mona wasn't a beer kind of girl. She looked out of place in the famous country music joint, with her hip-hugging miniskirt barely covering her ass, and her hair teased out in punk rocker style. In an attempt to go somewhat country, she wore black cowgirl boots and, for a top, she had donned a black bandanna. She was so petite that she could fold a bandanna in half, corner-to-corner, tie it behind her back, and it would pretty much cover her small, firm breasts.

In contrast to Mona and her attire, Gilley's was packed with real and wannabe cowboys and cowgirls in jeans and straw Stetsons, though there were some businessmen in suits and a few tourists in short britches. You may know a thing or two about Gilley's because of the movie *Urban Cowboy*, which came out a few years after the summer of '75. In its heyday, Gilley's was an amazingly popular place located on Spencer Highway in the Houston suburb of Pasadena.

Pasadena was a blue-collar town peopled largely by refinery and petrochemical plant employees who labored hard by day and partied hard at night. It was a country music town in '75, and Gilley's was the hottest of all the redneck hangouts in the whole Greater Houston area. The co-owner of the place, Mickey Gilley, was the front man on stage. He had a great band, a fantastic voice, and a Jerry Lee Lewis style on the piano. He was, in fact, Jerry Lee Lewis's cousin. However, Mickey Gilley's partner, Sherwood Cryer, was the real brains and muscle behind the success of the dance hall.

Sherwood had been born a poor boy in the East Texas Piney Woods, but through hard work, big gambles, some ruthless conniving, and creativity, he had become a wealthy man by 1975. He had originally moved to Houston to work as a welder, but soon went into business for himself with liquor stores, corner mini-marts, and small bars. Then he heard a relatively unknown performer named Mickey Gilley playing at a Houston club one night, and invited the now-legendary musician to be the talent at a new venue he had envisioned. Mickey accepted the offer, and Sherwood Cryer began fashioning Gilley's from an existing club that had gone belly-up.

As a welder, Sherwood naturally appreciated the sprawling structure of steel where he and Gilley began their honky-tonk ownership careers. To make the place look more like a club than like a warehouse, the exterior steel siding had been covered with unpainted rough cedar, which gave the impression an old-time country dance hall of wood. The gravel parking lot covered several acres.

At the front door there was a sign that read:

IF YOU LEAVE THE BUILDING FOR ANY REASON, YOU MUST
PAY ANOTHER COVER CHARGE!

Once you were inside, there were no windows to the outside world. The place was like a bunker, or a cave. But a fun one! Gilley's sported a huge wood parquet dance floor, several polished hardwood bars scattered here and there, scores of wooden tables and hundreds of chairs, dozens of pool tables and pinball machines, and all sorts of other amusements. The most famous amusement, of course, was that renowned mechanical bull.

Most folks don't realize it, but Sherwood Cryer built that mechanical bull, and developed a nice little sideline business manufacturing the remote-control bucking bovines for other establishments. Under his guidance, spring-boarded by Mickey Gilley's talent, Gilley's Club would soon become world famous as the largest honkytonk on the planet. It employed an army of bouncers on Friday and Saturday nights, when the place could turn into a madhouse of fisticuffs. Dan had worked at Gilley's briefly as a bouncer after he returned from Nam. He was one of the few people who could get along with Sherwood Cryer, the cantankerous co-owner.

Dan had told Mona and me to meet him in the "back forty"—the bar beside the mechanical bull. As Mona and I waited with our drinks, we were entertained by the idiots who were getting bucked off the mechanical bull. It was happy hour on the first Friday in June 1975, and the place was already hopping.

"I want to ride that thing," Mona said, looking at the bull.

"Don't let me stop you."

"As if I would," she said. She looked at me, doing a double-take.

I was wearing a straw Resistol cowboy hat, pulled low over my face, and dark glasses, though the light was dim in the dance hall.

"Do you really think you're gonna be mobbed by your fans?" Mona said, rolling her big blue eyes in her flashy way. "Take those shades off."

"Hey, when you're cool, the sun's always shining on you," I said.

"Oh, please," she answered.

I slipped the sunglasses into my shirt pocket, a little disappointed that no one *had* recognized me from my album covers or the bit parts I had had in a few movies.

Dan showed up right on time. There was some small talk and hugging among the three of us. To a certain degree, we were all posturing, getting ready to sweet-talk the investor, Archie Zeller, who was due to arrive any minute. Dan ordered a double Jameson Irish Whiskey, neat, and we continued to practice our roles as investment worthy entrepreneurs in need of capital.

"Here he comes," Dan said, tossing a twenty to the bartender as he grabbed his third double. "Now, remember. We ain't kin."

"I got it!" I said. "You don't have to keep reminding me." Dan had coached me on this. We were not to tell Zeller that we were cousins, or had grown up together. He wanted to make it look as if he had already landed a major investor—me—a hit song-maker.

"Put your arm around me," Mona ordered. "It's showtime." She was more excited about this scheme of Dan's than she ever had been about going to one of my performances. I really don't think she ever liked my music that much, but she had no problems with the rock-star lifestyle.

"I've got my game face on," I assured them both, draping my arm over Mona's bare shoulder.

As Zeller approached, he shot a cocksure grin at me alongside the cigar butt he had been chewing on all day. "I'll be goddamned!" he said sticking his hand out at me.

"You will be if you keep talking like that," I replied. Begrudgingly, I shook his hand.

"I knew I recognized you last night. Just couldn't place that mug of yours. I'm a pretty big fan of yours, boy!"

Zeller was older than Dan and me, but the "boy" part still rubbed me wrong.

"Actually, I'd say you're about average size for a fan," I replied in a wasted witticism that went right over his head.

"That last song you put out was the best thing you ever done. You ought to do more stuff like that, and leave that rock-and-roll shit behind."

Funny how some people conceal criticism in left-handed compliments. He was referring to my song "If Love Was a Pawnshop," which had been played on country radio, as well as on pop stations. What he was really suggesting was that it was the only good song I had ever recorded, in his opinion.

"I like rock and roll!" Mona declared, though she didn't say she liked mine. Her taste in music actually leaned more toward the Ramones than the Half Breeds.

Zeller's road-map eyes swiveled slowly over to Mona, then coursed up and down from her high-heeled boots to her blow-dried do. "Now, who's this green-broke filly?"

Mona backhanded me in the chest. "You never introduce me as your girlfriend," she accused.

"Oh, yeah. Mona Derringer. This is Archie Zeller."

"Call me Wildcat," he said, leering at Mona as he caressed her hand. He looked toward me. "So, you know me."

"Oh, yeah," I said. "I've heard your name since I was a kid. You're something of a legend around here."

"That so? And what am I legendary for, son?"

I shrugged. "Everything from wildcat drilling to high-stakes gambling."

Zeller seemed to like that answer. He swelled up like a puffer fish, a creature he somewhat resembled.

He was also well known for having a new gold-digging sugar baby hanging on his arm about every six months or so, which explained the way he now admiringly sized up Mona at the bar by the mechanical bull in Gilley's.

"Where in creation did you come from?" he said lustily.

"L.A." she said. "I met Ronnie there."

"Dan introduced us," I said. "We're together, you know. As in boyfriend and girlfriend." I snapped my fingers at Zeller. "You listening?"

"I heard you," Zeller said, finally releasing Mona's hand.

"Now that we all know one another," Dan said, "let's get a table in the corner where we can talk business."

We all followed Dan to a quieter area away from the mechanical bull and the loud jukebox.

"Aw, hey, darlin'," Zeller said to Mona as he plopped down in a chair. "I forgot to order at the bar. You don't mind being my beer wench, do you?"

The nerve. I just wanted to slap the guy, but Mona quickly handled it.

"Do I look like a *wench*?" she said, propping her fists on her hips with a snaky move. "Hell, no, I'm not going to be your beer wench. Now, I'll be your beer *bitch,* but don't ever call me a wench, *Wildcat.*"

Zeller grinned and began to laugh. He slapped the table hard with his hand. "She'll do, son!" he said to me. "That one's a pistol!"

"Her name *is* Derringer," I replied. I smiled at Mona. "Honey, can you wench me another Lone Star while you're bitching Wildcat a beer?"

"I'll bring a round, *sweetheart,*" she said sarcastically.

Zeller watched Mona's miniskirt twitch away, then seemed to remember that Dan and I were there. "So," he said, glancing at a knockoff Rolex. "Give me the skinny. I got a poker game tonight."

"Here it is," Dan said, obviously delighted to be getting down to business. "We all like to gamble. That's one thing the three of us have in common, right?"

I nodded. Zeller shrugged, not yet committing to anything.

"Ronnie has played high-stakes cards with the Hollywood elite and even the real pros in Vegas. Wildcat, you're notorious for fleecing hotshot cardsharps all over Texas. Like you two high rollers, I've played poker all over. I've won a few more than I've lost, and that's fine. But I've come up with a way—a surefire way—to make a killin' off poker. And it's all legal."

"In Nevada?" Zeller asked.

"No, sir. Right here in Texas."

"Gamblin's illegal in Texas."

"Only if you play for money," Dan insisted.

"What the hell else is there to play for?"

"The championship."

"Of what?"

I decided to chime in: "Poker. We're talking about a legal tournament to determine the champion of poker in Texas."

"And, therefore, the world!" Dan added. "It's gonna be called *The World Championship Series of Texas Hold 'Em Poker.*"

Mona arrived with the drinks and shoved them at us.

"And it's legal?" Zeller asked with a sneer, as if the very idea of legal poker disgusted him.

"It's no more illegal than rodeo," Dan claimed. "I noticed your buckle, Wildcat. You've probably ridden a bull or two in your time."

Zeller grinned at Mona. "I've shot more bull than I ever rode."

"Haven't we all. So, you know how it works. You want to ride, you pay your fee. The top winners split the pot. Champion gets the bigger cut. After expenses, of course."

"Expenses?"

"Operating fees," Dan explained. "You know. We'll have to rent the venues, pay for advertising. Hire dealers, security, beer wenches . . ."

Mona laughed and threw back a gulp of her third Cuba Libre. For a tiny gal, she could sure put away the booze. She snuggled a little closer to me and looped her arm through mine.

For the first time since entering Gilley's, Zeller took the gummy cigar butt from his mouth. He sipped his beer suspiciously. "So, you want me to enter this tournament, or what?"

"Hell, yes," Dan said. "You may become the first world champion of Texas poker!"

"It won't be easy," I boasted. "You'll be playing against me, and several other handpicked high rollers from all over the world."

"What's it cost to enter?"

"Ten grand. Chicken feed. But—"

"Uh-huh," the old slant driller said grimly. "Here comes the 'but.' "

"We need a silent partner. We need seed money to get this thing off the ground."

"How much?"

"Fifty thousand for starters."

Zeller scoffed. "You gotta be shittin' me."

"I'm already in for fifty grand myself," I said. "I sold my house in L.A."

"It was a crappy little dump, anyway," Mona added.

"You can smooch that money adios," Zeller opined.

I smiled confidently back at the old schemer. "I don't think so, Wildcat. You haven't heard the rest of Dan's business plan."

"I haven't heard anything but BS."

I turned my attention to Dan. "Maybe we shouldn't divulge any more. Maybe Wildcat's not our stake horse after all."

"We could sure use his notoriety," Dan said, talking about the millionaire as if he weren't sitting right there.

"Are you kidding?" Mona said, pointing at Zeller. "Can you imagine this guy on TV? He's pure gold."

"Like I said," I growled, elbowing Mona, "maybe we shouldn't divulge any more."

Mona clapped her hand over her painted mouth, having spilled the clincher.

"Television?" Zeller said, intrigued.

Dan's eyes twinkled. "That's where the *real* money is. Imagine this—" Dan spread his open palms across the smoky barroom air. "—Ronnie Breed presents . . . *The World Championship of Texas Hold 'Em Poker*! Starring Archie 'Wildcat' Zeller!"

"You'd get top billing among the players in the tournament," I explained. "You're the quintessential Texan." I almost gagged saying that. What I was thinking was that Zeller was the quintessential *crooked* Texan. But we needed the seed money, as Dan had said.

Zeller stared right through my eyes. "So, if I get top billing, what's in it for you?"

"Free publicity," I said, as if I couldn't believe he hadn't figured that out. "I'm the celebrity host. I provide the music. This will kick-start my new career as a solo artist."

"The advertisers for the TV show are already lined up," Dan said. "And I mean a dozen major, national corporations. It's a thirty-minute show. There are ten spots per show, and the advertisers will pay tens of thousands for those spots every week."

"I thought the advertisers paid the networks," Zeller said dubiously.

"This is not a network show," Dan admitted. "Not yet, anyway. That's down the road. This first season, it's designed as a syndicated show. We keep the advertising money, and sell the show to the local affiliates. We leave a couple of spots open for the affiliates to sell local commercials."

"Uh-huh," Zeller said. He took a long drink from his beer, paused, belched, and put his cigar back in his mouth. "How many of these affiliates do you expect will pay for this pipe dream?"

Dan smiled. "Thanks to Ronnie's name, we already have commitments from over two hundred stations coast-to-coast, including every major market in Texas. It's a lead pipe cinch, Wildcat."

Zeller was running low on suspicion. "How long you been workin' on this thing?"

"Months," Dan said.

Zeller was mulling the thing over. "I don't know. . . . Televised poker? Seems like it would be boring as hell."

"It's not about the gambling, it's about the gamblers. The BS. The interviews away from the poker table. The personalities. The jawing between high rollers during the game. You know. You've been there."

"I don't know. . . ."

"I'll make you a deal," Dan said, leaning conspiratorially in toward the center of the table. "If you ante up at fifty grand, I'll *guarantee* that you will win *The World Championship of Texas Hold 'Em Poker.*"

"How are you gonna do that?"

Dan's voice was almost down to a whisper. "I know dealers who could baffle a magician. Trust me. If I say you're the champ, you're the champ."

"How much does the champ win?"

Dan waved a hand at the annoying triviality of the question. "A hundred grand, but that's nothing. TV is where the money is. You'll be in as a one-third silent partner on all that TV profit."

Zeller chewed his cigar butt. "Let me make sure I've got this straight: I invest fifty grand, and you guarantee me one hundred grand in winnings, plus a third of the television profits?"

"Plus the title of champion," I added.

He ignored me. "You say you've got the other high rollers lined up. They all paid ten grand to enter?"

"Yes, sir," Dan said.

"And you got fifty grand from our celebrity here?"

"That's right."

"Then why do you need me?"

"Two reasons," Dan said. "First, it takes a lot of capital to get a gaming tournament off the ground, not to mention a television show. We need fifty grand more. We've got to pay the film crew, the venue owners for the poker games, the hotel rooms, the meals, the beer wenches—"

"Wenches don't come cheap," Mona agreed.

"And the other reason?" Zeller said.

Dan sighed and glanced at me and Mona. "I hope you don't take this the wrong way, Wildcat."

Zeller guffawed. "You don't really think you can hurt my feelin's, do you?"

"All right. Every television show needs its villain. You're the heavy. You're the guy every other player wants to beat."

"But not necessarily the guy all the viewers want to lose," Mona purred. "Some of us root for the bad boys to win."

Zeller took the cigar stub from his mouth, poured the rest of his beer down his throat, and dropped the stogie butt into the empty bottle. He reached into his shirt pocket and pulled out another Swisher Sweets, unwrapping it slowly. He threw the plastic wrapper on the floor and put the new cigar between his yellow teeth.

"Gentlemen . . . Miss Mona . . . You're looking at the next world champion of Texas hold 'em poker. I'm in."

4

THAT NIGHT, after Archie Zeller wrote Dan a check for sixty grand and left for his poker game, Dan and I did something we hadn't done together in years. We went out on a spree. I asked Mona if she wanted to go with us.

"Hell no. What is it, seven o'clock? And it's still so freaking hot here, I can hardly breathe. I'm going back to the bus and go to sleep until it cools off."

"That'll be about October," I informed her.

"Geez, I miss California," she whined as she strutted toward my tour bus, parked in the back of the parking lot at Gilley's. Its diesel generator was running, belching black smoke, powering the on-board air conditioner. It was a real sweet, state-of-the-art tour bus, and Mona, who did not like the humidity or heat of Houston, spent most of her time in there, sleeping and putting on makeup. She could put on makeup for hours.

Having sold my bungalow in L.A., I had used part of the money to buy this new tour bus. I was only starting to figure out the music business in those days. I had decided I needed to own my own tour bus. Normally, the record company management would lease a tour bus for the band, for way too much money, and take the expenditure out of the profits the band earned on tour. I had figured out that if I owned the bus, I could lease it to the record company while I toured and then lease it to other acts while I wasn't touring. Today, I own my own tour bus company, with a fleet of fifty-one coaches, but I got my start with that one bus in '75.

Dan watched Mona hike for the cool oasis of my bus. "How the hell could she possibly be hot in that outfit?"

"Oh, she's hot," I assured him.

"Well, enjoy it while you can. You know she's not your type, and it ain't gonna last long."

I nodded at the reality of the situation. "I know. But she makes me look like a rock star."

"Cuz, you are a rock star, remember? Come on, my T-Bird's over here."

The next thing I knew, we were barreling down Spencer Highway in Dan's perfectly maintained 1959 Thunderbird convertible. It was his first car from high school, and his true love. Of course, the top was down as we rocketed over the blacktop. The sun was sinking across the vast flatlands of the Texas Coastal Plains as we drove among croplands interspersed with creek bottoms thickly timbered with pecans and hackberries, shrubs and vines. The sunset illuminated some distant clouds, making them look like the kind of flaming balls of fire that you'd paint on the side of a hot rod.

"Reach back into that icebox behind the seat," Dan suggested, going too fast for comfort around a curve.

I fished a couple of cold beers out of the cooler. "Feels like old times. Where are we headed?"

"Rodeo in Lake Jackson. I'm sure some of our old pals are still around."

About then, I heard the siren. I glanced at Dan's speedometer. Eighty-five. I looked over my shoulder and saw the state trooper's lights behind us.

"Oh, hell," Dan said, as if pestered by something akin to a phone call he didn't want to answer. He pulled over, took the beer from between his thighs, drank a gulp, and then put the Lone Star can on the dashboard so he could shift in the seat and fish out his billfold.

The trooper stopped behind us and approached the convertible. "Evenin'," he said.

"Howdy," Dan said.

I nodded, looking at the officer under the brim of my straw hat, through my dark sunglasses. I took a drink of the beer in my hand. The trooper looked as if he had been on the force a few years and didn't put up with a whole lot of nonsense.

"You know how fast you were going?"

"This dang thing gets away from you," Dan lamented. He patted the dashboard and grabbed his beer can for a swig.

"How many of those have you had?"

"First one of the day." He didn't mention the two Irish whiskeys at Gilley's.

"Just gettin' off work?"

"Yeah, and late for the rodeo in Lake Jackson." Dan checked his wristwatch.

The officer was looking over Dan's driver's license and the expired military ID he had included with it. He looked at me. "You look familiar," he said.

Dan laughed. "You don't recognize him yet? Listen to this!" Dan had installed an eight-track tape player under the dash. He used the toe of his boot to shove in one of my tapes, which was sticking out of the player. Ronnie Breed and the Half Breeds began to play one of the hits I had penned.

"This is Ronnie Breed. Take your disguise off, Cuz. Show him!"

I sheepishly removed my hat and shades, and smirked at the trooper almost apologetically.

"Son of a gun," the trooper said. "My oldest son is a big fan of yours."

"No kiddin'? How old?"

He handed Dan's license and ID back to him. "He's eleven. Hey, I don't reckon you'd . . . If you don't mind . . ."

I autographed Dan's eight-track tape for the trooper's son and we were soon on our way to the rodeo again, with a warning ticket. Dan took another Half Breeds tape from the glove box and slid it halfway into the eight-track player, poised for the next officer we might meet.

When we arrived at Lake Jackson, we drove around back of the rodeo arena on the outskirts of town. The gatekeeper recognized Dan from our rodeo days and let us in to park among the pickup trucks and horse trailers of the rodeo competitors. Here, Dan was more of a celebrity than I was. He had been a pretty successful steer wrestler, bareback competitor, and bull rider, and had also spent his senior year in high school as a rodeo clown.

I could never match Dan's raw athleticism in the rodeo arena, but thanks to Uncle Bubba's well-trained roping horse, I had made a name for myself as a calf roper during high school, and of course I was Dan's hazer for the steer-wrestling competition. So, everybody knew us and we were greeted behind the chutes as long-lost compadres. My music business successes didn't hurt our image any, either, but these rodeo cowboys were more impressed by the great Dan Campbell than they were by his sidekick, pop-music singer-cousin. Now, if I had been George Jones, that might have been a different story.

We made our way slowly through the trailers, then around the pens full of bucking stock, bulldogging steers, and calves for the roping competition, shaking hands and slapping shoulders as we gravitated toward the bucking chutes. When we finally climbed up behind the chutes, where we could see the arena and watch the rodeo, one of our old high school rodeo pals was getting ready to buck out on a saddle bronc. His name was Jim Billings.

Jim smiled and nodded at us before they opened the chute. He lasted about seven seconds, then flew over the bronc's head and landed on the ground, where that brute stepped on him and broke his leg.

"Jim's hurt," Dan said. "Come on."

The two of us scrambled over the chutes and ran into the arena to help Jim to his feet, each of us looping an arm over our shoulders.

"Leg's broke," Jim said casually. "I heard it pop."

"Then we better get your lame ass out of the arena," Dan said.

"Can't you see we're trying to run a rodeo here?" I added as we carried Jim toward the gate where the ambulance waited.

The rodeo announcer's voice blared over the harsh loudspeaker: "Folks, give that cowboy a round of applause. It's the only pay he'll be getting tonight."

"You want my bulldogging runs?" Jim asked Dan. "I already put up the fee."

"Hell, yeah!" Dan announced. "I got my hazer right here."

I felt a pang of nervousness. I hadn't even sat a horse in several years, much less competed in a rodeo. But I wasn't about to chicken out. Luckily, I didn't have long to think about it. The bulldogging was the next event, and Dan was the first competitor slated to wrestle a steer.

Dan rode Jim's horse, and I borrowed a mount from the guy who had planned to haze for Jim. It all happened pretty fast. Suddenly, I was horseback in the arena, and I felt the old addictive lure of the rodeo. The smell of dirt and manure filled my nostrils. The lights around the arena swarmed with June bugs and moths. The murmur of the crowd hummed from the old wooden grandstands. A scratchy old Bob Wills record was playing on the loudspeaker. Someone jerked the needle off the record with a scratch, and the announcer's voice rattled the speakers:

"Our first competitor in the bulldogging competition is Jim— What? Oh . . . Been a change? All right, our first competitor, filling in for Jim Billings, who busted his leg in the saddle bronc competition is . . . Dan Campbell, out of Friendswood, Texas!"

By this time, a six-hundred-pound Corriente steer had been prodded into the chute and was poised to be released into the arena. Dan was in the box to the left of the chute on his borrowed mount. There was a rope stretched tight in front of his mount. He was not allowed to break through this rope barrier without being penalized ten seconds. I was on my horse to the right of the chute. My only job would be to keep that steer running straight between Dan and me so Dan could pounce on its horned head.

Our borrowed horses were well trained, and knew what was about to happen. They both pranced under us in anticipation of the chase.

"Ready, Cuz?"

"Yeah." *Be ready,* I was saying to myself. *Be aggressive.*

Dan nodded. The release gate opened and the steer shot from the chute. The spring-loaded barrier rope released Dan's mount from the box a mere fraction of a millisecond before his horse touched it.

I had already laid my borrowed spurs into the flanks of my loaner horse. Dan and I shot forward on either side of the steer, catching up to it with two great leaps of the muscled-up quarter horses we rode. From the corner of my left eye, I saw Dan drop gracefully from the right side of his saddle, his chest landing on the steer's head, between the horns, his right arm hooking under the right horn of the beast.

I slowed my mount and turned to watch. Dan's heels and hip pockets hit the dirt as he used his weight to stop the steer while twisting its head to the right. The steer fell on its left side, and Dan grabbed its nose to roll it all the way over, completing the run. I felt a whoop escape from my lungs, as this was one of the fastest bull-doggings I had ever witnessed. It had all happened in seconds just twenty yards or so from the gate that had released the steer.

A spontaneous eruption of applause from the crowd joined whatever the rodeo announcer was saying over the distorted loudspeakers. Dan got up, waved at the audience, and got back on his horse.

"Good job, Cuz," he said as I trotted up.

"That time's gonna be hard to beat, folks! Four-point-one seconds!"

"What took you so long?"

He grinned back at me. "I'm a little rusty."

The time stood up to the competition, and Dan collected the first-place money for bulldogging, which he forced on Jim Billings, who was going to need to pay for a cast on his leg. After we watched the last of the bull riders, we jumped back into the T-Bird and sprayed gravel across the parking lot to beat the fans out onto the highway. I noticed Dan did not take the first highway that would have led us home.

"Where we headed now?"

"Galveston!" he shouted over the wind roaring past our ears. "Henry's playing a gig tonight at the Wooden Nickel."

Henry Campos had been our bass player in our high school garage band. Dan told me that he was fronting a cover band now, and they played every Friday night at the Wooden Nickel Cafe. Henry had never gotten into writing his own music. He was satisfied to play chosen country and pop hits at his weekly gig for fun and a little extra cash. He was a pipe fitter in real life.

Dan parked in the alley behind the club, reserved for employees and band members, and we slipped in through the kitchen, avoiding the cover charge at the front door.

"Hey, you can't come through here!" a cook said, flipping a burger and pointing his spatula at us like a weapon.

"This is Ronnie Breed," Dan said. "He used to play here. He's gonna sit in with Henry."

"Ronnie Breed? Of the Half Breeds?"

The cook gave us a free beer and made me promise to send him an autographed publicity photo for the wall. The band was on break when we walked in. We found them enjoying beers and getting geared up to play the last set of the night.

When he recognized us, Henry Campos was absolutely thrilled. "Hey, you want to play a few songs? We know all your hits. You can join us for the drunk set. Dan, you still play drums?"

"Once a drummer, always a drummer."

The Wooden Nickel was packed with revelers who were drinking and not paying much attention to the band as we started our first song. Soon, however, people began to recognize my voice as the one from the record they had heard played on the radio as I sang "If Love Was a Pawnshop." The band knew the song well, and Dan still had a great touch on the drums. I had forgotten what a smooth bass player Henry was, and he was modest, too, never cranking his amp too loud.

"Turn that thing up a little," I told him between verses. It was always funny to watch Henry play. He was sort of a scrawny, wiry guy, and a big ol' Fender Jazz Bass looked huge on him. Plus, he made all sorts of bizarre faces while playing, though between songs he wore handsomely the dark features of his Chicano heritage. His black hair, which was still sixties-long, whipped all around his shoulders as he played.

The lead guitar picker and the keyboard player—two guys I didn't know—knew the songs well enough but didn't possess the talent

Henry had. They were part-time pickers having a good time once a week in the same old bar. I had no cause to think poorly of them. Though we were playing my songs, this was their gig. Dan and I were the ones horning in.

On the second song, Dan abdicated his throne behind the drums and let Henry's drummer take over. The guy was not half the drummer Dan was. Still, it was the right thing and the classy thing for Dan to do. The drummer had been pouting beside the stage. It was his drum kit, after all, and his gig, and some guy he didn't know had muscled in to play with the closest thing to a rock star that had stepped into the Wooden Nickel since Jerry Lee Lewis got drunk there back in fifty-something.

It wasn't easy sitting in with Henry's band, as I was accustomed to the Half Breeds. Yes, there had been personality issues within my old band, but I never doubted them for talent. It's hard to say what makes one guy, or gal, better than another when they can both play the same notes. The really talented players just have a certain snap to what they do. They can take a note or a riff or whatever, and add some kind of sizzle, or maybe a mournful cry, a soulful wail, a crispness, an energy, an attack, a surrender. The great ones have an instinct for dynamics, tone, and a million other nuances that the amateur picker may understand, but just cannot achieve. Henry had it on the bass guitar. The rest of the guys in the band did not.

So, I just pointed my pearly whites at the crowd, sang my songs, and locked in with Henry, grateful that the band was well rehearsed enough to know the structure of each of my half dozen hits. We played them all, to the growing joy of the crowd. These six hits of mine were pretty good little ol' pop tunes, and I was singing them about as well as ever, through a good Shure 58 microphone, and a fairly decent PA system. But it was the familiarity of the songs, bred by radio airplay, that thrilled the listeners. Without that, I would have been just another weekend crooner to the bar patrons. As it was, I was treated as some kind of hero, and that made me feel pretty good until I glanced over to see my cousin Dan smirking at me in admiration—a real, decorated war hero who never knew a fraction of the adulation I received merely for voicing a popular ditty. That knocked me off my high horse.

By the time we got to the last song, the drunken celebrants were all singing along and hanging all over each other at the foot of the little stage. I signed a bunch of autographs and drank some free beer. Finally, the bar closed and the surly cook, who turned out to be the owner of the place, chased off the remaining customers. The Wooden Nickel got mercifully quiet. Dan and I sat down and talked to Henry as the other guys in the band packed up their gear.

"You want us to help you load out?" Dan asked.

Henry laughed. "We don't load out, man. This is our only gig. We just leave the PA set up for next week."

"Oh. Pretty good little band you got," I said.

Henry shrugged. "They're good, reliable guys. We just do this for fun. We all have day jobs. The piano player's a kindergarten teacher, for Christ's sake." He laughed. Henry had been raised by parents who immigrated from Mexico. It was good to hear his Texas-Mexican accent again. It made me feel at home.

"Hey," I said, glancing at Dan for approval. I knew he was reading my mind, because he nodded his agreement before I even finished the thought. "You want to play bass for me this summer? Dan's got this series of gigs lined up. You'll have to take a hiatus from the Wooden Nickel for a couple of months."

Henry's dark brown eyes drilled me. He had a way of looking into your brain and your soul when he pierced you with his gaze— his face expressionless, as if using ancient *Indio* medicine to decipher your heart. "What kind of gigs?"

Dan explained the poker-tournament idea, and said the money was already there to pay the band, so he might as well sign on for the summer.

"Well, I got some vacation time and sick days saved up," Henry mused. "I could take some time off from the refinery."

"Good, because we're going to work up some new songs," I said. "We'll need a lot of rehearsal time."

"Oh, cool. New tunes. Okay, man. I'll gig with you. Damn plant is hot in the summer anyway."

"You don't need to check with your wife?" Dan prodded.

"You mean ex?"

"Perfect."

I shook Henry's hand on the deal and left with Dan for Pasadena.

5

BY NOW, it may sound to you as if I were having the time of my life with my cousin Dan. Sure, it was fun. But when I think back after all these years, I can still remember the worry that nagged my heart in the summer of '75. There were a lot of reasons for it. Much of it rose from the very real possibility that I might have dumb-assed my way out of my lucrative music career by breaking up the Half Breeds. The music business had spit out more talented guys than me.

Still, mine was not the kind of personality to sit and wait for things to happen. So, while Dan prepared for the first shooting of his televised poker tournament, I lined up some meetings. I flew to New York, where a bunch of record-company suits glad-handed me but made no offers. Same thing in L.A. My former label, Walnut, had told me in no uncertain terms that the only way I was getting another contract out of them was to go crawling back to the Half Breeds and beg them to put the band back together. That wasn't going to happen. Walnut did not see me as a solo artist.

So I returned to Houston in defeat. Mona had sweet-talked me out of enough money to fly to Canada for a break from the Houston heat, so I was making my tour bus my headquarters, parking it out behind my mom's barn. My mom had a nice old family place she had inherited—a hundred acres and an old farm house overlooking Chocolate Bayou. So, her life was mortgage free, and she still collected a small pension from the oil company because of my dad's death on that cursed rig. She lived modestly and made good money as a secretary for Houston Lighting and Power. She was a wise woman.

One evening, I was having iced tea with my mom on the screened-in back porch, grousing about the way I had been snubbed by record companies on two coasts.

"Why don't you go to Nashville?" she said, a tone in her voice that asked why in the world I hadn't thought of that on my own already.

All I could think of in reply was a boyish, "Wul . . . I don't know."

At that time, a snooty attitude still prevailed in the pop world that looked down upon country music as hick drivel. Though I had grown up on the finest classic C&W—Hank Williams, Lefty Frizzell, Patsy Cline, Floyd Tillman, the Sons of the Pioneers, and many others—I realized that through my years in la-la land, I had subconsciously adopted an unfair, lowly opinion of Nashville talent. With the so-called progressive-country movement, the walls were beginning to come down between rock and country, but my mom clued me in to the sad fact that I was still caught up in the pop world's pompous air of superiority.

"You've already had a crossover hit," my mom reminded me. "And those new songs you've been playing for me . . . Well, maybe it's just me, but I hear them as country songs with twin fiddles and steel guitars."

I threw my arms up into the muggy evening air. "Everybody's a producer," I complained.

"How long did it take you to produce your last record?" she asked.

"A year and a half or so. Why?"

"Well, it only took me nine months to produce you. So, there. I guess I *am* a producer!"

"Touché," I said.

"What would be the harm in talking to somebody in Nashville?"

"All right, I'll make some calls. Maybe somebody knows somebody. In the music biz, it's all about who you *know,* who you can *snow,* and who can open the *do',* " I reminded her.

"Yeah, well, in the real world, it's all about who you *are,* how hard you *work,* and when are you gonna mow the *lawn?*"

"That doesn't even rhyme."

"Real life isn't always a pretty song, son."

"I'll mow the lawn first thing in the morning."

"Good. Then, call Nashville."

A COUPLE of days later, I found myself hoofing the sidewalks of Six-teenth Avenue in Nashville—Music Row. This wasn't my first trip to the home of country music. I had recorded some sides in some great studios there and had done some radio promotion for my one crossover hit.

My crossover hit, "If Love Was a Pawnshop," was a bit unusual. Occasionally, a country song will have enough popular appeal to "cross over" to the pop radio charts. In my case, it was a pop song that crossed over to country. It happened quite spontaneously, with-out any marketing strategy behind it. Certain country deejays just liked the song, and started playing it. (This was back in the day when a deejay had more leeway to spin what he or she wanted to spin. Nowadays, it's all canned by corporate bean counters, and the deejays have to play what they're told to play. Worse yet, some stations have done away with deejays in favor of computerized programming. Don't get me started on that. . . .) Inspired by the progressive-country movement, I had produced "If Love Was a Pawnshop" with a steel guitar and fiddles, making it country-friendly enough to warrant crossover airplay. Plus, I let my Texas twang come through on the vocals on this particular tune, and that didn't hurt the country airplay possibilities, either.

Music Row had once been a residential neighborhood. Over the years, record labels, production outfits, recording studios, and man-agement companies had converted the old houses to offices, so the row had sort of a hometown look to it. The renovated houses still had front yards and shade trees. You couldn't let that fool you, though. It was a cutthroat, moneymaking business, just like Wall Street or Hollywood. I had lined up three meetings with some label A&R guys, and all of them turned out to be idiots.

The first one told me I was too young.

The second one told me I was too old.

The last one said, "Nashville ain't the place for hippie music, boy."

My fruitless meetings all over, it was about four thirty on a humid afternoon, and I just wanted a beer, so I walked across the Vanderbilt University campus to a place called Bishop's American Pub on West End Avenue, where I knew a lot of music business movers and shakers liked to hang out. I sat down at the bar and ordered a draft of Hamm's beer. It was cold and foamy, and it didn't last long, so I ordered another.

Just as I grabbed that second foamy beer, I heard a sweet, sultry, Southern voice over my right shoulder.

"I'm sorry, but . . . are you—?"

I turned, the mug still affixed to my lips, and saw the face of a woman who was so beautiful that I gasped. When you gasp with a mouthful of brew, the next thing you do is choke, then cough, then you spew beer foam into the face of anyone in front of you. The gorgeous woman flinched, then began to laugh as I sheepishly dabbed at her face with little paper cocktail napkins. At least my coughing prevented me from saying something stupid as I tried to repair the damage I had already created. This also gave me a chance to look this gorgeous creature over.

She was a little younger than me, I judged. She stood about five-seven, with long, straight, silky, shiny, auburn hair. Her lips were full, and her lipstick was smeared a little, but that was my fault because I smeared it, trying to dab away the beer I had gasped into her face. Her eyes were big, dark brown, and mischievous. The beer foam complemented her skin.

She was wearing a red dress with a V cut in the front—appropriate for business attire in that day and time—but her laughter only accentuated her endowments. I dropped one of those little paper napkins and stooped to pick it up. Skirts were short that year, so I couldn't help noticing a pair of well-shaped legs on top of patent leather pumps with heels maybe three inches tall—that was pushing it for office attire, but it worked for me.

A young Sophia Loren came to mind. I thought she might be of Italian descent.

"I am so sorry," I said, still wheezing a little from having inhaled my Hamm's. "I didn't even ask you if you wanted a beer."

"I don't mind sharing one with you," she said, "but next time, just hand me the mug."

Okay, a young Sophia Loren with a Tennessee drawl so thick, you could almost taste it.

I ordered another beer and told her she probably should check her lipstick. She looked in the mirror behind the bar, wiped away the smear, produced her lipstick from a little purse that hung on her shoulder with a thin strap, and took the beer I ordered for her.

"So, you were saying . . . ," I said. "Before I started foaming at the mouth . . ."

"Yes." She took a dainty sip. "Did anyone ever tell you that you look like a young Ronnie Breed?"

This woman knew how to sweet-talk a man. "About ten years ago, maybe. When I *was* a young Ronnie Breed."

"So, you *are* him! Mr. Breed, I'm your biggest fan. I have all your records!"

We had the typical star/fan conversation for a while—favorite songs, the time she saw me in concert, permission to call me Ronnie rather than Mr. Breed. . . . I decided that was enough about me. I wanted to talk about . . . whatever her name was.

"I'm sorry, I didn't get your name," I said.

"It's Dorothy." She said it the three-syllable, Southern way: DOOR-oh-thay. "Dorothy Taliaferro."

"Italian." So, I was right!

"On my daddy's side."

"Do you speak Italian?"

"Some. It's one of my goals in life to learn to speak it fluently."

So, she had goals in life. Interesting. "Are you from Nashville, originally?"

She took another sip of beer. I couldn't help staring at her mouth as she licked the foam away from her lip. "I'm from a small town in Kentucky. I moved here five years ago."

"Are you a singer?" For a person who had a track record in the music business, this was a frightening question to ask someone in

Nashville. What if she was indeed a singer, and a horrible one who thought she was the next Patsy Cline? I could already imagine her reaching into that little purse for her cassette tape full of Loretta Lynn and Tammy Wynette covers.

But she laughed and said, "Only in the church choir, back home. No, I moved here to attend Vanderbilt University."

If you have never watched a sexy Southern girl's mouth, and listened to her drawl enunciate "Vanderbilt University," you have not led a full and complete life.

"Did you graduate?"

"With honors."

"What keeps you in Nashville now?" I continued.

"I caught the country music bug living here."

"I've heard it was going around town."

"It's chronic, I'm afraid."

"How'd you get infected?"

"When I was in school, studying business, I landed an internship working for Lefty Frizzell's manager. When I graduated, Lefty offered me a full-time job, and I took it. We were trying to revive Lefty's career, and get some of his songs cut by some up-and-coming country singers."

I smiled a sad smile. "Lefty is one of my heroes. How's he doing?"

She sighed. "Not well. He won't take his blood pressure medicine, or cut back on the hard liquor. He quit performing. His office wanted to keep me on with a pay cut, but I opted to step out on my own. I started my own management company."

"Artist management?"

"Precisely."

"Why?" The tone in my voice made up for the fact that I had left out the words,

. . . in God's name would you ever voluntarily sign up for that brand of hell?

"I think music is important."

"How's it going? Your business, I mean?"

"Rocky," she admitted matter-of-factly. "Still looking for that first big, breakout artist to establish some clout."

I started to get nervous again. A management company looking for a springboard artist might prove more clingy than a chick singer looking to get discovered. But she had yet to put the hard sell to me.

"So," she began, leaning toward me, her eyes sparkling.

Uh-oh, here it comes, I thought. But her question surprised me.

"Any advice for me?"

"More than you'd probably ever want to hear." I nodded at the bartender, who had offered another round with a well-placed gesture.

"I'm sure you've worked with your share of management teams. Tell me what I need to know."

I looked into those beautiful, dark, Mediterranean eyes. I was clearly attracted to her, but I had nothing to prove to Dorothy Taliaferro. I had Mona in my life right now in a very public relationship. That situation was going to have to play itself out. I had no reason to sugar-coat anything for an aspiring artist management expert whom I might never see again. So I gave it to her straight:

"Above all else, remember this: You work on behalf of your artist. You don't work for the record label, the venue owner, or the booking agent. And don't *ever* make the mistake of thinking your artist works for you."

She sat back, a bit shocked at my intensity, but she took in what I had said and replied, "Okay . . . Go on. . . ."

"All those bloodsuckers—the labels, the venues, the agents—and the so-called publishers—all those insatiable parasites are all going to expect you to jump through all kinds of flaming hoops for them." I wagged my finger at her as I shook my head. "Uh-uh. It doesn't work that way. You've got to train *them* to jump through the hoops for your artist. And you have to jump through the flaming hoop first just to show those greedy profit-eating leeches the way."

Her eyes narrowed, as if she was considering downgrading herself to maybe my sixth or seventh biggest fan. "And then there's the dark side, right?"

"Oh, there's more, but it'll contradict everything I just told you."

"How so?"

"Don't ever give your artist the impression that you work for him—or her."

"Even though you've already said I work for my artist, and no one else."

"No, I said you work on *behalf* of your artist, and no one else."

"So, if I don't work for my artist, and my artist doesn't work for me . . ."

I drank deeply from my frosty mug and waited.

". . . we're equals."

I slapped my hand down on the bar. "Equal partners! Now you've got it! Nothing else will work. Don't ever take any crap off a temperamental, prima donna, troublemaking, exhibitionist glory hound who thinks he possesses a voice that is God's own gift to the human ear. They're not worth it. And if they get busted for drugs, or if they're a raging alcoholic, or just can't stay out of trouble? In what other business would you tolerate such nonsense?"

"None other."

"Exactly. Dump 'em faster than you'd dump a truckload of horse manure! Faster than you'd dump an abusive husband!"

"I'm not married," she said, almost defensively.

"That was hypothetical. I already checked your ring finger. Furthermore, assuming you can find a star-quality artist capable of mutual respect, you've got to realize that he might be a genius when it comes to music and showmanship, but a blithering idiot when it comes to almost everything else. Some of the geniuses I've worked with can't get on and off an elevator, much less the freeway. Some of them need a lot of hand-holding."

"Nothing wrong with a little innocent hand-holding," she said. Looking back on all this, years later, I can clearly see that she was attempting a subtle flirtation. I was just not in the frame of mind to process it at the time, so I brushed it aside.

"So, you put all that contradictory advice together, and you still don't have a chance in hell of succeeding in artist management if you don't have an ear—and an eye—for talent. And I can't help you there. Nobody can. Either you can recognize it, or you can't. It's an innate, instinctive thing. You can't learn it from somebody else any more than you can learn to fly by watching birds do it."

She smirked and finished her first mug of beer. "Rosy future you've painted for me, Ronnie. But I'll have you know I don't scare easily. And as for recognizing talent, the first time I heard your voice, I knew you had it made in this business, so you see I do have the ability to judge star quality when I see it."

"Oh, you're good," I said admiringly. "Stars love it when you appeal to their ego. You'll do just fine, Dorothy, if you can hang in there until you find your first moneymaking client."

"Speaking of which . . . I'd be crazy not to ask. . . ." She reached for the second mug the bartender had brought.

"So, ask. . . ."

"You wouldn't happen to be in the market for a new manager, would you?"

Subconsciously, I had already anticipated this question and considered my reply. I knew nothing about this woman, other than what she had told me in the last fifteen minutes. She was well spoken and motivated, but could she handle one of the toughest jobs in the world? I couldn't take an all-out professional risk on her just yet. For all I knew, she may have pissed off everybody in town by now. So I played hard-to-get.

"What if I told you I might be?"

She seemed encouraged, but remained cool. "Then I would tell you I'd be interested in working on your *behalf*."

"Even though I'm not a country artist?"

She shrugged. "Your music has always had country influences in it. If you're really looking for management—country, pop, crossover, whatever—I want a shot at it. Good music is good music. I don't get hung up on categories."

I decided to tell her that I had broken free from the Half Breeds. This news would be all over town in a couple of days anyway. I told her I was seeking a new direction, and a solo career.

She got real businesslike and spoke in a hushed tone. "Tell me what you need for me to make that happen for you in Nashville. You must have come here for a reason."

Oddly enough, this sort of stumped me. I didn't really know what I was doing there. Not exactly. Not with any kind of specificity. Maybe that's why I was floundering. I had been putting a lot of thought and energy into Dan's poker tournament, but my career beyond that was still hidden in the fog of my mind.

"I came here looking for the reason," I admitted. "I don't know what I expected to find."

"I see two avenues opening up for you here," Dorothy announced in a surprisingly authoritative tone. She held up one finger: "Song-writer." Then, a second finger: "Country recording artist. It's an and/or situation. I can make either or both happen for you."

"Elaborate," I suggested.

"First, songwriter. I know of a dozen songs you've written, some of them buried as album tracks on your Half Breeds records, that would make Top Forty country hits. That's mailbox money waiting to happen."

"You want to pitch them for me?"

"Sure. But we'll have to recut them."

"Huh? I produced all those songs. They're all great sides."

"Yes, but they're not country. Pop rock won't sell here. You know how the suits are in this town. They have no imagination. You have to show them the product in its final *country* form or they won't get it."

"You're right," I admitted. "But I don't have the jack for studio sessions right now. I've got all my cash tied up in other investments, and I sold my studio in L.A. I've got nowhere to record."

"Don't you worry, I'll handle that. Now, step two: Country recording artist. Do you have some fresh tunes no one has heard before?"

"Yes, ma'am. I've got a whole new album of material just waiting for a two-inch tape machine."

"I'll arrange the studio time. You give me those new demos and six months. If I don't have you a sweet, major-label, country-crossover record deal in six months, you can take your business to another management firm."

I pondered this. Six months. On one hand, it was almost impossible to get anything done in a mere six months in the music business. It was a minuscule fragment of time. A lightning bolt. A blink. It was outlandish for this Dorothy Taliaferro to claim she could make anything happen in a fleeting 180 days.

On the other hand, six months out of the national spotlight was a terrifying eternity in the life of a celebrity. You could be forgotten, replaced, presumed dead, even shuffled to the half-price rack. Hell, in six months you could hear yourself on the oldies station!

Logically, I could not possibly have agreed to give Dorothy Taliaferro any more or any less time than six months. She had nailed it. I was impressed.

"This is not exclusive," I said. "If some other offer crops up, I've got to go with it."

"Purely speculative," she agreed.

I gritted my teeth. I remembered that all my most lucrative business proposals had begun in bars. I stuck out my hand. "Six months on spec," I agreed.

I never knew a person could smile so wide. Those perfect teeth beamed like stage lights.

THE NEXT day, I was back home on the bayou. My mom returned from work and asked me how my Nashville meetings had gone.

I smirked and shrugged. "I may have found a new manager."

"Oh?" my mom said. "Is she pretty?"

How do they know?

6

THE FLAGSHIP Hotel was a Galveston landmark, though I'm not sure the term "landmark" is accurate, because it wasn't situated over land. It stood on a thousand-foot-long pier jutting out into the Gulf of Mexico off Galveston Beach. The Flagship was billed as the first hotel in the world built over tidewater when it opened in 1965. That may or may not be true. A Texan rarely lets the truth stand in the way of a good boast.

In the summer of '75, the Flagship was in its heyday. The restaurant was among the best on Galveston Island, the bar featured nationally known jazz acts, and the accommodations were like those of a luxury cruise ship, except the rooms were bigger, and you didn't get seasick.

Cousin Dan's decision to use the Flagship as a shooting location for our first segment of his proposed televised poker tournament was logical. He had sold the idea to the hotel manager with his usual good ol' boy charm and promises of filling the hotel with poker fans. And, Dan had told the manager, should the TV series actually take off, the Flagship would get free national publicity.

It was a Saturday in mid June when Dan and I met at the Flagship for an orientation tour and local television interview. Mona came with me. Dan brought Archie Zeller and one of the other high rollers he had recruited for the tournament, a fellow named Luis Sebastian, who said he was from Brazil. He was a dark, handsome rascal who didn't say much. Dan introduced us to the Brazilian.

"Brazil, huh?" Archie said. "I spent some time in Rio."

"Holiday?" asked Luis Sebastian, his poker face suggesting that he was just making conversation, and didn't really care.

"No . . ." Archie chuckled sheepishly. "I was thinkin' about takin' up permanent residence there, if you know what I mean."

"I understand," said Luis, seeming to warm up to Zeller a little.

"Anybody want a Bloody Mary?" Dan asked. "The hotel manager will be here in a few minutes."

The gamblers agreed to Bloody Marys, so Mona led them to the hotel bar, which was just opening up.

"How's the band coming along?" Dan asked me as we walked along behind the others.

"I'm working on it."

"Working on it? What does that mean? We shoot next week. Are we gonna have a band or not?"

"Of course we're gonna have a band. I got it handled."

This claim was something of a stretch. Henry Campos and I had been rehearsing my new songs and auditioning musicians. Henry had learned the tunes quickly, and composed some brilliant bass parts, but the players he brought to the auditions just weren't good enough. I had been working with some of the best talent in the business over the past several years, and these part-time pickers around Houston and Galveston just weren't cutting it. So, in truth, we didn't have a band, and I didn't quite know where I was going to get one in the next week, but I didn't dare admit that to Dan within earshot of everybody else involved. Luckily for me, the hotel manager showed up about that time and distracted Dan from further interrogations.

We toured the ballroom and the private room Dan would use to interview the poker players on camera. We reviewed catering, audience seating, room reservations. Dan had arranged it all. He had been working this thing hard. About the time we got finished with the Flagship tour, a young hotel receptionist came running up to the manager. She smiled at me, starstruck, and whispered something to the manager.

"Mr. Breed," he said, "there seems to be a phone call for you at the front desk."

"Really?" I couldn't imagine who might know where to find me just now.

"It's your *mother*!" Mona said, rolling her eyes. "She's the only one who knows you're here." She and my mother didn't have much in common other than XX chromosomes.

"Excuse me, y'all," I said, walking with the receptionist back to the front desk.

"Can I have your autograph?" she gushed as she handed me a Flagship Hotel notepad.

"Sure." I scrawled my name and handed the pad back. "So, is it really my mama on the phone?"

"She didn't say, but it didn't sound like your mother."

"You know my mother?"

"No, but it sounded like a younger lady."

I was completely baffled until after I said, "This is Ronnie," into the receiver. Then I recognized that seductive Southern drawl.

"It's Dorothy. I've got good news."

"How did you know I was here?"

"I called the contact number you gave me. You didn't tell me it was your mother's house. Anyway, she told me where you were. Nice lady. Don't you want to hear the good news?"

"I'm only staying with my mother temporarily," I explained, feeling a bit like a mama's boy.

"That's your business. Do you want to hear the good news, or not?"

"Sure, what do you got?"

"I've got thirty hours of free studio time lined up at Topaz Studios. It's only good for the next couple of weeks, though, because then they get real busy. And I've got some great session players dying to make the demos with you, free of charge."

This news stunned and concerned me. I wasn't accustomed to someone else putting my band together for me, or picking my studio. "I don't know," I said. "I'm real busy the next six weeks. I'm shooting a television pilot."

There was a pause at the other end of the line. Then: "Perhaps you missed the part where I said 'free studio time.'"

"Free is good," I admitted, "but they're bound to want something in return."

"They simply want to be first in line when you choose the studio to record the real album—your first country LP."

"Okay. But I always pick my own players, Dorothy. Even for demos."

"Well, then, I suppose you don't want to work with Slim Musselwhite, Mojo Stevens, and Warren Watson Warren. I'll just tell them to look for work elsewhere."

"Slim Musselwhite? I worked with him in L.A. What's he doing in Nashville?"

"Going country, like you."

"Mojo and Warren are great players, too. Those guys are top-notch." I looked up and saw Dan stalking toward me across the lobby.

"Did I mention that they, too, were willing to cut the demos for free, just for a chance to work with you? Free studio time and free top-notch players. I haven't found a bass player yet, however."

I thought about Henry. He was good enough to step up to Nashville. "I've got a bass player already. Don't worry about that. I just can't believe you got Mojo, Slim, and Warren in the same band! How did you do it?"

"I'd like to take the credit for it, but it's actually your doing."

"What do you mean?"

"All I have to do is drop your name, and doors open. You're extremely well respected among your peers."

"That may be, but how did you know which players to ask? Those guys are the cream of the crop."

"Someday you'll stop underestimating me. So, when are you coming back to town, Ronnie?"

Dan was in my face: "Ronnie! What the hell! Do we have a band for next weekend, or not? This thing has got to look like a real TV show!"

I fended him off with a gesture as I spoke into the receiver: "Tell the boys in the band we rehearse Monday afternoon at the studio. Three-ish." I covered the mouthpiece and looked at Dan. "I told you I was on it, Cuz."

Dan looked over his shoulder. "Don't call me Cuz. Get off the phone—*Eyewitness News* is here."

Sure enough, a news van for a Houston television station pulled up in front of the Flagship. Dan went to greet them.

"Three-ish?" Dorothy sounded uncertain.

"That's musicians' time. They'll understand. And tell them I've got some good-paying gigs for them in Texas. It's all part of this TV pilot."

"What's this TV thing all about?" she said.

"I'll tell you all about it Monday. I gotta do a TV interview right now. See you soon." I hung up the phone and strolled dreamily toward the news van, thinking of the world-class band Dorothy had somehow put together for me. I wasn't worried about adding Henry. He was solid—a naturally gifted musician who was going to step into the big leagues. He had the advantage of already knowing the tunes. As for the other guys—Slim, Mojo, and Warren—collectively, they had played on dozens of Top 40 hits with several different acts. This was going to be an all-star dream band.

On top of all that, something else had me feeling even giddier. At first, I didn't even know what it was. Then it came to me. I was going to see Dorothy again the day after tomorrow. What was I thinking? This was no time to be falling for an Italian Southern belle. Especially if she was going to be my manager.

"You didn't look like you were talking to your mother." Mona snapped me out of the haze, falling in beside me as I approached the news crewmen, who were quickly setting up in the lobby.

"It wasn't Mama."

"Ma-ma," she said, mocking me in a baby voice. "Who was it, then?"

"My manager."

"I thought your manager dumped you when you fired the Half Breeds."

"I found a new manager. In Nashville. She wants me there Monday to cut some demos."

"*She?* When were you going to tell me about *her?*"

"I just did, Mona." I could see that the TV crew was ready to in-terview me. Dan was waving me over.

"Well, don't get cranky. I don't care if you have a girl manager. Is she pretty?"

"That's what Mama wanted to know."

"So, she *is* pretty."

I saw a camera pointing at me, so I stopped and faced Mona. "Yeah, but she's got nothin' on my feisty little firecracker." I grabbed her around her tiny waist and pulled her close.

"Easy, rock star. You don't think I'm really jealous, do you?"

"Come on, play along. The cameras are rolling."

Her eyes lit up. She stood on her tiptoes and gave me a big kiss with her little mouth. "Now, go dazzle them with your celebrity bullshit."

"That's my job."

She smiled crookedly and shook her head at me.

I ambled over to Dan and the camera crew. Dan made introduc-tions. The reporter said it was a busy news day, and she had only a few minutes to spare. She wanted to interview Dan, but he refused, saying I was the official spokesman for the poker tournament. The reporter was a young, smart, attractive, redheaded gal who was all business—almost to the point of rudeness—until the camera lights lit up. Then she turned on the girl-next-door charm that had gotten her the job.

"This is Diane Krenek reporting from the Flagship Hotel in Galveston, with Ronnie Breed, of Ronnie and the Half Breeds, the official spokesman for the proposed television pilot slated to shoot here next week. Ronnie, this is an unusual idea for a TV show." She stuck the microphone in my face.

"It's a *unique* idea," I began. "It's called *The World Champion-ship of Texas Hold 'Em Poker.* And what better place than Galves-ton to begin shooting this pilot? Not so long ago, there was an infamous gambling den on a pier just down the beach called the Balinese Room. We're going to re-create that gaming ambience at the Flagship, but here, it will be totally legal, because the gamblers won't be playing for money, they'll be playing for the champion-ship."

"But there is prize money involved."

"Sure, just like a rodeo, or a golf tournament, or bingo. The best player wins. We've invited gamblers from around Texas and the world to compete—winner-takes-all."

"Where do you fit in?"

"Well, I don't how long I'll last, but I'm going to compete at the poker tables. And I'll be showcasing my new band for the live audi-ences, and the television cameras."

"*New* band?" she said, sensing the scoop.

"I've taken a break from the Half Breeds. Trying something a little different. The rest is top secret. Folks will just have to come out to the Flagship next weekend to check it out and get in on the shooting of our television pilot."

"Interesting breaking news! One more question: What charity organization does your poker tournament benefit?"

Reporters! Even on a fluffy little story like a televised poker tour-nament, they have to try to stir something up. Dan had no plans to benefit any charity, and Diane Krenek knew that. But I was the one on camera, and I wasn't about to come off as the money-grubbing celebrity benefiting only himself.

"Good question," I said, my mind scrambling. "Thanks for ask-ing. . . ." My brain groped. "We're benefiting . . . a really great cause. The DeBakey Heart and Vascular Center." Dr. DeBakey was a household name in the Houston–Galveston area—a celebrated heart surgeon and world-renowned medical genius. Back in the sev-enties, his research center was making great leaps in technology—most notably with heart transplants. If Dan and I managed to get our uncle Bubba a heart transplant, the DeBakey Heart & Vascular Center would be involved.

"Great cause!" Diane said. "Folks, that's next weekend, here at the Flagship in Galveston. You can get in on the shooting of a TV pilot, see Ronnie Breed's new band, and benefit the DeBakey Heart and Vascular Center. For *Eyewitness News,* this is Diane Krenek."

The moment the camera shut down, Diane turned to me and

thrust her notepad at me. "My sister is a huge fan. Would you? To Nancy?"

"Sure." I signed the autograph.

Meanwhile, Dan and the hotel manager had set up a poker table and recruited some Flagship patrons to stand around as if they were enjoying watching other people gamble. Dan and I, Luis Sebastian, and Archie Zeller played a few pretend rounds so the camera could shoot some footage. For a Hollywood effect, Mona leaned on my shoulder like some saloon girl in a movie. Then the news crew was off to the scene of a bank robbery. Zeller and Sebastian left the hotel together, talking about finding a poker game somewhere. The hotel manager went back to work. That left me, Dan, and Mona.

"The DeBakey Heart and Vascular Center?" Dan said, grilling me.

"Well? What was I supposed to say? That we don't benefit any charity? Just our own pockets?"

"All right, I see your point. Quick thinkin'. If we don't get bumped by the bank robbery or some goat-ropin' or something, that'll be great publicity."

"They're not going to bump us," Mona said. "Did you see Red's eyes light up when Ronnie said he had a new band? I can't wait to see myself on TV tonight!" She started jumping up and down like a junior high cheerleader.

I looked at my wristwatch. "I've got to pack for Nashville. Got rehearsals day after tomorrow." I clapped my hands together and rubbed them vigorously. "Dan, I just put together the band from heaven on high!"

" 'Bout time. What are you callin' it?"

I hadn't even thought about a new band name, but I was on a roll that morning. My mind just whirred into gear and cranked it out. I was done with half-breeds. It was so obvious that it just tripped right off my tongue. What can I say—sometimes genius just strikes.

I smiled at Dan and said, "Ronnie and the Truebloods."

He grinned. "Oh, that's *good*, Cuz."

I looked over both shoulders. "Don't call me Cuz."

7

BENJAMIN FRANKLIN Talmage woke up feeling old.

"Well, you *are* old," he chided, goading himself to get out of bed. He pushed the cotton sheet off his body and sat up. Even that little bit of physical effort made him short of breath. A few minutes later, he stood and made his way slowly to the bathroom.

It irked him something fierce not to be able to just jump out of bed the way he once had. He was only fifty-nine, but his heart condition made him feel a generation older. As he stood urinating over the toilet bowl, new vocabulary words floated in and out of his head—words like "cardiomyopathy"—terms the likes of which he never dreamed he'd have to learn until a year ago.

Before his fainting spell last summer, he had never spent a day in a hospital. He had rarely even visited with a doctor, and even then the doctors were friends with whom he occasionally hunted and fished. He had met a lot more doctors since his "episode."

Ben Talmage needed a new heart, and he was a good enough candidate for a transplant. The rest of his body was healthy. The problem was money, and the fact that Ben didn't believe in taking charity. He didn't care if it killed him, he wasn't going to die a burden to his family. People ought to take care of themselves, he believed.

"I'll come up with the money myself," he had told the hospital administrators. "How much is this operation gonna cost, anyway?"

The administrators had avoided answering that.

"Well, everything has a price tag, just tell me what it is."

It wasn't that simple, they had said. There was a wide range of things he might need once the procedure started, not to mention ongoing care after the surgery.

"Well, ballpark it for me. Am I the customer here, or not?"

So they told him. They gave him a range of somewhere between seven hundred thousand and a million dollars.

"You tryin' to give me another heart attack?" he had barked. "That's one way to drum up business."

They had tried to convince him that there were organizations in existence that might be able to help with some of the costs. Government programs and charities. Those were the wrong words to use to persuade Ben Talmage.

Now, as he shuffled out of the bathroom, he reminded himself that he had led a full life. He inched his way into the kitchen of his little frame house, now slowly falling into disrepair, as Ben just didn't have the strength to keep things up. He stared longingly at the coffee percolator, remembering his old life, always up before dawn, putting the coffee on.

Nowadays it was Sanka. The doctors had warned him off caffeine. He filled the percolator with water from the kitchen sink, poured the Sanka in the little perforated basket on top, put the lid on, and plugged it in the wall outlet. All this took a while. He had to stop to rest occasionally.

Before his heart began to fail, he would have spent two hours on his bulldozer by this time of the morning. He had savings to live on. He had seen to that over the years. But his savings were nowhere near enough to pay for the heart transplant he needed. Ben was an entrepreneur who had had the discipline to put 10 percent of his income in savings every year for the past thirty years. But, being self-employed, he had no health insurance. He couldn't afford both a savings account and health insurance, so he had gambled on good health and opted for the savings account. He wondered now if he had made the right move.

The good folks at the hospital had tried to convince him that the bills would get paid by someone. But Ben was not going to take charity. They had tried to put him on the transplant list, telling him he was a prime candidate, likely to survive five years or more with a new heart from a donor. He would have none of that.

The thought of them cutting him open and sewing in someone else's heart was weird enough, though he wasn't opposed to it, as long as the donor had signed up for it. But to take money he had not earned on top of that was unthinkable. If this was God's will, so be it.

As the percolator began to brew the Sanka, he shuffled out onto the porch to listen to the birds sing. He lowered himself down into his rocking chair. A mockingbird chattered in a huge pecan tree near the house, and out in the pasture he heard a bobwhite quail. He smiled. He had led a good life on this little piece of ranch property. He had worked hard and played hard. He had seen a good portion of the world and the nation, as a soldier and a traveler. Never a tourist, for he avoided those traps. He liked the word "sojourner." He continually reminded himself of his past adventures to take his mind off his present condition.

He had hunted elk in the Rocky Mountains. He had caught blue marlin off the west coast of Mexico. He had jumped out of perfectly good airplanes to save the world. He had visited bars and cathedrals in a dozen countries. He had taken care of what family he had as best he could. He had loved some women. That gal from Mexico was on his mind a lot these days. He had almost married her. That would have been a disaster, but she was a nice memory the way he had left it.

On top of all that, he had spent every moment he could spare acting as a steward to the acreage upon which he lived. He had never overgrazed it with too many head of livestock. He had created cover for the bobwhite quail, planted prairie grasses, dug a little pond for migrating waterfowl, and fertilized with manure instead of those chemicals everybody else was overusing.

If a man had to, he could almost live off the land here. He kept a grass-fed calf every year to take to the slaughterhouse and fill his own freezer. He could catch bass, catfish, and crappie out of his pond or the creek that wandered along the back pasture. He could hunt doves, teal, ducks, geese, and quail when in season, and could bag cottontail rabbits and squirrels year-round. There were enough pecan trees on the place to keep him supplied with nuts all year long, with enough to sell besides. It was just a little ol' patch of flat, Coastal Bend prairie, but this stock farm with its pastures, hardwood creek bottoms, and brushy fencerows was a thing of beauty to Ben Talmage.

But now, as his eyes drifted across the landscape, they fell upon that rusty old pumpjack across the fence, and his damaged heart sank into melancholy that quickly twisted into a familiar hatred.

Archie Zeller, he thought. That old son of a bitch. He remembered well the first time he had met Zeller. It was the spring of '59. Zeller drove onto the property in a Ford pickup and introduced himself. He had shaken hands with the man, a decade or so younger than him. Zeller dressed like a workingman and his face was tanned by the sun. He seemed like kindred at first.

"Well, what can I do for you, Mr. Zeller?" Ben had said.

"I'm a driller. Wildcatter. Lookin' for oil. Do you own this place?"

"Yes, sir."

"You own the mineral rights, too?"

"One hundred percent," Ben had answered.

"You mind if I do some testing? Could be oil under this dirt. It won't cost you a thing, and there's a chance you could make a lot of money."

Ben shrugged. "I don't mind."

"I'll be here in the morning with my equipment."

"I'll be gone to work before sunup, but I'll leave the gate unlocked."

The next night, Ben got a phone call from Archie Zeller.

"I'm sorry, Mr. Talmage, but the tests on your property just didn't look good. Didn't look good at all." He had rambled on about some kind of seismic testing he had tried.

"Well, I hope you have better luck down the road, Mr. Zeller. Keep a tight line, now, you hear?" That was oil field jargon Ben had picked up somewhere.

It wasn't six months later that Ben came home to find a crew preparing a drilling pad on his neighbor's property to the south. He knew exactly what they were doing, for he had built many a drilling pad himself as a bulldozer operator. The rig was going in right in the middle of the tract, almost a mile from Ben's fence line.

"Huh!" he had grunted to himself. "I guess ol' Archie had a little more luck with his tests over there."

The neighbor who owned the property in question lived in the city, and never visited his land. Ben had never even met him. The landowner leased the field out to a farmer whom Ben knew pretty well from the occasional conversation over the barbed wire fence, or the chance meeting at the feed-and-seed store. The farmer typically grew corn or sorghum, which made for some great dove, duck, quail, and goose hunting for Ben.

Over the next couple of weeks, Ben came home daily to see the drilling rig take shape. From his porch, he could watch through his binoculars. He recognized Zeller strutting around, giving orders, saw the wildcatter's pickup coming and going. When the rig started actually drilling, the hum of the big machine sang him to sleep at night. Ben was philosophical. He hoped the well would come in for the neighbor's sake. He thought about what he would have changed in his own life, should he become oil rich. Nothing. He had everything he wanted.

Then, at a Friday-night high school football game, he saw the farmer who leased the field, and the farmer told him that the property had been *sold* to a wildcatter named Archie Zeller.

"Huh?" Ben had said. "I figured he was just leasing that land. I didn't know he had bought it!"

"He bought it," the farmer had assured him. "He won't let me farm there no more."

"There goes my bird huntin'," Ben had lamented.

Over the next months, more rigs cropped up on the four-hundred-acre piece of erstwhile farmland, and one of them was awful close to Ben's fence line, only a couple of hundred yards from his house. Things got noisy. Still, Ben was usually tired when he got home. He'd have a beer or two and make himself some supper. He'd listen to the radio or watch the news on that grainy black-and-

white TV for a while before he went to bed. He had a clear con-
science. He slept well in spite of the new rig, closer to his house and
louder. He remained philosophical. Rigs didn't drill forever. They'd
either hit oil and put up a not-so-noisy pumpjack, or they'd go bust
and close the well.

One day, Ben saw Zeller across the fence, yelling at the drilling
crew, so he strolled over there to get the lowdown on the well. Zeller
saw him, and condescended to approach the fence for a discussion.

"Howdy, Mr. Zeller," Ben said.

"Mr. . . ." Zeller snapped his fingers, trying to recall.

"Talmage. Ben Talmage."

"Right." He shook Ben's hand over the barbed wire fence. "Sorry.
I meet a lot of people."

"Looks like I was just right on the edge of the oil, huh?"

Zeller took off his felt cocksucker hat and mopped a grimy bandanna across his face. "I tell you what," he lamented, "I have taken
a bath on this property. There's a little pocket of crude down there,
but these wells are low-yield. I'm just trying to pump enough out of
here to break even, then I'll have to sell this tract at a loss. I have
lost my shirt on this deal."

"Well, I guess that's the wildcatter's life," Ben said.

"True enough," Zeller replied. "Well, Mr. Talmage, I've got to get
on down the road and make enough money somewhere else to pay
for this boondoggle." He swept his arm across the landscape he had
sullied with rigs and pumpjacks.

"Better luck elsewhere."

That well on the fence line came in. A pumpjack started grinding
and squeaking within easy earshot of the house. Oh, well, it wouldn't
last forever. If it was low-yield, as Zeller had claimed, it would play
out in the near future. Ben soon grew accustomed to it. He had
other things to think about. He didn't pay it much mind. Still, as the
months dragged by, he'd look over at the former grain farm every
now and then and notice that all those pumpjacks were still seesaw-
ing crude from the earth. He wondered when it would end.

Then, one morning at four thirty, the same time Ben woke every
day, he got up to a god-awful commotion going on over there at the

little oil patch next door. He got his binoculars out. There was a cement mixer backing up to the near well, other concrete trucks running all over the property in the distance. They seemed to be sealing the wells. Wasn't that unusual? Ben had never worked as a roughneck or roustabout, but he had heard them talk. He had heard they would "work over" a well when it played out, trying to get some more out of it. But did they pour the old shafts all full of concrete when they ceased to pump crude? He had never heard of such a thing. It also seemed like an odd time to do the job, at four-something in the morning, but maybe they had a full day elsewhere.

That night, the news broke on TV. They called it the East Texas Oil Field Slant-Drilling Scandal, and Archie Zeller was right in the middle of it. He had been accused of using a device called a whipstock that allowed him to angle his drilling shafts under the properties of neighbors, stealing millions of gallons of crude without having to pay surface leases or oil royalties.

"Well, I'll be a cross-eyed mule," Ben growled.

He followed the story as the weeks went by. Zeller hired the best lawyers, who made motions for delays. Come to find out that Zeller had done time for running confidence scams, but that information couldn't be used against him in court. Then, right before the trial started, the prime witness for the prosecution—one of Zeller's disgruntled drillers—dropped off the face of the earth. Disappeared without a trace.

Zeller beat the rap, but the talk around town—at the high school sporting events, the barrooms, the churchyards, and the cafés—held that Zeller had gotten away with larceny on an epic scale, and was probably guilty of murder, as well.

Ben knew he was a victim of this scam. Zeller had scrambled to seal the wells with slanted shafts, to cover the evidence of the whipstock use. He was sure Zeller had angled that well near his fence under his property and stolen many months of oil field royalties from him that he would never see. He asked around about the average yield and value of a typical oil well per month. It varied wildly. But no matter how conservatively Ben figured it on the low end,

Zeller could not possibly owe him less than a million dollars in royalties and surface-drilling lease fees. He had been shafted.

So what? Archie Zeller was a thief. Ben Talmage was an honest philosopher. He wasn't any poorer; he just wasn't as rich as he could have been. He lost no sleep over it. He went on with his life, joking about the whole incident, refusing to let the scandal embitter him. That had worked fine until his anemia drove him to schedule a doctor's appointment. Cardiomyopathy. His heart would gradually enlarge, they told him. He would grow weaker and weaker.

Death could come at any given moment. He needed a new heart. And there was but one thing standing in the way of his signing on to the transplant list: money. Now Archie Zeller was not just a thief anymore. He was a murderer. He was slowly killing Ben Talmage. Ben could feel the grimy hands of the wildcatter tightening the grip around his throat. As he sat on the porch and glared at that old, rusty, abandoned pumpjack, Ben began to boil with hatred. Somebody ought to make Archie "Whipstock" Zeller pay for what he had done.

The Sanka was perking in the kitchen, but Ben didn't have the strength just now to get up and pour himself a cup.

8

THE FAMOUS Topaz Recording Studio took up all three floors of an old brick office building just off Music Row. It included five different control rooms, meaning that five projects could be recorded there simultaneously. Thanks to Dorothy Taliaferro, Topaz had agreed to grant thirty hours of recording time to me in one of their lower-end demo rooms, called Salon D. Even this facility had better equipment than the top-flight rooms of most studios.

As I toured the entire facility—ushered about by a pretty young receptionist who had met all the big country stars and was not impressed by my pop celebrity—I tried to keep a running tally in my head of how much money the owners of Topaz had invested in equipment. I lost count somewhere around ten million dollars.

At length, I settled into Salon D and familiarized myself with the Harrison recording console, the compressors, reverbs, equalizers, and other electronic gizmos I would have at my disposal. A rookie engineer had been assigned to the project. His name was Jimmy Williams, and he claimed he was kin to Hank. He couldn't have been over twenty-one years old.

"Who's paying you?" I asked him.

"Sir, I volunteered."

"Why?"

"I figured if you liked how I handled the studio, you might let me engineer the real album. And if not, I'd probably learn a lot from you, as a producer."

I patted the kid on the back. "I already like you, Jimmy. You've got a good attitude. But it's gonna take more than attitude for me to request you, should we record a real project here. I've got to like your work. I've got to like it a lot."

"I understand, Mr. Breed. I just appreciate the opportunity, sir."

"Just call me Ronnie. Don't call me sir."

"Yes, sir, Mr. Ronnie."

"Yeah, *that's* better. Now, listen, Jimmy. . . . I know that we're recording for free, so they've relegated us to Salon D. But if we use our heads, we can improve this facility to the C or B level. You get my drift?"

"Not really, sir."

"It's all about getting a clean signal path, Jimmy. So if we could, like, *borrow* a microphone or two, or some preamps, or whatever is not in use in the better rooms, we can upgrade this room until it's almost as good as the A room."

I saw a grin stretch across Jimmy's face. "I'll keep an eye on the schedules and see what I can sneak out of the other rooms when they're not in use."

"Good. This could mean a lot of late hours. We have to cut when nobody else is working so we can get ahold of the better mics and stuff."

"This is my life," Jimmy said, spreading his arms and slapping his palms against his thighs in a sign of resignation.

Slim Musselwhite was the first band member to show up. He got there about four o'clock in the afternoon. Slim was an Alabama guitar picker who had cut his teeth playing blues on a National guitar. His father, a hardworking farmer, appreciated his son's musical talent so much that he had traded a Model T pickup for the first electric guitar he had ever seen, and the Musselwhite farm did not even have electricity.

I had worked with Slim on some blues-rock projects that I had produced in L.A., and liked him a lot, on top of being awed by his genius as a guitarist. I was thrilled to have him in the studio. After some small talk, Slim's face got real serious.

"Lemme axe you a question, Rawn." I always liked the way he pronounced my name. "On these live gigs down there in Texas . . .

what's folks gonna think about a black man being in a country band?"

The question stumped me. I hadn't looked at it from a black man's point of view, I guess. "No more of a problem than it would be in Alabama," I said.

"That bad?" His countenance grew grim.

"I wouldn't drag you into anything dangerous. We're going to be playing some nice venues. Big hotels, mostly."

Slim smiled. "All right, then. I'll just pack a peashooter."

"We're shooting a television pilot. We're the band for the TV show."

His smile grew wider. "I'll get my shoes shined." Slim was known for stylish apparel onstage.

"And, also . . . I'm not so sure we're going to be a *country* band. I don't know what we're going to be yet."

"I like it," Slim drawled. "The canvas is clear."

The drummer, Mojo Stevens, showed up next. Mojo was born in Detroit, but he had Southern roots, his daddy having moved north to work on the assembly line instead of remaining in Kentucky to die of black lung, like his own father. Mojo had grown up on his father's music. Hillbilly music. But he had also absorbed some Motown funk. His gift was perfect tempo and innovation that never got too busy.

I grabbed an acoustic guitar off the wall and started playing some of my new songs that we were going to demo. Mojo played the back of a legal pad with his drumsticks.

"You want to do the verses half-time, and go to full-time on the chorus? That chorus really soars, man."

"You're reading my mind, Mojo."

Warren Watson Warren showed up next. He was one of those West Texas players who had moved to Nashville to save country music in the sixties. Around Music City, he was a well-known studio fiddler, brought up on Bob Wills music.

"I've always wondered, so I've got to ask," I said. "How come your folks named you Warren Warren?"

"My mama was from England. She was a war bride my daddy

come home with. Well, my grandfather on my mama's side had the first name of Warren. He insisted I had to be named for him, even though my last name was already gonna be Warren—my daddy's last name. So, like the Brits say, I was 'made redundant' the day I was born. Been looking for a steady job ever since."

"Where'd the Watson come in?" Mojo asked.

"My mama loved those Sherlock Holmes books. Thank God she didn't name me Warren Sherlock Warren."

I continued to showcase my new songs for the new band until Henry finally showed up. Henry was afraid of flying. He had driven the fifteen hours up from Houston the night before, and had over-slept in the motel room I had rented him. He looked as if he had just stepped out of the shower when he arrived.

"Man, those dark window shades in that motel room fooled me," Henry said, by way of apology. "I couldn't see no daylight."

With this one statement, Henry unwittingly let it slip that he had never toured with a band before. The other three guys looked at him askance.

"I've known Henry since I was in high school," I said. "He knows the tunes already. He can talk you through 'em as well as I can."

"Whatcha been doin' since high school?" Slim asked, still dubi-ous of Henry's track record.

"Pipe fittin'," Henry said proudly.

"*Humph,*" Slim grunted. "I done a little of that myself." His tone of voice suggested a different kind of pipe fitting.

We ran through all the songs for a broad overview. We were try-ing to decide which song to choose to begin arranging, when Mona stepped into the doorway. She had insisted on coming with me to Nashville, and had been driving around town in our rental car all day, looking for excitement.

She had dressed in what she considered a country style, wearing a faded pair of boys' overalls with a filmy tank top on underneath, and Converse tennie shoes. She had tied her hair up in pigtails, like Mary Ann on *Gilligan's Island*.

As she stepped into the control room, all the guys sprang to their feet. I thought young Jimmy Williams was actually going to drool on her. She faked a smile and put up with the obligatory handshakes as I introduced her all around. Then she looked at me.

"This town is boring," she said to me, as if it were my fault.

I spread my arms to indicate the studio surrounds. "Welcome to the exciting world of recording."

She rolled her eyes and sat in a plush armchair in the corner that Warren had vacated.

"Oh, somebody has a hot tush!" she said, tucking her legs up on the seat. "The chair is warm!"

As we got back to work, discussing the tunes, I saw Mona lay her head on the arm of the chair. She closed her eyes and was quickly asleep. One thing Mona could do was sleep. Especially during daylight hours. She had more trouble sleeping at night.

For the next hour or so, we worked on one song in particular, creating an arrangement for the demo. The musical minds in the room seemed to click well together, and I was feeling good about this gathering of talent that was possibly going to evolve into my new band.

Finally, Slim looked over at the young studio engineer, Jimmy, who had been listening attentively but hadn't said a word since he said hi to Mona.

"So," Slim said. "Rawn tells me you want to be a producer someday."

"Yes, sir," Jimmy said.

"Well, you could start by producing me a Scotch and water." Slim smiled, his eyes twinkling the plea for a drink.

Jim jumped to his feet. "Yes, sir. There's a wet bar downstairs. Do any of you other sirs want anything to drink?"

"I'll take a coffee with cream and sugar," I said.

"Cream and sugar?" Slim repeated. "You ain't no real cowboy."

"I'll take a Coke," Mojo said.

"I'll have a beer with a splash of tomato juice in it," said Warren Watson Warren.

"Why would you mess up a beer with tomato juice?" Slim demanded.

"Why mess up the tomato juice with the beer?" Mojo said.

"It's a West Texas thang," Warren explained. "Y'all wouldn't understand."

Just then, Mona sat up and—without opening her eyes—said, "Vodka and tonic, Jimmy."

"Got it," Jimmy said, and he trotted out through the door and down the hallway toward the elevator.

The band members began discussing the song again, but with my keen producer's ears, I heard Jimmy's voice speaking to someone down the hall. (When you've been producing records long enough, you can hear a glitch in the guitar part while talking to someone on the phone and simultaneously eavesdropping on a conversation in the control room.) Then I faintly heard heels clicking on the marble floor. Somehow, I knew the cadence of that long-legged stride.

My heart skipped a beat when Dorothy appeared in the doorway. She was wearing a low-cut gold satin top with ruffles, a tight-fitting sandy taupe skirt, stockings, and gold pumps. Her auburn hair was strewn all about her shoulders as if some Madison Avenue fashion photographer had just arranged it so.

"I thought I'd stop in and see how you gentlemen are coming along."

When she heard that sultry Southern drawl, Mona's eyes flew open like those of a she-cougar who had just sensed the presence of a rival lioness entering her den.

"We're off to a pretty good start," I said.

As Dorothy greeted the men, Mona pulled herself out of the armchair in the corner and stood. Dorothy towered over her as they shook hands. Mona must have felt sorely underdressed in her overalls and tennie shoes.

"So you're the new manager," Mona said, as if it were an accusation.

"I'm still on probation, hon," Dorothy answered.

Mona's lip snarled. "Well, at least we have that in common."

Jimmy arrived with the drinks, and being a good Southern boy, he handed out the ladies' drinks first. "Vodka and tonic . . . and whiskey sour."

Dorothy sipped her drink. "I thought y'all might be ready to break for supper," she suggested. "All the nice restaurants will be closed before too very long."

I looked at my wristwatch. "You're right. I lost track of the time."

Mona guzzled her entire vodka and tonic. "I'm going back to the hotel to dress for dinner. I'll be back in twenty minutes." She ran from the control room, her Converse shoes squeaking on the floor.

"That means at least forty-five minutes," I said. "Maybe an hour." I set my coffee aside. "Jimmy, on second thought, I think I'll have a bourbon, if you don't mind."

"On the rocks?"

"Neat."

"Uh, what does that mean?" he said.

"That means just put some bourbon in a glass all by its lonesome."

"I'll be right back with it." He bolted from the control room and ran back toward the elevator.

Dorothy looked at the musicians in the room and smiled. "It's just amazing to see this much talent in one room," she said. "I don't know what exactly will become of it, but I know it will be good."

"I don't hardly see how we could go wrong," I added. "But I will tell y'all this: There's been some talk around town about me going country. That's BS. I was *born* country. I don't have to *go* country."

"Amen, Rawn. I still got sharecropper dirt under my fingernails."

"So," I continued, "we're gonna take these songs of mine and put our style on them. So, what we need . . . is a *style*. But I don't want to go looking for any particular kind of style. We're going to let the style find us."

Mojo nodded and punctuated my idea with a short roll of his sticks on the legal pad.

"Y'all know how it works in this town. The record-company suits and the A and R guys have zero imagination. They see whatever act is at the top of charts this week and go out looking for a copycat band."

"We ain't no copycats," Slim said, picking up on my point.

"We're the band they'll be copying next year," Warren suggested.

"Make that six months from now," Dorothy added.

As we waited for Mona to return, we continued to talk about the possibilities. We all agreed that we were tired of trying to force our talents into pigeonholes created by other people. We weren't going to worry about being country, rock, blues, pop, folk, or whatever. We were going to do whatever the hell we wanted to do with these demos and play a few live shows together for the poker tournament television pilot. If we all clicked, so be it. If the band flopped, at least we would know that we had approached the project with integrity and tried our best.

Mona arrived in record time, wearing a devastatingly sexy black dress over black suede buccaneer boots, all accented by flashy silver festooned with fake diamonds on her fingers, her choker, and her earrings.

"Cute outfit," Dorothy said to her, and we all left to dine at Maude's Courtyard on Division Street.

There was an interesting dynamic at the dinner table that night. Mona seemed bent on competing with Dorothy, just for the sake of the competition. It had nothing to do with me. Mona just had to be the center of attention wherever she went, and that was tough to accomplish with a tall, willowy Southern belle seated at the same table. Dorothy, on the other hand, had a way about her that said she had nothing to prove to anyone, though I knew that she was campaigning intensely for my business as a client.

I just sat back and enjoyed the whole thing, refusing to get caught up in it. I knew Mona would stay with me for the summer, as she was keenly into the whole television-pilot project. I also knew that she and I would go our separate ways soon enough. We were not meant to spend our lives together. As for Dorothy, I didn't know enough about her personal life to even know whether or not she had a steady boyfriend, but I had to assume she did. Women that gorgeous did not stay unattached very long.

I did know that I felt my stomach flutter every time I heard her voice. There was no doubt that I was infatuated with Dorothy. But I wasn't about to let my guard down and make a fool of myself. Mona was, I realized, a convenient reason for me to maintain my distance from the incredibly desirable Dorothy Taliaferro, and that was probably a good thing during the summer of '75. I had too much going on in my life that summer to drag a new love into the mix. So I looked at Dorothy as forbidden fruit, which, of course, only made me want her all the more.

9

REHEARSALS AND recording went well over the next three days. We fell into a routine. We'd pick a song to arrange, learn it, rehearse it, perfect it, then cut it live. All the players would be in different isolation booths when we cut, so if one guy made a mistake, we'd just keep going to the end of the song, and then that one guy could come back and overdub his part, fixing the mistake.

On some songs, Warren would use an open track to play a second fiddle part, harmonizing with his own original track. Or Slim would use a track to add a second electric guitar, a Dobro, or an acoustic guitar. I added some piano and mandolin parts on a couple of songs. We were recording on a two-inch, twenty-four-track tape machine, so we had plenty of tracks for the drums, bass, guitars, some percussion, fiddles, and vocals.

Ah, yes, those now-famous vocals. All the guys in the band had good singing voices, and could all find harmony parts. As we began to experiment with vocals, we discovered that our voices blended incredibly well. We all possessed very different vocal styles that nevertheless complemented one another. When we started overdubbing for harmonies, we were stunned with the results. When we had three-, four-, or even five-part harmonies going, our vocals sounded like some kind of human accordion, or a church organ or something.

"I didn't know we were starting a vocal band," Mojo said.

"The blend is like Canadian whiskey," Warren added.

"It's *skeery,*" Slim concluded.

By Thursday, we had a demo album in the can—a sparsely produced project that, once mixed, Dorothy could use to try to get a
record contract for us. We recorded four songs per day, cutting the
sides mostly as a live band. The players were so good that an overdub was seldom necessary. By the time we were through with the
demos, Henry Campos had been accepted as a true talent by the
seasoned hit-makers. We were, at least, a studio band. But the un-
spoken question remained: Could we play live?

We would find out Saturday, at the Flagship Hotel.

THE INITIAL taping of Dan's proposed television pilot at the Flagship
in Galveston could only be characterized as sheer pandemonium.
Only Dan seemed to know what was going on, and I was pretty
sure he was faking it. His film crew had arrived from God-knows-
where—three guys who ran around with cameras, lights, and boom
mics as if they knew what they were doing. One of them was the
director—a brash, effeminate little fellow who called himself by one
name and one name only: Bartholomew.

On Friday night, the last two star gamblers arrived. They went by
the names of Jack Diamond and Lady Daniela. Diamond was an
older gent from Canada, and Lady Daniela was an attractive French
woman who said she made Monte Carlo her home. These two characters, along with me, Luis Sebastian, and Archie Zeller, would be
featured players, and were expected to advance to the championship. In fact, Dan had guaranteed it. I don't want to say the whole
thing was rigged that way, but Dan had handpicked some very talented dealers from Vegas, if you know what I mean.

Dan had everyone attend a meeting in his suite at the Flagship
Hotel on Friday night. We had a great view of the moon beaming
down on the Gulf of Mexico from his window. There was an open
bar, so we all poured drinks and made a little small talk. Then Dan
called the meeting to order.

"Now, I know I sent you all a detailed prospectus on this event,
but I also know none of you are the type to read that kind of crap,
so I'm going to go over it all for you here.

"For the next five Saturdays, we're holding one-day-long tournaments in five Texas cities: Galveston, San Antonio, Corpus Christi, Fort Worth, and Houston. Greater Houston, that is. The final grand champion show will actually be at Gilley's in Pasadena, a Houston suburb. That's five cities in five weeks, folks, so brace yourselves for a hell of a ride across half of Texas.

"The Saturday schedule will be pretty much the same for the next five Saturdays. At noon, Ronnie Breed and his new band, the True-bloods, will play a couple of songs to get the attention of the crowd. Then we'll begin shooting the first round of poker. Each of you will sit at your own table and you'll play against four local yokels who bought tickets to the event. I expect you to beat all these local yokels."

The players chuckled as if that would not be a problem.

"After each of you five high rollers defeats the local challengers, we'll take a break for supper—that's what we call the evening meal in Texas: supper. Dinner is at noon. After supper, we'll shoot the championship round for that city—wherever we are. One of you will win.

"I've developed a point system to keep track of who performs the best over the five weeks, but I can almost guarantee you that you five gamblers will be playing for the finals at Gilley's in five weeks. Don't disappoint me."

Again, the confident chortles filled the room.

"Ronnie and his band will play a few songs at various times during the tournament, and of course they'll put on a concert or a dance at each city on Saturday night, after the championship round is over. We're relying a lot on Ronnie's celebrity to bring out a crowd for the filming of the poker."

"No pressure there," I mumbled.

"Okay. Everybody understand the schedule?"

Everyone in the room either nodded or shrugged or stared out at the Gulf.

"I'll take that as a unanimous yes. Don't worry, I'll be here to constantly remind you what to do next. Now, about the game itself. This tournament is going to be a hold 'em tournament. If you're not familiar with hold 'em, don't worry. It's the easiest poker game there is to learn. I'll deal a few practice hands tonight so everyone will know how it works. Each table will have a dealer, so you don't even have to worry about knowing how to deal it."

Jack Diamond raised his hand. "Hey, Dan, why hold 'em? Why not draw poker or stud or something we all know?"

"Because hold 'em was invented in Texas. In fact, we're not going to call it hold 'em, we're going to call it *Texas* hold 'em. Texas sells. And a new game will arouse curiosity. So it's a Texas hold 'em tournament, and that's all there is to it. You'll all learn to love this game."

"Fine," Jack said. "Just asking."

"Now, keep in mind that gambling is illegal in Texas, so we'll be betting with chips in front of the camera, and playing for points, not money." Here, Dan lowered his voice and said, "So if you want to make any side bets, do it discreetly. I don't want any of my star gamblers arrested.

"That's about it, I guess. Oh, one more thing. I want to see some charisma on the camera. Talk a little trash at the tables. Take a few shots at each other. Let's make it fun. All right! Any questions?"

"I got one," said Zeller. "Where's my blindfold?"

"What blindfold, Arch?"

"I cut my teeth playin' hold 'em. You're gonna have to blindfold me just to make it fair to these poor saps."

"That's it!" Dan said. "Save it for the cameras, Wildcat!"

AS NEAR as I have been able to find out, hold 'em was invented in the small burg of Robstown, Texas, down around Corpus Christi, near the turn of the twentieth century. Dan and I had learned to play the game from our uncle Bubba, but not a whole lot of people knew it. The star gamblers Dan had invited to be televised had the benefit of some practice rounds that Friday night, giving them a huge advantage over the locals who would come to play on Saturday at the Flagship.

As you probably know by now, Texas hold 'em has become a hugely popular game all over the world, thanks to television and the Internet. You may know how it's played. I could write a whole book on the game and how to play it, but if you're not familiar with it, here are the most simple basics of how it works:

There's a system of "blinds," which I don't need to get into in depth. These so-called blinds are the first two players to the left of the dealer. There's sort of a forced wager you have to make if you're one of the blinds. That gets the betting going. So much for the blinds.

The dealer deals each player two cards, facedown. These are his "pocket cards" or "hole cards." After each player peeks at his two hole cards, there's a round of betting. If a player doesn't like what he's got in the pocket, he can fold right then and there.

Next, the dealer deals three cards, faceup, on the table. This maneuver is called "the flop." These three flop cards can be used by any player to finish out his or her hand. More betting follows the flop.

Now the dealer turns a single card faceup, beside the flop cards. This is called "the turn." The card revealed on the turn can also be used by any of the players. More betting, folding, raising, calling . . .

The dealer deals one more card faceup, for all to use should they find it helpful in fleshing out their hand. This card is called "the river." A final round of betting ensues, after which the players must start revealing their hole cards if they want to win.

So, in Texas hold 'em, you have your own two hole cards, plus five common cards lying faceup on the table to use in putting together your hand. The entire game is geared toward driving the pot up through round after round of betting.

If you're a hold 'em player, you know that I've breezed over a bunch of details. For example, before the dealer deals the flop, the turn, or the river, he "burns" a card. That just mean that he tosses aside the top card on the deck. All this burning of cards is supposed to make it more difficult for a slick dealer to stack the deck.

Those are the basics. There are nuances to this game that you could spend a lifetime learning, but that's it in the proverbial nutshell. The game is more about the players than the cards: who's bluffing, who's hot, who's cold, who's nervous, who's cocky. So after our practice rounds Friday night, with Dan dealing and explaining, all the gamblers seemed to feel comfortable with the game and ready for the tournament to start the next day.

THE FIRST round of the tournament wouldn't start until after lunch, but Dan had a full schedule for the star gamblers, and the film crew, starting after breakfast on Saturday morning. Makeup, interviews, and that sort of thing. I was busy with my band, on top of all that, so it was a crazy day.

About eleven that morning, I was doing a sound check with the Truebloods. We were dialing the sound system in with the hired sound man, and running through the intros of all the songs. In addition to our new demos, we would be playing some of my old Half Breeds hits. We finally got the PA system sounding about as good as it was going to in the cavernous ballroom where we would entertain later. We were playing "If Love Was a Pawnshop" when Dan burst into the ballroom with Archie Zeller. He waved his arms at me as I sang up onstage, then pointed to his wrist watch.

The song ended.

"That sounds pretty good," I said to the audio guy over the mic. "It'll be better with live bodies in the room to absorb some of that echo."

The sound man gave me a thumbs-up, relieved to be done with the lengthy sound check. I guess I was somewhat of a perfectionist when it came to audio.

"Come on, Ronnie!" Dan said, tapping the face of his watch. "I've got you and Archie scheduled for your on-camera interviews!"

"Sorry, Dan. I lost track of the time." I racked my guitar and trotted across the dance floor to join Dan and Zeller.

"I'm going to put Archie in front of the camera first," Dan said as we rode in the elevator to the fourth floor. "You need to comb your hair or something. You look whupped."

"I've been working. Don't worry, I'll perk up."

When we reached the suite where the camera crew had set up, Dan cautioned us: "Be quiet now, the cameras may be rolling."

When we opened the door, I saw the Brazilian, Luis Sebastian, in front of two cameras. He was sitting with a view of the Gulf of Mexico behind him, the interview obviously in progress. I noticed Mona standing behind a camera. She had gotten a job with the TV crew as a makeup artist. Apparently, their usual makeup specialist had failed to show up.

As we stepped in, the snooty TV crew director, Bartholomew, turned toward us and put his finger to his lips, a threatening look in his eyes. We closed the door behind us quietly.

Luis Sebastian was smoking a cigar and holding a toddy with a lime slice on the rim. ". . . this is why," he was saying, in his lush Brazilian accent, "a gambler never goes anywhere without his passport in his pocket." As he was saying this, he set his drink down, reached into his jacket, and pulled what looked like a passport from within.

"And . . . Cut!" the director said. "What a great story!" He led the tiny film crew in a round of applause. "Dan," the director announced, "this Brazilian stud is pure gold! He's like camera candy!"

Dan nodded. "Told ya, Bart."

"It's Bartholomew. *Bartholomew!*"

"All right! Shit! Bartholomew, then. I've got another couple of characters for you right here. Archie 'Wildcat' Zeller is next."

Mona pranced over to me. "Hi, honey!" she said, giving me a peck on the lips. "This is fun! Maybe I finally found my calling!"

"Good for you, babe. You're a natural."

Mona turned to Archie Zeller. "Right over here, Wildcat." She swung her arm toward her makeup chair. "I'll just dab a little powder on that shiny red nose."

"They didn't bring their own makeup gal with 'em?" Archie complained.

"She had a gallstone, so I'm filling in."

"Mona carries enough makeup in her purse for a troupe of circus clowns," I added. "She knows what she's doing."

"Well, all right," Archie allowed.

Mona tugged at his arm. "Sit down, Wildcat. We're on a schedule."

Soon, Archie Zeller was in front of the camera, looking as if he thought he was God's gift to cinema. To tell you the truth, he was pretty good at being the guy you loved to hate. Every TV show needed a villain. With Zeller, it was typecasting. He was so obnoxiously sure of himself and his gambling prowess that his every pore seemed to ooze arrogance that stank like a fetid week-old gut pile.

With the cameras rolling, Bartholomew said, "Just tell us about yourself, Mr. Wildcat—as a gambler. Ready . . . and . . . action!" He then cued Zeller with his index finger.

"I tell you what," Archie declared, chewing a gummy cigar butt, "these amateurs are about to step into the world of Wildcat Zeller. They call theirselves gamblers. Crap. They don't know the meaning of the word. Not one of these lightweights have ever bored a hole in the ground, bettin' their fortune on the off chance a gusher might come in. Now, *that's* gamblin'! I've got thirty years experience staring at that beast. I can look right through that Brazilian's dark glasses and glare a hole in his brain like a drilling rig. You won't catch Wildcat Zeller wearing sun shades at a poker table. My eyes are my drill bits. Whiskey's my mud. This is my championship to win. I *will* be crowned the champion poker player of Texas, and therefore the world . . ."

Right about then, I fell asleep in the makeup chair. The obligatory applause from the film crew woke me up a few minutes later. Zeller was wearing a Cheshire wildcat grin that would have put a possum to shame.

"I think we found our heavy!" Bartholomew sang.

Mona unclipped the microphone from Zeller's lapel and escorted him to the door, stepping out into the hall with him.

"Enjoy your siesta?" Dan asked.

"It was delightful," I grumbled.

"Okay, it's time for our sleepyhead!" Bartholomew announced, turning toward me with his hands clasped daintily.

"Where'd you find this guy?" I asked Dan under my breath.

"Hey, he's good at what he does," Dan said through his teeth. "He came highly recommended."

"Makeup girl!" the director shrieked. "Makeup girl, get in here!"

I saw Mona step back into the room, giving Wildcat a seductive little wave through the narrowing crack in the door as she shut it.

That was almost too much to take. I mean, Mona was a confirmed flirt, but . . . with Zeller? I gave her a look that screamed something like: *You've got to feel so dirty right now.*

She pouted back at me and shrugged. "I'm just doing my job!" she hissed.

10

I WOULD like to believe that every person alive possesses a special gift. Some guys can make broken motors run. Some people have an inexplicable ability to catch fish. I once knew an old man who could pull his car over, walk out into a strange pasture or field, and pick up an ancient flint arrowhead that had somehow called to him. Some individuals possess enough wit to make a man laugh in a coma. There are bona fide geniuses in universities who can figure out, with hieroglyphic symbols on a chalkboard, how fast the universe is growing. Some souls have a knack for making money, others for making gourmet fare, still others for creating beautiful works of art.

But I also harbor an unfortunate belief that too many of us get our gifts beaten, scared, or simply talked out of us by narrow-minded know-it-alls who have, in turn, long since had their gifts bullied out of them. The survivor who recognizes, accepts, develops, and celebrates his or her unique gift in the face of incessant criticism, doubt, and misguided advice is a truly courageous champion of self-belief.

I think I am safe in claiming, without boasting, that my gift lies with music. It just makes sense to me, without even having to try to understand it. I'm not saying I've learned it all. Music is one of those things—like poker, horses, or fishing—that you can study your whole life and never know everything about. I also believe that I have made the most of my gift, and that has brought me the rewards of wealth, fame, acceptance, praise, and joy.

Even so, I am, to this day, still sometimes frustrated at how many people just don't get it. Everybody hears music, but not everybody listens, or even knows how to listen. Many people have to be told what music to enjoy, to purchase, to like, to dance to, to talk about. They are thus instructed by record-company marketing campaigns, Top 40 charts, awards shows, and incessant, repetitious radio airplay of a handful of songs that become drilled into their heads as if by skilled and evil brainwashing experts.

Do you realize how much room there is in the world for people to make music? Do you realize how few are allowed to occupy the most visible surfaces of that space? It's a fragment of the whole. An iceberg makes a poor analogy. You can see way too much of it jutting above the surface of the sea.

But there are precious few enlightened, confident, intelligent people in the world who possess the gift of making up their own minds about what is worthy, what is good, and what constitutes talent. At our opening show at the Flagship Hotel in Galveston, Texas, in '75, Ronnie and the Truebloods enjoyed no such gifted individuals in our audience. Zero.

Now, this wasn't your normal gig. It wasn't a club that attracted avid music fans. It wasn't a theater or a big outdoor music festival. It was a ballroom in a fancy hotel, and the real attraction was supposed to be poker. About 150 folks had bought tickets for this thing. A few of those probably had bought tickets to hear my music, though we had done precious little advertising. Others were attracted by the opportunity to be on a television show. But most were there to try their hands at gambling with some high rollers. So the crowd was disjointed, and took some work to whip into shape as an audience.

I looked out over this crowd as Dan introduced us. Our stage stood at the far end of the ballroom. Most of the people were clustered around two cash bars that the hotel had set up. Beyond the bars, at the other end of the ballroom, was the filming set for the poker tournament. As Dan's introduction echoed through the huge room, we kicked off our gig with one of our new songs, and I must say, we fairly nailed it. It was slick, and we sounded good. But only one guy went to the trouble of putting his drink down to applaud, and we got only three claps out of him.

So we went on to the next song—another new one, and one that would a couple of years later be a smash hit. Same results.

Some lady walked up to the stage and said, "When is Ronnie Breed going to play?"

Irritably, I answered, "Lady, I *am* Ronnie Breed."

"Well, play your good songs!" She meant the ones she had been force-fed over the radio, of course.

"Rawn," growled Slim Musselwhite. "You gonna have to do the Half Breed thang to get 'em goin', man."

"All right," I grumbled.

Mojo clicked off the tempo for my biggest pop hit, and when Slim launched into that familiar guitar lick in the intro, the crowd lit up like a refinery fire and gravitated toward the stage like lemmings headed for a cliff. The TV cameras swooped in, now that people were acting like they were having fun, and I started to feel like something akin to a rock star again. This was the first live gig I had played in almost a year, but I shook the rust off with a couple of moves I had stolen from Elvis, and reclaimed my calling: that of a mood-changer, a note-painter, a story-singer; an eraser of cares, a rhymer of pictures, a strummer of truth. I could go on and on, but I'll spare you.

After playing a couple of my past hits, I addressed the crowd.

"Folks, I have a new band, and a new album coming out soon." I was aware that the latter might well be a bald-faced lie, as we didn't have a contract yet. "How would you all like to be the very first fans to hear my next hit song?"

They screamed and gesticulated to the point of spilling drinks. We played a song we had cut in the studio two days before, and sold it to the audience as best we could. The cameras helped the crowd get into the music. Most people are natural hams and know how to at least try to play a role on camera. These people played the role of fanatics. I was proud of them.

And that was it. Like I said, it wasn't your normal gig. Dan had explained that the cameras just needed a few snippets of music to edit in. But everybody understood TV production. They were here for a televised poker tournament.

"Ladies and gentlemen," I said, "we'll be back onstage later tonight to play some more tunes for you—some old ones, and some new ones. But right now, it's time for all of you lucky players to take your places at the poker tables. Let the games begin!"

THREE HOURS later, I was still sitting at my assigned table, playing against the last opponent left—some bartender from Sugar Land. Dan had picked twenty players among the ticket holders, and these were the lucky contestants who would play in front of the cameras. Supposedly, the names had been drawn randomly. In reality, Dan handpicked the contestants he wanted to play in the first round. The amateurs he chose were invariably attractive young women, or guys who looked as if they couldn't tell an ace in the hole from a hole in the ground. Dan seldom did anything with just one agenda in mind.

There were five tables. One each for me, Luis Sebastian, Archie Zeller, Jack Diamond, and Lady Daniela. So, each table included one of us handpicked high rollers, four of the contestants who had won the "random" drawing, and a professional dealer.

One of the two cameras rotated over to my table to watch me beat the bartender, whose name was Dean. Dean was a pretty good poker player, but the cards were stacked against him. I knew I would beat him. The dealer, a master card mechanic Dan had found somewhere, was instructed to deal me the winning hand. Hey, there was too much at stake here to make this a fair tournament. But Dean the bartender would get his money's worth for his ticket, and would go home with some nice prizes. We weren't playing for real money, so it wasn't like we were ripping off the contestants. In fact, everybody had a real good time.

Dean knew he was in trouble with his last hand, so he bluffed and went all in, trying to get me to fold. It was a pretty smooth move, but it didn't work. The river turned, and the queen I needed to win appeared. Dean was good-natured about it and shook my hand. People applauded.

Dan, who shared directorial duties with Bartholomew, hollered

"Cut!" and that was it for the taping of the first round. Dan was sort of the fill-in director when Bartholomew went to the production van, where he spent much of his time doing whatever TV directors do in their production vans. But now, Bartholomew came bursting back into the ballroom.

"People! Listen, people!" he yelled. "We're going to break for dinner, then shoot the final round at eight o'clock sharp! I'm going to need extras in the audience, so if you local people want to see yourself on TV, stick around!"

"Dinner?" said Dean the bartender.

"He means supper." Dan said, "He ain't from around here."

Dan corralled all the high rollers, plus Bartholomew, to have supper with him in the Flagship's five-star restaurant. There I got better acquainted with Lady Daniela, from Monaco, who was very beautiful and mysterious and held both her clove cigarette and her salad fork in the European way. Not at the same time, though.

"I am most pleased to make your acquaintance," she said in what I took for a French accent.

"*Enchanté,*" I replied. That was about all the French I knew.

"*Parlez-vous français?*" she responded.

"*Oui,*" I joked, slathering on an accent of my own making. "Cordon bleu. Seafood plate."

"You are a funny man," she said without laughing.

The Canadian, who called himself Jack Diamond, for overly obvious reasons, was less exotic. He drank blended whiskey, ordered his steak well done, and spread mounds of butter on his dinner roll. He was of good humor and laughed a lot, but was not very funny. He acted like a bit of a goofball, but that was the way some poker players played you—making you think they were buffoons while they systematically fleeced you like a cross-eyed lamb.

After we had ordered, Dan dinged his spoon on a wineglass to get everyone's attention. "First, a toast," he said, raising his glass. "Ronnie!"

He was always putting me on the spot like that, but I came through with an old Irish toast I had squirreled away in my brain. "Here's to lying, stealing, cheating, and drinking," I began. "Now, when you lie—lie to save a friend. When you steal—steal a lady's heart." I looked at Lady Daniela. "Or a gentleman's heart."

"Either/or," she quipped. "Why limit oneself?"

"Whoa!" blurted Jack Diamond.

"When you cheat," I continued, "cheat death. And when you drink—drink with me, my friends!"

"Ah, bravo!" cried Luis Sebastian.

"Here's a better one," declared Archie Zeller, who had not even bothered to drink to my toast. "Here's to horses, and here's to women. And when I die, tan my hide and make me into a lady's sidesaddle so I can ride between the two things in life I loved the most. Here's to horses, and here's to women!"

The gamblers all laughed like crazy, and Archie looked satisfied that he had out-toasted me.

"Now, I want to go over our schedule before the main course gets here," Dan said. "We're off to a good start. Good job, so far, everybody. Now, after supper, we're going to shoot all of you together at the championship table for the Galveston finals."

"Yes," Bartholomew interjected, "and I need you guys to really turn on the ol' high roller charisma. This is what's going to sell the show to the advertisers, and the public. And I don't mind a little animosity between players. People like conflict. We'll all have a drink or two afterwards and laugh about it, but let's make it look a little seedy and dangerous for the cameras."

"What comes next, after tonight?" Jack Diamond asked.

"The schedule hasn't changed, Jack. Next weekend, we do the same thing in San Antonio. The following week, it's Corpus Christi, the birthplace of hold 'em. Then, Fort Worth. Then, the final location just outside of Houston, at Gilley's Dance Hall. Five cities in five weeks."

"We'll edit it down to ten episodes," Bartholomew said. "That's our first season. If we're lucky, we'll get picked up by one of the networks, and you'll all be big stars."

"Except for Ronnie," Dan said, blowing cigar smoke out of the side of his mouth. "He's already a big star."

"Not big enough," I admitted.

"Nobody has ever done anything like this before," Dan said. "We're going to shoot Texas hold 'em poker like a sporting event. We'll patch in your interviews during the show, so rehearse your favorite stories, your most clever sayings, or whatever. It'll be a real-life drama, with a lot at stake—the championship of the world!"

"May the best man win!" Jack Diamond said.

"Don't mind if I do!" Archie drawled. Damn, he was a cocky bastard.

But the others just laughed and played along, so I did, too. It occurred to me that if I hadn't had so damn many things on my mind, I would have been having one hell of a good time that evening at the Flagship. But most of my burdens were of my own making, so I had no cause to complain. I had no way of knowing, however, that the burdens would only multiply as the weeks passed, and that I would come close to destroying everything in my personal and professional life before the end of the summer.

11

DAN HAD scripted the tournament to a tee. He knew who was going to win at every city to host an episode of *The World Championship Series of Texas Hold 'Em Poker.* He had already decided that Archie Zeller would win at Galveston. So, of course, he did. Dan had taken a play out of the professional wrestling playbook for his hold 'em tournament. Some folks may have thought it was real, but it was all rigged. It was designed to keep the five high rollers in the spotlight so that they would all end up playing in the finals at Gilley's on the fifth Saturday.

So, that night at the Flagship, Dan's expert dealer eliminated the gamblers, one by one, with some sleight of hand that allowed him to manipulate the deck and deal the winning hole cards wherever he wanted them. The Canadian, Jack Diamond, was the first to go. Then, Luis Sebastian. Next, it was Lady Daniela who went all in and lost out. Only Archie Zeller and I were left still playing.

I knew Zeller was going to win. So did he. We were both in on the script. So it was more like shooting a movie about gambling than actually gambling. I played the role as best I could, betting my whole pot on what I knew would be the last hand. And, of course, Zeller won when the hole cards were revealed.

So, using Dan's system, Zeller had scored five points. I had scored four. Daniela three, Sebastian two, and Diamond one. At the end of five weeks, the top five scores from the four previous weeks would play for the world championship of Texas hold 'em. And you can bet that Dan had it figured so that those top five scorers would be the five high rollers he had handpicked from around the world. No one was going to break into our little circle from the outside and surprise us. There was too much at stake.

After Zeller beat me to win the Galveston finals, I still had to front my band and entertain the crowd with an hour-long set of music. That hour turned out to be my favorite chunk of the day. The band performed phenomenally, and the crowd loved us. We had proved that we could stand up as a live band and win over new fans. I felt we were on our way to great things.

At the end of the night, we all gathered at the hotel bar and drank and laughed about the activities of the day. Mona was sitting beside me, and ol' Whipstock Zeller was on the other side of her. The more Mona drank, the more she laughed at Zeller's stupid jokes and draped herself on him. Finally, there was nobody left in the bar but Dan, Zeller, me, and Mona. The bartender gave us the last call signal, and we drank up.

"Well, I gotta hand it to you, Dan," said Zeller in a rare complimentary tone. "You pulled it off pretty smooth. Looks like your show is off to a good start. Hell, I might just turn a profit on my investment!"

"Actually . . . ," Dan began. "Oh, well, never mind. . . ."

I waited for Archie to react, but he seemed not to have picked up on Dan's less-than-positive tone of voice. So I replied in his stead.

"*Actually* what?" I demanded. "You don't sound so optimistic."

"Well, actually," Dan repeated, "we're running out of money. I'm not sure we can continue shooting after the next episode."

"Huh?" Archie demanded.

"I'm new at this television business," Dan explained, shrugging innocently. "There are expenses I didn't see comin'."

"Well, cut some expenses!" I suggested.

"I've tried. I asked Bartholomew and his TV crew to work on speculation, but they wouldn't have any of that. This is your fault, Ronnie. You're not selling enough tickets. I counted on you being a bigger draw."

"On the basis of what?" I said defensively. "We have no advertising budget!"

"Boys!" Mona scolded drunkenly.

"The bottom line is, I need y'all to put in a little more seed money. I mean, if you want to see this thing through to the big time."

"I can't, Dan! I gave you all the liquid assets I had."

"You could sell one of your tour buses."

"Yeah, you got four of 'em," Mona slurred.

"Those buses are making money for me. Anyway, they're all leased out to touring bands for the summer."

Mona stamped her foot like a spoiled five-year-old. "But I like my makeup girl job!"

All this time, Archie's face had been growing darker. "I want my money back right now!" he demanded, his tone belligerent.

"I can't do it, Archie. I don't have it. But if you kick in some more, I *guarantee* you'll see a profit on this thing in the end."

"How can you guarantee it?" Zeller snapped.

"I can't tell you that."

"You didn't seem too all-fired worried about this today," I said, picking up on Archie's anger.

"Well, I was sure that I could approach the both of you tonight and get some more seed money to keep this thing going. I'm telling you, the profits are going to be huge!"

"The lawsuit I slap your ass with is gonna be huger!" Archie said. "This is bullshit!" He stood, prepared to stalk out.

"Come on, settle down, Wildcat . . ." Dan groaned.

"I've got to agree with Zeller on this one," I said. "I can't afford to sink any more money into this pipe dream. It's only week one, and we're already broke?" I threw some small change on the bar as a tip. "Come on, Mona."

"You'll hear from my lawyer," Zeller said, turning to walk away.

"You mean . . . ," Mona whined. "It's over? I don't want it to be over! Come on, Ronnie. Please! I like TV. Make it keep going!"

"I can't, Mona. I just can't."

Archie was almost to the door when Dan hollered: "Okay, wait!"

Zeller stopped and scowled over his shoulder.

Dan dropped his chin on his chest in defeat. "All right, I guess I'm going to have to let you two in on the real profits behind this thing."

"What are you talking about?" I said.

"Come on, I'll show you."

We joined Zeller, who was still fuming mad at the barroom entrance.

"Follow me if you want to get rich," Dan said, turning down the hallway toward the elevators.

"I'm already rich," Zeller replied.

"Okay, that would be rich*er* in your case, Archie."

Mona picked up on the hopeful development. "Goody," she said, prancing along. "Come on, Ronnie. Come on, Wildcat."

Zeller and I exchanged a cautious glance.

"This better be good," I said.

"I won't disappoint you," Dan replied, sounding confident. "Come on."

We boarded the elevator and rode in silent anticipation up to the top floor. Dan whipped a key from his pocket and unlocked the penthouse suite of the Flagship Hotel.

"This is a hell of a lot nicer than our rooms," I complained as we entered.

"No shit," Zeller said.

"Hey, a bar!" Mona squealed. "Anyone want a drink?"

We all nodded.

"What are we doing here?" Zeller demanded.

"This way," Dan said, leading us into the living area of the sprawling suite.

When I stepped in, I saw a desk strewn with ledger sheets, pencils, notes, and an ashtray full of butts. In addition to the normal hotel room television set, I noticed a small, portable TV monitor perched on the corner of the desk. There was a whiskey tumbler and not one but two telephones in the midst of the squalor.

"This is the reason I needed the suite," Dan said, putting his hand on one of the phones. "It has two separate phone lines, so he can take twice as many calls."

"Who?" I asked.

"What kind of calls?" Zeller said suspiciously.

Mona handed out drinks—whiskey on the rocks for everyone.

Zeller looked into his glass and began fishing out the ice cubes. "Darlin', I don't see any reason a piece of frozen water should ruin a perfectly good whiskey." He threw the cubes on the plush red carpet of the suite.

"Sorry, Wildcat," she purred. "I'll remember next time."

Zeller took a gulp. "Now, what the hell is it you're trying to show us, Dan?"

"Have a seat." Dan gestured toward the cushioned, crushed velvet, purple armchairs gathered around a hardwood table.

We sat down. Dan looked at us earnestly. "You boys are good poker players. No, really, you're pretty darn good. But I handpicked you to be here for other reasons. Archie, you're here because you have the money to bankroll this outfit and make it work—plus you've got a Texas mystique that's interesting to people around the world. Ronnie, you're here because you had some cash to invest, too, plus you're a celebrity. But the other three players I picked—do you know why they're here?"

I shrugged. "Same reasons?"

"No . . . All right, listen, I don't want to insult y'all, but as poker players, you two are minor-leaguers. The other three I brought in are major-league, international superstars in the world of gambling."

"Then how come I've never heard of 'em?" Zeller asked.

"Yeah?" I added.

"Believe me, if you were a major-leaguer, you would have heard of them. The highest of high rollers in the world know who Jack Diamond, Luis Sebastian, and Lady Daniela are."

"So what?" Archie said, insulted. "What's this got to do with getting my money back?"

"You're going to get more than your money back," Dan said. "You're going to get ten times your money back, or more, because I'm about to let you in on a little secret."

I saw Archie glancing at the phones and the ledger books on the desk. "I'm listening."

"The TV show is for real," Dan began. "I have no doubt it'll be a big hit, if we can just keep the shooting funded for another four weeks. But there's more going on here than meets the eye. The real moneymaking happens right here in this room, and it's already begun."

Mona was crunching a piece of ice in her mouth, her big beautiful eyes looking out under lazy drunken lids. "Huh?" she said.

"Every top-flight high roller in the world knows what's going on here tonight," Dan bragged. "And they've been calling in, making bets on the outcome." He jutted his thumb over his shoulder, toward the desk with the phones. "That's where my bookie sits. He watches a live camera feed of the poker tournament on that little monitor so he can keep up with the action. He takes the calls, keeps the books, collects the money."

"And smokes a lot of cigarettes," Mona mumbled.

"How do you collect money over the phone?" I said.

"Account numbers, routing numbers. The money is all wired in. Happens all the time, Ronnie."

"Where's all this money wired to?" Zeller asked.

"Swiss bank account, of course. It's untraceable. Tax free."

I shook my head, as if to clear the fog from this whole nebulous concept. "So you're saying that you're making money off other people gambling on us gambling?"

"You got it, Ronnie. The house—" He pointed both index fingers at himself. "—gets a cut of the pot."

"How big of a cut?" Archie asked.

Dan shrugged modestly. "Ten percent. The phone-in gamblers know that, and don't mind it. That's just a little ol' administrative fee they're willing to pay."

"All right . . . ," I said. "So how much . . . How much are we talking about?"

"How much what?" Dan said.

Archie took over the questioning. "How much did the house take in tonight?"

"I didn't get the final tally from my bookie, but the last time I checked, about midnight, it was almost two million."

"Dollars?" Mona blurted.

"You're shittin' me," Archie said, his eyes rolling like wheels in a slot machine.

"So you made ten percent of two million?" I said, gasping at the mere mention of the amount. "You made two hundred thousand dollars tonight?"

Dan chuckled. "No, Ronnie. Wildcat asked what the *house* took in. I *am* the house. Two million *is* the ten percent. The Swiss bank account took in almost twenty million."

Archie shoved his empty glass at Mona. "More whiskey."

"Bring the bottle," I added. I could feel the blood rush from my face and sink into my guts, sensing an approaching point of no return in this enterprise. It was scary but intriguing. "Let me get this straight," I said. "A bunch of high-rolling gamblers from all over the world phoned in twenty million dollars' worth of bets tonight?"

Again, Dan shrugged. "A million-dollar bet is chicken feed to these guys."

"Wait a minute," Zeller protested. "If you made two mil tonight, why the hell do you need me to invest more of my money to keep the TV crew shooting?"

"Because I can't touch the money in the Swiss account until after the final championship. Those are the rules of engagement. The pot builds and builds. The high rollers from around the world reinvest their winnings each week, until the finals. The excitement grows. After week five, these guys will be making enormous bets."

"How would they know if you did take a little out of the Swiss account? Just to keep the tournament funded?"

"These people aren't fools. They all have access to the account information. I'm the only one who can draw on the account, but everyone else can monitor it. You won't catch me drawing a single Swiss centavo out of that bank until this is all over and the money is distributed to the winners. A lot of these high rollers are guys you don't want to mess with. I mean, I'm a tough guy, but I gotta sleep sometime."

Mona sloshed more whiskey into our glasses and set the bottle down on the table. "We're in!" she said. "When do we start?"

"Now, hold on, Mona. . . ." I swirled the liquor. "How legal is all this, Dan?"

Archie snorted at the question.

"I like to look at it this way: It's so international, and so untraceable, that it's not all that illegal."

"What about tracing the phone calls?"

"That's the beauty of it. My bookie here works with another bookie in Vegas. The Vegas bookie takes all the international calls. It's legal there. I really don't think we're breaking any laws. Besides, we move to a different city each week, so no one county sheriff or police chief pays us much mind. And thanks to your quick thinking, Ronnie, we're benefiting a charity, so we look totally legit."

"Ronnie-hon," Mona said, "you have that nest egg you set aside when you sold your Lake Tahoe place."

"Mona," I growled.

"Tahoe?" Dan said, grinning. "I guess you forgot to mention that, buddy. Lakefront?"

"Right on the water," Mona said. "It was so pretty."

"Mona!"

"You want to make that nest egg grow to the size of an eagle's roost?" Dan said.

"Who all knows about this?" Archie said.

"Us, my bookie, the Vegas bookie, and some foreign investors."

"Luis? Jack?" Zeller snapped his fingers. "That gal from Morocco?"

"Monaco," I corrected.

"Whatever. The foreign gal."

"They're not in on it. Hey, I don't want to split this thing *too* many ways."

"I want to meet the bookie," Zeller demanded.

"No. Absolutely not. Nobody meets my bookie. He remains completely anonymous, for obvious reasons."

"I don't want to know anything about him," I said. "I feel like I know too much already."

"Oh, come on, scare-dee-cat!" Mona chided.

"Nobody meets the bookie," Dan repeated. "Period."

"Then this must be for real," Zeller said. "I was gonna call bullshit on you if you were to let me meet the bookie. You know what you're doing, don't you, hotshot?"

Dan simply smiled and spread his arms in acceptance of the compliment.

"So, let's talk turkey."

Dan sipped his drink. "I need another twenty grand from each of you."

"What's my cut?" Zeller asked.

"Ten percent of the house take."

"No way. I want a third."

I was surprised that Zeller was going along with this so readily. Apparently, he had money to throw around.

Dan sighed and bowed his head. "Twenty percent of the house, and that's all I can do."

"What's to keep me from calling the Texas Rangers right now?" Zeller threatened.

I saw Dan's temper kick in, but he held it together. "I'm not an amateur, Archie. I have an exit strategy. Besides, you'll only implicate yourself if you blow the whistle."

"Twenty-five percent."

Dan grinned. "Done! Ronnie? I'll let you in at the same percentage if you kick in another twenty grand."

"I don't know," I said, my stomach fluttering with warnings.

"Why would you *not* do it?" Mona urged.

"So, it's twenty-five percent of the house's ten percent?" I asked.

"Very good, professor. As long as you put in as much as Archie. Are you on board the Flagship or not?"

I almost choked when I said, "Okay, I'm on board." We were committed now. This ship was sailing forward under the skull-and-crossbones.

Dan slapped his hands together. "I *knew* I could count on y'all! Bring the cash to San Antone Friday, and this show will continue to roll. We're gonna make so much friggin' money that we'll never have to work another day in our lives!"

Archie jumped up, looking satisfied at his horse-trading. He grabbed his whiskey and headed for the door. "Not a problem," he bragged. "I got that much stashed in the cookie jar." He left the suite and slammed the door.

I released a huge sigh.

"You all right?" Dan said.

"I think I might puke," I said.

"You lightweight!" Mona sang, laughing at me as she mussed my hair.

"I don't know if I'm ready to live the life of a pirate."

Dan put his hand on my shoulder and gripped me tightly. "You remember the story of Jean Lafitte, Cuz?"

"Vaguely." I rubbed my face, feeling the exhaustion and the whiskey slam together in my brain.

"They said he was a pirate. He ruled Galveston Island a hundred and sixty-some-odd years ago. Right here, Cuz, on this same strand. But Jean insisted he was a *privateer*, not a pirate. He had a legitimate beef with the Spaniards, and he only raided their ships. They were pompous, arrogant, greedy gold-mongers, and Jean saw it as his duty to take their ill-gotten riches."

"Like Robin Hood!" Mona declared.

"Yeah, sort of. And he was a patriot, too, Ronnie. He helped Andrew Jackson rout the British at New Orleans in the War of 1812."

"I saw the movie with Yul Brynner," I said. "What's your point?"

"We're privateers, not pirates. There's a difference. Keep that in mind. Now, go get some sleep. You look like hammered shit."

Ah, sleep. That sounded good. I rose laboriously from my chair.

And that was how I became embroiled in a secret scam that I've had to remain silent about for thirty years. I know what you're thinking of me now. I was greedy. It was probably criminal. I was stupid. It was risky. I caved in to peer pressure from a pretty face and a fast-talking cousin. But, like the dealer in a hand of Texas hold 'em, I have yet to turn the last cards in this game for you to see. You never know how your final hand will play until you get past the flop, the turn, and the river.

12

MY MEMORIES feel like whirlwinds in my head every time I think back on the summer of '75. Imagine a barnstorming stunt pilot doing barrel rolls in the eye of a hurricane. That's what those five weeks during the poker tournament felt like. It wasn't just the gambling and the scheming. I had my career and my personal life to think about, too. While Dan headed west to San Antonio with the TV crew and the film set, I spent a couple of days at my mom's farm, then flew back to Nashville. On Wednesday, I met with the band at Topaz Studios.

As we settled in and got ready to listen to the demo tapes from the week before, Slim said, "That was a weird gig at the Flagship, Rawn."

I smiled apologetically. "Maybe San Antonio will be better this weekend."

"Hey, I ain't complainin'," he said. "The bread was good, and the rooms were cool. I'm just sayin', it was a weird gig, man."

"I'm going to do a live radio spot in San Antone. Maybe get some more music fans to the hotel there."

"Yeah, well, do me a favor and call ahead to the hotel and tell 'em I don't work for them. I had three different fools point me toward the kitchen door at the Flagship."

"It's San Antonio, man," Henry said. "They'll be shoving *me* to the kitchen there."

I was mortified to think that I had failed to make my minority band members feel comfortable, and promised it would not happen again. This was 1975. Segregation was a recent memory, and some folks in Texas were slow to move forward into the new era of equality. I had been thinking too much about my own issues and not enough about the safety of my two band members whose skin happened to be darker than mine.

As we began listening to the demos and liking what we heard, the weirdness of the Flagship gig drifted away, and we began talking about the future for the band.

"These demos are badass," Mojo said. "I mean, there are some things we can smooth out on the real album, but this stuff rocks."

The band agreed. We listened to side after side, and continued to compliment one another on a stellar demo recording. Just as we were celebrating the last song in all its glory, Dorothy Taliaferro stepped into the studio, carrying a notebook. She was wearing an Atlanta Braves baseball cap, her ponytail bobbing along behind her; a generic team jersey bearing the number ten, which she definitely was; faded cutoff jeans and the highest-heeled, most ornate, floral cowboy boots I had ever seen. She was showing a lot of shapely leg between the tops of those boots and the white fringe of the cutoffs.

"I thought I heard a construction worker whistle outside," Warren said.

Dorothy brushed the comment off. "Those guys? They'd whistle at *you* if you wore this outfit, Warren."

"Hey, why don't you try it on and see?" Henry suggested.

Warren grinned sheepishly. "Not my size, I'm afraid."

After some niceties, Dorothy said, "Ronnie, can I talk to you privately?"

"Sure," I said.

"In the break room?"

"Let's go."

We went down the hall to the break room, where we found a long, narrow table. She went to one side, and I went to the other, so we could sit across from each other, face-to-face. We sat in molded plastic chairs with chrome metal legs, the smell of scorched coffee and stale doughnuts hanging in the air.

"So, where's Mona?" Dorothy asked, settling into her seat.

"She went to the mountains to cool off for the week."

"Oh, too bad. I was going to invite her out for a drink while you and the guys fine-tuned the demos."

"I'll tell her when I see her in San Antonio this weekend. I'm sure she'll take you up on it next time, if there is a next time."

"She doesn't like Nashville?"

I sighed, and smiled. "It's hard to tell what Mona does or doesn't like from one minute to the next. She's a free spirit. She does what she wants to do, when she wants to do it."

Dorothy smirked, intrigued, and nodded slightly. "How long have you two been together?"

"Not long, but probably longer than we've got left together."

Dorothy bunched her perfectly plucked eyebrows. "You don't seem too upset about that."

"Maybe I'll have the opportunity, someday, to explain my relationship with Mona to you. It's probably not exactly what you think. In a lot of ways, it's a relationship of convenience, and the moment it becomes inconvenient, it'll be over."

"Hmm," she purred, piercing me with her big brown eyes. Then she shook her head as if to clear her thoughts. "I didn't come here to grill you about your personal life. That's your business. I want to talk to you about the demos."

"They sound good, huh?"

"Yes, they sound great. But I want them to sound better than great. I want them to sound fantastic!" She smiled and fluttered her lush eyelashes, flashing me with the crystal clear brilliance of her eyes.

Her comment, however, let a little helium out of my dirigible. "You don't think they're fantastic?"

"They're on the verge of fantastic." She got up and started around to my side of the table, opening her notebook as she rounded the end of the long table.

"The verge?" I could not prevent my eyes from tracking her. I had never seen hip pockets on a pair of cutoff jeans move quite that way.

"They have the potential to be marvelous," she continued, sitting down beside me with her open notebook. "I have a few notes and suggestions."

A hint of perfume wafted into my nostrils as I looked at the first page of notes. She had timed each song, and marked the changes she wanted by the minute and the second. There were more than a few notes there.

"What is this?" I asked, pointing at a reference to a "KB."

"Oh, sorry, that's my shorthand for 'keyboard.' There's one note that's just a little bit late in the second chorus."

I flipped through some of the following pages. There were dozens of improvements she wanted on every song. "Dorothy," I complained, "it's only a demo."

"Yes, I know, Ronnie. And I know you know what you're doing, and I know you've had some big record deals in your career. But I want to sign you to the biggest deal of your life. To do that, I need the best demo you've ever recorded."

I would have paid money to sit in a room, look at Dorothy, and hear her sexy drawl say the word "recorded" over and over and over again. I sighed. "What kind of perfume are you wearing?"

"It's called Le De. It's from France. Don't change the subject, Ronnie. I believe in these sides. I really do. They have more soul, more heart, more raw talent than anything I've ever heard, with the possible exception of Elvis on his best day. What they need is a little polish in the right places. Just a little precision overdubbing here and there—judiciously, surgically."

"Yeah, but they're demos. This is not a final project. We didn't use the best room in the studio. It's just a sales tool."

"Ronnie . . . Honey . . ."

I knew it was just a Southern courtesy for her to call me honey, but it made my heart double-clutch.

". . . You've had some success as a pop star. You've earned your celebrity. But that's not enough. As a solo artist, you're a risk to a major label. Especially as a crossover, country solo artist. A *sales-tool* kind of demo is not good enough. You have to dazzle them with something better than Conway Twitty's best finished project. Better than Glen Campbell, better than the Eagles."

I looked over the notes. Page after page. "This is going to take days. Maybe weeks."

"I've negotiated with Topaz for fifty more hours of free recording time. They really want you to do the project here."

I shook my head. "I thought we were ready to mix these demos. I really did. The boys in the band thought so, too." I was flipping blindly through the pages of Dorothy's corrections. I shut the notebook. "What if I refuse?"

She never batted an eye. She would have made a great poker player. "If you want to be a *mediocre* recording artist, then you'll have to find a *mediocre* manager."

It was so adorable, I almost giggled. The word sounded like "meaty okra" when she said it. I thought about the poker schedule over the next four weeks. The band could travel back and forth between Nashville and Texas, make the demo fixes during the weekdays, and play the tournament gigs on the weekends.

Then, too, there was the thought of extending my plans in Nashville. And that meant seeing more of Dorothy. This was an easy call to make. Improve the demos, increase my odds of getting a bigger deal, rehearse more with the band, and smell more of Dorothy's French Le De.

"No 'meaty okra' for me, please. I'll make the changes, Dorothy."

The memory of her smile would light up my world for days.

13

THE MENGER Hotel in downtown San Antonio stands right next door to the site of one of the most famous battles in the history of the North American continent. There, in 1836, 189 Texans chose to fight to the death rather than surrender to the tyrant, Santa Anna. Twenty-three years after that fabled struggle at the Alamo, William A. Menger built a two-story hotel just south of the hallowed ground. They say the Menger is haunted. I don't doubt it. Many a conscripted Mexican soldier must have died from Texas rifle and cannon fire on the ground where the venerable hotel stands.

In the summer of '75, the Menger was 116 years old. Over the decades, some famous people had slept there, including Robert E. Lee, Ulysses S. Grant, Teddy Roosevelt, Mae West, and Babe Ruth. In the early twentieth century, the Menger would become the gathering place for members of the Texas Trail Drivers Association— aging Texas cattlemen and cowboys who had gone "up the trail" in the days of the Wild West. I had no doubt that mucho poker had been played there among them. It was an obvious choice for Dan's second round of poker in his floating hold 'em tournament.

When I checked in to the Menger on Friday, I hunted down the hotel manager, the head chef of the restaurant, the maintenance engineer, and the janitorial supervisor. I showed them all a Polaroid photo of my band. I pointed out to them that some of my band members were minorities, and they were not to be insulted by being directed to the kitchen or the loading dock because of their skin color.

I was confident that I had made my point, so I went on up to my room. Mona had already checked into the adjoining room. Mona and I always booked two adjoining rooms. There were a lot of reasons for this. For example, Mona insisted on her own private bathroom. Secondly, she liked to sleep at odd times, and wouldn't tolerate a roommate barging in while she was napping. Of course, the fact that her luggage took up half a hotel room was reason enough. It was amazing how such a petite, scantily clad sprite of a woman could fill a room with her wardrobe. And there were other reasons for our sleeping arrangements, but that is a discussion for another time.

After getting unpacked in my room, which didn't take long, I rapped on the door to the adjoining room and cracked it open. "Mona? It's five o'clock," I said. "I'm going down to the bar for the meeting."

"Thanks for the news flash, Ronnie," she sang, a note of sarcasm in her voice.

"See you down there."

I went down to the Menger Bar, located just off the lobby. Back in 1887, the then-manager of the Menger had decided to add on an ornate bar, and make it a replica of the House of Lords pub in London. The architect in charge of the new addition installed a paneled cherry wood ceiling, beveled glass and hardwood booths from France, and a polished oak bar and back bar. A decade later, Teddy Roosevelt used the Menger Bar to recruit soldiers for his Rough Riders, who would soon charge up San Juan Hill in Cuba, taking the summit and ending the Spanish–American War. The tavern had been known as the Teddy Roosevelt Saloon ever since.

Having been to this historic pub before, I was looking forward to stepping back into it, even though I knew Archie Zeller would probably be waiting there for "the meeting." I entered and breathed in the cigar and cigarette smoke. (It seems odd to recall this now, but I once loved the smell of a smoky bar. Nowadays, I detest the odor of tobacco smoke, especially in an enclosed room. But back then, before we had realized the dangers of secondhand smoke, it smelled like money to me, as I had earned a small fortune playing music in clouded taverns.)

The mounted longhorn steer heads and Western paintings on the walls of the saloon gave the place a combined Old World–Old West feel. I could hear the ghostly echoes of rattling chips and shuffling cards from poker games long past. I was looking forward to getting my lips pressed against a frosty mug of beer.

The bar was crowded with Friday's happy hour clientele, laughing and drinking and smoking. Being alone, I sat on a stool at the bar and ordered a Lone Star. From my seat, I could watch the crowd behind me in the mirror of the back bar, and I saw the reflection of Archie Zeller emerge from the darkest of dark corners. He sat beside me at the bar.

"Where's Dan?" he asked.

"Well, howdy-do to you, too, Arch," I said. He looked at me with a dead catfish face, so I answered his question. "I haven't seen Dan yet."

"I've been waiting half an hour."

I returned the fish stare. Conversation between Zeller and myself did not come easily. He tapped his empty tumbler on the polished oak to get the bartender's attention.

"Did you ante up?" he asked, a new shot of bourbon in hand.

I knew what he meant: Had I given Dan the twenty grand I had agreed to invest last week in Galveston? I nodded. "I brought the money with me. You?"

"I'm way ahead of you. I already gave it to him."

We sat there uncomfortably for a couple of more minutes until Mona thankfully showed up. Zeller swept his cocksucker hat from his head when he greeted her and gave her a lingering hug.

"Dan called the room," she said, straightening her ruffled sundress after the mauling Zeller had given her. "He can't make it to the bar right now. He wants you two to meet him in the loading dock."

"The loading dock?" I complained.

"Said he's unloading the cameras and stuff for the set. Come on, he told me how to get back there."

We told the bartender to keep our tabs running and followed Mona out the door to the street. This exit faced the south approach to the Alamo. She turned right on the sidewalk and led us toward the back of the hotel.

Zeller pointed at the Alamo. "That there is hallowed ground," he said.

That seemed to be one of the few things on which Archie Zeller and I could agree.

In the alley around back of the Menger, we found the film crew's equipment truck backed up to a loading dock. I spotted Dan stepping backwards out of the back of the truck, carrying one side of the gaudiest of the poker tables—the one we had all sat around while filming the championship round at Galveston.

"Watch your step, Dan!" I shouted.

Dan looked my way, missed a step, and fell backwards. I could hear the TV crew guys yelling "Whoa!" and "Watch it, Dan!" but Dan lost his hold and the table upended, flipping toward him, and landing upside down on top of him as he failed to scramble out of the way on his back.

Bartholomew rushed out of the truck, screaming, "Don't damage my set! What are you doing?"

I rushed to get the table off Dan as he lay pinned between the green felt table cover and the concrete loading dock.

"You all right?" I said, shocked at the blow he had taken, hoping he hadn't broken something.

But Dan was incredibly tough. He started laughing under hundreds of pounds of crushing weight that had just slammed him to the concrete. "I fold!" he wheezed. The crewmen and I helped hoist the table. Even Mona lifted an edge. Zeller was slower to climb the loading dock stairs, and all the heavy work had been done by the time he arrived. The table stood on edge as I help Dan to his feet.

"Anything broken?" I said, truly concerned.

"Maybe a rib or two. Nothing new."

"Hey!" Zeller shouted. "What the hell?"

I turned to see him looking into the exposed underside of the table. My eyes followed his to see what looked suspiciously like video cameras installed under the tabletop at every position where the players sat and played their hands—cameras that pointed up through the bottom of the table surface. Each camera was apparently wired to its own videotape machine.

"Shit," Dan said. "Turn that thing right-side-up before somebody sees those."

"I've already seen 'em," Zeller scolded. "You want to explain that?"

"Now, don't get excited, Arch. That's just for the TV audience. Those cameras catch glimpses of what each player has in the hole. Later on, we can edit shots of the hole cards into the show, so the audience can get in on the strategy of the game—see who's winning, who's bluffing." Dan winced and held his palm to his rib cage.

The cameramen righted the table, and Zeller crept forward to examine the tabletop. Along the edge of the rimmed table ran a row of flashy glass disks that seemed to be there only to lend a casino-like air to the set. But if you looked closely enough, you could see that five of those glass disks were actually camera lenses, each belonging to one of those video cameras under the table.

"Why weren't we told about this?" Zeller demanded.

"It doesn't affect the live play. It's just there to edit in later."

"I don't want my hole cards filmed!"

"He has a point," I said. "This is highly unusual."

"Of course it's unusual!" Dan shouted, his temper flaring. "It's televised poker! It's never been done before!" The outburst really seemed to hurt his rib cage.

"All right, take it easy," I said.

Dan beckoned for Zeller and me to step aside. Still holding his ribs, he walked over to his old military duffel bag, which he had already unloaded and thrown against the loading dock wall. He reached into the duffel and pulled out a bottle of Jim Beam whiskey. He gulped enough to make bubbles rise in the upturned bottle. He wiped his mouth on his sleeve and passed the bottle to me. I took it, of course.

"Look, gentlemen, it's like this. By showing some camera shots of each player's pocket cards, we're teaching the viewers how to play hold 'em, so they'll get into it. That means, next season, we'll have bigger crowds at our live events, and more people tuning in on the television stations. Everybody will want to play."

Zeller shook his head adamantly. "I didn't agree to having my pocket cards filmed," he persisted.

"Actually, you did. Read the fine print on your contract. Page three, paragraph four: 'Subject'—that's you—'grants permission to producer'—that's me—'to use images of subject's person and possessions, including, but not limited to, clothing, accoutrements, and handheld objects—'"

"That's bullshit!" Zeller yelled.

"Boys!" Mona chided.

I looked over both shoulders and spoke low. "What's the big deal? We know who's going to win anyway." I took a pull from the bottle and tried to hand it to Zeller, but he pushed it away.

"I don't cotton to everybody watching the goddamn electric teevee knowing my strategies."

"Fine!" Dan shouted, giving in. "If you don't want me to use the footage from your hole cards, then I won't, Archie. It's not that big of a deal."

"That settles it, then!" Mona sang. "No longer a problem."

Dan took the whiskey bottle from me. "Let's just keep the pocket cameras our own little secret, though, okay?" He took a swig.

"I love a secret!" Mona whispered.

"Fine with me," I said. "I don't care."

"All right, I guess," Zeller agreed. "As long as you don't film my pocket cards."

Dan nodded. "Okay. New business. Did you bring the cash, Ronnie?"

I reached into the breast pocket of my blazer. "Got it right here." I pulled out an envelope full of cash.

Dan took it, shook it, and threw it into his duffel.

"Aren't you going to count it?" Zeller said.

"Not here on the loading dock. Anyway, Ronnie wouldn't cross me. I'm betting it's all there. Now, here's why I wanted to meet with you two: I've been getting calls in my room all day from interested parties around the world—some are new players that didn't bet last week. This thing is beginning to build."

"I can smell fresh blood," I said.

"I better start smelling some money," Zeller warned. "Lots of it."

"It'll be a good weekend. I guarantee it." Dan dropped the bottle on top of the money in the duffel. "I need to get the set unloaded, boys. I'll see you in the bar later."

"Come on, Wildcat!" Mona said. "Let's go drink some whiskey!"

This prospect seemed to brighten Zeller's mood.

"You two go ahead. I'll stay and help Dan."

Dan rubbed his ribs. "I appreciate that."

Mona hooked her arm around Zeller's elbow, and they walked down the loading dock steps and disappeared in the alley.

"Don't worry," I said. "She'll cheer him up. How bad are you hurt?"

Dan smirked at me. He pounded his fists against his rib cage. "That was all for show, Cuz. I've had worse things than poker tables fall on me." He slapped me on the shoulder. "Come on, let's get this crap unloaded."

14

THAT NIGHT, Dan took our whole bunch—TV crew, gamblers, and band members—out to the Fig Tree Restaurant. A nice stroll down San Antonio's famous River Walk led us there from the Menger Hotel. The restaurant was on Villita Street, across from La Villita, which was San Antonio's original neighborhood from the early 1700s. The old homes in La Villita had been converted into a collection of shops and eateries.

We sat out in the courtyard of the Fig Tree, where we could watch the pedestrians amble by on the River Walk, and wave at the excursion boats that catered to the tourists. I had an excellent beef Wellington. Mona enjoyed the seared scallops. Dan devoured a rack of lamb. Several bottles of wine were opened, and we all had a great time.

Dan footed the bill for everything, using Zeller's seed money, of course. So, basically, Zeller was buying us all dinner, and didn't realize it. You may think my seed money was being spent, too, but I'll come clean on that matter:

Though Zeller thought I was an equal investor in this TV poker scheme, I had not actually put in any cash money. Not a dollar. As Dan put it to me, in private, "Think of it this way, Cuz: What you're investing is tens of thousands of dollars' worth of your celebrity."

Earlier that day, back in the loading dock, after the poker table turned over, revealing the hidden cameras, you may recall that I had handed Dan an envelope full of hundred-dollar bills. It was actually Zeller's money—the cash that he had already given to Dan. We just wanted to make it appear that I was an equal investor. I admit now that the deception makes me a bit of a rascal, but Dan and I had our reasons for doing things the way we did.

So, anyway, without knowing it, Zeller bought the entire outfit dinner at the Fig Tree Restaurant down on the River Walk, including a big tip, which was unheard of for Zeller. When we left the restaurant, Dan stopped me at the front door and pointed across the street at La Villita.

"Right here is where Santa Anna lined his cannon out to besiege the Alamo," he said. "That rogue, Santa Anna. He called himself the Napoleon of the West. No ego there."

So our unlikely entourage walked a cannon shot back to the Menger Hotel and retired to the Teddy Roosevelt Saloon. As the night dragged on, individuals drifted away to their rooms, one by one, until only the die-hard night owls were left in the barroom. As usual, that amounted to me, Dan, Mona, and Archie Zeller. Dan was sitting with his back to the corner like a gunfighter, laughing his head off at some joke he had just told. I happened to be looking at him when his eye caught sight of something or someone over my shoulder. The smile dropped from his face like a wrench from a windmill. Rarely had I ever seen anything that close to shock register on Dan's face, but I saw it now. He recovered quickly, the old steel spark returning to his eyes.

The next thing I knew, someone was sitting down in the empty chair to my left. I looked sideways to see a man who was a stranger to me, but obviously not to Dan. The man possessed Hispanic features. He looked a little older than Dan and me, physically fit, and well dressed in a black suit and a white shirt with an open collar and a loosened necktie. You can tell a lot by a man's eyes. This man's eyes were intelligent, sad, resigned, skeptical, and fearless all at once.

"Hello, Dan," he said.

"Bruno," Dan replied, a strange smile on his face.

"You look good."

Dan grinned. "I've put on a few pounds since last time you saw me."

A peculiar statement, seeing as how Dan didn't have an ounce of fat on him.

"You always were a survivor."

"Well, now," said Mona, sounding more than a little tipsy, "just who are you, *señor*?"

"Bruno Marques, FBI." He winked at Mona as he whipped a badge from inside his blazer, flashed it, and returned it to its pocket.

"You two seem to know each other," I said. I glanced at Zeller and saw him shifting his eyes nervously around the table. Archie had been investigated by the FBI before, in the slant-drilling scam and some of his other confidence games.

"Bruno and I first met in the Corps in Vietnam, but we got better acquainted in Chile a couple of years ago. I was smuggling guns to the Patria y Libertad movement."

"I warned him not to do it," Bruno said. "It was too dangerous. But Dan wasn't finished fighting communists after Vietnam."

"I got caught by Allende's commie troops. That was the worst six months of my life." Dan chuckled.

"When we got him out of prison, after Pinochet's coup d'état, he looked like a scarecrow," Bruno said.

I vaguely remembered hearing reports of the right-wing coup, led by a General Pinochet, that had deposed the communist government in Chile under President Allende. I was on tour with the Half Breeds at the time, and hadn't paid it much mind. Had I known Dan was mixed up in it, I would have been worried sick. This was, I realized, one of those trips abroad that Dan would never talk about.

"That's the reason my days as an international arms dealer are over," Dan declared. "Forever!" He slapped the tabletop and laughed. "Now I'm in the entertainment business."

"Ah, yes," Bruno said. "Television."

"Televised poker. It'll sweep the nation, amigo."

Bruno shook his head and smiled. "If you say so, Dan."

"So, what brings you here?" Dan asked, rather casually.

"San Antonio is my hometown, remember? I'm taking a little time off to visit my family."

"And you just happened to see your ol' buddy Dan at the Menger saloon?"

Bruno smiled. "Not exactly. Your little gambling ring popped up on the bureau's radar."

"I'm a blip?"

"Not a very big one. I volunteered to look into it."

"Oh. Well, first of all, it's a poker tournament, not a gambling ring. The only bets are with chips. The players play for prize money. There's no gambling."

"Except for the calls coming into Vegas."

"Now you're just fishin'."

Bruno shrugged. "That's the way I'd do it. That would be perfectly legal. Those gambling junkies in Vegas will bet on anything."

"I don't have time to get mixed up with a bunch of Vegas thugs. Oh! And we benefit the DeBakey Heart and Vascular Center in Houston. We're legit, Bruno. Look, we even have our own celebrity spokesman." He pointed me out, as if to gesture toward a visual aid. "You've heard of Ronnie Breed and the Half Breeds, haven't you?"

Bruno looked at me. "Hell yeah. Big fan." He shook my hand and smiled warmly.

Dan introduced Mona and Archie, and ordered a drink for Bruno. The two former compatriots lightened up and started telling stories about when they were both special ops grunts sneaking around behind enemy lines in Vietnam.

Finally, the bartender gave the last-call warning, and Bruno stood to leave. "Pleasure meeting all of you," he said. "Dan, good luck with your TV show. Televised poker." He shook his head again doubtfully, but clasped Dan's hand across the table. "Just do me a favor and keep it clean."

"We're cleaner than boiled soap, amigo. Go hassle some real crooks." He smiled at his old pal.

Special Agent Bruno Marques waved and left the bar.

"FBI?" Archie said after Bruno had gone.

"Relax, Arch. He's an old friend."

"I saw the look on your face when he walked in," Archie protested.

"It was a shock to see him here," Dan allowed. "That guy turns up in the damnedest places. The jungles of Cambodia . . . my prison cell in Santiago . . . the Teddy Roosevelt Saloon . . ."

"I don't need the FBI snooping around my business," Archie hissed.

Dan waved off Zeller's objections. "He just gave us a free hall pass. He's got nothin' on us and he knows it. Like I said, he's an old friend."

Zeller downed his drink and got up to leave without saying good night to anyone.

"I'll smooth it over," Mona said, trotting out the way Zeller had gone, into the hotel lobby.

Finally alone with Dan, I looked him in the eye. "What the hell was that all about?"

Dan shrugged. "I've been expecting some investigation from somewhere. I just didn't think it would come from the bureau. And I damn sure didn't think they'd send Bruno."

"So he's the real deal?"

"They don't come any realer than Special Agent Bruno Marques."

I wouldn't admit it to Dan, but I was about as nervous as Archie Zeller over being a blip on the FBI radar—even a small one. "You don't think he'll make trouble for us, do you?"

"There's no law against playing cards for plastic chips, or shooting a television pilot. This is good news, Cuz. Bruno's a friend. Once he gives us a clean report, we can refer any local yokels or county mounties or state troopers to the FBI. That's a pretty good recommendation."

I put my trust in Cousin Dan and shrugged off my concerns. It was late, I was tired, and we had a big day ahead of us. I said good night to Dan and left him alone in the bar. I went up to my room and got ready for bed, then heard Mona enter her adjoining room. I knocked on the door between the two rooms and cracked it open.

"I was beginning to worry," I said.

"You were not."

I smiled. "Did you get Zeller settled down?"

"Just leave Wildcat to Mona. We're not going to lose our stake horse."

I drummed my fingers vacantly on the door. "Are you tired?"

She sighed and nodded. "Jet lag. I'll see you in the morning, Ronnie."

"Sweet dreams."

She guffawed in an unladylike way. "I don't dream sweet."

I clicked the door closed between us.

15

THE NEXT day, Saturday, I was up early, and off to the local country radio station for a live interview I had lined up over the phone. I brought a cassette tape of one of our Nashville rough mixes to play on the air, much to the deejay's delight.

"Folks," he said to his listeners after playing the song, "that's a brand-new release from Ronnie Breed, and you heard that one here first! Sounds like you're going country to me, Ronnie!"

"Oh, I don't know," I said with aw-shucks modesty. "I just make music and let other folks sort it out."

We went on to plug the live concerts later that day in the lobby at the Menger, and to explain the shooting of the poker tournament. Then I raced back to the Menger in Dan's '59 T-Bird. After a light lunch, the band had a smooth sound check on the stage the hotel employees had set up in the ornate Victorian lobby of the Menger. There was a wall of glass windowpanes behind the stage, revealing the lush courtyard garden behind us. In front of the stage, rows of columns supported the broad lobby in the historic structure. There was a small dance floor in front of our stage. The poker tables had been scattered up and down the lobby, and the cameras were poised, cranelike, above them.

I was standing around with the other gamblers and the TV crew, waiting my turn for Mona to powder my nose, when Dan approached me with a smile on his face.

"We've actually got people lined up around the corner out there to see the tournament," he said. "I asked around, and most of them said they heard you on the radio this morning. Good job, Cuz!"

I shrugged modestly, but was glad to hear we might have some actual music fans at the tournament. My band needed a confidence builder. We knew we could play, but I needed for the boys to start having fun in this band. If not, I might lose them, no matter how great we sounded or how good the money was. Nobody wanted to stay in a band that couldn't draw a crowd—even if the band was good and the money was great.

The gig went about the way it had in Galveston, except better, as there were more music fans among the poker enthusiasts. The band was tight, the cameras seemed to be getting some great shots, and the audience was highly enthusiastic. I made a mental note to arrange more radio interviews in Corpus, Fort Worth, and Houston.

After a few songs, I grabbed a Bloody Mary at the bar and went to take my place at the gaming tables. Just as in Galveston, Dan had handpicked twenty ticket-holding spectators who would get to play poker with the high rollers, and that included the prettiest girls out of the crowd under the pretense that they were "camera-friendly." In reality, he was hoping they'd be "Dan-friendly." And sometimes they were. Dan was a good-looking rascal and a smooth talker, and women just seemed to fall all over him.

He also kept a close eye out for any real ringers out there who might be able to beat one of our high rollers. I don't know how he could pick them, but he could. Being a ringer himself, he could just spot them. These were the kind of characters he intentionally did *not* choose to play in the tournament.

So, I was walking toward the gaming tables, and Dan joined me to tell me where to sit and against whom I would play, when suddenly we found Special Agent Bruno Marques standing in our way.

"You couldn't give a brother a shot?" Bruno said. He was in his civvies—jeans and a plaid shirt, but still had the look of a lawman, clean shaven and crew cut.

Dan played innocent. "A shot at what, amigo?"

"The tables. I thought maybe you'd see my name in the hopper and pull some strings for me."

Dan smirked. "It doesn't work that way. Luck of the draw, Bruno. It's totally random."

"Hmm," Bruno said, looking toward the tables. "I see a lot of random amateurs taking their seats. Not to mention three of the prettiest random girls in the room."

"Lady luck smiles where she will," Dan declared.

Bruno sighed. "I guess I'll just have to try again in Corpus next week."

"You do that, amigo. Right now, you'll have to excuse us. We're fixin' to shoot this round."

Bruno stepped politely out of our way.

"Uh-oh," Dan said after we were out of earshot.

"I hate it when you say 'uh-oh,' " I groaned.

"Here's the thing: I'm going to have to tell my dealers to play this round on the level. You'll have to win your table without the dealer's help, Cuz."

"What? Why?"

"Because Bruno is not only a high-stakes gambler, he's one of the world's best at busting dirty dealers and slick card mechanics. He knows all the tricks and he can spot them a mile away."

"Crap."

"Hey, cowboy up," Dan scolded. "You can beat these hacks. Just play it like your ass depends on it, because it sort of does."

"No pressure there."

"You always come through under pressure. Three weeks ago . . . at the Lake Jackson Rodeo . . . when you hazed the bulldoggin' for me. We hadn't practiced that in years, and you nailed it under pressure, so go do it again."

"The horse did all the work. I just sat there."

"Well, you didn't fall off. That's all there is to it here. Just don't fall off your chair, and you can beat these rubes."

I swallowed a little courage, put my game face on, and went to sit at my designated table. There were four amateur poker players waiting there—three working-class guys and one pretty girl. They all seemed thrilled to be playing against a celebrity from the music world. I greeted them all cordially, but I was sizing them up as opponents all the while. Dan came around and whispered to the professional dealer who would shuffle and dole out the cards. The dealer nodded.

Bartholomew chose my table to start shooting. "And . . . action!" he shouted.

We all started with a thousand hypothetical dollars' worth of chips. My stack took a couple of small hits on the first two rounds, as the cards the dealer dealt to me were quite useless. Then, on the third hand, I started with a pair of kings in the hole. Two other players apparently had promising pocket cards, too, judging from their raises, but the dealer improved my hand to three of a kind on the flop, and I found myself holding a full house when the river turned. I won several hundred fake dollars, and my roll began.

The rest of the world shut down, and the poker table became my whole universe. I got into the rhythm of Texas hold 'em, absorbed the strategies, juggled a hundred possible scenarios at once through the gyroscope of my mind. It wasn't just about the cards. It was also about the players. Body language they could not hide. The pretty girl at the table didn't even know the rules, and the dealer had to constantly school her. Of the three working stiffs at the table, only one possessed the potential to rival me, but little experience at hold 'em. Dan was right. I could beat these hacks.

I played cautiously, with occasional bold moves, and the cards continued to benefit me often enough. I felt my gambler's wit sharpening again, as I analyzed the gestures and attitudes of my opponents, and judged their responses to checks, bets, calls, and raises. The hum from the rest of the room seemed to disappear, and all I thought about for a while was the game at hand. It was therapeutic in a way. My concerns over my career, Mona, Dorothy, the band, the tournament, Dan, and everything else that weighed upon my shoulders somehow went on vacation for a spell, and I just played poker.

One by one, my opponents lost their chips to me, and I won my table quicker than any of the other high-rolling gamblers recruited for the event. I was feeling pretty good about Ronnie Breed as I walked away to the applause of the onlookers and went to fetch my first beer of the day.

Just then, a hotel bellboy came running up to me. "You're Ronnie Breed, right?" the gangling kid said, his Menger Hotel uniform fitting him poorly.

"Yes, I am. I guess you want my autograph?"

"You need to call your manager in Nashville. She's called the front desk half a dozen times!"

"So, I take it that's a no on the autograph," I muttered, a bit embarrassed at jumping to that conclusion.

"I don't collect autographs." The kid hustled away.

With the tail thus snipped from my kite, my ego took a little nosedive. But I rallied at the thought of calling Dorothy. Not only did I relish hearing that Southern purr over the phone, but I also reasoned that she must surely have good news for me if she had called the hotel six times. Probably a record deal. Maybe a cut by some star. I went to the front desk and had them charge the long distance call to my room.

"Talent Fire Agency. This is Dorothy speaking."

This was the first I had heard of Dorothy's agency's name. I hadn't even thought to ask. "I like that," I said. "Talent Fire."

"Ronnie?"

"The one and only. I just won a poker match. What are you doing on this fine Saturday?"

"Damage control."

"Damage?"

There was a pause. Then Dorothy said, "Ronnie . . . Honey . . ."

"Uh-oh. What did I do now?"

"Were you on the radio this morning?"

"Well, yeah. Doing some publicity for the poker tournament."

"And does your publicity include playing rough-mixed, unfinished demo tapes live, on the air, on one of the hottest country music markets in the nation?"

"I didn't exactly look at it that way. I was just plugging my new band."

"It's not time to plug yet, Ronnie. We plug when we have an album deal, and an album ready to release. You're getting way ahead of yourself."

"Sorry," I said, rather defensively. "What's the big deal?"

"There's a process to be followed here. A business plan. A formula. If you will allow it to work, you will see how effective it will be. Playing a work in progress live, on the air, is not part of the formula. It's difficult enough that this poker tournament of yours is interfering with my planning. Playing unfinished sides on the radio is simply not going to work for me."

"All right!" I said. "I won't play any more demos on the radio. But I mean, really, what was the harm in it?" I was wondering how the hell she even knew about it.

"Have you heard of Baldemar Huerta?"

"No, I can't say that I have."

"He's an up-and-coming country singer. He has a big Nashville record deal. Do you know where he lives?"

I shrugged, even though I was on the phone. "I don't have a clue, Dorothy."

"Baldemar Huerta lives just outside of San Antonio. I pitched the song you played on the radio this morning to him last week. Last week, he liked it. He was all but set to record it. But Baldemar Huerta listens to the radio, Ronnie. He heard the song that he was looking forward to recording and debuting to his own hometown, and decided that since you had stolen his thunder, maybe he wouldn't record the song after all. Oh, by the way, Baldemar Huerta's stage name is Freddy Fender."

My heart sank into my guts. I had heard Freddy Fender's first couple of hits on the radio. It was clear that he had a hot career going. "Oh, shit," I said, feeling a door slam on my future. To a songwriter, a chart country hit was worth tens of thousands of dollars—maybe hundreds of thousands.

"Those were my words exactly, when he called me this morning to tell me. Now, all is not lost. I got him to reconsider. He may still want to record the song. He's a fan of yours. Not as big a fan as he was yesterday, but still a fan."

"I'm sorry, Dorothy. I had no idea. I'll be more careful with the demos. I swear."

"Thank you, Ronnie, dear. This business is like the poker match you just won. You've got to play your cards close to the vest. Congratulations on your win, by the way."

Feeling a smidgen of forgiveness, I sighed into the receiver. "Thanks."

"Will I see you back in Nashville next week?"

"Of course. We have to get back on those changes you wanted." Now I was really kissing up, wondering how she had so effortlessly maneuvered me into this subservient role.

"Give my love to Mona. Call me when you get to town."

"Okay, Dorothy. Till then . . ."

"Good day, Ronnie."

I hung up the phone. Good day? What? No "tootles"? No Southern "bye-bye, now"? She was really mad and I felt particularly stupid.

"Hey!"

I turned to see Mona standing there with her hands on her hips. "Where the hell have you been?"

"On the phone with Nashville. Dorothy sends her love."

"I am so freaking charmed." She grabbed me by the arm and pulled me back toward the lobby. "Dan wants me and you to distract the FBI guy so the dealer at Wildcat's table can deal him back into the game. He's losing his ass against some cowboy."

"You'd be a better distraction than me." I was stumbling forward as Mona pulled me headlong like a sled dog.

"You're supposed to be the celebrity hotshot."

She dragged me up a few steps behind Bruno, who was watching the filming of Zeller losing his stack of chips to some rancher or cowhand—a plainly dressed leathery gent with a well-worn Stetson pulled low over his eyes. How had Dan let this guy in the game? He had poker experience written all over his face. Jack Diamond, Lady Daniela, and Luis Sebastian had managed to win at their tables, and were all standing around watching, but ol' Whipstock was having trouble with the cowboy. Zeller was clearly angry and frustrated, nervously shuffling his shrinking stack of chips as the cowboy raked in another pile of little plastic disks. The dealer was shuffling.

Mona looked at me. "Brace yourself," she whispered through clenched teeth.

"Huh?" I said.

"Bullshit! I've had it!" she shrieked. Then she slapped me. Hard.

"Hey!" I yelled, stunned, hearing gasps of surprise all around me.

"Dorothy, Dorothy, Dorothy! That's all I ever hear about anymore is your brown-eyed bombshell, Dorothy!"

From the corner of my eye, I saw that Bruno had turned away from the poker table and toward the commotion we were causing. "It's business, Mona. Damn. She's just my manager!"

"Oh, I know what she wants to manage!" She loaded up for a swift kick at my groin, but I saw it coming and blocked her pointed pump with my knee. It was still a painful blow to my leg.

"Ouch!" I yelled.

As Mona strutted off like a majorette—something no one could turn an eye away from—I heard some tittering laughter around me.

"You all right?" Bruno Marques said in my ear.

I turned, and glanced at the poker table just long enough to see that the game had continued through the distraction, though one of the cameras had turned toward me.

"I'm fine, Bruno." I rubbed my knee with one hand and my face with the other.

He chuckled. "You want to press charges?"

"No, I'm used to it by now."

"She's a little hot-blooded."

I forced a grin. "Sometimes that's fun. Hey, let's get a beer in the bar, you want to?"

"Hell yeah," Bruno said. "I'll buy the first round."

It was always surprising to me how some people, like Bruno, yearned to rub shoulders with a celebrity like me. We spent the next hour in the bar, entertaining each other—Bruno with his tales of crime fighting and international intrigue, me with my stories of rock and roll and Hollywood stars.

Meanwhile, Archie Zeller—with the help of a slick dealer—reversed his fortunes and mounted an astounding comeback against the cowboy who had almost beaten him. He would sit with the rest of us high rollers tonight at the championship table for the San Antonio finals.

16

THAT NIGHT, Mona accompanied me to the lobby for the taping of the San Antonio finals. We stepped out of the elevator as if we had no recollection of the minor spectacle we had made of ourselves earlier in the day. Mona was wearing a stunning red sequined flapper dress and matching retro hat, and I wore a nine-hundred-dollar gray pin-striped silk suit with a tie that matched Mona's chosen shade of crimson. On our way to the camera set, we ran into Bruno Marques.

"Did you two kiss and make up?" the lawman asked.

"And then some," Mona lied, a wicked grin on her face.

I swaggered on toward the championship table and the camera lights.

Dan was waiting. He motioned Mona and me aside.

"How did you like our distraction today?" Mona asked.

"A little over the top, but it got the job done. Mona, *please* go do the makeup on the players."

"Okay!" she said. "Geez!"

Dan leaned in close. "Now, listen, Cuz. Bruno's still hanging around here observing, so the dealer will have to deal this round legitimately. I don't care who wins, as long as it isn't Zeller. He already won at Galveston, so somebody else has to win tonight so we don't stray too far from the script. If Zeller wins twice, it'll bump somebody else out of the final grand championship round at Houston in three weeks, and we'll have some unknown loose cannon sitting in."

"Why are you telling me?" I complained. "I have no control over who wins."

"You do now. Remember that trick we used to use when we'd go to out-of-town poker games and pretend we didn't know each other?"

My cousin was referring to a set of signals we would use to tip each other off, across the table, as to what kind of pocket cards we held. Often, this little bit of knowledge would enable one of us to know what the other players *didn't* have in the hole, and allow one of us to win. We didn't think of it as cheating in the days of our misspent youth. We thought of it as teamwork. You've seen baseball coaches sending in signals from the dugout. That's what we did, except much more subtly. A touch of a cuff. Three rattles of a stack of chips. A sniff. A particular word thrown out in casual conversation.

"What good will it do for me to use the signals when you're not even playing?" I asked, more than a little exasperated at this new turn of events.

"Daniela will be sitting across from you. I taught her all the signals."

"Lady Daniela?"

"Yeah. Bruno will suspect her the least."

"When did you teach her the signals?"

"I've spared you some of the details on this deal, Cuz. It just so happens that Lady Daniela and I have a bit of a history together."

"I don't even want to know."

"You're right, you don't want to know. Just make sure Whipstock loses, then you're off the hook."

"Dan, I haven't used those signals in years."

"They'll come back to you. Anyway, it's hold 'em. You only have two pocket cards. How hard could it be to signal what they are?"

"Crap." I sighed. "All right, I'll do it."

Dan slapped me on the back.

"Ronnie, honey!" Mona yelled impatiently, waving a powder brush at me. "Makeup!"

"I'm coming, baby."

DAN WAS right. The signals came back to me. I never even looked up at Lady Daniela, but as long as I was in the game, she had a slight advantage, thanks to my signals, and she used it to build up the biggest stack of chips on the table. However, I was learning that Archie Zeller was a pretty darn good card player, and he held on. Then, in one incredible hand, in which Daniela and I had already folded, and Luis and Jack both went all in with all their chips, Zeller threw together a surprise four of a kind on the river and knocked both Luis and Jack out in one lucky stroke. Oh, you should have seen him gloat!

We were down to three players. Me, Zeller, and Daniela.

It was crucial that I stay in the game, to keep feeding information to Daniela, and she knew this. She managed to help me build my stack of chips whenever Zeller folded early. She'd bet big to build up the pot, then fold on the river, so I could win and retain enough chips to stay in the game and continue to help her.

Finally, Daniela got Zeller to shove all his chips in on a hand in which she knew he could not possibly have built anything higher than three jacks. I don't remember all the cards from the flop, the turn, and the river, but there was one ace showing, faceup, on the table—the ace of hearts—and one jack—the jack of spades. There were no kings or queens showing on the table; not enough of any one suit for a flush; not enough in sequence to build a straight; no pair showing. I held the ace of clubs and the jack of diamonds and had signaled that intelligence to Lady Daniela. After Zeller went all in, I folded. Daniela then called Zeller's bluff and won, for she herself held the ace of spades and the ace of diamonds. She had beaten his three jacks with her three aces.

Zeller was not a good sport. He stomped off like a little kid, refusing to shake Lady Daniela's hand when she offered it. Some of the crowd actually booed him for his rudeness.

Now it was down to Lady Daniela and me, and I knew what to do. Lose. The script said I wasn't supposed to win the championship round until week three, and go on to the grand championship with the other handpicked high rollers in week five. So, with the pressure off me, I set about the process of losing my chips. I still had two hours of music to play with my band that night, so I was intent on getting the poker game over with as quickly as possible.

So I sat back, relaxed, bantered with some of the onlookers, shrugged off my bad "luck," and enjoyed the game while orchestrating my losing streak. I had some time to look over the attendees who had come to watch the tournament. It was a better crowd than Galveston. I saw a couple of faces I thought I recognized from Galveston, so I asked, "How many of y'all were at the tournament in Galveston?"

About a dozen hands rose in the air. "How many of you are coming to Corpus next week?"

About half the crowd waved a hand. "All right," I said. This thing just might build up into something huge by the time we got to Houston, I thought.

I kept losing to the ever-so-classy Lady Daniela until I decided to go all in on a lame hand. "Who wants to hear some music from Ronnie Breed and the Truebloods?" I asked.

A round of applause erupted.

"If I don't win this one, you'll get your wish very soon."

The crowd laughed, the cards were revealed, and Daniela had become champion of the San Antonio finals. The cameras swooped in on her. With a grandiloquent bow, I kissed her hand and then made my exit to get onstage. Within five minutes, I had made a pit stop in the men's room, grabbed a glass of water for the stage, strapped on my guitar, and kicked off the first song with the band.

The gig was fun. The band was tight, and the music fans I had courted over the radio got into the new songs, as well as the old Half Breeds tunes. There was dancing and beer-drinking in the ornate lobby of the Menger Hotel. I think the ghosts of some old cowboys, some vanquished Mexican soldiers, and some heroes of the Alamo joined in on the celebration.

During the third song in the second set, I saw a man approaching the stage. The man stuck out, as people with star quality do. He looked Mexican, his face very brown. His most striking feature was his thick shock of wiry black hair—hair that seemed to have an energy all its own. He ambled up to the stage, toward me, and arrived at the end of the song.

"Hey, Mr. Ronnie Breed," he said, his border Tex-Mex accent playing prominently with my name as his eyes pierced mine. "I heard you on the radio this morning. I'm a fan of yours."

He didn't exhibit the infatuation of the typical fan. "Is that so?" I offered him my hand.

"I'm Freddy Fender."

My eyes lit up. "Then I'm a fan of yours, too. Your song—'Wasted Days and Wasted Nights'—that thing's going to gold, amigo."

He shrugged. "I wanted to cut one of your songs, but I heard you play it on the radio this morning. Now, I don't know . . ."

"I want to apologize for that," I said. "That was a mistake. I grabbed the wrong tape on my way to the studio. I didn't realize it until the song started playing, and then it was too late. I didn't want to undercut you if you were going to record the tune, man. I hope you didn't change your mind about covering it."

"I don't know, man. . . ."

"Hey, you want to play a song with my band? Do 'Wasted Days,' Freddy. The crowd will go crazy!"

"Is this gonna be on TV?"

"I'm not the TV producer . . . but . . . it looks like the cameras are rolling. You can use my guitar."

Freddy glanced at my players. He knew I was schmoozing him, but he couldn't resist a stage, a good band, and a television camera. He shrugged. "¿Por qué no?"

"Ladies and gentlemen!" I announced, handing the guitar to Freddy as he stepped onstage. "Have I got a special treat for y'all! We have a surprise guest star for you here at the Menger Hotel tonight!"

I heard Freddy telling the band what key the song was in and explaining that he would kick it off with his vocal. Warren and Mojo both said they knew the song. The rhythm section was in, and that was half the battle. The song was simple. The rest of the band would be all over it in half a verse.

"We have a country superstar in our midst. Please give a big welcome to San Antonio's own Freddy Fender!"

"Wasted days and wasted nights . . . ," Freddy belted.

Holy guacamole, I thought. *This guy's got pipes!*

I eased over to Slim's microphone to sing the harmony on the chorus. Freddy's eyes widened when I sang along, and he shot a smile at me. Singing harmony is one of my favorite things, and I've been called one of the best in the business.

As I predicted, the crowd did go a little crazy. By the time Freddy was finished with the song, they were crowding the stage, hooting and hollering for the hometown hero.

"Are you still going to cut my song?" I asked, taking my guitar back from him.

"I'll tell you what, man. I'll cut it if you sing the backup on it."

"You got it, amigo. Just tell me when."

"But you gotta keep it *escondido,* man. You know what I mean?"

"Yeah. Under wraps. I hear you."

"Cool. I'll be in touch."

I couldn't wait to get back on the phone with Dorothy and brag about the damage control *I* had pulled off.

The Truebloods ran through the rest of our set like a well-lubricated locomotive. When talent like Freddy Fender steps up onto your stage, you have to step up yourself. You might think I'm competitive. I like to think of myself as being inspired by great influences, even though I was the more seasoned hit-maker between Freddy and myself at that point in both our careers.

As we played, I watched from the stage like a hawk on its roost. You can see a lot going on up there while you're performing. I spotted Dan and Bruno sitting together in the corner, knocking back shots of tequila, and reliving old adventures. I noticed Mona in a dark corner, schmoozing our stake horse, Wildcat Zeller. Mona had an eye for money, and how to get hold of it. I didn't kid myself into thinking there was any other reason for her to be sporting around with me, posing as my girlfriend. It was all about the money, and Zeller had a lot more of it than I had. I knew where this was going.

We played a solid two hours, and ended with our most up-tempo number among the new Truebloods songs.

Slim Musselwhite grinned at me. "Cool gig, Rawn. And nobody handed me no dishwasher's apron."

"Slim, if we hit the big time, you can hire your own dishwasher," I said.

"Maybe a little French maid action," Mojo said from behind the drum kit, punctuating his quip with a rimshot.

"Hey, Ronnie, can we get paid now?" Warren asked. "I got a date with one of these señoritas in the crowd."

"Sure," I said, reaching for my wallet, which was full of hundred-dollar bills. I looked out over the milling audience members. "Which one?"

"I don't know yet," Warren admitted. He grabbed his pay and waded into the midst of some attractive Latina fans.

"It's nice to have choices," Henry observed.

"What's next, Ron? Topaz?"

"Tuesday," I said. "See y'all in Nashville."

"Right on." Slim folded his bills and slid them into his trouser pocket. "Mojo, let's me, you, and Henry go run the town together. Black, white, and brown, ain't nobody can mess with us no ways."

It was good to see the band bonding.

Mona was nowhere to be seen, so I spotted Dan and Bruno, and went to join them at a table.

Dan saw me coming and poured me a shot of tequila. "Drink up, Ronnie, you're several shots behind."

I obliged.

"So, old pal," Dan said, resuming his conversation with Bruno. "Are you gonna remove our blip from the FBI radar now? You can see it's just an innocent little tournament."

"A charity tournament at that," I added, shuddering involuntarily from the tequila shot.

"Yeah, charity," Dan echoed.

"I've got to be honest with you, Dan. Anytime your name surfaces at headquarters, red flags pop up faster than hard-ons in a titty bar."

Dan laughed. "I know I've run a shenanigan or two past your

periscope, but this is a legit operation, Bruno. It's totally public, for Christ's sake. There's nothing to hide."

"You've got to do one thing for me," Bruno said, getting serious. "One thing, then I can give this whole crazy gaggle-flock of yours my FBI rubber stamp of approval."

"One thing? Name it!"

I poured myself another shot of tequila.

"You've got to do the drawings for the amateur contestants in the open, in full view of the audience and the cameras. It looks like it's rigged if you do it in some back room."

"That's it?" Dan said. "That's all?" He sounded sincerely cooperative, but I could always tell when he was bluffing.

"I'll come to Corpus next week, to observe the drawing, then I can go back to headquarters and tell them you've gone straight."

"Done!"

Bruno shook our hands and departed to a room he had booked upstairs.

After he had gone, Mona and Wildcat appeared out of the dark somewhere in the lobby.

"Oh, boy! Tequila!" Mona squealed.

Dan faked a smile and aimed it at Zeller. "That was quite a hand, earlier, Wildcat. You wiped out two opponents at once."

"So much for your high rollers." He sat down clumsily. "I want to know how much money we made tonight."

"Well, let's see, we sold over two hundred tickets at fifteen dollars a head—"

"I'm talking about the *big* money," Wildcat said.

Mona slugged a shot of tequila and shoved one in front of Zeller.

"I don't drink that Meskin shit," he said, sloshing it aside.

Mona howled a fiery lungful of breath at the ceiling.

"Y'all get Wildcat some whiskey. I'll call up to the bookie's room and get a tally."

I bribed a bartender to hand over a half bottle of Jack Daniel's whiskey as Dan went to the nearest house phone. Meanwhile, Mona, in a tequila-brightened mood, went on and on about how wonderfully Zeller had played at the poker table that night.

"What about me?" I said. "I stayed in longer than he did." I was surprised to hear a note of jealousy in my voice.

"Wildcat lost on purpose, to follow the script. You just lost," Mona said derisively.

"Yeah, you let yourself get beat by a woman." Wildcat laughed and drank from the neck of the whiskey bottle. Mona joined him in ridiculing me.

"Maybe I lost on purpose, too. To follow the script."

"Sure you did!" Mona chortled.

"Does a bear piss in the Vatican?" Zeller snickered.

I looked up and saw Dan coming, much to my relief. It had been a long day, and I was about ready for it to be over.

"Well?" Zeller said when Dan sat down.

Dan did not look ecstatic. "We didn't do as well as last week."

"Well, just how well did we do?" I demanded.

"The Swiss account only took in about one-point-two."

"One-point-two whats?" Mona said.

"Million."

"Hey, last week you said it was over two million!" Zeller hissed.

"No, it was almost two million. I don't know what happened to-night," Dan said. "I can't figure it out."

"Maybe it had something to do with an FBI agent hanging around," I offered.

Dan shrugged. "Or could be the losers from last week are licking their wounds."

"You mean to tell me we have to split a measly hundred and twenty thousand three ways?"

"That ain't bad, Wildcat. You doubled your investment."

"I expected a lot bigger return than that!"

Dan shook his head, his brows bunched, puzzling it over. Suddenly, he slapped the tabletop. "Oh, I know what it was! It's the holy day of Eid al-Adha!"

"The what?" Zeller said.

"Our biggest bettors are oil-rich sheiks. In the Arab countries, they're sacrificing goats today!"

"Aw, poor goats," Mona whined.

"You better not be shittin' me," Zeller warned.

Dan ignored him. "Next week, the pot will be back up, you mark my words."

"But we did double our money," I said. "Right?"

"Absolutely," Dan assured me.

"Well, I expected more from my investment than a hundred percent profit," Zeller said.

"It'll get better next week. I promise. Those Arab holidays are so hard to keep up with. They have a different calendar, you know. It's a lunar calendar, so it doesn't jibe with our solar calendar."

Sometimes I wondered if Dan was all BS, or if he really did know what he was talking about. "Well, if we can double our money on a bad day, I can't wait to see what a good day looks like!" I sang.

"That day's comin'," Dan prophesied. "And it's gonna dawn pure gold."

17

SITTING BEHIND the huge Harrison control console in Salon D of the rambling Topaz Recording Studio, I felt like a blend of alchemist, symphony conductor, and air traffic controller, with a touch of that man behind the curtain in *The Wizard of Oz* thrown in for dramatic effect. I played the Harrison like a church organist, my fingers going to the right control without even having to look.

Jimmy Williams, the young recording engineer assigned to our project by Topaz, had relinquished his throne to let me find the EQ I wanted for the fiddle, as Warren prepared to fix some pitchy notes on one of the songs. Something had changed with the room or the fiddle, and the EQ was not matching the part we already had on tape, so I was trying to make today's sound match the tone of last week's recording. Warren was in the isolation booth, behind the glass, but I could see young Jimmy's reflection in that same glass as he stared, mouth open, at my maneuverings on the board.

I remembered the first time I saw such a control board, when I was a teenager in Houston and visited a recording studio to see about cutting my first demo. I was aghast at the hundreds of tiny knobs, buttons, lights, meters, and sliding control thingies covering an area of about three by eight feet on the tilted console. It completely unnerved me as to what I did not know about recording. I'm sure I had had a look on my face like the one Jimmy was sporting now.

But I am a big believer in demystification. (I don't look forward to dying, but when my time comes, I'm going to look at it as the ultimate demystification.) Like almost anything else, a recording console can be demystified. First, you break it down into channels—twenty-four of them, in the case of the Harrison. Already you've diminished a great deal of the mystery, for each channel represents an instrument, a voice, a drum, or whatever you've got hooked up to record through that channel. That channel carries the electronic signal to a narrow strip of the two-inch tape on which you're recording. There's enough space on that two-inch magnetic strip for all twenty-four channels.

Now all you have to do is learn the knobs, buttons, lights, and things for one channel. Oh, and those sliding thingies I mentioned are called "faders." They allow you to change the volume on that channel—fade it up or fade it down. Of course, I'm talking about 1975 technology here, and everything has now gone digital, and recording is often controlled with a mouse and a computer monitor. But even the computer monitor has a representation of the old control console, like that on the Harrison, which I had now assumed authority over as lord and master, like a puppeteer making twenty-four marionettes dance in my own bizarre little ballet.

Not all musicians get into the electronic side of the business as engineers or producers. Some couldn't care less about it. Like Henry, for example. As I tweaked the EQ on channel seven (the fiddle), Henry sat on the couch, perusing a *Playboy* magazine some other band had left in the studio. To tell the truth, I don't think he was actually reading it, but he was looking at the pictures.

Slim had an excellent ear, and knew what needed to change among the vast array of sounds. He spoke the electronic lingo, but never touched the board. He had no desire to produce records.

Some movie actors become directors. So it is with musicians. Some of us become record producers. I'll admit that I'm a bit of a control freak. Hopefully not to the point of micromanaging, but I do like to have my say over anything that's got my name on it. That's why I learned to produce my own records. I like gadgets, and I like to demystify things. So, I produce.

"Why is the sound different this week?" Jimmy asked. "I didn't move anything in the room."

"Who knows," I answered. "Maybe it's the humidity today. Maybe the extra hours on the fiddle strings. Maybe it's what Warren had for breakfast."

"He had grits," Mojo said, lying on the floor, his eyes closed.

"Well, that explains it," I replied, continuing to roll off a little bottom end on the EQ knob for channel seven.

"Oh, yeah," Slim said, sitting behind me on the couch. He had been listening to Warren's fiddle as I adjusted the EQ. "That's it, Rawn!"

I pushed the talk-back button so Warren could hear me in his headphones. "We got you dialed in, Warren. Let's go ahead and punch that turnaround."

"Ten-four, good buddy," Warren said. He was a CB radio enthusiast, like millions of other Americans in the seventies.

I started the tape and punched the red record button in the exact right place as Warren played along. Then I punched him cleanly out of the mix. After the twenty minutes of adjusting, tweaking, and listening, Warren nailed the ten-second part we wanted fixed in one pass. We rewound the tape and listened back to make sure.

"That was a take, Warren. Get out of there! It's supper time!"

"That's a big forty-roger," Warren said.

I got up and turned to Jimmy. "Thanks for letting me engineer that one," I said.

"Hey, I'm learning from you!"

The door opened and Dorothy stepped in. "Gentlemen," she said.

Slim stood, Mojo got up off the floor, and Henry slid the *Playboy* facedown on the coffee table.

Something happened in the electronic connections in my mind, and I ever so briefly saw Dorothy as a fully dressed *Playboy* model about to get naked for a photo layout. I flinched as if stung by a bee, and shook off the image. But she did have the body for it, after all. Any fool could see that, as she had dressed for dinner in a short, clingy, emerald blue dress with a plunging V neckline. A lucky gold locket on a braided chain homesteaded the valley of the cleavage. Blue patent leather stilettos lengthened her already gazelle-like legs and accented her shapely calves.

"How's it coming along?" she asked casually.

"Slowly but surely," I answered. "We're about halfway through with the changes."

"No rush."

"You look stunning," I blurted.

The band members all grunted in agreement.

"Thank you!" she sang, in two descending notes. "Do you have dinner plans, Ronnie?"

I shrugged. "I was just going to have some beers and a steak with the boys."

"I need to steal you tonight for a dinner meeting. Someone important wants to meet you."

"Okay," I said, curious. "Who?"

"You'll see. Sorry for the short notice. It all came about just now. You have half an hour to change. Did you bring a suit?"

"Uh, not exactly."

FORTY-FIVE MINUTES later, after a quick shower and a quicker change, I stepped out of Dorothy's cherry red, '64 Mustang in front of one of the swankest restaurants in Nashville—Mario's, at Twentieth Avenue and South Broadway. It was a three-piece-suit kind of place, but I was a rock star, and could get away with wearing jeans and boots, a pressed white shirt, and a tan blazer I had borrowed from Warren.

"You look splendid," Dorothy said after handing the keys to the valet. "But I need to print up a wardrobe list for you so Mona will know what to pack for you in the future. You've got to be prepared for any eventuality in your travels."

I laughed.

"Did I say something amusing?" she asked, smiling at me tauntingly with one corner of her perfect mouth.

"Only the part about Mona packing for me. So, are you going to tell me who we're meeting?" We walked inside the white brick building and past the hostess stand, turning toward the bar.

"I didn't want you to get nervous."

"Dorothy, I haven't been nervous since Elvis shook my hand in Hollywood, and even he thought I was the coolest thing since the mood ring."

"Oh, you're way cooler than the mood ring," she gushed. "You're almost as cool as the Pet Rock."

"Ah, stroking the client's ego. You're good."

"You have no idea how good I am at stroking."

I do believe I may have been blushing at that remark when I met Morris Witherspoon, who had been waiting for us at the bar. He turned suddenly on a barstool to face us, and there he was.

"Ronnie, this is Morris Witherspoon," Dorothy said.

I knew very well who Morris Witherspoon was. Everyone in the music business knew him as the genius promoter behind more hits than Mickey Mantle. He wore an expensive navy blazer with a red silk handkerchief leaping from the pocket. His iron gray hair was perfectly parted, combed back in waves like furrows in a plowed field, and held in place with some kind of hair oil.

As I shook his right hand, I pointed at the distinctively shaped glass in his left. "Dirty gin martini?"

Witherspoon smiled. "Mercury gin, Noilly Pratt dry vermouth, a twist of lemon rind, and two picholine olives."

"With a dash of olive brine? Chilled, shaken, and strained?"

"It's the only way."

"I'll take one of those," I said to the bartender, who was waiting to take our orders.

"I think we're going to get along just fine," Witherspoon said.

Over the next couple of hours—at the bar and the dinner table—I enjoyed getting acquainted with Morris Witherspoon. He had grown up in a wealthy cigarette family, he said, but smoked only Cuban cigars. He had sold his interest in the family tobacco corporation to an uncle and invested in the music business in Memphis, and later Nashville. He had discovered and launched the careers of some great blues, rockabilly, and country stars.

Major Morris Witherspoon was renowned as a Hemingway-esque sort of adventurer—deep-sea fishing, big game hunting, globe-trotting. He dated Hollywood starlets but had never married.

He had played one year of major league baseball in 1941, before becoming an army fighter pilot in World War II. He was an expert on Italian wines and had even written a book on the subject. He was just about the most affable man you could imagine meeting, and the fact that he was picking up the tab didn't hurt his likability, either.

"So, anyway . . . ," he said, finishing a bowl of cioppino, which wasn't even on the menu, but which the Italian chef loved to prepare for him, "we searched everywhere, found the snake—the largest python yet on record—killed it, cut it open . . . and would you believe that little boy was still alive?"

"Nah!" I gasped.

"Yes! I saw it with my own eyes. He recovered fully and is now the high priest of his tribe in the jungle. He said he had visions in that snake's belly. *Visions!*"

"I don't doubt it," I said, polishing off my last bite of seafood Alfredo lasagna.

Witherspoon refilled our three glasses with a wonderful vintage of Montepulciano d'Abruzzo, taking great care to ensure each glass was equally filled. He finished each pour with a practiced twist of his wrist. "So, Ronnie. What about *your* vision?"

"My vision?"

"For your career. Your music. Your life."

Witherspoon struck me as the kind of guy you didn't want to bullshit. "I wish I could see it more clearly. I guess I'd have to say I'm currently seeking my vision."

"An honest answer," he said, sipping his wine. "Let's start with your music. That is, after all, the important thing."

This simple statement impressed and somewhat staggered me. How easy it was to forget what was important, in light of contracts, record deals, concerts, hit charts. . . . Major Witherspoon was right. The music was the most important consideration. All other things would fall into place if you just got the music right.

"Well, I've got the best band right now that a guy could ask for. Dorothy recruited the musicians for me."

"We did it together," Dorothy said modestly.

"She's told me," Witherspoon said, smiling in admiration of the combo we had assembled. "I know them all, except your bassist."

"Henry and I go way back. He's doing a great job. As good as the others."

Witherspoon took a cigar from his pocket. "Do you mind?" he said to Dorothy.

"Not at all," she replied, daintily pushing aside her finished plate of baked basil-and-prosciutto-wrapped halibut.

"Ronnie? It's a Cuban." He offered me another stogie that seemed to magically appear in his hand.

"Sure, Morris. Don't mind if I do. Where do you get Cubans?" I asked as I took the hand-wrapped cigar.

He glanced at me over the end of his smoke as he lit it with a gold-plated Zippo lighter. "Cuba," he replied matter-of-factly.

"Of course." I took the Zippo and the stainless steel cigar cutter he offered.

"Now, where were we? Your band."

"The Truebloods." I snipped the end off the Cuban.

He nodded. "I like that name. And your men are top-notch players."

"There's more to it than just that," I said. "Unlike my old band— the Half Breeds—the Truebloods actually get along." I lit the smuggled stogie.

He nodded. "You've got to be careful with band names. I always thought that 'Half Breed' moniker would doom your band, even though I understand the raw rock edge your label was going for. Still, the name was too negative. Borderline offensive, even. I like the Truebloods much, much better."

I puffed on the incredibly smooth cigar. "Yeah, me, too. The band just feels better. Our voices blend. Our instrumental talents complement one another. The creativity has been energizing." I saw Dorothy beaming at my choice of words.

"I've asked your lovely manager to describe your band's music, but she refuses to do it."

"One cannot pigeonhole a peregrine falcon," Dorothy drawled eloquently.

"How would you describe it?" Witherspoon asked.

I sat back in my chair. "Take some boys from the country, dust 'em with a little rock and roll, pay their dues with the blues, and put a pinch of gospel in their soul."

"You better write that down, son," Witherspoon gushed.

"I already have. Part of a song I'm working on."

I saw Dorothy holding back her giddiness. "Those wheels just never quit turning in his little ol' head!"

For the life of me, I thought for a moment she had ended the sentence with, "Hey, Ed!"

Major Witherspoon elegantly rolled a wheel of ash from the end of his cigar into the tray. "Let me ask your view of something going on in the industry, Ronnie. What do you make of this so-called progressive country movement?"

I waved it off like a wisp of Cuban smoke. "It won't last. They're trying to manipulate the market. They're trying to create a climate for crossover hits. I think the whole progressive country scare will drift into a sort of soft rock, and what does soft rock do? It crumbles. Country music must remain country music, unapologetically. It doesn't need to progress. In fact, I'm in favor of a little *regressive* country."

Dorothy's eyes shifted to gauge the major's reaction.

Morris Witherspoon chuckled, smoke puffing from his lips like a locomotive. "But you just described your band, in your beautiful lyrics, as a combination of country, blues, rock, and gospel. That's got crossover written all over it."

"Yes, but it's not a contrived movement of any sort. It's just who we are."

He nodded as if profoundly satisfied. "I'm anxious to hear your demos. Dorothy has teased me with them, but won't let me listen until you've done some polishing."

"We're working on the overdubs."

"When will you be finished?" He blew a perfect smoke ring over the table.

"Hard to say. Three . . . four weeks."

"Why so long? I could crank out two or three records in that time." The major smirked, but he was only half-joking. He was known for his efficiency in the studio.

"We only have a couple of days a week to work on them, between gigs in Texas."

"You've been playing live shows in Texas?" He sounded mildly alarmed.

"Sort of." I then felt obligated to describe the televised poker idea to him as briefly and vaguely as I could.

"Now, *that* sounds interesting," he said, leaning toward me through his own cigar smoke.

His obvious fascination with the unpredictable world of televised gaming made me a little nervous, so I tried to knock some chrome off the concept: "Actually, it's pretty boring. But the live gigs are great practice for the band."

"Could you get me in on the poker tournament?" he asked, undaunted. "I mean, just as a player, not as a producer."

I could feel my brows gathering in worry. "I don't know, Morris. I'm just the band leader, and one of the poker players. I'm not in charge of the television production." I felt the pointed toe of Dorothy's shoe gouge my shin. "I mean, I'll do my best, but I can't promise."

"I think that would be splendid fun—win or lose. I wouldn't be opposed to making a charitable contribution to the heart research center, either. Maybe that would help a fellow win a spot at the tables?" He shot a wink at me.

I was silent until the pointed pump goaded me again. "Yes!" I gasped, and choked on cigar smoke. "That would be most generous. Okay, I'll see what I can do."

"It would give me a chance to hear your band, see you work live."

"Of course!" Dorothy agreed. "A showcase!"

"Not the best time of year to visit Texas," I muttered. "The heat."

"When will you let me know?" He was staring through his own smoke ring at visions of poker tables and TV cameras.

"I'll talk to the producer this weekend. If not this season, next season is wide open."

Dorothy raised her glass. "Ronnie can be very persuasive. He talked Freddy Fender into cutting one of his songs." She kicked me again, but not so hard this time. "I'm sure he can get you a seat at the poker tables next weekend."

I was obliged to touch my wineglass to those of my dinner companions, which produced a perfect three-note chord.

"B flat?" the major asked.

"You do have the ear," I said, forcing a smile. The chord was actually a C.

"I look forward to seeing you operate in Texas. If this band glows like Dorothy's description of it, I'm going to want to take a very serious look at signing the Truebloods to a development deal. I've had my eye on you a long time, Ronnie. I always suspected, somehow, that the two of us would work together."

Yeah, sure, I was thinking. *That's what they all say.* Still, if Major Witherspoon was just blowing smoke . . . well, at least it was Cuban smoke.

18

WHEN MAJOR Morris Witherspoon's chauffeur brought the Rolls-Royce limo around to the front of Mario's, I couldn't miss the huge set of cattle horns affixed to the grille of the automobile. The horns spanned the entire breadth of the vehicle, and the base of each horn was about as big around as one of Dorothy's thighs—an easy comparison to make, as she was standing nearby in that short dress. This circumference was the perfect size for a woman's thigh, by the way, but seemed awfully large for a bovine's horn.

"Damn, Morris," I said. "If those are real, they must have come off the world's biggest Texas longhorn."

"Oh, they're real, but they didn't come from any longhorn," he explained, sliding into the backseat. "They came from a Watusi bull that I had to shoot in Africa when it charged me. Those horns fell at my very feet, if you can imagine that."

"Wow."

"I then hunted over the carcass of the dead bull until I got what I was really after."

"What was that?"

"A rogue, man-eating lion that had been terrorizing a remote village. Poor beast had a wounded paw and had resorted to eating slow prey—humans. I'm still regarded as a demigod in that village."

"Holy cow."

"See you in Texas, Ronnie. Good night, Dorothy." He slammed the door.

We stood there, waving and smiling until the limo turned the corner.

"Are you as pumped as I am?" Dorothy asked, turning toward me.

I shrugged. "About what?"

"He all but offered you the deal of your life!"

The valet brought Dorothy's Mustang around, and we stepped in.

"Some mother hen is going to have to sit on that egg for a while before we go to counting a new chicken," I said, feeling a tad loopy from the wine. "I'll believe it when the contract is signed."

"Ronnie!" she scolded. "Where is your optimism? You performed beautifully tonight."

"Performed?"

"You know what I mean. Your conversation was brilliant. You said all the right things. Except . . ." She put the car in gear.

"Uh-oh. What did I do now?"

"I was a bit mystified at your reluctance to get the major involved with the poker tournament. What were you thinking?"

"I was thinking that I don't want to get Morris embroiled in something I can't control, and this poker thing is a loose cannon."

"Oh, pish-posh. You're playing cards on television in luxury hotels."

"There's more to it than that, Dorothy."

"Such as?" She turned the car onto Broadway, toward my hotel.

"International intrigue."

"Oh, now you're just mimicking the mysterious Major Wither-spoon."

"He is a fascinating guy. I'll give him that. How did you even get a meeting with him?"

"It's a long story."

Her vagueness made me suspicious, and my suspicion made me unexplainably jealous. "You didn't do anything . . . I mean, you didn't make any promises—"

She read my mind. "Ronnie! How dare you. I am a professional. I don't use feminine wiles to get my way."

"Well, then how did you line up the meeting?"

"If you really must know, I found out that his secretary's sister teaches Jazzercize at the gym where I work out, so I made friends with her and got myself invited to a girls' night out, where I met the secretary and casually mentioned your name, and promised her that I would introduce her to you if she would introduce me to the major."

"Oh, so you used *my* feminine wiles!"

"I guess you could say that. Anyway, don't drop the ball on this poker thing, Ronnie. Let the major play a hand or two of cards. He just wants to be on television."

"Don't we all?"

"Not me. I'm a behind-the-scenes kind of girl."

"Ironic, huh?"

"What do you mean, ironic?"

"I mean, you'd think that you, of all people, would jump at the chance for some TV airtime."

"What are you saying?" She glanced at me as she steered the car around a corner.

"I'm saying you're drop-dead gorgeous, Dorothy. The cameras would feast on you like a lion on a Watusi!"

She drove in silence the next block to the Hermitage Hotel on Sixth Avenue, where I was staying. When she stopped, she put the car in park and turned toward me. "Do you really think I'm gorgeous?"

I laughed. "What red-blooded American man wouldn't think you're gorgeous? You're hotter than a firecracker. You make Sophia Loren look like a second runner-up in a plain Jane pageant."

"Oh, stop."

"No, I won't stop. Haven't you ever seen one of those things called *a mirror*? Brigitte Bardot would kill Raquel Welch for your looks."

She started laughing. "Then why hasn't anybody asked me out for a date in months?"

"You're too pretty. Guys are intimidated."

"That's not true."

"Of course it's true. There's no other explanation."

"If you didn't have Mona, would you ask me out?"

"You better believe I would."

"But you just said guys are intimidated."

"I'm not a guy. I'm a rock star. I would have asked you out the moment I met you, if it wasn't for Mona."

"So, if Mona wasn't in your life right now, you'd ask me out for a date?"

"Well, not now, because we're working together now. It's a professional relationship."

"I know couples who work together."

"I do, too. They fight all the time."

"Maybe they make up all the time."

It was getting a bit steamy in the Mustang, so I cracked the window open. "Maybe you're right. Okay, never mind that we work together. If it wasn't for Mona, I'd ask you out right now."

"Really?"

"Absolutely."

The glow from a streetlight burned in her eyes. "So, about you and Mona . . ."

This was dangerous, man-eating-lion territory, but I couldn't stay out of it. "It'll never last. But now she's working for the TV crew shooting the poker tournament, so I can't very well just dump her if she's going to be hanging around the set. That would be a recipe for a televised ass-chewing. Excuse my French."

"Excused. Well, I won't wait around forever, and I'm not a home wrecker. Just so you know."

"It's not as if Mona and I actually have a home."

"When was the last time you had a home?"

"You mean, without wheels under it?"

"I mean a real home. With a cat and a dog and a garden? When was the last time you had some home cooking other than your mother's?"

"Maybe at my aunt's house, when I was seventeen."

"You know, you can have your life as a star, and have a home, too."

"Really? With a billiards room?"

"Sure."

"And a pool?"

"Why not?"

"And a wet bar?"

"Wouldn't be a home without one."

"And a recording studio?"

"That's a given."

"And a helicopter pad?"

"Now you're pushing it."

"I've been known to push it."

"I bet you have."

I stared at her incredibly attractive mouth for a few seconds, wishing I could kiss it. "So, what it boils down to is this: If it wasn't for that cotton-pickin' poker tournament, I'd already be done with Mona, and the demos, and I'd probably have an offer for a record deal from Morris, and a date with you."

"Life throws hurdles in our path."

I seriously, but only briefly, considered asking her up to my room. Dorothy wasn't a groupie. She was a Southern belle. A gorgeous Tennessee babe who was starved for romance, and who actually liked me. Anyway, how would she ever trust me in the future if I did anything with her behind Mona's back now. I forced myself to open the car door, lest I stay long enough to say something stupid.

"I look forward to my first conversation with you after Mona's out of the picture." I got out of the Mustang and leaned over so I could see Dorothy, still sitting inside.

"Be gentle with Mona," she said. "She's probably not as tough as she acts."

"She's already looking for a way out."

"Breaking up is never easy."

"I guess I'll see you next week?"

"I'll plan a home-cooked meal for the band. You can even bring Mona if she decides to come with you."

I smiled. "Sounds absolutely lovely. Good-bye for now, gorgeous."

"Good night, handsome."

19

I WENT to bed with a frustrated smile on my face. I woke up the next morning thinking, *What the hell was I thinking*? She was my manager, for heaven's sake! I almost called her from the hotel to say something like, *"About that silly conversation in the car last night. I didn't mean a word of it."*

But that would have been a lie. I had meant every word of it at the time. But now, by the light of day, I had to wonder what had gotten into me, other than the Montepulciano d'Abruzzo and the dirty gin martini. We had all but signed off on the blueprints to our first house! I barely knew this woman!

At the airport, while waiting for my flight to Houston, I dialed Dorothy's number, but hung up before it rang. What would I have said? She was probably out shopping for a wedding gown anyway, but what if she *did* answer? I was either going to screw up my personal or business relationship with her, or both, if I hadn't already.

On the airplane, I tried to catch some sleep, but I kept thinking of those luscious Watusi-horn-circumference thighs and that addictive Scarlett O'Hara–meets–Dolly Parton drawl. Arriving at Houston Intercontinental, I drove to my mom's house to collect the tour bus.

"How was Nashville?" she asked.

"Fine," I muttered as I repacked my suitcase for the weekend in Corpus Christi, taking advantage of the laundry my mother had washed for me.

"And Dorothy?"

"Fine."

"Oh, my Lord," she said. "What happened?"

"Mama! I said, 'Fine'!"

"Tell me what happened!" She grilled me until I told her a version of the conversation in the car.

"Oh, honey, you've got to give Mona her marching orders first. You got way ahead of yourself with Dorothy. Don't mess it up."

I sighed as I shut the suitcase. "I feel like an idiot."

"Oh, now, don't you worry. The next time you hear from Dorothy, I'm sure it will all be fine. She's a sweet girl."

"How do you know? You haven't even met her!"

"A mother just knows these things. I'm so glad you're finally thinking of settling down and starting a family."

"Settling what? Starting when?"

"Don't gag! I said settling down and starting a family."

"I am not!"

"You know, you'll want to be young enough to still be able to roughhouse with your grandchildren."

"Grandchildren! Good Lord, Mama!"

"You'll thank me, if I'm still alive."

"Oh, for heaven's sake." I grabbed my luggage and marched out of her house for the bus.

"You don't know it, but you're settling down." She hummed Mendelssohn's "Wedding March" as I passed through the screen door she was holding open for me.

ON THE long, solitary drive to Corpus Christi, I went over and over the Mustang meeting in my mind. Finally it dawned on me. The helipad! If I couldn't have a helipad, then we would just have to call the whole thing off! At the same time, I was reveling in the feeling that I might be falling in love with Dorothy Taliaferro. But what if Mona, and this crazy poker tournament with all its hidden layers, got in the way of my finding my one true love? Perhaps it was better. I barely knew Dorothy. But I *wanted* to know her.

"For cryin' out loud!" I railed alone in the bus as it rumbled over the bridge spanning Copano Bay. "What the hell is wrong with me?"

———

CHECKING IN at the Crest Hotel on the beach in downtown Corpus, I found a message waiting for me at the front desk. The Mexican-American girl behind the reception counter smiled at me and arched her eyebrows a couple of times as she handed me an envelope. "I couldn't help reading this as it came off the fax machine," she said. "It's pretty juicy." Then she shoved a piece of paper and a pen in front of me. "Can I have your autograph?"

Bemused by her invasion of my privacy, I nonetheless signed the autograph dutifully. The girl was all of nineteen and probably didn't know better. Opening the envelope, I found the electronic facsimile of a handwritten note. I had never seen Dorothy's handwriting before. Beautiful penmanship:

> *Dearest Ronnie,*
>
> *I don't quite know what got into us last night, other than the wine. We seemed to have let our little ol' sulky get out in front of our Thoroughbred. Let's just keep our minds on our career moves right now, and let whatever else is supposed to happen take its course. Thank you for a beautiful evening.*
>
> *Enchanted,*
> *Dorothy*

How perfect was this woman? Enchanted! If she had signed off with "sincerely" or "cordially," I would have contemplated throwing myself off the hotel roof. But her note had put me at ease and melted my heart all at once.

Through all my worry over my managerial situation, I had forgotten to inquire with the front desk whether Mona had checked in yet. She had flown to San Diego for the week. So when I got to my room, I knocked on the adjoining door. No answer. No Mona yet. I left my side of the double adjoining door open.

My room at the Crest Hotel looked out over the beach and the bay and the Gulf beyond. For some reason, I caught myself wishing

I could share the view with Dorothy. This was ridiculous. I picked up the phone and called Dorothy's number. She didn't answer, but I left a message on her answering machine.

"Hi, Dorothy. It's Handsome. I mean Ronnie. Thanks for your fax. I agree with every word you wrote, especially 'enchanted.' Okay, I better go now before I say something stupid. I'll be in touch. . . ."

I hung up. "I'll be in touch?" I said to myself. "She signs off 'enchanted,' and I sign off 'I'll be in touch'? What a dipstick!" Disgusted, I threw myself onto the bed. Why was I behaving this way with this woman? Yes, she was gorgeous, but I had met a lot of pretty women. She was actually kind of bossy, I reminded myself. Did I, subconsciously, need a controlling woman in my life? What had gotten into Ronnie Breed? Exhausted—physically, mentally, and emotionally—I fell asleep.

I dreamt that I was in a recording studio, and none of the knobs or buttons or faders worked on the board. A huge python stretched across the back of the control console, with a boy-sized bulge writhing in its belly. Dorothy was in the isolation booth, behind the glass, talking to me over the microphone, but I couldn't hear her. No matter what I tried, I couldn't get her microphone turned on, and she was obviously telling me something incredibly sensuous, judging from the gleam in her green eyes and mischievous smile on her face. Frustrated, I pushed some unknown button, and was appalled to hear Mona's voice instead of Dorothy's:

"What the hell is this?"

I woke to see Mona standing over me with the fax in her hand.

"Oh . . . Uh . . . ," I said.

"Yeah, 'oh, uh,' indeed! What happened in Nashville with Daisy Mae?"

"It's Dorothy," I grumbled, rubbing my eyes, "and that's a personal note."

"I can see that!" She wadded up the fax and threw it at me. "What happened?"

"Nothing! Just some random talk after too many glasses of wine."

She pounced on top of me on the bed, straddling me, pinning me down with her hands on my chest. "If you think I'm going to tolerate you sporting around Nashville, in public, with that long-legged temptress while you're still supposed to be my boyfriend, then you don't understand what's at risk here!"

"Nothing's at risk, because nothing happened," I argued, looking up at her fierce glare. "I told her she wasn't bad-looking, and if I didn't have you, my lovely Mona, in my life, that I might even ask her out on a date. I was just being nice."

"No hanky-panky?"

"Of course not."

"No kissy-face?"

"No!"

"Don't lie to me!"

"I didn't even hold her hand. If I didn't know better, I'd think you were jealous."

She jumped off me. "What if the paparazzi had caught you? We don't need any extra scrutiny until the world championship poker show is over."

"I just had a simple meeting with my manager and a heavy-hitting promoter, that's all. You know, my career has to go on after this poker tournament is over."

"That's your problem, Ronnie. You're still thinking of this as a simple poker tournament. You're in denial. Remember what you signed up for. This is a high-risk, high-reward, million-dollar—" The phone rang, and Mona snatched it. "What?" she demanded. She listened, her eyes shooting poison darts at me. "He's right here. Maybe you can talk some sense into him." She covered the receiver and said, "Next time you go to Nashville, I'm going with you, and I guarantee I'm not going to let you out of my sight!" She threw the phone receiver down on the floor.

I grabbed the curly phone line and hauled it in. "Hello?" I said in a weary voice.

"What the hell was that all about?" Dan's voice asked.

"Just a little lovers' quarrel."

"Save your quarrels for the next time I need a distraction. Now, you and Mona get down here and help me wrangle Archie. He just got here and he's in a piss-poor mood."

"All right," I said. I hung up the phone. What had I gotten myself into? I looked in the mirror. Mona was right. I needed a dose of reality. I was too deep into this thing that I kept thinking of as a poker tournament to back out now. I realized that I'd better get my head on straight, stop thinking about Dorothy and my music career—at least for the weekend—and fulfill my promise to Cousin Dan to make this thing work. It seems I was always loyal to Dan above all else. I tucked in my shirt and combed my hair.

"Mona, the game is afoot!" I hollered through the door to the adjoining room. "Get your cute little ass downstairs, pronto!"

She peered into my room. "That's more like it."

WE PLIED Zeller with booze and promises of a big payoff on Saturday. The other poker players, TV crew members, and musicians began to arrive, and we feasted on seafood and steaks, then drank toddies in the sea breeze at the open-air poolside bar until the wee hours. Mona went upstairs before me. When I finally made it to my room, I started kicking my boots off and unbuttoning my shirt, ready for some sleep. The door to the adjoining room opened, and Mona was standing there, wearing a wisp of lingerie no bigger than a hankie.

"Mona!" I said, my eyes bulging like those of a cartoon character.

She switched the light off, allowing the moonlight to bathe the room. "I think I know what you need," she purred.

"You do?"

"You need a little incentive to keep your hands off your manager."

"Incentive?"

"Here are the rules," she said. "Just do as you're told, and you won't be disappointed. Understood?"

I nodded. She came slinking toward me, and helped me pull my second boot off. The rest is rather personal, but I will say this—she was right on two counts: I definitely wasn't disappointed, and she knew exactly what I needed. I thought about Dorothy briefly, but I didn't feel guilty. Dorothy probably thought this was what Mona and I did on a regular basis anyway. I'm sure my fans and the gossip

columnists thought the same thing about Mona and me that summer. The truth was that that night was the first, last, and only time I
ever made love to Mona. I know that sounds crazy, but that was
one wacky, mixed-up summer—that summer of '75.

20

THE NEXT morning, feeling a new spring in my step, I made the rounds at the radio stations, did the sound check with the band, and got ready for the shooting of the tournament. This was week three, and the Saturday schedule was becoming somewhat routine, though we had to adjust to a new city and a different hotel setting each week. At Corpus, because the weather cooperated, we set up outdoors on the sundeck next to the pool so we could film the poker games with the open water in the background.

The Crest Hotel had been built in such a way that the hotel building hung over the poolside area, providing much-needed shade to escape the Texas sun. If you wanted to work on your tan, you could stroll out of the shadows onto the sundeck. This made a perfect setting for our poker tables. The camera lenses could take in the open sea beyond or the bathing beauties around the pool, and Dan had somehow seen to it that all the bathers were beauties.

Much to my satisfaction, the event continued to draw an increasing number of music fans, thanks to the radio publicity I had been doing. In fact, I think the crowd was almost double that of the San Antonio audience. Some of the fans even requested the new True-bloods songs that we had recorded as demos but hadn't released yet.

As we finished our first set of three songs—the short set just to kick off the show and set the mood for poker playing, Dan approached the stage with his ol' buddy Special Agent Bruno Marques in tow.

"Hey, Bruno," I said, shaking his hand as I stepped off the hotel's rickety temporary risers we were using as a stage.

"Kick-ass band," Bruno said.

"Thanks, man." It was easy to be cordial with Bruno. I truly liked the man.

"Ronnie," Dan said, beaming a big grin, "your publicity is really starting to pay off. These crowds are getting bigger, and that makes us look a lot better on camera!"

I nodded. "It's coming together."

"When's the drawing?" Bruno asked.

"Right here and now," Dan said, "right in front of the audience and the camera, just like I promised you."

"Who's going to draw the names?"

"Mona. She's camera-friendly."

Bruno looked at Mona, who was all dolled up in a bright green spangled evening gown for her moment in front of the camera. She looked so good that Bruno could not possibly have rejected the idea of her drawing the ticket stubs out of the big hopper Dan had acquired somewhere.

"And . . . action!" Bartholomew sang.

Mona lit up like a Dallas Cowboys cheerleader and began cranking the handle on the hopper, which was a big cylinder of some kind of wire mesh just a grade or two above chicken wire, but spray-painted gold. It was filled with ticket stubs from the fans, each ticket including the name of the purchaser. It occurred to me that Dan had probably made the hand-cranked hopper in his woodworking shop over the past week.

After a final turn of the stage prop, Mona fixed her eyes on the sea in a dramatic Hollywood stare and reached blindly into the hopper through a little door in the wire mesh. Drawing a ticket out, she read the name handwritten on it. "Mauricio Benavides!" she said quite clearly, with perfect enunciation.

A man hooted in the audience, and the camera panned toward him as his wife and friends celebrated the drawing of his name. I had to admit that this was excellent theater.

Mona repeated the process twenty times, until all the amateur players had been chosen from the ranks.

Bruno Marques threw his ticket stub on the floor. "Damn! I wanted to play this week!"

"Sorry, Bruno." Dan said, "Luck of the draw."

Mona came sprinting toward me. "How'd I do?" she sang, bright-eyed. She was in a particularly good mood today.

"Baby, you were fabulous!"

"I wasn't asking about last night!" she quipped, then growled like a tiger kitten.

"Aw, I don't want to hear this," Dan said.

"What's wrong, Dan, the old producer's charm didn't work on the local girls last night?" Mona seemed to enjoy taunting him while she was draped all over me.

"Thanks for reminding me. Now, you two get to work, and I don't mean on each other. I was afraid this might happen." He walked off to tend to his production.

"You know, I wasn't just saying that," I assured Mona. "You really were fabulous last night."

"You were an animal."

"You were a machine."

"Yeah, well—" She slithered off me. "—don't get used to it. It'll probably never happen again."

I feasted my eyes on her. You wouldn't think a man could be distracted from a sight such as Mona all dolled up and in a frisky mood, but something, somehow, from the extreme corner of my peripheral vision, drew a glance from me. That glance led to an astounded stare, for Dorothy Taliaferro had stepped out of the hotel, onto the poolside patio where the video shoot was taking place, and the sea breeze was blowing her short, canary yellow, chiffon skirt up around her thighs.

Mona's eyes must have followed mine. "Oh, now I can assure you it will never happen again!" she blurted. "You have got to be kidding me!"

Dorothy corralled her skirt before the whole crowd saw the color of her panties, and caught sight of me staring at her. She risked a brief wave and came gliding gracefully toward Mona and me.

Just before Dorothy reached us, Mona stalked past her, saying, "Nice fax, Daisy Mae!"

"Oh, my," Dorothy said. "I am sorry, Ronnie."

"Don't worry about it. That's just Mona. What are you doing here?" I smiled to let her know how happy I was to see her.

"You didn't get my messages?"

"I've been busy with the poker thing." I gestured vaguely to the gaming tables around me.

The wind whirled Dorothy's garments about her thighs again. "Chiffon is not sea-breeze-friendly," she said, penning down as much fabric as she could.

"On the contrary, the breeze seems to be enjoying the hell out of itself with your chiffon. So, what did I miss in your messages?"

"He insisted I come along."

"Who?"

"The major. Morris Witherspoon."

"He's here, too?"

"Checking us in right now."

"Checking you in!"

"Separate rooms, of course."

"Well, that's a relief. But I thought he was coming *next* week!"

"It appears the major is a man of whims. His limo picked me up and spirited me to his private jet, and the next thing I knew, the Gulf breeze was blowing up my skirt."

"It's not that I'm not thrilled to witness that, but what does Morris think he's going to do here?"

"He wants to play poker, Ronnie. He talked about it all the way here. And if you really want that record deal, I suggest you find him a seat at one of these tables."

I slapped my palm against my forehead.

"Hey, rock star!" Dan said, rushing toward me. "The cameras are ready to roll! Sign the autograph and tell the groupie you've got to go to work."

"I beg your pardon!" Dorothy said.

I shot Dan a tense look. "Dan, this is my manager, Dorothy."

"Oops," Dan said, putting on a sheepish grin for my sake. "My apologies, Dorothy. Ronnie said you were stunning, but, wow!"

"Really?" she said, looking coyly at me.

"Dan, we have a problem." I boiled the issue down to its crux as succinctly as I could, but by the time I was finishing up my explanation, I saw Major Morris Witherspoon step out of the building and onto the poolside sundeck. He spotted Dorothy and me, and began to walk our way.

There was something almost supernatural about the way Major Witherspoon commanded attention when he stepped into any given arena. He made more people gawk than Dorothy had with her incredible, swirling chiffon skirt. He simply carried with him an inherent air of greatness. He just had it, whatever "it" was.

"Dan," I said, "this is Major Morris Witherspoon."

Dan shook his hand. "Pleased to meet you, but the answer is no." Dan was suspicious of anyone whose charisma rivaled his own.

"He's prepared to make a sizable donation to the DeBakey Vascular Center," Dorothy offered.

Dan shook his head and looked at his watch. "Not gonna happen. Maybe next week, sport." He slapped Morris on the shoulder.

Morris placed a cigar between his teeth and, with his signature sleight of hand illusion, produced another one magically, out of thin air, which he handed to Dan. "Cuban?"

"Ah, a Julieta. One of my favorite vitolas." Dan took the cigar.

"You know your Habanos," Morris said admiringly.

"Yeah, but you're still not sitting down at my tables, especially with those kind of magic cigar tricks up your sleeve."

"If there's a problem, I'm sure we can arrive at a solution," the major said, gesturing with his cigar. "How does ten thousand dollars sound as a donation to your charity?"

"It's the DeBakey Heart and Vascular Center," I said.

"I'll write the check. You can fill in the pay-to-the-order-of line any way you wish."

Dan's right eyebrow rose, almost imperceptibly. The offer hooked him, but he was still resistant to the idea of letting a stranger sit in at the tables. "I can't just sit you at one of the tables on the spur of the moment, sir. These people bought tickets and got drawn in a lottery. I can't ask one of them to give up a seat."

"Of course not, Dan," said Morris, assuming an instant first name familiarity. "But I can." He stepped toward the tables.

"What's he doing?" Dan said.

Dorothy and I shrugged.

"May I have your attention!" the major bellowed in a commanding tone. A hush fell over the poolside patio, and all the players looked toward Morris Witherspoon. "I came here to play poker. Who will sell his seat to me for one thousand dollars?"

The hush transmogrified into a grumble.

"No takers?" Morris said. "All right, then. Two thousand dollars!"

It was Mauricio Benavides—the owner of the first name Mona had drawn from the hopper—who stood first. "Cash?" he said.

"Of course!" Morris reached into his pocket, pulled out his money clip, and strolled toward Mr. Benavides. In thirty seconds, the major was seated, and Mauricio Benavides, two grand richer, was walking away with his wife, who was thrilled with her husband's mastery of the odds.

Now, it just so happened that Mauricio Benavides had been seated at my table to play hold 'em against the celebrity know as *me*. In his stead, I was now to face Major Morris Witherspoon and three other amateur contestants. Only, the major didn't do anything amateurishly. This concerned me because I knew I needed to win this first round to keep our tournament in line with Dan's script, which meant I needed to beat the one person in the music business who gave a hoot about springboarding my career into the big time. Secondly, I had to do this without any help from our crooked dealer, because Special Agent Bruno Marques was still observing the proceedings.

As he watched Witherspoon sit down, Dan said, "What the hell just happened?" This was not something I heard Dan say very often.

"Let him play," Dorothy said. "Ronnie's career depends on it."

I followed Dan as he stalked over to Morris's chair.

Dan leaned low to converse with the major. "You realize you're playing for chips, not money, right?"

"I understand perfectly. Ronnie told me all about the tournament in vivid detail."

Dan rifled a glare at me. "You'll have to sign a contract." Dan snapped his fingers at one of the camera guys, who was carrying a clipboard.

Morris rolled his eyes toward Dan and smiled. "My lawyers can get me out of anything you could possibly get me into, Dan. Show me the dotted line."

"About that contribution to the vascular center."

From his jacket pocket, the major pulled out his checkbook and a pen, signed his name on a check, tore it out of the book, and handed it to Dan. "I trust you'll remember our arrangement when you fill in the details."

The clipboard guy pointed out the dotted line on the contract, and Morris signed that as well.

"We're losing our perfect daylight," Bartholomew whined.

"Let's roll!" Dan shouted.

"Makeup for the new guy!" Bartholomew shrieked. "Makeup! Makeup! Where is that makeup girl?" he demanded.

"Mona's not here," I groaned. "She left in a huff."

Dorothy, standing nearby, said, "I'll powder his little ol' nose." She reached into her beaded clutch for a tiny brush and some base and took the shine off Morris's perfect features.

Meanwhile, Dan pulled me aside and led me to my seat next to the dealer. "Beat this guy!" he said under his breath. I could tell he did not appreciate Morris's intrusion here.

"I will if I can, but—"

"Beat him like a cheap snare drum." He put his cigar in his mouth. "This guy is so full of crap. This ain't no Cuban between my teeth. It's Honduran."

"How do you know that?"

"It doesn't taste or smell like a real Habano, it's rolled too tight, and there are veins in the wrapper. This guy may be a star-maker in the record biz, but everything else he says is bullshit. Beat him! He won't respect you if you don't!"

So I went from thinking my career hinged on losing to Morris to believing with all my heart that success would come only if I drubbed him without mercy. That's the kind of influence my cousin Dan had on me. It had always been that way.

21

MONA CAME screaming out of the hotel, where she had obviously been watching developments through the glass wall between the pool and the lobby. "Oh, no, you don't!" she wailed.

She sprinted in short but rapid steps in the tight green evening dress, rather like a quail on the run, past the swimming pool and toward the poker table where Dorothy was powdering Morris's nose in preparation for the filming of the poker game.

"That's my job, Daisy Mae!" she shrieked at Dorothy. Gaining speed, she snatched a rat-tail comb from the makeup tray she had stowed behind one of the cameras, and flew into the midst of the action at my poker table.

"Just trying to help," Dorothy said, ignoring Mona's frenzied tone as she continued to work on the major.

Grabbing the comb by the teeth, Mona use the rat-tail handle to jab at Dorothy as if wielding a dagger. I had no trouble imagining that Mona may have parried her way out of a knife fight or two.

"Lands!" Dorothy said, backing away.

Looking back on all this, I know Mona was only doing her job. She had to keep Dorothy on the outside of our poker tournament. Letting just anybody into the inner circle of what we were doing could have led to disaster.

"That's enough, Mona!" Dan shouted, trying to calm the little firebrand.

At this moment, I happened to look past Mona to see a guy shooting pictures with a Nikon camera. I recognized the photographer, an aggressive paparazzo named Rudolph Richards, who had dogged me throughout my rock-and-roll career. He was easy to identify. His nose had been broken, maybe more than once, and was uniquely crooked. He had one goofy eye, but I could never tell which one—neither ever seemed to be looking at me when I confronted him. Over his T-shirt he wore a frazzled fly fisherman's vest that possessed all the pockets needed for his photographic equipment. The rest of his attire consisted of short pants and running shoes. He seemed to be shooting some wild photos of me, Major Witherspoon, and Dorothy, all reacting to Mona's antics with her makeshift weapon.

Photography was strictly forbidden inside our tournament for security and secrecy purposes. So when I saw the camera and recognized Rudolph, I jumped up, pointing and screaming, making a bigger scene than Mona had.

"No photos!" I yelled. "Security! Get him! Get that guy!" I then recalled that we had no security, other than Dan.

The legendary Rudolph Richards, who did this sort of thing all the time, was way ahead of me. He was already running for the exit. He had positioned himself in such a way that he had a head start to the parking lot through an open gate, whence he fled, jumping into a waiting car that sped away with him, leaving the rest of us stunned.

"Who the hell was that?" Dan demanded.

"The Great Rudolph. He's a legendary paparazzo."

"You mean paparazzi?" Dan said.

Morris, apparently enjoying himself, spoke up in my defense. "Actually, Ronnie is right, Dan. 'Paparazzi' is plural. 'Paparazzo' is singular."

Dan bit his lip and wheeled on the crowd. "No photos!" he yelled, causing the entire audience to reel back one step, as surely as if they had rehearsed it. Then he turned on Mona. "Mona, drop your weapon!" he ordered.

She sneered back at him.

"Drop it!"

Mona reluctantly obeyed, tossing her plastic dagger onto the poker table near me.

"Step away from the comb!" Dan ordered.

She didn't budge.

"Mona! Step away from the rat-tailed comb!"

She snarled at him and condescended to shuffle one small step away from the table. I picked up the comb and slipped it into the inside pocket of my blazer.

Dorothy bowed out of her temporary makeup artist position, Bartholomew screamed, "Action!" and we finally began playing Texas hold 'em. I had three amateurs and Major Morris Witherspoon sitting at my table. I knew I had to beat them all.

Morris was no slouch as a poker player. He lasted longer than the three locals. The game boiled down to a tug-of-war between him and me. But I consistently won two hands to his one, for I was a craftier wagerer. Being filthy rich, Morris was accustomed to throwing his money around, in life and at the gaming table. I wouldn't play his game. I refused to let him draw me into any huge bets unless I had a sure winning hand. When he tried to highball me, I'd just fold and we'd go on to a new hand, so I gradually built up my stack of chips while whittling away at his. I made my bets like a sniper. He dropped his like a bombardier.

It came down to an interesting hand that I could afford to take a chance on. After the dealer lay the river down aside the other cards from the flop and the turn, Morris bet about half his remaining stack of chips. I called his bet and raised him—doubling his bet. Everybody knew this meant that Morris would either have to fold or shove all his chips into the pot.

With the cameras zooming in, and the spectators silently waiting for Morris's reply to my raise, the major looked at me and smirked. "Let's make this a little more interesting, Ronnie."

I reached for my Cuba Libre and took a sip. "How's that, Morris?"

"I'm going all in. But in addition to these colorful little plastic chips, I propose a personal wager between you and me."

I glanced at a camera. "Gambling in Texas is illegal, Morris."

"It's not a cash bet. I'm wagering something else."

I drummed my fingers on the felt. "I'm listening." I willed myself to relax, refusing to let my body language telegraph any frustration or nervousness to my opponent.

"If you win," Morris said, "I will guarantee you and your band a recording contract with my label, Silver Spoon Records, at the standard industry royalty rates, full marketing push, international tour, radio and magazine support, billboards, the works."

"You haven't heard my new band yet."

"I admit it's a bit of a risk, but not a very big one. You're Ronnie Breed, after all. I trust your talent, and I know all your players, except the bassist. Besides, I'm going to win this hand."

"I think you're bluffing. But if I were to lose this little side bet of yours, what do *you* win?"

"You sign over the publishing rights to your catalog to me."

This amounted to roughly half the royalties to any of my songs that might get recorded in the future, making this a multimillion-dollar risk for me. "No way I'd sign over my publishing to anyone, Morris."

He shrugged. "Win this hand, and you won't have to. How confident are you in your poker skills, Ronnie?"

I had the makings of a pretty good hand, but it was not necessarily unbeatable. The question was whether or not Morris was bluffing. I believed he was. Dan had planted the idea in my head that the flamboyant Morris Witherspoon was so full of crap that his blue eyes were forever on the verge of turning brown. I was going to win this hand. I just knew it. I almost took him up on the side wager.

But then I happened to look up to see Dorothy staring at the table, petrified at the possible outcome. Then I glanced around to see Mona biting her nails in a rare display of nerves, hanging on Archie Zeller's arm, no less. Dan was looking on, too, the pseudo-Cuban almost bitten in half between his teeth, his jaw muscles flexing.

I looked at the bigger picture. I was not here to make side wagers with Major Witherspoon. This was no way to win a recording contract. I was here to win round one at Corpus, and go on to the finals tonight with the rest of the high rollers, all of whom had not surprisingly won their tables. I realized that the major was playing me, testing me. He was gauging me for backbone, spirit, and confidence. I knew how I had to reply.

"Major, with all due respect to your gaming skills, I'm going to win this hand." I put on a cocksure smile. "However, I refuse your side bet. When I win my recording contract with Silver Spoon Records, it will be on the basis of my talent, and that of my band. I won't have it said that Ronnie Breed had to win a card game to get a record deal."

A murmur of approval rippled through the audience, followed by a smattering of applause.

Morris drilled me with a stare that revealed nothing. Then he let his genuine, infectious smile spread over his face and wrinkle the corners of his eyes into perfect crow's-feet. "Very well," he said. "All in." He pushed his stack of chips toward the center of the table.

"Cut!" Dan yelled. "All right, let's reset the cameras. Take five."

The audience groaned in complaint, eager to see the poker hands we both held.

It may seem peculiar that Dan always called for a break during the most pivotal moment of the game—the revealing of the hole cards by the players who thought they had winning hands. But Dan had explained that he needed to make sure that the cameras were in the right positions to catch the reactions of the players at the climactic moment. That was Dan's story, anyway. I knew there were other reasons behind this unpopular, anticlimactic momentum-killer.

"I'm running to the men's room," Dan said, taking his headphones off and hustling away.

Five minutes later, we were set for the revelation of the pocket cards, and the makings of the winning hand.

"And . . . action!" Dan ordered.

I reached for my cards first, pausing dramatically like Dean Martin in 5 Card Stud. Turning over my hole cards, I revealed my baby straight. I knew, realistically, that if I had a baby straight, Morris could possibly have a higher one. With instinctive showbiz flair, the major stalled, flipped the corners of his pocket cards for a moment, then pushed them forward without revealing them, effectively folding his hand as he shoved the two facedown cards in with the burnt wood.

"Well done, Ronnie!" he said, standing suddenly to give me a congratulatory handshake.

People started slapping my back as I glanced around the scene of my victory. Dorothy looked stunned. Mona looked relieved, and she whispered something in Archie's ear that made his eyes perk up.

"Let me buy the winner a drink," Morris said magnanimously, leading me away by my arm.

As we walked to the bar, the crowd parted to let us through. Elated with my win, I breathed in the salty sea air. I wondered briefly if I should have taken Morris's side bet, but decided not to think of that again. What was done, was done.

Bruno Marques stepped up beside me as we approached the bar. "Great round," he said to Morris and me both. "I'll see you pukes next week in Fort Worth."

"You're not staying?" I said, surprised.

Bruno frowned. "I got to go to a wedding in San Antonio. My piece-of-crap nephew got a girl pregnant." With that, Special Agent Marques left us to our devices, which were multifarious. This meant we could let our card-mechanic dealer decide the outcome of the championship round later tonight. That meant it was my turn to win one for Texas. This was the good news. The bad news was that Bruno's eagle eye would be trained on us again next week in Fort Worth.

As Morris ordered our drinks, Slim appeared beside me, smiling, his gold tooth gleaming. "That was smoove, Rawn," he said in his ultracool blues-speak.

This was a relief. I was worried the band members might bust my chops for not taking the side bet and winning the band a recording deal. Slim seemed to understand that Morris was testing me, and that I had passed the test. I wasn't so sure that Dorothy would share this view.

I would find out soon enough, because I saw her approaching. Dan was a couple of steps behind her, looking a mite befuddled still, which was unusual. Morris, who seemed always a step ahead of everything, had already ordered Dorothy a piña colada. He handed me a dirty gin martini, the way we both liked it.

"Well, *that* was interesting," Dorothy said in a classic Southern understatement. "I couldn't tell whether or not I was about to be made rich and successful, or redundant and obsolete."

Morris laughed. "Aren't either of you curious?"

"About your pocket cards?" I asked.

Morris nodded, sipping his martini.

"The point's moot now."

"*I'm* curious," Dorothy admitted.

"Let me just put it this way," Morris said. "If Ronnie had taken my side bet, I would have revealed those cards. But since we were playing for mere chips, I decided to let them remain a mystery. I have no time for a new career as a television poker celebrity."

Dan stepped up just in time to hear that statement. He rolled his eyes behind Morris's back, then shook my hand vigorously and slapped my back as if I had a tarantula on it. "That was one hell of a shoot-out, boys!" He looked only at me when he said this. I knew he was proud of me. "That will play great on the tube." He turned to Dorothy. "Miss Taliaferro, I want to apologize again for my rudeness earlier. My mama raised me better than that, and I hope you'll forgive me."

Dorothy held back a smile. "You're lucky I don't know your mama, or I'd tattle on you."

"Please, not that," Dan said. "Anything but that."

"Well, you just be on your best behavior from now on, Mr. Dan, and perhaps I'll find it in my heart to forgive."

"Whew," Dan said, sweeping a little sweat from his brow. "Now, I hate to be a hard case, but we're behind schedule. We're expected in the restaurant for supper in five minutes." He tapped the face of his wristwatch.

"Then I had better take my drink to my room and freshen up," Dorothy announced.

"I have your key," Morris said, patting his jacket pocket. "I'll escort you up, dear. I'm in the room next door."

Dan and I watched them walk away, Dorothy's arm looped around the major's.

"You think he's pounding that?"

"No!" I said.

"Whoa, don't blow up on me, Cuz. You sweet on her?"

"No!" I repeated.

"Liar. She's more your type than Mona, that's for sure."

"You think?"

"Yeah, but play it cool, like you played that shoot-out. Keep your mind out of your pants and on the game."

I sighed as Dorothy disappeared from my sight. "Did you get a look at Morris's hole cards after the shoot-out?"

"I think so. They were shoved in with the dealer's burn cards, so I can't be sure."

"And?"

"Can I get a beer?" He shifted his eyes from the bartender to me. "You had a baby straight, right?"

"Yeah."

"Well, he may have had an adolescent straight."

"He had me beat?"

"Maybe. I can't be sure. Like I said, the cards were shoved in with the burnt wood. But if you had taken that bullshit side bet, he just might have burned your ass for a few million dollars. You played it just right, Cuz. I was afraid we were in trouble when he dangled that recording contract, but you kept your eye on the ball, just like in Little League when we went to state."

"We lost at state."

"We should have paid the ump. The other team did."

"Is nothing pure anymore, Dan?" I sipped my gin and vermouth.

"No. Everything's a little dirty, like that martini you're slurpin'. Still, it can be enjoyable."

"Nice metaphor."

"We're doing this for a reason, remember?"

"I know."

"Don't let these greedy bastards get in our way."

"I won't. Just promise me we won't take any money from Morris."

"Don't worry. Archie's our only stake horse." Dan reached into his summer blazer and pulled out the check with Morris's signature on it. "Send this to the DeBakey Heart Center, like he said."

I took the check. "Okay, Cuz."

He looked over both shoulders. "Don't call me Cuz. See you at supper, pronto."

22

THE OFFICIAL Corpus Christi Hold 'Em Supper went well, except that I was jealous of Morris Witherspoon, who was sitting with Dorothy. Every time I looked their way, Mona would kick me under the table. (What is it about women, and kicking under the table? Do they kick each other under the table? I can't remember ever being kicked by a man under the table. In fact, if a man's foot even accidentally touches another man's foot under the table, both of them are liable to draw back as if snakebit. You just don't violate another man's sub-table space.)

After supper, the championship round went by Dan's secret script. It was my turn to win. That meant I had to sit there for hours, eliminating the other players, one by one. Considering the fact that Morris was in town to showcase my band, I would much rather have lost early so that I could go upstairs and prepare for the gig.

It finally came down to me and Luis Sebastian. The dealer provided the cards I needed, and I got Luis to go all in on the final showdown. I won, as I knew I would. I spent some time in front of the camera, consoling Luis and gloating over my victory. As quickly as I could, I attempted to make my exit so that I could relax alone in my room, go over the set list, change my guitar strings, shower, and put on some fresh clothes.

But Dan prevented all that.

"Good work," he said, pulling me aside.

"Thanks. I'll be in my room."

" 'Fraid not, rock star. There's a local news gal here to interview you."

"Aw, crap," I said with a groan. At this stage of my career, it was crucial that I remain in the public eye whenever possible. "Tell her to meet me onstage."

I found my band members milling around onstage, all of them getting their instruments ready, casually sipping some drinks, and talking about the good-looking girls in the audience.

"Here's the new set list," I said, stepping among them. "I changed a couple of things around, so y'all let me know what you think."

As the band looked over the set list, I saw the local reporter assigned to the story trotting toward me with her cameraman in tow. She was a pretty, young Hispanic woman. Back in those days, the attractive young women coming out of broadcast journalism schools often had to endure a rookie year covering fluff stories, which of course included local entertainment. I met a lot of young female journalists back then.

"Hi, I'm Alicia Ramos, KCTX News," she said, "big fan of yours, and we're going live, on the air in thirty seconds. May I interview you?"

I was still shaking her hand when I said, "Sure, Alicia."

"May I call you Ronnie?"

"I don't see why not."

She listened to her headset for several seconds, gave me a three-two-one countdown with her fingers, then flashed a smile that came on like a neon light. "That's right, Frank," she said to some anchorman in the studio, "and I've got a Texas rock-and-roll legend, Ronnie Breed, with me here, live at the Crest Hotel. Ronnie, why did you decide to bring your new televised poker show here, to Corpus Christi?"

"Well, Alicia, it's not really my show. I'm just the musical entertainer for the first season, and I also happen to be one of the participating poker players. But the producers wanted to come here because we're featuring a poker game called hold 'em that originated around the turn of the century in Robstown, which is, of course, just a few miles outside of Corpus. So we're paying homage to the birthplace of this incredibly exciting poker game."

"What's the name of the show, Ronnie?"

"We're taking hold 'em nationwide, and we want the country to know where it comes from, so we call it Texas hold 'em. The show will be called *The World Championship Series of Texas Hold 'Em Poker*."

"Are there cash purses involved for the winners?"

"Gambling is illegal in Texas, of course, so we don't allow cash bets. The contestants play for chips, and the tournament winners take home a little prize money. So we're not any more controversial than Bubba's rodeo, or Grandma's bingo game."

"And you perform during the poker tournament?"

"My new band, the Truebloods, will be kicking off here any minute."

"Is there a new album in the works for this new band, the Truebloods?"

"We've been in the studio for the past three weeks. And we're going to insist on touring through Corpus Christi when the record comes out." I smiled right through all my own BS. We hadn't even been offered a contract yet.

"Anything else you'd like to add, Ronnie?"

"Only that our traveling poker tournament benefits the DeBakey Heart and Vascular Center in Houston. We raised over ten thousand dollars here in Corpus Christi alone!"

She turned away from me to face the camera. "Frank, apparently we live in a very generous community, and an exciting place for television productions, as well. This is Alicia Ramos reporting for KCTX News." She stared and smiled at the lens for a few seconds. "And, we're clear. . . ."

"That was painless," I quipped.

"You've done this before," she said, as if impressed.

"A time or two."

"Can I ask one more favor?"

"Sure."

"We sign off at ten twenty-eight. Can your band being playing a song that we can cut to, live, for a few seconds at the end of our news broadcast?"

"Just tell me when to kick the song off."

She smiled, almost seductively. "Maybe just one more favor?" She pulled a pen from her notepad. "An autograph for my nephew? He plays guitar."

"What's his name?" I reached for the pen.

A FEW minutes later, guitar tuned and ready, awaiting Alicia's signal to kick off our first song, I saw Major Witherspoon step out of the hotel, onto the pool patio. "He's here," I said to the band. "You know what to do."

"Jus' do what we do," Slim said.

Morris Witherspoon ambled toward the stage. I glanced toward Alicia and caught her eye. She held up two fingers, like a peace sign, signifying that we were somewhere inside of two minutes to going live on the air. The major walked up to me. I hoped he wasn't intent on a long conversation.

"I came down to offer my apologies, Ronnie."

"For what?"

"I have to fly to L.A."

"Now?"

"One of my artists, Big Al Brothers, had an automobile accident. I'll fly to Fort Worth next week and hear your new band there."

"Can't you stay for one song?"

He shook his head. "My mind is on Big Al. It sounds like a bad wreck."

"What about Dorothy?"

"She's packing right now."

"She's going with you?"

"From L.A., we'll fly back to Nashville."

"Oh . . ." I glanced toward the local reporter to check our progress. She flashed one finger at me. "I was hoping she could stay."

Morris beckoned me closer. "Are you entangled with your manager, Ronnie?"

Suddenly, we were back at the poker table, trying to read each other. I wondered if the question was business related, or personal.

Was he interested in Dorothy? I mean, what man wouldn't be? Or was he simply wary of an artist/manager team screwing things up with a romantic relationship?

I tried bluffing. "I'm here with Mona. You know that, Morris."

He scoffed. "How long could that possibly last? Are you entangled with Dorothy, or not?"

"Define 'entangled.'"

"You know what I mean."

"Are you asking for business or personal reasons?"

He shrugged. "One or the other. Perhaps both. I simply want to know what I'm stepping into with you, Ronnie. Just tell me the truth."

"The truth is, I don't know. And if I don't know, I guess that means the answer is no, we're not entangled."

He smiled, and my heart sank. What had I just done? Had he outplayed me this time? I had all but given him my permission to have his way with the desirable Dorothy in his private jet on the way to L.A. I had visions of them frolicking on Venice Beach. Morris was old enough to be my dad, but he was a dashing character, fabulously wealthy, and younger women flocked around him. Had I just driven Dorothy into his flock?

"That's all I wanted to know," Morris said. "I look forward to hearing the band next week. Oh, one more thing . . ."

What now, I wondered.

"There *will* be a waltz on the demo project, yes? It's part of the Silver Spoon formula. There must be a waltz on every country album."

"A waltz? Of course, Morris. I've studied your formula." I was lying outright. I knew nothing of the Silver Spoon formula, and I didn't have a waltz demoed.

He nodded and turned. As he walked away, Alicia Ramos, the local reporter, started a countdown from ten seconds to zero. Just as we kicked off one of the new up-tempo Truebloods songs, Morris disappeared through the glass doors into the hotel.

The audience cheered the song, and my band launched into it like a fighter jet blasting off the deck of an aircraft carrier. I was in the pilot's seat, but parts of my mind were wandering around elsewhere:

A waltz? I hadn't written a waltz in years. . . .

Morris was gone, and Dorothy was leaving with him.

Morris had missed our showcase, and the Truebloods would have to wait until next week. . . .

Unless . . . What if Dorothy—not my music—was what he was really after? He might not even be interested in a showcase by next week, for all I knew. . . .

Was Dorothy my manager or was she using me to snare Morris?

Was Morris—not me—what Dorothy was really after?

Though I felt as if I had a block of ice inside my guts, I smiled and winked at the camera as I knew Dorothy would want me to do— if she really was my manager, and not just some gold digger chasing the multimillionaire. I imagined that she might be watching through the glass wall as she prepared to fly off with the most fascinating gentleman on the face of the earth. If I hadn't been onstage, I might have puked my heart right out of my chest. That's how helpless and lost I felt at that moment. And yet, I faked a smile and belted out my lyrics.

What's done is done? Easy come, easy go? Better luck next time? No poker-related cliché could help ease my anguish. I looked out at the audience. I saw Mona trying to teach Archie Zeller how to dance. Still grinning shamelessly, I noticed Dan in the middle of the crowd, doing the bump with that cute reporter, Alicia. He shot me a smirk and gave me a thumbs-up.

I felt a sudden flash of emotion I had never experienced before— resentment toward my cousin Dan. This made me feel guilty. So I was resentful and guilty, insecure and jealous, faking a smile, and playing a song to a crowd when I really wanted to be alone, scream- ing into a pillow, and tearing my hair out. I had always followed Dan's lead. That had gotten me into some trouble in the past, but nothing too lastingly serious. This was different. This stupid poker tournament, my sham of a love affair with Mona, and Dan's schem- ing might very well have cost me more than I cared to lose this time.

What would Dorothy think if she knew what we were really up to with this televised tournament? Would that even make a differ- ence, now that I had handed her over to Morris on a silver platter?

I had lost control of my life. No, even worse, I had willingly relinquished control to Dan. I wasn't a rock star—I was playing at a beachside hotel in Corpus Christi, for heaven's sake! I was getting too old for this nonsense. It was time to start thinking for myself. I had to learn to say no to my favorite cousin. I just hoped I hadn't learned too late.

23

I CAN perform in the most miserable state of mind. If you're in show-biz, you have to sometimes. You just shove your emotions aside and do your job. Actually, as a musician, the job can be therapeutic if you let it. After all, if you're playing your own songs, and getting paid for it, and the band's getting along great and playing well, and the fans are partying like crazy, how could you not forget your troubles for a while?

So by the end of the gig, I had cheered up a little, even though Morris Witherspoon had not stayed to hear the band and might never contact me again, for all I knew. Even though Dorothy had run off with the major to L.A. Even though I realized I had allowed Dan to kidnap my life for the summer and hold my soul hostage for a ransom I couldn't afford to pay.

In spite of all that, I stepped off the stage into a small throng of adoring fans, many of whom had rushed down to the hotel after the live interview on the local news. The band had played flawlessly, and didn't seem the least bit upset that we weren't signing contracts with Silver Spoon Records at that very moment. I had had a couple of drinks toward the end of the last set, and had just the right alcohol buzz going to improve my outlook.

I was even beginning to think I had overreacted to everything earlier. Dorothy had gone with Morris because it was a free ride on a private jet. Why wouldn't she? Morris had missed our showcase because one of his stars was in trouble, and he was the kind of guy to take care of his people—or at least protect his investments. Dan knew what he was doing with this poker tournament, and had made me well aware of the risks before I signed on. I decided to lighten up and join the party.

After the balmy afternoon on the patio, the night breezes coming off Corpus Christi Bay felt refreshingly cool. I mingled with fans and the band, the television crews from our shoot and the local media, and the poker players. We drank and talked and celebrated another city conquered by *The World Championship Series of Texas Hold 'Em Poker* until the usual die-hards—Dan, Mona, Zeller, and I—were the only ones left poolside.

"How'd we do?" Zeller asked after my fiddle player, Warren Watson Warren, finally left us to stagger on up to bed.

"I don't know," Dan said. "Let's go up to the bookie's room and get a tally.

"We're going to meet the bookie?" I asked.

"Hell no. He's in bed by now. He sleeps in another room in another hotel. He's a very careful guy. Come on."

We took the elevator up to a suite on the sixth floor. The room possessed similarities to the one we had seen at the Flagship Hotel, in Galveston. In addition to the normal hotel television set, there was the small TV monitor installed by the film crew. Hand-scrawled notes were scattered about, and the ashtray was filled with cigarette butts. Mona found the wet bar and started opening tiny bottles of booze to provide us all with yet another nightcap. Dan started flipping through a ledger book as Zeller looked over his shoulder.

"Is all that chicken-scratchin' supposed to make sense?" Zeller asked.

"Give me a minute, will you, Wildcat? You're making me nervous, reading over my shoulder."

"Come here, Wildcat, honey," Mona said, patting the seat on the couch next to her. She had a straight shot of bourbon waiting for him.

I opened the sliding glass door to the balcony to let some fresh air in. I stood out on the balcony alone a few minutes. I wondered why

Dorothy had not said good-bye before she left. I thought about her and Morris in L.A. I felt myself slipping into doubt and self-pity again.

"Well, crap," I heard Dan say, inside the room.

I stepped back in to see Zeller glaring at my cousin.

"What do you mean? 'Crap' what?"

"Well, it's not as good as I had hoped, Wildcat. The betting's still down from the first week. A little better than last week, though."

"Goddamn-it, you promised me more profits than this!" Zeller yelled.

"Easy, Wildcat! There's always next week in Fort Worth, and then the big show in Houston. There's plenty of time for the big payday."

"Bullshit! I've had it. I want my winnings now!"

"You know I can't touch the money until the tournament's over, Arch. You'll get paid in two weeks. And it'll be a big payday, too, because the betting will pick up next week."

"You don't know that."

"My gut says things will improve. Hey, it ain't like you're losing money. You're making a tidy profit."

"It ain't worth my time and money to keep this up. I could turn a lot higher profits than this in the oil patch."

"Wildcat, baby," Mona whined. "Come on. Play another week."

"Actually . . . ," Dan said. "Y'all ain't gonna like this, but . . ."

"What now?" I asked, a growl in my tone.

"Well, there won't be another week, unless we get another infusion of cash. Our TV crew goes through money like the Pentagon buying claw hammers."

"How much?" Zeller prodded.

"I think another ten grand from both of you will get us through."

"You think?" Zeller said.

"No way!" I said, putting my foot down.

"Ronnie!" Mona snapped, as if I had blasphemed.

"This is bullshit, Dan. This thing has turned into a bottomless pit of losses."

"Easy, Ronnie. You're thinking 'losses' when you should be thinking 'investments.' You've probably tripled your money already. It's just waiting for you in the Swiss account."

"I want it now."

"Me, too," Zeller said.

"Y'all know I can't do that. Look, in what other kind of investment can you control your dividends? Just like any other business proposition, you've got to let the investment mature. If you two just stick with me two more weeks, you'll see profits you never dreamed of!"

"No," I said. "I'm not putting in any more money."

"Me, either," Zeller insisted.

"Boys!" Mona said, distraught. "What about me? What about my TV career? I want to see myself on TV!" She stomped her foot like a spoiled child.

"Then you better come up with twenty grand," I said.

Mona threw herself facedown on the bed and began weeping angrily like a two-year-old. I was disgusted with the whole scene. I just wanted out.

"I've got a career to worry about, Dan. I should have been concentrating on my next record deal all summer, instead of this fiasco."

"Stick with my fiasco, and you can buy your own record company."

"You have no idea how much a record company even costs, Dan."

"Sure I do. I own one in Brazil."

"Bullshit," Zeller said.

"I've heard enough of this crap," I announced, walking for the door. "Mona, are you coming or not?"

She sat up on the bed, mascara smeared all over her face. "Ronnie! Are you just going to quit? Listen to Dan!"

I looked at my cousin. "I think I've listened to Dan long enough. It's time I do my own thinking for a change."

"I'm goin', too," Zeller said.

"Wait!" Dan said. He ground his teeth and clenched his fist. "Damn, I hate to do this."

"Do what?" I demanded.

"Let you in on my *other* little secret."

"What are you talking about, Dan?"

"I guess I'm going to have to include you two in my profits again. Damn-it, you're milking me like a Jersey cow."

"Every time you let us in on profits, it ends up costing us more," I complained.

"This is different. I guess it's high time I told y'all about the hospitality room."

"The what?" Zeller and I said in unison.

"The hospitality room! Come on."

Dan opened the door and waited for us to follow. Mona jumped off the bed and bounced into the hallway. "Hospitality room!" she sang.

Dan tossed his head toward the exit. "Come on, guys. Y'all won't be sorry."

We took the elevator up to the top floor. Dan produced a key to the penthouse suite and opened the door to let us in. Inside, the evidence told the story of a lively party. Shot glasses, beer mugs, and snifters—empty and half-full—were scattered around on the bar and on the coffee tables. The place smelled of tobacco smoke and spilt booze. The ashtrays held a variety of butts and a cigar stub or two. A large platter on the bar held a few surviving finger sandwiches. Bowls of assorted nuts and bar snacks were scattered here and there. As in the bookie's room, an extra television monitor sat beside the room's standard set.

"This is the hospitality room," Dan said.

"What kind of hospitality are we talking about?" I asked.

"Free drinks and grub. And some pretty lively side betting."

"Who's doing the betting?"

"Your opponents in the tournament. And a few Texas high rollers."

Mona picked up a finger sandwich and nibbled on it. "What are they betting on?"

"Mostly the tournament. But these yahoos will bet on anything animate or inanimate. It doesn't matter to them."

"Let me get this straight," I said. "When Jack Diamond got eliminated first in today's final round, he came up here and started making bets on the players who were still in?"

"Yep."

"Why didn't you tell us about this before?" Archie grunted.

"Yeah," Mona said, her mouth full of stale pimento cheese.

"I had intended to let y'all in on it next week, but I guess now is as good a time as any. I really didn't think you'd be interested until the pot got up into the millions."

"Millions?" Zeller said, his bloodshot eyes widening.

"Oh, yeah. Several million by now."

"But this is illegal," I said.

"You sound like a big ol' Boy Scout," Dan scolded. "Which one of us hasn't done our share of illegal gambling?"

"Yeah," Mona chided. She washed her sandwich down with a bourbon and Coke.

"What about this pot you mentioned?" Zeller demanded.

Dan crooked his finger and led us into the bedroom. The king-sized bed was still made, though it looked as if it had been sat upon. Leading us around the bed, Dan pointed toward the corner of the room. Stepping around him, I saw a large safe sitting on the floor.

"Did you haul that thing up here?" I asked.

Dan dropped to one knee and began dialing in a combination on the safe door. "Yeah. It takes me and two bellboys to move it. Nobody's gonna carry this baby off without busting a couple of hernias."

Zeller pointed at a set of scales on the dresser—a rather large device that looked capable of precise measurements of weight. Not the sort of thing you usually found in a hotel room. "What's with the scales?" he demanded.

"Oh, are you a Libra?" Mona said.

"No, Mona," Dan replied, still concentrating on the safe's combination. "I'm not a Libra. Sometimes we don't have time to count when the betting is hot and heavy."

"So?" I asked.

"So we weigh the money instead of counting it. For example, twenty-three pounds of hundred-dollar bills equals a million bucks."

About then, Dan turned the handle on the safe and swung open the door. It looked to be about half-full of bundled banknotes. He took a bundle out and tossed it to Zeller. "That's ten thousand."

Zeller sniffed the cash and thumbed through the stack, checking the corners of the bills. "How much is in there?" he asked, pointing at the safe.

"I'll have to check with the hospitality room host to get a new total. But I can tell you this: I, personally, won three million betting on Ronnie's shoot-out against Morris Witherspoon."

"Wait a minute," I said, remembering the day's events. "You were standing right there at the table during that round. How could you have placed a bet up here?"

"Remember the production break? When we always take five to reset the cameras? That gives me the chance to phone my bet up to the hospitality room host."

"So that's the reason for the production break," Zeller said.

"You're sharp, Arch."

"He's about as sharp as the edge of town," I muttered.

Zeller jutted his thumb at me. "So you won three million on this choirboy? Why the hell would you bet on *him*?"

Mona cackled, spraying her drink across the room. "Choirboy! I love it!"

"Let's just say I had a hunch," Dan answered.

"My ass sucks canal water if you bet that much on a hunch."

Dan opened the nightstand drawer, pulled out a handy Gideon Bible, put his hand on it, and said, "I swear to God. But it wasn't as risky as you might think. I had a little hunch-maker on my side."

"Huh?"

Dan slammed the nightstand drawer and stood. "You two are forgetting something. I'm surprised it hasn't dawned on you yet."

"What?" I demanded.

"Think!" Dan said, clearly enjoying this. "It's obvious!"

"What is?" Zeller was glaring at Dan.

"I know," Mona said, raising her hand, as if she were in class. "The cameras."

"She's smarter than both of you put together!" Dan said, laughing.

"Cameras," I said. "You mean—"

"Under the table," Zeller slurred. He stared a thousand miles away, as if he had just cast his eyes upon the true meaning of all human existence. "How does it work?"

"Give me that cash back and I'll tell you."

Zeller fondled the bound stack of bills, then reluctantly tossed the ten grand to Dan, who tossed it into the safe, shut the steel door, and spun the combination wheel. He gestured back toward the living room area of the suite, and we all went back to the bar. Motioning for us to sit, Dan grabbed the straight-backed wooden desk chair, reversed it, and straddled it, his elbows resting on the chair back.

"It's pretty simple," he began. "Bartholomew's TV crew cameras broadcast the game to this room so all the high-rollin' gamblers can see the flop, the turn, and the river. Then we bet on who's going to win when they reveal the hole cards. Only, I have quite an advantage."

"The cameras under the table," I said.

Dan nodded.

"But where do you see the shots picked up by the pocket cameras?" I asked, feeling uneasy about this whole new angle being exposed.

"I don't. Bartholomew does, out in his production van. Have you noticed that he always turns the director duties over to me toward the end of each round, supposedly so he can watch the camera angles from the production van?"

"I've noticed that," I said.

"Well, he's watchin' the camera angles, all right, including the ones nobody else can see."

"The pocket cameras," I said.

Dan nodded. "Bartholomew can see who has the winning hand before the final bets are placed. He tells me who to bet on over my headset. That's why we take the production break to reset the cameras right before the players reveal their hole cards. That break gives me a chance to get to the nearest house phone and call my bet up to the hospitality room host."

"Who's this host?" Zeller demanded.

"You'll meet him next week in Fort Worth," Dan promised, letting his mouth slip into a wry grin.

"Who-all knows about the secret pocket cameras?" Zeller said, his eyes narrowing with greed and lust.

"Only the four of us, and Bartholomew. I have to split my winnings with him."

Zeller threw his whiskey back, clapped his hands together once, and started rubbing them together vigorously. "I can smell the money already! I can't wait to walk away with my three million dollars next week!"

"Whoa, Wildcat," Dan said. "Nobody walks away with any money until the final championship round at Houston. All the winnings go back in the safe. That way, the pot keeps growing, building the excitement. The payday in Houston is going to be phenomenal."

"Whatever," Zeller said. "I want to win one of those three-million-dollar pots next week!"

"I can't let you do that," Dan said matter-of-factly.

"You did it!" Zeller said, an ugly leer replacing his miserly grin.

"Sure I did. But I was trying to lose! That's the reason I bet on Ronnie. Morris had the better hand, but for some stupid reason, he let Ronnie take the pot."

"What?" I blurted. "Bullshit! Why would you try to lose your bet?"

"I've got to lose as often as I win to make it look good. Next week I'll lose most of today's three million on purpose so nobody will get suspicious of me. We can't get greedy just yet."

"I can't help it," Zeller admitted. "I was born greedy."

"You'll have to be patient. Next week, in Fort Worth, you can win a little, lose a little, and maybe recoup a little on one last bet. But you can't raise suspicions by breezing into the hospitality room and making a multimillion-dollar score right off the bat."

"So we start our betting with the ten thousand we talked about downstairs in the bookie's room?" I said.

"No! Hell no!" Dan sprang to his feet. "The ten thousand we talked about downstairs is to keep the production going. You invest that with me. You have to bring your own cash money to the hospitality room."

"You've got to be kidding!"

"Hey, I'm not giving either one of you a tip from my pocket cameras until I see that ten grand apiece. That's only fair."

"What am I? A money tree?"

"Ronnie, honey!" Mona whined. "Look ahead to Houston. Big money!"

"I was right about her," Dan said. "She is smarter than the two of you put together."

"How much can we bet next week?" Zeller said.

Dan shrugged. "Start with five grand. That's what Bartholomew and I started with. We've been careful not to get too greedy. We've intentionally lost some bets. But our share of the pot has been gradually growing through the tournament. Keep in mind, it's not a lead-pipe cinch, even with the pocket cameras. Sometimes the player with the losing hand successfully bluffs his opponent into folding what would have been the winning hand."

"How much are we talking about winning, when it's all over?" Zeller asked.

Dan smirked, looking characteristically cocksure. "My plan all along has been to wait until after the river is revealed in the final shoot-out of the world championship hand at Gilley's in two weeks. When that happens, I'll put down a large bet on one of the two final players before they show their hole cards. The way I've got it scripted, nobody is going to want to make the same bet I'm making. I'll win the bet and pocket a nice profit. You can do the same—*if* you'll come up with twenty grand more to keep the shooting of the show funded another two weeks."

"How much could we win?" Zeller asked.

"Depends on how much you bet. The odds will be about twenty-to-one, the way I have it scripted."

"So if I bet a million, I win twenty million?"

"That's the plan."

"If I won twenty million, that would make me twice as rich as I am," Zeller muttered under his breath.

I snorted. "That would make me twenty times as rich as I am. I can't scrape up a million dollars in two weeks."

"Half a million will do," Dan said. "Your payday will be about ten million, then, if you only bet half a mil."

"Well, maybe I could manage that." It was strange to hear my own voice talking about this, as if I was really considering it.

"Lightweight," Mona grumbled.

"Hey, million-dollar hits don't grow on trees," I said defensively.

"Wildcat pumps his up from underground," Mona said, as if jabbing the handle of a rat-tail comb deeper into my guts.

"Everything is relative," Dan said. "The odds will be twenty-to-one. Probably, we'll be the only three betting on the long shot that I've scripted for the final hand. Of course, we'll also split the ten percent house commission from the Swiss bank account three ways. That ought to be worth a couple of million more."

"I know a con when I see one," Zeller said.

Hearing that word—"con"—made my guts go glacial. We all stared at Wildcat, waiting for the next words to cross his lips.

"Might as well admit it," he continued.

"Admit what?" Dan asked.

"This is a con." Zeller smiled. "And a good one. Us four, and that limp-wristed TV producer, Bartholomew, are conning a lot of high rollers out of a fortune with those hidden cameras."

Dan looked smug. "That's one way to look at it. I see it as a well-deserved by-product of our success with the TV show."

A silence fell over the hospitality room. We all looked at each other.

"So . . . ," Dan said, "are you boys in or out?"

"I'm in," Zeller said, nodding.

"You realize what that means, don't you?" Dan replied.

"Yeah, it means I'm gonna score twenty million bucks."

"True," Dan said. "But it also means you can't be world champion of Texas hold 'em poker."

"Why the hell not?"

"You can't be in the hospitality room, placing a million-dollar bet on the final outcome, if you're one of the last two players sitting at the poker table holding cards."

Zeller frowned his disappointment. "Oh, well. I'd rather be a rich loser than a poor champion any day. Count me in."

I sighed. "I'm in, too."

"Yes!" Mona said, pumping her fist.

"Good," Dan said. "That way, I don't have to kill either one of you for knowing too much." He laughed. "Let's drink to our new partnership!"

24

"RAWN . . . ," I vaguely heard Slim saying.

My mind was out in nebula somewhere, looking for Dorothy. Since she had neglected to say good-bye to me in Corpus Christi, I had not heard a peep from her.

"Rawn?" Slim's distant voice was laced by my head's own reverb.

Dorothy had run off with Morris Witherspoon, and hadn't answered her phone since. I wasn't even sure if she was my manager anymore, much less my would-be heartthrob.

I heard the sound of someone thumping loudly on a microphone. "Rawn! This thang on?"

I found myself sitting at the Harrison control console in Topaz Studios' Salon D in Nashville, staring at the knobs and faders. I looked up through the glass into the isolation booth where Slim stood with his guitar strapped on. We had been fixing some guitar parts on the demos.

"Sorry, Slim. There's so much snoring going on in here, I can hardly hear you."

It was true that Henry, Mojo, and Warren were all snoozing on the sofas, but it was a lame excuse for my having drifted away mentally toward the end of the session. I had sent Jimmy home an hour ago, and was engineering the fixes myself.

"Yeah, right," Slim said. "I know where your head's at. Was that a take?"

"It sounded good," I said, remembering the guitar intro we had just put down on tape. "You're done. In fact, we're all done. That was the last of Dorothy's fixes." Her name hurt crossing my tongue. Why hadn't she called? Where had Morris taken her?

Then I remembered that other thing. The waltz. We needed to add a waltz to the demos, and I didn't have a handy waltz lying around anywhere just now. I would have to write one. But why go to the trouble, until I heard from Dorothy or Morris. Limbo. That's where I was stuck. Music City limbo.

Slim unplugged his guitar, exited the isolation booth, and strolled into the control room. "Hey, man," he said, scratching the back of his neck and looking vaguely at the floor. "I got to axe you a question."

"About what?" I said, making a note on the track sheet for the song we had just finished.

"You heard from the man?"

"The man" was Morris Witherspoon. "No. Not since Saturday."

"Look, man. I gotta know somethin'. This deal gonna float?"

He was asking about the record deal. "I think there's a real good chance it'll float, Slim. I've got to mix these demos and give them to Dorothy to give to Witherspoon. Then we'll know something. But you know what they say: 'It ain't final till it's vinyl.' "

"I gots to know somethin' soon, man."

"What's the rush?"

"I got another offer."

A pang of dread sank into my stomach. Slim's guitar tone was a huge part of the Truebloods' sound. "From who?" I asked, rather defensively.

"This cat—you know him—Joe McLeod."

"Know him?" I railed. "He hit me in the head with a Neumann microphone a month ago!"

I had raised my voice enough to wake up the guys on the sofa.

"What's going on?" Mojo said groggily, stretching his limbs.

"Joe McLeod is trying to steal Slim from us. Any of you other guys get offers from McLeod?"

They all shook their heads.

"He got him a record deal with Walnut," Slim explained, a bit apologetically. "It's your old band, but he wants me in it, too."

"Of course he does! He knows you're working with me!"

"Said he didn't know that."

"Bullshit! That backstabbing son of a bitch!"

"Uh, the name of the band . . . ," Slim said, trying to break something to me gently.

"What about it?"

"He said you stole the name from him. He's usin' the same name we usin'. They done got a deal with Walnut as Joe McLeod and the Truebloods."

"Mother . . . ," I began, standing up and kicking the producer's chair across the room. My lips had loaded up a capital F for the next word, when the studio door opened to reveal a smiling Dorothy Taliaferro, followed by a swaggering Morris Witherspoon.

". . . Fudgin' fiddlesticks!" I railed, grabbing myself with both fists by the hair of my head.

The smile dropped from Dorothy's face. "Everything all right, Ronnie?"

Now, I'm usually a pretty cool customer, but I came as close to losing it at that moment as I ever have. I mean I was on the verge of going ballistically berserk right in front of Dorothy and Morris, who were staring at me like two hoot owls in a tree, wondering if I had lost my mind. One held my professional career in his hands, and the other, my romantic future in her heart. So what did I do? Did I cash in my chips? Did I go all in? No. I bluffed. I pulled myself together and remembered what Dan had told me to do with Dorothy. Play it cool, like a poker hand.

"You just caught the punch line of a bad joke," I lied. "Pretty funny, right, boys?"

The band caught on and humored me with some halfhearted chuckles.

"Looks like you're putting them to sleep to me," Morris said, a wry grin bending one side of his mouth.

"I never claimed to be much of a comedian. Come on in! We were just about to celebrate!"

"Celebrate what?" Dorothy asked.

"We finished the overdubs. I'll have the demos mixed down and ready to hand over to Morris next week."

"Wonderful! Isn't that marvelous, Morris?"

"That's splendid," Morris said in his deadpan poker voice, as if calling a bet. "So, I'll hear the band live in Fort Worth this weekend. And maybe play a little more Texas hold 'em—" He raised a knowing eyebrow at me. "If that goes well, I can listen to the demos next week."

I nodded my approval. "So," I said, trying to sound casual, "where-all have you two been?"

"Oh!" Dorothy squealed. "It's been an absolute whirlwind. First we went to check on Big Al Brothers in L.A."

"Yeah?" I asked with manufactured politeness. "How's Big Al?"

"Two broken legs and a collapsed lung," Morris said. "He'll be all right, but we had to cancel his autumn tour with Conway Twitty."

"Aw, too bad."

"Morris is looking for a replacement band to tour with Conway," Dorothy said, reining in some of her giddiness. "The Truebloods are up for consideration."

"We shall see," Morris said cautiously. "We shall see. One step at a time."

Dorothy shoved Morris playfully. "Oh, they're a shoo-in, Spoony." Dorothy looked at the band. "Y'all might as well block out your fall calendars now. The tour is nationwide."

Spoony? Did she just call Morris Witherspoon "Spoony"?

"We'd have to rush to get our first album recorded," I said, "but it's doable. I mean, we've done the preproduction work with these demos."

"I'm sure it'll take less time than you think," Dorothy said, as if she knew more about the process than I did.

"So, about this celebration?" Morris said. "Where are we going? How about dinner at the Hermitage Hotel? My treat."

AN HOUR later, the band members and I were all showered and changed into dinner attire, and were busy carving into our steaks at the Hermitage Hotel's five-star restaurant. Dorothy had reminded me that I had asked, back in the studio, where-all she and *Spoony* had been since Saturday night.

". . . So, after visiting Big Al in the hospital, we flew Morris's jet down to Mazatlán for a piña colada and some beach time."

"I eschewed the piña colada in favor of some Herradura Reposado," Morris said, "chased with a cold Sol."

Chased with a cold soul, indeed, I thought. Sounded like a song to me. "I thought you looked tanned," I said to Dorothy.

"Thank you, Ronnie, but I stayed under the palapa in a hammock most of time, while Morris went spear-fishing for our supper."

The band members were chewing away ravenously at some excellent victuals, as if they were relieved to have an excuse to stay out of the conversation, but their eyes darted about the table quizzically.

"We only stayed in Mazatlán two nights," Dorothy continued. "Then Morris insisted that we simply had to fly up to Coeur d'Alene for some splendid fly-fishing. He caught a huge rainbow, but I never quite got the hang of it."

"You did very well for your first time fly casting," Morris said.

"Oh, please, Spoony, I'd be better off with a cane pole."

There was "Spoony" again! *Play it cool, Ronnie,* I reminded myself in Dan's voice. "I've got to ask," I said. "Spoony?"

"My old Ivy League nickname," Morris said. He glared a warning at the boys sitting around the table, including me. "Only Dorothy can get away with calling me that." Then he smiled at her.

"So, after Idaho, there was just enough time to pop over to the Big Apple and catch a Broadway show."

"I love Broadway!" Mojo said, venturing into the conversation. "What did you see?"

"Yet another production of *West Side Story*," Morris said in a mournful tone.

"Oh, Spoony, it was wonderful!"

"That's one of my favorites," Mojo announced.

"I never got into it," said Warren.

"We left New York this morning, and here we are!" Dorothy sang, as if in a Broadway finale, complete with sweeping gestures.

"I got a question," Slim said, gesturing toward the major with his steak knife. "How much was in that pot of gold?"

Morris tilted his head like a curious Labrador retriever. "Which pot of gold was that, Slim?"

"The lady said you caught a rainbow." His mouth broke into a grin, a gold tooth leading the way.

Morris erupted in laughter, and the rest of the table followed his example, including me, though I had to force it.

"Let me tell you something, Slim. It's not the gold that interests me. It's the catching of the rainbow that keeps me going." He raised his glass flamboyantly, and we all toasted to catching rainbows.

I had to admit that Major Morris Witherspoon—my rival for Dorothy's affections, and my possible future career-maker—had a pretty classy line of bullshit. I liked and respected him. I wondered briefly, if it came right down to it, if I had to make an either/or choice, would I pick the career or the girl? Or would the girl even want me without the career?

25

LATER, AFTER brandy and cigars in the bar, the boys in the band had the bartender call them a cab for their hotel, leaving me with Dorothy and Morris. Morris offered us each a ride home in his limo, but Dorothy declined for both of us, much to my surprise.

"No thank you, Spoony, I need to have a little ol' business meeting with my client," she said. "I'll make sure he gets back to his room in one piece."

"Please do," Morris said. "We don't want him ending up like Big Al." Morris stood, kissed Dorothy on the cheek. He shook my hand, and when he did, I found a spare Cuban cigar included in the handshake. Or maybe it was Honduran.

As the major left, I saw Dorothy looking longingly after him, her eyes sparkling. I thought I was going to have a jealous conniption fit, but I kept my poker face intact. She gazed upon his form until he was completely through the door; then she wheeled to face me.

"Oh, my God!" she said in a stage whisper. "Can you believe this?"

I was a bit stunned. "What?"

"Morris Witherspoon is on the verge of signing you to the deal of your career! We've already worked out virtually every detail of the contract!"

I looked at her dubiously. "Whoa, Dorothy. Don't get your hopes up too high. Morris hasn't even heard the band yet. Or the demos."

"At this point, that's a mere formality. The man loves your work."

"You mean my past work. I've seen this happen before in this town, and in L.A. Nobody wants to tell you no. Nobody wants to

burn any bridges, so they string you along with free dinners and cigars as long as they can, hoping that something more marketable
pops up in the meantime. Then you're yesterday's wannabe. Hell,
you're not even a wannabe anymore, you're a has-been wannabe."

"Ronnie Breed!" she scolded. "That kind of pessimism will not
be tolerated by the Talent Fire Agency."

"I'm a realist. Not a pessimist. I like Morris. I really do. But until
he puts his name on the dotted line, we've got nothing but free
lunch and fake Cubans."

"Fake?"

"It's Honduran. I can tell by the veins in the wrapper."

"Oh, it is not. And dinner at the Hermitage, for the whole band,
is quite a step up from free lunch."

"So is a whirlwind trip to L.A., Mazatlán, Coeur d'Alene, and
New York City!"

"Oh, so you're jealous?"

I thought we were really about to get into it now. "Jealous? Is there
something to be jealous about?"

"You are! You're jealous that I got to go to L.A., Mexico, Idaho,
and the Big Apple, while you were stuck in the studio, fixing the
sides. Well, let me tell you something, rock star, I was working on
our contract with Morris the whole time."

"Well, you could have checked in to let me know."

She looked at me as if I had gone crazy. "I did check in. I left you
messages daily."

This news stunned me. "Where?"

Dorothy propped her hands on her hips. "Ronnie Breed. You are
in such big trouble."

"With who?"

"Do you mean to tell me that you haven't called your mother
since Saturday?"

"What does my mother have to do with any of this?"

"That's where I've been leaving the messages, silly! On her machine. Well, I spoke to her in person on Sunday, and she was just
certain that you'd check in, like a good son would, but you haven't,
have you?"

Now I felt the scolding was actually warranted. All this time, I had been thinking that Dorothy was out there gallivanting with Morris—or even worse than gallivanting—and that she hadn't even called. If I had phoned my own mother, I might have known better. I might not have been worried about any of this at all. Why shouldn't Dorothy have a good time traveling the continent while she worked out the contract with Morris? Maybe she was right about this deal. Maybe it was imminent. Maybe I had become a jaded pessimist in this business.

"Well, I've been busy with the demos," I said.

"What a lame excuse. I want you to call your mother first thing in the morning."

"Yes, ma'am," I mumbled.

"Now, when can you have the tracks mixed?"

"Next Wednesday. I promise."

"Good. We need to strike while the iron is hot. And trust me, Ronnie, it is red hot."

My jealousy flared again. Was she saying that her relationship with *Spoony* was red hot? I couldn't stand it. I had to up the ante and ask. "So, does *Spoony* treat his date like a gentleman should?"

She smirked at me. "How would I know? I spent my time modifying drafts of the contract. You'd have to ask his date."

"He brought a date?"

"No, he didn't *bring* one. He had one *waiting* in every town. There was a starlet in L.A., a señorita in Mazatlán, a cowgirl in Idaho, and a ballerina in New York."

I felt the relief crash over me like an ocean wave hitting a drunk man in the face. "Oh," I said stupidly. And I did feel stupid for ever doubting Dorothy's fidelity.

"If you'd call your mother, you'd know all of this. I left a message with her every day."

Now that all that was cleared up, I felt a sudden, unbounded optimism in all things romantic and professional. "Well . . . Okay!" I said, sipping my last, incandescent swallow of fine Courvoisier brandy, courtesy of Dorothy's purely platonic colleague, Morris Witherspoon, aka Spoony.

Then I remembered Slim, and Joe McLeod. "We have a problem," I began. I told Dorothy about Joe's attempt to steal Slim from the band.

Dorothy listened to me vent as she finished a glass of wine she had been milking for an hour. "I'll talk to Slim tomorrow. We'll match anything McLeod offers him."

"We can't promise that until Morris makes *us* an offer."

"Which he will, after he hears the band and the demos. Surely Slim will give us a week."

"I hope. But what about the band name?"

Dorothy gave me the most provocative smile—sexy and all-knowing. "I'm way ahead of Joe McLeod on that one. I'm already in the process of having the Truebloods registered, trademarked, copyrighted, and patented, coast-to-coast and border-to-border. Morris's lawyers will eat McLeod for breakfast if he tries to use that name."

The refreshing surf sobered me anew. I smiled at Dorothy. "We should talk more often."

"If you had a home, with a phone, we would. I can't very well call your bus."

"I'll have a home again. Someday soon, I hope. I just have to figure out where my place in the world is."

"Nashville, silly. This is your place. You're home and you don't even know it."

"I hope you're right, Dorothy."

She melted. "I love the way you say my name in your Texas accent."

"Texans don't have accents. Everybody else does."

She rolled her eyes as she set her empty glass on the bar and took her car keys from her purse. "I'd offer you a ride, but you remember what happened last time."

"I'm taking a cab back to the studio, anyway. I'm rarin' to get started mixing. But if you had offered the ride, I would have taken it."

She slid off her barstool. "That's what I was afraid of. Now is not the time."

This struck me as a not-so-subtle hint that the time would come. I felt as if I had a rainbow on the hook, and I was playing her for the pure joy of the catch, regardless of the pot of gold. Still, I knew she would never be mine unless I could swoop her up in my net, and that would take some reeling. (Sorry to belabor the metaphor, but I am a fisherman in addition to being a songwriter.)

"I'll walk you out to your car," I said.

The Mustang was parked around the corner, under a streetlight. As we approached it, I cupped my hand around Dorothy's as if to engage in a little innocent hand-holding, but I only stole her car key from her grasp so I could open the door for her. Not to be outdone, she pretended to slip off the curb in her stilettos, falling wantonly into my arms, her ample breasts pressing up against my chest as her hair engulfed my face.

A heat-seeking missile could have found those luscious lips, and that's what my tongue turned itself into: a heat-seeking missile. Our first kiss exploded in fireworks that showered the streetlight with shame for its feeble attempt to illuminate the scene below . . . our embrace . . . the warm cocoon of our bodies heating the blended aroma of Le De perfume and Old Spice after-shave . . . the private world of our lips locked together, our hands seeking new destinations . . .

"Hey, get a room!" somebody yelled from a passing car.

Dorothy pushed away from me. "Oh, my," she said. "I must have slipped."

My lips and tongue felt numbed by pleasure, unable to form words. "Wow may wombat," I uttered. I have no idea what I was trying to say.

"I agree," she replied. "Until then. Good night, Ronnie." She smiled like a moonbeam and stepped into the car. Before she drove away, she kissed her finger and pressed it against the glass window.

I waved as she drove away. When she was gone, I said to myself: "Uh-oh."

I don't know how long I stood there, but eventually certain realities began to sink in. Not only had my desired romance with Dorothy escalated a notch, but there was still a shot at a record contract with Morris, too. Then I remembered the other problem I had forgotten to mention to Dorothy. Now that the deal was back on with Morris, I had to write and record a waltz in one week's time. "What are the chances of that happening?" I said to myself. "*What Are the Chances*"? Hmmm. That was as good a title as any for a country waltz.

As I turned back into the Hermitage Hotel, the melody, the tempo, and the first handful of lyrics rained down on me from nowhere:

> *What are the chances of you giving me one more chance?*
> *What are the odds that you'd even consider a dance? . . .*

I had the bellman call a cab. As I waited for the taxi, I scrawled more lyrics on a hotel notepad.

> *I lost a bet with your heart*
> *I was a fool from the start*
> *What are the chances of you giving me one more chance? . . .*

"Come on, second verse," I begged.

The cab showed up, and I told the driver to take me to Topaz Studios. I thought about Dorothy and how she might like this song.

> *What was I thinking when I placed a bet with your love?*
> *I should have held you as close as a hand in a glove.*
> *As close as a heart to the vest*
> *The hand that I held was the best.*
> *What was I thinking when I placed a bet with your love?*

I paid the cabbie at Topaz and beat on the door until the night watchman let me in. I rushed to Salon D and switched on the tape machine. I already knew the key and chord progression even though I had not picked up a guitar nor sat down at the piano. I spent the rest of the night in the studio, recording "What Are the Chances." I played all the instruments myself. I got away with it because I kept everything dirt simple. The rimshot and the kick drum—simple. The piano chords—basic. The bass notes, the rhythm guitar, and the Fender Telecaster—all fundamental. I couldn't fake Slim's tone on the electric, so I just played the melody, pure and plain. It wasn't fancy, but this was a song any garage band in the world could play, and someday many would. I threw in a modulation and some harmonies. Done.

By dawn I had our waltz recorded, and nobody knew it but me.

26

FORT WORTH always struck me as either the biggest little town in Texas, or the smallest city. In the summer of 1975, downtown sported a collection of office buildings twenty or thirty stories tall, giving the impression of a sort of kindergarten for skyscrapers. A traffic jam was a rarity in "Cow Town," yet the place teemed with activity. Cattle, horses, cotton, oil, aviation, education—they had all driven the Fort Worth economy at one time or another. The population was just a little too large for everyone to know everyone else, but it still seemed as if that were the case anyway. If you were from there, you couldn't walk two blocks down the street without recognizing somebody. People who had grown up in Fort Worth tended to stay.

Not far north of downtown, on Exchange Street, lay the remnants of the old Fort Worth Stockyards—one of the industries that had fed Fort Worth's boomtown economy in its early days. Back in the days of the Wild West, the fabled Chisholm Trail passed through Fort Worth. One section of town was so wild that it was known as Hell's Half Acre. Later, when the railroads arrived, the town grew into a thriving cattle-shipping center. Meatpacking plants came next, providing thousands of factory jobs.

In 1907, city planners decided that the busy Fort Worth Stockyards needed a modern coliseum in which to exhibit quality cattle and other livestock. They built it in eighty-eight days, and it still stands today. The Cowtown Coliseum, as it was dubbed, hosted the first indoor rodeo, the first nighttime horse show, the first radio broadcast of a rodeo, and the first bull-riding event in a rodeo. Besides all that Western stuff, the coliseum also served as a cultural center for the city. Over the decades it featured performances by the Russian Ballet, the Chicago Grand Opera, Enrico Caruso, Elvis, and even Bob Wills.

You can bet that a lot of poker had been played in the bars along Exchange Street in the days of the Wild West. But before 1975, the coliseum had never hosted a poker tournament. My cousin Dan changed all that. The arena dirt on the floor of the coliseum could be covered over with flooring for all kinds of events. It was a perfect place for a TV shoot, poker tables, a dance floor, and a live band.

Mona and I met Dan at the coliseum on Friday to check things out for the Texas hold 'em tournament. Dan and I found a large stage waiting for us.

"This beats the hell out of our last three locations," I said. "I like this wide-open setup."

"And the air-conditioning," Mona added. "I thought the humidity was going to kill me in Creep-us Chorsti." She refused to call Corpus Christi by its real name. (If you're from Corpus, don't be offended. Mona could find something to complain about on a sunny day in Honolulu.)

"I just hope we can fill this place," I said. "A space this big sure feels empty just half-full."

"Ticket sales are up," Dan said. "It's weird. The whole tournament thing is actually drawing a crowd."

"Or maybe my new band," I suggested.

"Oh, yeah, I bet *that's* it." Mona could squeeze sarcasm into a comment like God packed stench in a skunk.

"Hey, Dorothy is on the verge of a big deal for my band!" I said defensively. Dorothy's name felt good in my mouth.

"Oh, Dorothy!" Mona stuck her finger in her wide-open mouth and made gagging sounds.

"You two squabble on your own time, will you? Who's with Zeller right now?"

"Lady Daniela," I said. "I saw them in the hotel bar."

Dan looked at his watch. "Mona, I thought you were going to take over the babysitting about now."

"I'm going!" Mona said. "Geez, the hotel's just down the street." She waved us off and strutted out.

Dan waited until she had walked away. "So, Cuz, how *is* Dorothy?"

"Fine."

"Really!" he said, as if he knew something. "You're on your way to second base, aren't you?"

"What? Shut up, Dan."

"Third?"

"It's not like that with Dorothy, Dan. She's my manager."

"Oh, I bet she could manage, all right."

"Grow up."

"Like hell I will. So, what's bothering you, Cuz?"

"Pressure, man. I really need for this record deal to come through. And I'm worried about Slim. He hasn't checked in. I'm not sure he's coming."

"So what? You can play a gig without Slim."

"Morris Witherspoon is coming to showcase the band. Without Slim, there's no record deal."

"That's a load of crap. Hire another guitar player if Slim quits. You're the talent, rock star. Anyway, you know you always worry too damn much. Slim will show."

"What makes you think that?"

"I can tell he likes you, even if you are a cracker."

I had to laugh a little, and that improved my mood. Dan always made me feel stupid for worrying the way I did. He didn't seem to let anything get to him.

"Come on. Let's go get a drink," he suggested.

We left the coliseum and walked west on Exchange Street to the Stockyards Hotel, a turn-of-the-century inn with an Old West feel. As a couple of ex–rodeo bums, Dan and I fit right in and loved the place. I stopped at the front desk to see if Slim had checked in.

"Not yet, Mr. Breed," said the twangy-voiced Fort Worth girl behind the counter. "Can I have your autograph?" she asked.

I signed my name for the girl and wandered into the bar. Dan was standing in the doorway.

"I don't like this," he said. "I'm not sure why, but I don't like it." He pointed.

I looked across the crowded bar and saw Morris Witherspoon sitting with Bruno Marques, the two of them facing each other over the table in a booth against the wall. "Now who's worrying? They're just having a beer together."

"Yeah, I guess. Hey, watch this. I'm going to stare at the side of Bruno's head. I bet he'll feel it, and look at me inside of ten seconds."

"He can't feel you staring."

"You wanna bet? Hunnerd bucks."

"You're on."

"Count to ten."

"One . . . two . . . three . . . four . . ." That's as far as I got before having to hand a hundred-dollar bill over to Dan. Maybe it was just coincidence, but Special Agent Marques really seemed to feel Cousin Dan staring. By the count of five, he had turned his head to look right at us.

Morris and Bruno waved us to their booth, both sliding over against the wall so Dan and I could sit on the bench seats beside them. I sat beside Morris. Dan sat beside Bruno.

"What are you two rascals cookin' up?" Dan said.

"Just getting acquainted," Morris said. "Bruno has been entertaining me with some fascinating tales."

"Any true ones?" Dan said.

"Gospel. Every word," Bruno said.

"Now I know you're lying."

From where I sat, I could see Archie Zeller and Mona at a table nearby. Lady Daniela and Jack Diamond sat at the table, too. Luis Sebastian was nearby, sitting with Bartholomew and the professional card dealers. Farther in the corner sat my band members, with the exception of Slim.

As if reading my mind, Morris said, "Any sign of Slim?"

"He hasn't checked in yet," I admitted.

"Dorothy told me about the offer that McLeod made to him. Did you tell Slim I'd match the offer if I sign your band?"

"Slim has dropped off the face of the earth," I lamented. "I haven't been able to talk to him since the other night when you bought us dinner in Nashville."

"Slim's gonna show," Dan said. "Quit worrying. Who wouldn't want to be in a band with Ronnie Breed? Hell, I wish I was good enough."

"We shall see," Morris said. "In the meantime, I certainly hope my name gets drawn to play poker tomorrow."

Bruno chuckled for some reason.

"Luck of the draw," Dan said. "You'll be in the hopper, like everybody else if you buy a ticket."

"I'm feeling lucky." Morris turned to me. "How does the stage look, Ronnie?"

"It's a real classy setup. I always wanted to play the Cowtown Coliseum."

He nodded. "And how's the mixing going at Topaz?"

"Smoothly. I'll have the demos to you by Wednesday."

"I hope I'll have reason to listen to them."

I took that to mean that if he didn't like the live show tomorrow, he wouldn't waste his time on the demos. "The band's tight," I boasted. "I think you'll like what you hear."

"Keep me informed about Slim," Morris said. "If he doesn't arrive, I don't intend to waste my weekend playing poker in Fort Worth."

I saw Dan's jaw muscles flex. He really did not care for Morris Witherspoon very much. "I thought you *wanted* to play," Dan said.

"I came here to showcase a band," Morris said. "The tournament is an amusing diversion. But if Slim Musselwhite doesn't perform, I have other bands to showcase in other cities."

Now I was worried. I mean, I was really worried.

"Slim wouldn't miss this gig," Dan said. "Cool your jets, Morris." With that, he slid off the bench seat and walked out of the bar.

27

THE NEXT day, Saturday, I did a couple of live radio interviews to pro-mote the poker tournament. By the time I returned to the hotel, Slim still had not checked in to his room. I began to get angry about it. If he had taken a job with that backstabbing ex–Half Breed, Joe McLeod, he at least might have called me so that I could find a re-placement guitar player.

Now I felt guilty for getting mad. What if Slim was in trouble, or hurt, or sick, and couldn't phone in? I hadn't known him personally very long, but he didn't seem the type to let his band down.

As time neared for the shooting of the tournament, I started get-ting very nervous about Slim not making the show. I tracked Dan down in the coliseum and pulled him aside.

"I got a problem, Dan," I said in a discreet tone of voice. "Slim still hasn't shown."

"I'm sorry, Cuz, but you're gonna have to go on without him."

"Can we have Mona draw the names before I do the short set? Maybe that would buy me a little time."

"Okay, but then we've got to shoot the short set and get on with the tournament, Slim or no Slim."

"If he still hasn't arrived by the time I do the short set, I want to do the set solo. That'll give us a chance for Slim getting here for the dance tonight."

Dan sighed, but nodded his approval. "I've heard you solo plenty of times. You'll knock 'em dead. I hope Slim shows up tonight."

"Thanks, Cuz."

"Shh! Not so loud with that 'Cuz' business!"

A crowd of about four hundred people showed up early at the coliseum. The first order of business was the drawing of names for the contestants. As Dan and I watched, Mona took her place in front of the camera, dressed fetchingly in a fringed cowgirl outfit, including tall boots, a short skirt with matching vest, and a pink hat.

"Action!" Bartholomew shouted.

Posing with one hand on her hip, Mona began cranking the handle on the hopper containing all the ticket stubs. The contraption was much fuller than it had been in Corpus. In fact, it seemed too full for the crowd on hand. In front of Mona, Morris Witherspoon and Bruno Marques watched, both of them looking hopeful.

Mona stopped the hopper, opened the little door in the wire cage, and reached in for a ticket stub. "The first lucky player," she announced, "is . . . Morris Witherspoon!"

"Bravo!" Morris shouted.

"That didn't take long," Dan grumbled.

Mona continued her on-camera chore that she seemed to love so much. She announced the next eighteen contestants, all of whom were thrilled to have been drawn to play against the high rollers from around the world. Mona then reached deep and pulled out the last stub.

"And our final contestant is . . . Morris Witherspoon?"

"Bravo again!"

"Cut!" Dan yelled at the cameraman as he stormed over to Morris. "What is this?"

"I simply bettered my odds," Morris said. "I bought a hundred tickets."

"You can't do that!" Dan shouted.

"Actually, I can, and I have. I had my lawyers look over our contract, Dan. There's nothing in it preventing me from buying all the tickets I want. You should be happy for my support."

"Well, we're going to have to draw another name. You can't play two tables at once."

"Not at all," Morris said. "I won the drawing. I won it twice. So I'll grant my second winning ticket to my friend Bruno Marques." He gestured toward the FBI man.

"Thank you, Morris!" Bruno said.

"I knew it!" Dan shouted. "I knew you two were up to no good! You stacked the deck on me!"

"Just make sure you don't stack the deck on me," Bruno said, laughing.

Morris and Bruno seemed very pleased with themselves. Dan was perturbed, but there was nothing he could do. He agreed to let the multimillionaire and the FBI agent play.

"But you two are not sitting at the same table!" he insisted. "No telling what kind of tricks you may have rehearsed."

"If we both win the first round, we'll be sitting at the same table!" Bruno said. "The championship table!"

"You underestimate the competition," Dan barked. He turned to me. "Ronnie, get up onstage and kick this thing off with some music."

With no word from Slim, I had to take the stage, solo. I saw Morris Witherspoon complaining to Dan about the absence of the band, but I had clued Dan in to cover for me.

"The band's not playing this short set," Dan would be telling the surprised major right about now. "We need some footage of Ronnie performing solo. The band will play tonight." This would buy me precious time.

The lights went down in the Cowtown Coliseum and a bright spot beamed down on me, as I had arranged with the house lighting crew. I stood there with my acoustic guitar. The spotlight made me feel like something of a star again, and I magically shut out my thoughts of everything beyond the light that now illuminated me.

"Ladies and gentlemen!" I announced, enjoying the cavernous reverb that the soundman used to bathe my microphone channel, and yet hoping simultaneously that he would remove it when I sang. "Welcome to the Fort Worth semifinals of *The World Championship of Texas Hold 'Em Poker*!"

The crowd clapped and hooted somewhere out there in the dark.

"My name is Ronnie Breed. It is my pleasure to entertain you with a few songs before we let the games begin. Here's a little tune I wrote a few years ago. Maybe you've heard it. It's called 'If Love Was a Pawnshop.'"

I strummed the chords as the applause died down. I sang the first line, grateful that the soundman had dumped the big echo in my mic channel. The crowd applauded at the first line, having recognized the song. Funny how they always do that—applaud familiarity.

I don't know what it was about that day, that place, that mic, that stage—but sometimes, as a singer, you just have moments when voice control comes as naturally as breathing. Looking back on my career, I don't know if I ever had a better solo performance anywhere else. I sang that song like I owned it. Of course, I did own it. I had written it. It was mine, and I proved it. To hell with missing guitar players and other things I couldn't control. I was Ronnie Breed. When all else failed, I could still stand in the spotlight and shine!

When I stepped off the stage, two songs later, Morris was waiting for me, looking huffy.

"You were to tell me if Slim wasn't going to make it," Morris scolded.

But I was already in poker mode, and I wasn't going to be bluffed. "No, Morris. You may have instructed me to keep you informed, but I never agreed to do it. I don't work for you just yet. Now, excuse me, I've got to shoot a TV pilot." I turned and walked away.

Talk about a risky bet! I had gone all in with one statement. I was about to find out just how interested Morris Witherspoon the starmaker really was at signing Ronnie Breed to a recording contract.

"Ronnie!"

I stopped. Slowly, I turned.

"You're right, of course," Morris said. "My apologies. Will Slim be here tonight?"

"I honestly don't know, Morris. I hope so. I hope I haven't wasted your time."

He tucked his hand into his pocket and struck a movie star pose, his composure back at his command. "To the contrary, those three songs you just sang were worth all the jet fuel I burned getting here. I'd say we're even, so far."

I nodded and smiled at him, then went to work.

When I walked to my table, I found Dan waiting for me, tapping the face of his wristwatch.

"I got here as fast as I could," I said.

I saw the other players seated. They included Bruno Marques. Great. I knew what was coming. Mona came to touch up my makeup as Dan gave me my instructions.

"You've got to beat Bruno."

"I was afraid you were going to say that."

"You can do it. He plays like a cop."

"What do you mean? By the book?"

Dan rolled his eyes. "I forget how clean you are."

"He's so clean he squeaks when he walks," Mona said, powdering my nose.

"I was clean until I got mixed up with this business," I complained. "What do you mean he 'plays like a cop'?"

"He doesn't give a damn about the odds. He plays his hunches, and he bluffs his ass off."

"All right, I'll call his bets."

"Be more aggressive than that. Raise him. Keep him on his heels."

I felt like a fighter taking his instructions from his trainer in the corner. Mona finished dusting me, and I stepped into the ring.

Dan was right. I easily kept Bruno on his heels. He seemed more interested in investigating Dan's dealer than he did in beating me. Still, he outlasted the rest of the amateurs at my table. By this time, Archie Zeller had won his first round and now came to watch the lingering struggle between me and Bruno. I had a huge pot built up and I soon finished Bruno off with a couple of jabs and a right cross. He took his drubbing cheerfully.

"You play clean, don't you?" he said, shaking my hand in front of the camera.

"I've been told I'm so clean that I squeak when I walk."

Dan came over to console his old friend and rival. "Nice try, jarhead."

"Yeah, yeah," Bruno groused.

Zeller and Mona walked up.

"I was hoping you'd beat this loser," Wildcat said to Bruno as he pointed his thumb at me.

"I was more interested in watching the dealer. Making sure this whole thing is legit."

"And?" Dan said, a confident grin on his face.

"You're clean, Dan. When I get back to headquarters, I'll tell them you're on the up-and-up this time."

"I only break laws in foreign countries," Dan replied.

"I see that now. Hey, you'll give me an alias when you air the show, won't you? I don't want my cover blown."

"I'll take care of you, Bruno. You know that."

"Likewise." He held out a hand for a shake with Dan.

"You leaving?"

"Yeah, I'm off your case now. My R and R is used up. I've got to go back to work."

"Watch your back out there, Bruno."

"Keep your nose clean, leatherneck."

With that, one of our more likable problems walked out of the Cowtown Coliseum. We watched him leave, and waved when he turned back around for one last look at us.

I looked at Dan. "Thank God he's out of here," I said. I could feel relief sculpting my facial expressions and body language. "He seemed like a good guy, but damn, he made me nervous."

"Good thing you got rid of him," Zeller lectured. "Today was gonna be my last day with this outfit if I had to look over my shoulder at a federal law-dog one more time."

"Lighten up, boys. This is the best possible development. We just got issued a clean bill of health by none other than the FB of I."

"Let's celebrate!" Mona was forever open to any excuse to party.

MORRIS WITHERSPOON lasted the longest of all the amateurs in the tournament. Dan had matched him up with Lady Daniela. Morris was a pretty good poker player, and managed to hang on, hand after hand. But the cards were literally stacked against him. Dan's best card mechanic was dealing at Lady Daniela's table, and he fed her the aces she needed to eliminate Major Witherspoon.

After kissing the triumphant Lady Daniela on both cheeks, European style, Morris sauntered over to me and said, "Well, that's that for this week. Perhaps you'll see me next week in Houston."

"You have to go?"

"Yes. Unless Slim is coming for the show tonight."

I hung my head. "I just checked the desk. No word from him."

"I hope he's all right," Morris said.

"Me, too."

He checked his wristwatch. "I can still make Bakersfield. There's a band out there I've been trying to catch for months."

My hopes of showcasing the Truebloods for Major Witherspoon sank. Where in creation was Slim Musselwhite?

28

AFTER A big steak dinner at the Cattleman's Steakhouse—paid for by that witless blowhard, Archie Zeller—we started filming the Fort Worth finals at the Cowtown Coliseum. Dan's script called for Luis Sebastian to win in Fort Worth, so Zeller and I made sure we got ourselves eliminated early in the game so we could make our maiden visit to the hospitality room. The TV crew was still buzzing around Lady Daniela, Jack Diamond, and Luis Sebastian when we left the set of the Fort Worth finals and walked down the street to the Stockyards Hotel.

Mona was supposed to meet us in the bar. When Zeller and I had had two drinks apiece, she finally showed up.

"Let's go up," Zeller said. "I'm champin' at the bit to make some easy money."

Mona hooked an arm around my right elbow, and Zeller's left, and we departed the bar. We took the elevator to the top floor, and found the hospitality room. Dan had given us the room number and the secret knock—three "long" knocks, a pause, then two more "short" knocks. When the door opened, I was hit in the face by a cloud of cigarette smoke and the cold stare of a tough-looking, muscled-up black man in a hideous leisure suit. The leisure suit was an appalling fashion development of the times to begin with, but this one—in baby blue—was particularly absurd. The man was also wearing about two pounds of gold chain around his neck.

"Dan sent us," I said.

"I know," said the man, with an accent and an attitude straight out of the ghetto. He sported a perfectly spherical Afro hairdo. "Get in here. I'm your hospitality room host." He waved us into the room, checking the hallway for prying eyes, and shut the door quickly behind us.

I stuck out my hand, sort of halfway between the white handshake position and the black handshake position, so the host could choose. "My name is—"

"We don't use names here," he snapped. He looked disdainfully at my indecisive hand. "I'm gonna call you Half-Cocked. You can call me Leisure Suit, or LS for short."

"You can call me Wildcat," Zeller said.

"Like hell I will." He looked at the stub of a cigar Zeller had been chewing on for hours. "I'm gonna call you Stogie." His eyes slowly turreted toward Mona, and lingered on her a second. "How you doin', Little Bit?"

"Fine," Mona replied, batting her heavily blackened lashes.

"Easy, there," Zeller said. "She's our girlfriend."

"'Our' girlfriend?" I complained.

"Oh, lighten up, Ronnie," Mona scolded. "We're in the hospitality room!"

LS ambled in a muscle-bound fashion back behind the bar, on top of which several stacks of bills were piled. Each one presumably belonged to one of the gamblers in the room, or perhaps some absent gamblers phoning in their bets. A couple of the stacks were quite large, the bills crisp. It looked as if some of the players had recently withdrawn bundles of cash from their banks or safes.

My eyes continued to sweep the smoky room—a large suite done up in western ranch-style furniture and trimmings. An elderly white lady sat at the bar, a bowl of peanuts at her elbow. She was chewing laboriously while holding a cigarette between her fingers.

"Look at that ol' biddy," Zeller said. "Shriveled up like a corpse."

"She might be a nice lady," I said, irritated at his negativity.

"She's a hag."

Beyond the old woman, I noticed three men with smokes and drinks in their hands, intently watching a baseball game on the normal hotel room TV set. None of their faces were familiar. I had

overheard Dan telling Zeller that these high rollers had been following the tournament since Galveston, betting on the games via
closed-circuit TV in the hospitality room.

"I need a drink," Zeller announced to the host. LS was apparently the watchman and the host. But not the bartender.

"You make your own drinks here," Leisure Suit said, pointing to
the booze bottles and an ice bucket wrapped in towels for insula-
tion. "I have to keep an eye on these bets."

Zeller frowned, but helped himself to a whiskey. I grabbed a Dos
Equis from a miniature refrigerator. Mona made herself a rum and
Coke. There was a television monitor behind the bar—the one Dan's
crew had installed to air the Fort Worth finals that were going on
just down the street. I glanced at the TV and saw a grainy image of
the dealer shuffling the cards for another hand.

"You gonna eat all those?" Zeller asked the elderly woman as he
sat beside her at the bar.

"What?" she said in a loud voice, cupping a liver-spotted hand
behind her ear.

"Those are for everybody!" Zeller shouted. "Not just you!"

She frowned and slid the bowl at him. "Hell, go ahead," she said,
sucking her teeth. She watched as Zeller threw a handful of the nuts
into his mouth. "I don't eat the damn peanuts. I just suck the chocolate off 'em and spit 'em in that bowl!" She showed him a bowl of
chocolates at her other elbow.

I thought Zeller was going to gag. He ran to the bathroom to
rinse his mouth out. Old Lady and Leisure Suit high-fived over the
bar and laughed until they had to wipe tears from their eyes. Even
with everything on my mind—the whereabouts of Slim, the appear-
ance of this illegal gambling, Dorothy, my career—I had to laugh
along with them.

Zeller came out of the bathroom, red-faced with anger. "That
ain't healthy!" he shouted.

"I've been waitin' to pull that on somebody all day!" she said.
"The chocolates don't even have nuts in 'em! It was just a joke,
sonny."

Zeller looked somewhat relieved. "Well, it ain't funny."

"It's that time, gents!" Leisure Suit announced. "And ma'am." He winked at the elderly woman. "Here comes the flop!"

The three baseball fans grouped around the television to watch the poker hand along with Old Lady, Zeller, and me. One camera angle showed the flop—the first three common cards used by all three players still alive in the Fort Worth finals. Other cameras collected shots of the players eyeballing one another.

"So, how does this work?" I asked the guard.

"If you want to make a bet on one of the hands, you have to put it down after the river, and before they show their pocket cards. There will be a break to reset the cameras, but it's also to make time for us to bet. It'll give you about five minutes to make up your mind."

"What if we lose?" I asked.

"You lose your bet. It goes in the pot."

"What if we win?" Zeller asked.

"You double your money. Simple as that. Until Houston, that is. Then the winners split the pot. Could be better than double-your-money then. A lot better."

"What's the limit?"

"You ain't got that much money in that cheap jacket, Stogie. I wouldn't worry about it."

"Lookee, there!" Old Lady rasped, pointing at the TV screen. "You see that smirk on Lady Daniela's face? She's got something good in the hole!"

"I bet she does," drawled one of the high-rolling baseball dudes.

Old Lady cackled right along with the lascivious snickers of the men.

We watched the turn, and the betting that followed. Opinions were expressed about who was bluffing, and who might hold the real winning hand.

"You know one thing for sure," Old Lady said. "Luis ain't bluffing. He *never* bluffs."

The dealer flipped the river. The cameras cut to the poker faces of each player, and the betting began. On the basis of the five common cards, the bets and checks and raises, and the expressions on the players' faces, we were supposed to make up our minds how to wager.

"I'll put five grand on Lady Daniela," Old Lady said, taking five bank-wrapped bundles of bills from her handbag.

One of the men bet a thousand on Jack Diamond. Another put two grand on Luis Sebastian. The third man declined to bet this round, saying he hadn't been watching closely enough.

"You gents gonna bet, or just sit there?" Leisure Suit asked Zeller and me.

Before we could answer, the phone rang. LS grabbed it. "Hospitality room. Yeah, Dan, it's all cool up here. You betting this round? No? Oh, yeah, he's right here." He handed me the phone.

"Dan?" I listened briefly. "The band's ready!" I said defensively. "We can play with or without Slim." You can guess what Dan might have been saying about now. I invented a reply. "I just want to put a couple of bets down—damn . . . Don't worry, I'll be onstage when the game is over." I handed the phone back to Leisure Suit. "What a slave driver," I muttered.

"What's that supposed to mean?" He frowned as he hung up the phone.

"Bad choice of words," I admitted. "I didn't mean anything by that."

The frown remained on Leisure Suit's face. "You got thirty seconds to make your bet, Half-Cocked."

Zeller laughed at my nickname.

I reached for some cash in my blazer pocket. "Well, I wasn't really watching, but I'll go with what the peanut lady says and bet a grand on Daniela." I lay the government notes on the bar, creating my own stack.

"Don't blame me if you lose, sonny," she warned.

"You, Stogie?" the guard said to Zeller.

"Lady Daniela. Ten thousand." Zeller pulled precounted packets of cash from pockets inside his threadbare dinner jacket.

"Them ain't just peanuts!" Old Lady blurted, as if impressed by the amount of Zeller's bet.

Everyone had a laugh at Zeller's expense over the peanut reference.

"Real funny, grandma," the old slant driller said.

With the bets made, we turned our attention back to the TV. This was an unedited version of the show, of course, because it was shot live, and we had to wait for the cameras to get reset. Finally, the players began showing their cards. Jack Diamond had a mediocre hand—two pairs: kings and deuces. Luis bested him with a full house—kings over sevens. Then Lady Daniela won the pot with four deuces and an ace kicker.

Old Lady and I celebrated our modest gain together, but Zeller acted as if he had won the Kentucky Derby. His obnoxious fist-pounding antics annoyed the fire out of me.

"How do you like *them* peanuts!" he hissed at Old Lady.

LS began settling up the debts, shifting money from one pile to another, the losers forfeiting their bets, and the winners doubling theirs. The gamblers watched him carefully as he shifted bills, but no one complained about the redistribution of wealth.

"The pot still owes you four grand," LS said to Zeller. "I'll get it from the safe. Y'all keep an eye on one another."

Zeller gloated in Old Lady's face. "Bet big, win big!"

"Lose big, too," she replied.

"Not a chance," Zeller boasted.

I tapped Zeller on the shoulder. "Come look at the view of Fort Worth from the window, Archie." I grabbed him by the sleeve and pulled him off his barstool, leaving Mona behind.

"Let me go," Zeller snapped, after we were out of earshot by the window. "What the hell are you doing?"

"You don't have to act so cocky," I said under my breath. "You know we're going to lose the next bet, right? Just to make it look natural?"

"Yeah, yeah."

"After the next phone call from Dan, just bet the way I do, and we'll both lose a little for now. We'll win big next week."

"I remember the scam," Zeller said, his yellowed eyes piercing me like a drill bit. "I cut my teeth on penny-ante flimflams like this."

"Well, I didn't, so I'm a little bit nervous about all this. Let's just play it cool."

"I'm a friggin' cucumber. This is easy money. Drink up and relax."

Leisure Suit announced that the next round would begin. He had returned from the bedroom, and the safe. Zeller's stack had leapt to twenty thousand. Mine was up to two grand. On the grainy, closed-circuit television, we watched the black-and-white action. The deal. The betting. The flop, the turn, the river.

"Jack Diamond went all in!" Old Lady said, pointing at the screen as if she just lived for hold 'em poker.

"He's bluffing," said one of the other high rollers. "It'll be down to Lady Daniela and Luis Sebastian after this hand."

"Get your bets in," LS said. "You've got five minutes."

The hotel room phone rang.

"Yeah?" said Leisure Suit into the receiver. "Yeah, Dan, he's still here." He handed the receiver to me.

"Hello . . . Yeah, Dan, I can see that Jack went all in. I'm paying attention. If he loses, I'll come down and get the band ready." I rolled my eyes to show Zeller how fed up I was with Dan's micro-management style. Of course, in reality, Dan was not saying anything about getting the band ready at the other end of the phone. "I'm a professional. Trust me." I hung up the phone.

Meanwhile, Leisure Suit had taken the bets of the high rollers. "You, Stogie?" he said to Zeller.

Wildcat scratched his chin. "I'm still thinkin'."

I knew, of course, that Zeller was not thinking. He was waiting to see which way I would bet, for I had just spoken to Dan, and Dan had made it clear to us that he had knowledge of each player's hole cards, via Bartholomew in the production van, and the secret pocket cameras under the table—knowledge he had promised to pass along to us via his phone calls to the hospitality room.

"You got about thirty seconds," LS said to Zeller. "Half-Cocked?" he said, looking at me.

"You know what," I opined. "I don't think Jack is bluffing. I think he actually has a hand right now. I'm gonna put a thousand on Jack."

The guard nodded. "Stogie?" he said, looking at Zeller. "Ten seconds."

"Fifteen grand on Luis Sebastian."

I can't say that I was shocked. According to Dan's plan, Zeller was supposed to bet the same way I had, knowing that we were supposed to lose this time, just to reduce suspicion. But Zeller's greed wouldn't let him do that. He had a fifty-fifty chance of doubling his bet, as long as he bet on one of the other two players. He chose Luis Sebastian.

"The bets are in."

We all turned to the grainy little TV. Jack's hand was trash. He was gone for the day. Luis had three eights and some change. Lady Daniela also had trips: fives. Luis Sebastian and Archie Zeller had won.

Mona did her cheerleading routine for Zeller, jumping all over him.

"Have a chocolate, loser!" Zeller said to Old Lady. His rasping, slobbering laughter was hideous. But in two bets, he had more than tripled his original wager.

I probably looked like a sore loser, but it was Zeller who had me perturbed, not the loss of cash. I looked at Leisure Suit. "I gotta go." I put my hand on my stack of cash.

The guard pinned my hand down on top of my cash with a grip like a vise. "You know the rules."

"Huh?" I noticed the high rollers glaring at me as if I were stealing something, and yet that was my own cash.

"Once you start bettin', you stay in until the grand championship round in Houston. When it's all over there, that's where we split the money."

"Well, this is just my original bet," I complained. "Can't I take that with me?"

Old Lady leaned in close. "Sonny, did you get the license plate number?"

"What license plate number?"

"The one on the turnip truck you fell off of after you were born yesterday? The idea is to build the pot! Build it up, big!"

"All right, I'll leave it!" I said, acquiescing. "What's a thousand bucks, anyway. Will you unhand me, sir?"

Leisure Suit lifted his powerful hand from my wrist. The rest of the gamblers in the room, including Zeller, looked down on me as if I were a rank amateur. "Come on, Mona," I ordered.

"I'm staying with Stogie," she boasted. "He's a winner."

Zeller's smug swagger made me want to punch his lights out.

"You're gonna miss a kick-ass gig."

"*Slim* chance of that happening," Mona slurred.

That was uncalled for. She knew I was worried sick about Slim having quit the band. I walked away from my thousand dollars and prepared to leave the room.

As I made my exit, I came face-to-fist with a hovering set of knuckles preparing to knock on the door I had just opened. My eyes focused on the owner of the knuckles. *What the hell?* My heart sank into my stomach. The last guy I wanted to drag into the illegal complications of the hospitality room was my future career-shaper, Major Morris Witherspoon.

29

"HELLO, RONNIE," the major said, slipping by me, into the room. "You saved me the secret knock." To illustrate that he knew the code, he rapped three longs and two shorts on the end of the bar.

"Who the hell is this?" demanded Leisure Suit. The look of shock he glared my way worried me. I knew Morris was not supposed to know about the hospitality room.

"I'm Major—"

"We don't give names up here!" the host barked. "Who invited you?"

"I did," Zeller said. "He's all right. Let him stay."

Leisure Suit glared at me some more. "Shut the door."

I obeyed.

"Did Dan approve this?"

"Dan may run your life, but he don't run mine," Zeller said.

"You'll have to go," the guard said to the major.

Morris, as suave as ever, shifted his eyes to the piles of cash on the bar. "Do you think it would be wise to kick me out after what I've seen here? Perhaps it would make more sense to let me incriminate myself, along with the rest of you."

"Who says there's a crime goin' on here?"

"The State of Texas?"

"I told him the score," Zeller boasted. "The man's got money, and he wants to make a bet or two. Let him stay."

"He looks all right to me," Old Lady said. "Peanuts?" She held the bowl out to Morris.

"No thank you, ma'am. I'm allergic." He looked at LS. "May I have a gin martini, my good fellow?"

"I ain't no *fellow*. I ain't good. I'm *bad*. And, I *ain't* no bartender. Make your own damn drink."

"Oh," Morris said. "I understand." He grabbed a bottle of gin and a glass. "It's a *hospitality* room in name only."

I stepped up close to Morris so I could keep my voice low. "Bruno doesn't know about this, does he?"

He looked at me as if the question both bored and insulted him. "Of course not. Do you think I'd alert the FBI? Bruno has left town."

"Dan ain't gonna like this," LS said.

"I see what's bothering you and I have a solution. Let me make the first wager on the next hand. I'll be the first gambler in the room to break the law. You could all testify against *me*, if you wanted to."

"Hell, why not?" Old Lady said. "Let him bet!"

"Yeah, let him bet!" Mona agreed, sloshing her drink as she gestured and staggered against Zeller.

Leisure Suit mulled it over. "All right, we'll do it your way. You bet first."

"Go Morris! Go Morris!" Mona cheered with drunken, moronic enthusiasm.

While the hospitality room host briefed Morris on the rules, I pulled Zeller aside. "What the hell are you doing? First you bet to win, when you were supposed to lose, then you tell Morris about the hospitality room?"

Zeller leered with self-pride. "I don't like losing on purpose. Besides, it looks funny if you and me bet the same way every time after you get off the phone with Dan."

I had to admit his argument was logical. "Okay, but why did you bring Morris in? Don't you see what kind of a conflict of interest that is for me?"

"That's your problem. The way I see it, he's got money, and we've got a foolproof system. Let's use our system to separate him from his money."

"You can't use the system without me, Archie. Dan calls *me* in the hospitality room because it looks as if he's riding my ass over the musical stuff. He's got no reason to call *you*. It wouldn't look right."

"I guess that means I'm done bettin' for the day, if you have to go."

"That's exactly what it means, unless you want to place a bet without the benefit of the pocket cameras. Next week, in Houston, you better stick to the script or I'll refuse to tell you what Dan tells me on the phone."

"I'll just follow your bet, dumb-ass."

"Then I won't bet."

"All right!" he said, giving in to my demands. "Hell, I was just havin' a little fun, Ronnie. Jesus H. Christ. Why don't you go tune up your guitar or somethin'. I'm gonna stay here and goad Witherspoon into some high-dollar bets. Build that pot up with his money!"

"You know I'm on the verge of signing a recording contract with him. Don't screw that up."

"That asshole's playing you like a blue cat on a cane pole. He ain't gonna sign your band to no contract. The only way you're gonna get any money out of him is to ream him with our system."

"You don't know what you're talking about, Archie. I'm sure you're a hell of an oil well driller, but you don't know the music business. He wants to sign my band so bad, he can smell the ink on the dotted line."

"A guy like that doesn't smell anything but money. You think he gives a damn about a song on the radio?"

Zeller was describing himself more so than Morris Witherspoon. "Yeah, well, I *do* care about the songs on the radio. *My* songs. Don't encourage him to lose a bunch of money to where he doesn't want to come to Houston next week."

Archie laughed in my face. "*Think,* choirboy! The Fort Worth money stays in the pot until next week, at Houston. You *want* Witherspoon to lose big here, so he'll come back next week to recoup his losses."

I couldn't argue with that logic, either. "I gotta go, Archie. Just don't do anything crazy, all right?"

He laughed again. "I'm a wildcat oil well driller. I don't do nothin' short of crazy."

"Great," I said. I turned my back on Zeller, who was still laughing at me, and went to the bar to speak to Morris.

"So, when did Zeller tell you?" I asked, trying to sound casual. "About the hospitality room?"

"In the men's room at the restaurant. Why?"

I tipped up my Dos Equis. "Just wondering. I'm on my way back to the coliseum. I'm gonna go check on Slim one more time. If he's here, will you come down to hear the Truebloods?"

Morris looked at me, his watch, the poker game on the closed-circuit TV. "If he arrives in the next half hour, maybe. I have just enough time to put one bet down here, then I'm taking a limo to the airport. My pilot is doing his preflight check right now."

It was something of a relief to me that Morris would have time for only one bet. How much could he possibly lose on one bet? But I was still devastated that he would not stay to showcase the band. "You know they don't let you leave here with your winnings," I warned under my breath. "It stays in the pot until next week, in Houston. They split the money there."

"Ronnie, Ronnie," he chided. "It's not the pot of gold that matters."

"I know, it's chasing the rainbow. I remember."

"Go play your gig. You always look worried unless you're onstage. I'll check with the lovely Dorothy on the Slim situation next week." Having dismissed me, Morris turned his attention to the poker game.

As I ambled toward the door, Leisure Suit shot yet another fierce glare at me, as if the unauthorized player's presence in the hospitality room were all my fault. "Aren't you supposed to be playing some songs somewhere?" he growled.

"That's where I'm going," I insisted. I had just put my hand on the doorknob when I heard Old Lady croak excitedly:

"He's all in! Jack Diamond's all in, boys! This could be the last bet of the Fort Worth finals."

"In that case," Morris said. "It looks as if I have some catching up to do. I'll bet half a million."

The room went silent. My heart pounded. I remember seeing Leisure Suit's eyes bulge.

"No, you won't!" LS snapped. "I'm sure you'd like to just breeze in here and start betting that kind of money with the odds at fifty-fifty. These three gents and this nice old lady have been making wagers for four weeks, beginning every week with five poker players in the game, four-to-one odds. Even these two lightweights," he railed, gesturing at Zeller and me, "got here when there were still three players left."

Morris was not fazed by the tongue-lashing. "Very well, sir. What's the limit?"

"For you? Right now? Fifty grand."

Morris sighed. "How very boring. I'll wager fifty thousand."

"On who?"

"I'm not sure. Still thinking."

I couldn't bear listening to any more, so I stepped out into the hall. Either Morris was going to lose fifty grand because of me, or Dan was going to have fifty grand shifted from his safe to Morris's pile of winnings. This whole thing was getting out of control. Dan never foresaw any of these complications when he dragged me into this wild scheme.

Then the reality hit me. He hadn't dragged me in at all. I had readily agreed to all this. I had to stop blaming Dan and accept responsibility for my own decisions. I made a pact with myself as I rode down in the hotel elevator. I was going to see this thing through with Dan. Then—provided we didn't get arrested—never again. No more shenanigans. I was going back to my honest career as a songwriting troubadour.

I found myself standing in front of the reception desk. "Could you check to see—?"

"I'm sorry, Mr. Breed," said the young lady on the other side of the counter. "He still hasn't checked in."

I sighed. "Thanks anyway."

I trudged over to the coliseum. My band was waiting backstage, with one obvious exception.

"We're gonna have to do this without Slim," I said to the boys. "Warren, that's going to mean a lot of fiddle breaks."

Warren shrugged. "Where's Witherspoon?"

"He doesn't want to hear us without Slim."

"There goes our shot, then," Mojo said.

"Not at all," I said, trying to prop up some optimism. "Witherspoon says he'll come see us next week in Houston. I'm sure we'll have the Slim problem worked out by then."

"Let's hope," Henry said. "Slim's got the right guitar tone, dude. His vocals blend. He's perfect."

"I know, I know," I said irritably. "Let's just get through tonight. Come on, let's get onstage and be ready when the last hole card is turned in the tournament."

We filed onto the darkened stage. I tuned up my guitar and made sure the other guys were tuned to me.

Across the Cowtown Coliseum floor I could see the camera lights hovering over the poker set. The last hand was still lingering between Luis Sebastian and Jack Diamond. I knew Luis was scripted to win here in Fort Worth. What I didn't know was whether or not Morris had placed a winning or a losing bet up in the hospitality room.

The crowd around the poker table erupted in applause, and I saw Luis Sebastian stand to the congratulations of the spectators. Our stage lights faded up. We tested our amps with a note or two, causing some of the spectators to look our way.

"Y'all ready?" I asked.

The boys nodded. Morale was low, but we had to play anyway. Striking his sticks together, Mojo clicked off the tempo of the first song, and we plowed into it. It was a miserable rendition without Slim, but the drunken revelers didn't seem to mind. They quickly gravitated our way. Those cowboys and cowgirls in Fort Worth could sure dance. They didn't care about a missing guitar player. They heard the bass and drums pounding out that two-step beat, and commenced tearing up the floor.

I was glad Morris was not there. We sounded the way we felt—like crap. Three songs into the set, I was praying for this gig to come to a merciful end. Then I looked up and saw Slim Musselwhite weaving through the dancers on the floor, running with his guitar case in his hand.

30

"HEY, LOOK!" Henry said. "It's Slim!"

I motioned for an early end to the song, and we all got out of that tune as quickly as we could.

"Folks, we're going to take a short break to get our guitar player, the great Slim Musselwhite, plugged in onstage."

The dancers grumbled, but sat down to their beers and waited.

"I'm assuming you're still our guitar player," I said to Slim, taking his hand to help him up onto the front of the stage. I was so relieved to see him that I couldn't muster any anger. I also couldn't help noticing he looked like hell. His eyes were bloodshot, his clothes wrinkled.

"Sorry I'm late, Rawn. It ain't my fault, though. It was that fool, McLeod."

"What did he do?"

Slim lay his case on the stage to open it and remove his guitar. "Flew me out there to la-la land and offered me a job. I couldn't take it, though. The money was good, but I didn't like the feel. This is my band, right here." He looked around at the musicians surrounding him.

Hearing that, I almost burst into tears with relief. "So, what took you so long getting back?"

"Mother—" Slim bit his lip as he slung his strap over his shoulder. "McLeod put something in my drink. Knocked me out, man. I woke up in a dark hotel room with no clock, shades drawn, sick as a damn whore. Missed my flight."

I shook my head at the gall of my nemesis, McLeod. "He knew we were showcasing for Witherspoon today. He sabotaged us!"

"Damn right," Slim said.

"Well, why didn't you call, Slim?"

He plugged his instrument cord into his Telecaster. "Man, there weren't no time to call. I just barely got on the last flight, man."

"You look like hell. Can you play?"

"If I don't fall out. Let's do it." He was tuning as he stepped toward his amplifier. He plugged the other end of his cord into the Fender Twin, wailed a note or two, and nodded.

The rest of the gig was better, but far from perfect. I was glad Morris had gone on to Bakersfield, or wherever, in his private jet. We were all out of synch with Slim's late arrival. Slim himself was exhausted, and playing at 50 percent of his enormous talent level. This was not the gig I had always envisioned playing at the Cowtown Coliseum. It was all I could do to suffer through it.

Toward the end of the show, Mona finally made her arrival at the gig. She had, apparently, gone back to the room to change clothes after her visit to the hospitality room. Perhaps she felt dirty for hanging all over Zeller, and had to shower. For some reason, she had decided to wear a little sailor's outfit complete with white bell-bottoms and a little white sailor's hat.

Dan drifted over to the stage, too, having wrapped up his responsibilities elsewhere. He looked pretty happy, though he frowned at me quizzically while we were playing. He could tell the band was out of sorts. No one even complained when I ended the show a little early, which didn't make me feel any better about the gig. There was no great outcry for an encore.

"Let's put this one behind us, boys," I said. "It's been a rough day. Especially for you, Slim. You better get some rest."

I went and sat down with Dan, knowing what was coming.

"That sounded like somebody pouring slop out of a bucket," he said. Dan always did have a metaphorical way about him.

"McLeod drugged Slim. We're lucky he got here at all." I grabbed a glass of champagne off a waitress's tray as she passed by.

"That's not important right now. What I want to know is when the hell did Archie get a chance to tell Witherspoon about the hospitality room?"

"In the men's room at the restaurant."

"Who was supposed to be watching him then?"

"Mona."

"Oh." He gritted his teeth and threw back a whiskey. "That was my fault, then. I don't guess Mona could very well follow him into the men's room to keep an eye on him. It turned out okay, though."

"It did?"

"Yeah, Morris bet the wrong way. He lost fifty grand. Left the cash right there in the hospitality room and went to get on his jet."

I put my elbows on the table and cradled my face in my hands. "Dan! You promised me we weren't going to take any of Morris's money!"

"Hey, I didn't tell him about the hospitality room, Cuz. Zeller did. Anyway, don't worry. I'll figure out a way to let him win it back next week. Here comes Archie. Act natural."

"Natural? What the hell is natural anymore?"

"Have a seat, Arch."

Zeller accepted the invitation.

Dan drilled Zeller with a fierce poker stare. "I heard what happened in the hospitality room, Wildcat."

"Did the choirboy tattle on me?" Zeller asked, jutting a thumb at me.

"No, I heard it from the hospitality room host."

"The colored boy in the funny jacket?"

"It's a leisure suit. Don't you keep up with fashion?"

"Not if it ain't khaki."

"Well, you're lucky that guy didn't just kill you. I've known him since we were in Nam together. He's bad news if you cross him, so don't pull that crap again, Archie. No more uninvited guests."

Zeller hissed. "You boys got no instincts for a good con. Why not pull in another mark?"

"We don't know enough about Witherspoon," Dan insisted. "I also heard you won all your bets. I thought you two were supposed to lose your second bet to make it look good."

"I lost mine," I said.

"*I lost mine,*" Zeller repeated, mocking me like some overgrown third-grader. "I don't want to bet the same way Choirboy does every time."

"You don't mind when you know you're going to win."

Zeller shrugged innocently. "Hell, nobody even got suspicious."

"Amazingly, you seem to be right," Dan agreed. "All the high rollers up in the hospitality room think you just lucked into a streak, but they all plan to fleece some skins off you next week. You must have rubbed them the wrong way."

Zeller ignored all that. "How big can we bet next week?" He was almost salivating.

"Leisure Suit and I just counted up the money in the safe and balanced the individual holdings against the hospitality room bank. I'm not going to tell you how big the bank is, but I will say this: There's enough in there to cover both of you if you were to make a million-dollar bet on the last hand."

"Holy crap," I said, wiping my brow.

"And how much will we win?"

"If you two are the only two guys betting on the underdog who we know is going to be the winner—and that's the way I've got it scripted—then you're going to make a fortune. You may win as much as ten times your bet."

"How are you gonna make sure we're the only ones betting on the underdog?" I asked.

"Good question. You may have noticed that Luis Sebastian never bluffs."

"Yeah. So?"

"On the last hand of the championship, he's going to go all in. Everybody's going to bet on him, knowing he doesn't bluff. But, he *is* going to be bluffing."

"How can you be so sure?" I asked, wringing my hands at the thought of losing a million-dollar bet.

"Luis and I have a deal."

"He's in on this thing?" Zeller said angrily, thinking of having to split the take yet another way.

"No. He owes me half a million from another wager. This is his way of paying his marker."

"Promise me nothing can go wrong," I pleaded.

"I'll have my best card mechanic dealing in the championship round. Plus, we'll have the pocket cameras as insurance. When Luis goes all in on the only bluff of his career, you two are going to be the only two idiots to bet on him."

"So, me and Choirboy split the pot?" Zeller said, jutting his thumb at me.

Dan nodded, a grin on his face. "It's winner-takes-all on the last bet. If you two are the only two winners, you split the pot. Everybody else loses."

"There's just one problem," I lamented. "Where the hell do I get a million dollars? I'd have to sell half my assets. I can't get that done in a week."

"You have a payroll, right?" Dan said. "For your band, managers, roadies."

"Yeah."

"You pay withholding taxes on them, right?"

"I have to."

"Well, that money you withhold from their pay is in an account somewhere, isn't it?"

"Yeah, but I can't touch that. Technically it belongs to the IRS. I have to send it in later in the year."

"Who's gonna know if you tap into it? You make a big bet with the feds' money, and you pay Uncle Sam back a couple of days later."

The very thought of this made me nervous. "My payroll is not that big. I don't have a million in my withholding account."

Dan threw his hands up in the air, exasperated. "It's just an idea."

"It's a damn good idea!" Zeller said, as if he had just seen the light.

Dan was still fixed on lecturing me. "You don't have to bet exactly a million, Ronnie. Whatever you can scrape up will do."

Zeller's enthusiasm turned to near panic. "Wait a minute, now. If I make a million-dollar bet, and he bets just half a million, I get a bigger share of the pot than he does, right?"

Dan showed him his open palms, as if trying to calm a spooky horse. "Don't worry, Wildcat, the split will be proportional to the bets."

"Who's going to figure all that out?"

"You may think LS is just an intimidating bank guard, but he's actually a mathematical savant. He's like a Texas Instruments calculator. He'll figure the split and explain it to you."

Mona came bouncing over to us out of nowhere and actually sat on Zeller's lap. "Hi, boys!" she shrilled.

"Mona, can you find us a bartender?" I asked, having finished the flute of champagne.

"'Hi, Mona!'" she said, suggesting a more fitting greeting.

"And get off Wildcat's lap!" I snapped.

"Yeah, get the choirboy another bubbly," Zeller suggested.

"I just grabbed that off a tray. I'll take my usual bourbon, neat."

"I'll have a boilermaker," Dan said.

"And you know what I like," Zeller said, grinning lasciviously.

Mona heaved a great sigh. "I'm getting tired of being the booze bitch." Nonetheless, she trudged to the bar like a good little sailor.

"Now, there's just one more thing," Dan said. "The hospitality room is going to be a little different next week."

"How's that?" I asked.

"We're shooting the championship at Gilley's dance hall. There's not a decent hotel nearby where we can set up the hospitality room. So, Ronnie, we're going to use your bus."

"Oh, we are?" I said, protest in my voice.

"Yeah, it's the perfect solution. We'll load the safe in there late tonight, so we can keep an eye on it all week."

"That makes sense," Zeller said.

"Where have you been keeping the safe up until now?" I asked.

"Well, I hate to tell you this, Ronnie, but I've been keeping it in your bus all along. There's a compartment under your bed where it just slides in perfect."

"Who said you could do that?"

"Forgiveness is easier to get than permission. Now, listen, there's going to be another change. The high rollers up in the hospitality room got a little nervous about Morris Witherspoon this evening, and his mention of the FBI. They asked me to make an adjustment for next week."

"What kind of adjustment?"

"Next week, on the final hand, all the high rollers want to come out of the bus and watch the flop, the turn, and the river being filmed. They want to watch it from the front row, so the cameras will film them watching. That way, if we're being investigated, they'll have film evidence that they're just watching the tournament, and not gambling in some back room."

"Whatever," Zeller said.

"Then," Dan continued, "when the final bets are in, we're going to take a break to reset the cameras."

"We always do that," I said.

"Yeah, but next week, the break will be longer."

"Why?" I asked, shrugging.

"I'm telling you why. During the break, we can all go back to the bus and place our hospitality room bets. Ronnie, you can bet first, then go back to the stage and play some songs with your band to keep people distracted. The rest of the high rollers will place their bets on the final outcome, then come back into Gilley's to watch Luis and Jack turn their pocket cards to decide the championship!" Dan spread his arms for dramatic effect.

"And to decide who wins the pot in the bus," Zeller said. "Which will be me, and Choirboy here."

"I don't like that nickname," I said.

"Well, I don't like having to split the pot with you."

"Hey, this is no time to start bickering," Dan hissed. "We've got to work together on this thing. There will be plenty in the pot to go around. Plus the house percentage from the Swiss bank account, which we're also splitting three ways, remember?"

"How's that money stacking up?" Zeller asked.

"Better this week. It more than doubled last week's take. Next week, it'll be off the charts. Now, listen up. This is the important part. If you two are the only two to bet on Luis—and that's what we're counting on—then the moment the tournament is decided, you two get on the bus with Leisure Suit and hall ass out of there. All the winnings will be yours, anyway. You don't want to have to deal with any sore losers. Let me handle them. We'll meet later and divvy up the take."

I looked at Zeller to see him squinting a suspicious glare at Dan, as if this whole thing suddenly seemed too good to be true from his point of view.

"So you're not gonna bet on the bus?" the crooked slant driller asked.

Dan shrugged off the idea. "I may give Ronnie enough of my money to flesh out his million-dollar bet, and share in his winnings. But it wouldn't look good for all of us to make the same bet. No, I'm not worried about the winnings in the bus. I'm getting other things out of this deal."

"Like what?" Zeller prodded.

Dan looked at him quizzically, as if Zeller should know the answer to his own question. "I get my TV show funded. I get my third of the house share of the Swiss bank account. And I get ten percent of the hospitality room pot before you two split it."

"Ten percent?" Zeller complained.

"That's fair," I said in Dan's defense.

"The hell it is! Five percent would be more than fair."

Dan glared at Zeller. "Archie, I invented the hospitality room scam. I think I've earned my ten percent. Anyway, I have to pay Leisure Suit out of my ten percent, and guys like that don't work cheap. And whatever I win from Ronnie's bet, I have to share with Bartholomew."

"I don't like you taking ten percent of my pot that Choirboy, here, is already horning in on."

That nickname was really starting to make me fume.

Dan got real serious and leaned in toward Zeller. Dan was a charismatic sweet-talker, but when he put on that serious face, you didn't want to tangle with him.

"Let me remind you how it works, Wildcat. This is a team effort. The pocket cameras pass critical information to Bartholomew. Bartholomew passes that information to me. I pass it to Ronnie, and you follow his lead. So I suggest you do your best to get along with Ronnie and me for one more week, then you can be rid of us forever, for all I care."

Zeller leaned back in his chair. "Hell, I was just horse-tradin' you a little, Dan. A feller's got a right to Jew another feller down a little. I guess I can live with you taking your ten percent."

"Good," Dan said, punctuating the conversation.

Mona showed up with a bartender and a tray of drinks. As we passed them around, she leaned on Zeller's shoulder like some bit-part Western movie saloon girl rubbing up on the bad guy in the black hat at a poker game in the Long Branch Saloon. Except for that sailor outfit, of course.

"Mona," I chided, "what if the paparazzi busts in here and takes a picture of *my* girlfriend hanging all over some other guy?"

"Oh, like the paparazzi follows *you* around anymore!"

"What about Corpus, when Rudolph Richards got that shot of me at the poker table?"

"That was all about Morris Witherspoon, not you."

"Oh, yeah?" My weary brain was all out of comebacks. "Well . . . Well . . . What's with the sailor outfit you're wearing?"

She snarled her lip and gave me her *you dumb-ass* look. "Duh. *Fort* Worth!"

"Fort Worth was an army post, not a naval base," Dan said.

"We're not even on the coast!" I added.

Mona stuck her tongue out at me, then said, "Army, navy—who gives a crap, *Choirboy*!"

Zeller threw his head back and laughed at me grotesquely.

"Come on, Wildcat," Mona said. "Let's go to the bar and shoot some hot damns!"

Zeller sprang to the invitation. "See ya, Choirboy!"

I watched them walk off, then looked at Dan. "He's gonna call me Choirboy one time too many, and then, *bam*!" I shot an upper-cut through thin air.

"Easy, Cuz. Wait till the time's right." He paused, watching them walk away, Zeller lumbering, Mona bouncing. "You gotta admit, she does make a cute little sailor."

I smirked. "You ought to see her out of uniform."

Dan stuck his trigger fingers in his ears. "I don't want to hear it. I might slip up and say something about it in front of Dorothy."

I sighed, feeling a world of frustration boiling in my viscera. "Not that it would matter. Dorothy will never forgive me if I screw this deal up with Morris, and I've probably already blown the opportunity of a lifetime. This tournament has got me so distracted, I can't take care of business with my personal or my professional life."

"Keep your eyes on the prize, and see this thing through one more week, Cuz. Then everything will fall into place for you: Morris, Dorothy, the Truebloods. Not long from now, you'll look back on the whole poker scam as a job well done for a noble cause. You do remember why you signed on, don't you?"

I let Dan's pep talk sink in. It was easy to forget why I *had* signed on, but now I remembered. I may have weaknesses of character, but failing to finish what I start is not one of them. I resolved anew to see this thing through just one more week.

"Yeah, Dan. I remember."

31

TOPAZ STUDIOS' Salon D proved my refuge. It was my dark cave where I could hide from my worries and throw my full attention into mixing the Truebloods demos. I worked with young Jimmy on the mixes, and he proved a good hand and a quick learner. It was refreshing to work with such an innocent kid engineer in contrast to all the shifty characters I had been associating with that summer of '75.

In those pre-digital days of analog recording on magnetic tape, we didn't have automated mixes that you could just store in a computer one change at a time until you had all the voices and instruments coming and going as you wanted them. You had to mix manually, in one pass, dumping the recorded signals from the twenty-four-track, two-inch tape to a half-inch tape that had two tracks only for the purpose of capturing a stereo mix.

Jimmy and I would rehearse the way we intended to fade this voice up here, that guitar down there, and so on. We'd mark these fader moves on long strips of masking tape stuck beside the fader to remind us where we wanted the gain levels on that track while mixing that particular song. One fader for one track might have two or three markers for two or three different changes, and there were twenty-four tracks to manipulate. We had four hands on the control panel. Doing the math, that gave us six channels per hand to fade here and there, to mute, to douse with a little extra reverb when needed, pan the stereo mix left or right, or whatever, all while the song was playing in real time. Mixing in this way was like a ballet in the middle of a calf scramble.

We would rehearse only once or twice before we'd attempt dumping a mix. I didn't want to run the two-inch tape too many times, because I knew that microscopic flecks got knocked off the tape every time we ran it over the tape heads, which could eventually affect the sound quality. You had to think quick and learn fast to get a good mix in the nonautomated analog days. I relished the chore as a way to take my mind off all the sordid distractions in my life.

We were mixing the last song, after two days of long hours in the studio. I was adjusting three vocals, the snare drum, a fiddle part, and the bass guitar. Jimmy was riding herd over the lead vocal, two guitars, and a tambourine. We looked like harpists, our hands moving all over the control panel, plucking the parts we had rehearsed.

We had decided to do a slow fade at the end of the song, as if the tune were drifting away into space as you listen to the chorus repeat over and over. I had given Jimmy the responsibility of making the final fade on the master fader as sort of a reward for his diligence and hard work. Everything went well with the mix to the end of the song, so Jimmy reached for the master fader. He began moving it downward ever so slowly.

"That's it," I coached. "Take your time. Milk it."

Jimmy looked like a surgeon making his first incision, his hand steady enough, his eyes keen to the task. It was like watching your own homemade ice cream melt as we heard our precious tracks begin to fade.

I closed my eyes. In a vision I saw the band, myself included, on a floating stage, on a perfectly still lake, on a windless day. It was as if someone had given our vessel the gentlest of shoves away from the shore, for we were drifting off. A fog rose on the lake as the band, and the music, embarked on a voyage into the unknown. As the haze engulfed the Truebloods, I saw my own eyes, happy and confident. The stage floated on and the song diminished in the distance, gradually becoming part of the beautiful strain of pure quietude. The hushed echo of nothingness embraced me like a pillow as my vision of the castaway band disappeared into the fog. Then there was peace.

"Was that a good take?" Jimmy asked.

My eyes flew open and I returned to Salon D. I reached out and pushed the buttons to stop both tape machines. I looked at Jimmy and smiled. "We're done."

It was just a demo album, but we were both swept up in the elation that comes with seeing something good through to the end. We gave each other a backslapping hug as if we had just won a championship ball game.

"Man, the tracks sound good," Jimmy said. "Don't you think they sound good?"

I nodded. "I just hope the real album has the energy of these demos. With any luck, we'll be cutting in Salon A as soon as next week."

"I sure hope corporate assigns me as engineer to the project."

"Don't you worry, Jimmy. I'm going to demand that they give you the job."

"Thanks, Mr. Breed!"

"Yeah, call me Ronnie, damn-it. You're making me feel old. But, hey, let's not get ahead of ourselves. We don't have a contract just yet. We've got one shot left at an audition with Major Witherspoon."

"He's gonna love the Truebloods, Mr. Ronnie."

"Yeah, if I can just hold the band together one more week. They've all had offers for fall tours."

The door to Salon D unexpectedly opened, and I saw Dorothy standing there, the red, green, and amber lights from the studio machines bathing her in impressionistic hues, some pulsing on and off, others glowing steadily. That auburn hair of hers tumbled everywhere around her shoulders. She wore a summer party dress in a bold floral print that gathered tight under her bosom and fell away like a stage curtain that was just barely long enough to hide the cast. My eyes continued cascading all the way down to her wedge sandals.

Some women, when angry, can look intensely beautiful.

"Wow," I said.

"Yeah," Jimmy agreed.

She had something rolled up in her hand. It looked like a newspaper. "Jimmy, would you take a break, please? I need to confer with my client."

I didn't like the tone of the word "confer." Jimmy left. Dorothy closed the door. With her eyes locked on mine, she stalked closer to me like a seductive runway model, except that she was a real woman, not just one of those stick figure girls the designers liked to drape clothes over like walking coat hangers. Just as she came near enough for me to smell her perfume, she reached out and whacked me on the head with the rolled-up newspaper.

"Ouch!" I said. "What the—?"

"Are you *trying* to sabotage this deal with Major Witherspoon?"

"Of course not! I just finished mixing the demos. They sound fantastic."

Ignoring that, she continued. "Morris told me that he's already lost fifty thousand dollars at your little poker tournament!"

"We're going to give that back," I assured her.

"Morris won't take charity! You'll insult him!"

"No, we're going to make it look like he's winning it back."

"So, the great Morris Witherspoon is going to *break even* like some amateur in Vegas? That's worse than losing. There's nothing worse than breaking even. What a waste of time. You don't even learn a lesson."

(Even in the midst of that heated discussion, I took note of Dorothy's philosophy, and it has stuck with me to this day. Never break even. It's better to lose trying than to tie playing it safe.)

"It wasn't my fault that Morris lost the money. He found out about the hospitality room gambling from somebody else. He's a big boy, Dorothy. It's not my job to babysit him."

"Why was there illegal, backroom gambling going on in the first place? Maybe you're the one who needs the babysitter."

"I'll be your baby, if you're applying for the job."

"Don't flirt with me right now. I'm mad at you." She reached out and whacked me with the newspaper again.

"Ouch! Stop that!"

"Oh, hush. That didn't hurt you near as much as this is going to hurt your chances of a record deal." She dropped the rolled newspaper onto the recording console, and it fell open to the cover of that most shameless of all celebrity tabloids, *The International Inquisitor.*

There, I saw a photo that took up almost the whole front page. A moment passed before it sank in. Then I recognized myself, Morris, Dorothy, and Mona. Mona was wielding a pointed object that looked for all the world like a dagger. Dorothy was lunging backwards to avoid being stabbed. Her long hair, frozen in time, suggested the extreme desperation of her maneuver.

I glanced up at the headline:

RONNIE AND THE MAJOR BET
ON DUEL BETWEEN BEAUTIES

I looked for the photo credit: "Rudolph Richards." Hell's own paparazzo.

The setting, as you may recall, was the poker tournament TV set at the Crest Hotel in Corpus Christi, Texas. The way the photo turned out, it really did look as if Mona and Dorothy were engaged in some kind of mortal combat. Morris was actually laughing at the time the shot was taken, as if this blood sport were great fun to him. Rudolph's camera caught me with my fist clenched and an expression that looked like a grimace on my face, as if egging the women on to fight to the death.

Dorothy picked up the tabloid and opened it to the first page. "Wait until you hear the story." She then began to read:

"'At a secret beach resort on the Mexican coast—,'" she said.

"Whoa!" I ordered. "The Crest Hotel? Secret?"

She silenced me with her index finger and continued to read: "'—lawless high rollers gamble not only for high-stakes poker winnings, but on which beautiful female gladiator will outlast her rival in hand-to-hand combat with deadly weapons.'"

"Oh, good Lord! It was a rat-tailed comb!"

"It gets better," she said. "'Our intrepid photographer, Rudolph

Richards, risked his life to catch this week's cover photo of record mogul, Major Morris Witherspoon, and aging rock star, Ronnie Breed, as they make wagers on this gruesome blood sport.'"

"Aging? I'm thirty-two!"

"You're missing the point. This is not exactly good publicity."

"It's not a total loss," I said.

"What could you possibly mean?"

"Well, Morris and I look like hell, but they caught your good side."

"This is no time to impress me with your wit."

"Sorry. Just trying to lighten the mood."

"How could you let this happen?"

"Hey, I've been accused of having brass balls, but never crystal balls. Look, Dorothy, this is what you signed on for, whether you knew it or not. This kind of crap happens all the time in the celebrity world. None of this is my fault. I'm not the one who invited Rudolph Richards to Corpus Christi. I'm not the one who invited Morris to do some backroom gambling. I'm just trying to keep a band together and mix some demos to win a recording contract. I've got the demos mixed. Now I need to work on the band. I've scheduled two days of rehearsal in Houston. I leave Nashville in two hours." I looked at my watch.

She stared at me for a few seconds. "We can't let Morris see this photo."

"He's probably seen it already."

"No, he hasn't. He's fly-fishing for salmon in a remote Norwegian fjord this week. He's flying straight from Oslo to London to New York to Houston to hear the Truebloods. I'm to pick him up at Houston Hobby Airport."

"He'll probably see *The Inquisitor* in some airport."

"Hopefully not in Oslo. I've called a friend in London and a friend in New York, and instructed them to meet the major during his layovers, keep him entertained, and steer him away from the newsstands that carry the tabloids."

"Attractive friends?"

"Sorority sisters. They'll charm him silly."

"He's going to see the photo eventually."

"Let's hope he sees it *after* he signs our contract."

I shrugged. "I promise I won't wave it in front of his face." I looked at the ridiculous photo again. "Hell, he might think it's funny."

"And he might think it will turn conservative, Bible Belt country music fans against his record label, and especially against Ronnie Breed."

"Come on, Dorothy, people know it's a tabloid. I've been libeled plenty of times by sensationalist rags like this one, and it's never ruined my career."

"Your rock-and-roll fans would love this. Country fans? You've got some explaining to do to them."

"So, when Johnny Carson has me back on his show, I'll explain it. You handle Morris. I'll handle the music."

She threw the newspaper in the trash can and turned for the door. "Houston is our last shot at this," she said on her way out.

"Good. I work well under pressure. Dorothy, wait!"

She stopped in the open doorway and turned back to look at me, still angry, still gorgeous. "What?"

"Sunday, the day after the poker tournament wraps, I've rented a studio in Houston so Morris will have a place to listen to the demos on some top-notch speakers."

"Fine. I hope he'll still want to."

"I'd like for you to sit down and listen to them before then. Jimmy will roll the tape for you here in the studio."

"I'm not in the proper frame of mind right now. Maybe tomorrow."

"Okay. Also . . ."

"Well?" She crossed her arms and tapped her foot daintily but impatiently.

"Just so you know . . . Mona and I have come to an agreement. After the poker tournament wraps next week, we're going our separate ways. Forever."

I had just raised the bet. Would she check, call, or go all in? I just hoped she wasn't going to fold her hand.

"Good," she said, quite emotionlessly. "She's a bad influence on you. Otherwise, your personal life is of no concern to me. . . ."

At that moment, I feared she had folded. Until she added, in her addictive Southern drawl:

"At least not just right now." She turned, flipping that luxurious mane of long hair around at me and leaving the studio without so much as a fare-thee-well.

32

I HAD told the band members to meet me at my mom's farm on Chocolate Bayou on Thursday evening. I had no real reason to believe they wouldn't show, because the Truebloods were all reliable professionals. Still, I knew they were being sought after by other bands. I also sensed that they had begun to think of me as something of a loose cannon, because of the weirdness of the poker tournament, my volatile relationship with Mona, and the baggage leftover from my old band, the Half Breeds—especially the Joe McLeod problem. And so, I was relieved and reassured when they all arrived on time at the old family farm.

We rehearsed in Mom's barn until after midnight on Thursday. Friday, we resumed at noon, tweaking every nuance of every song. Our morale began to bounce back and we started acting like a band again instead of just a bunch of egocentric pickers. After she got home from work on Friday, Mama came out to the barn to listen to us play a few songs. I knew she was partial to her only baby boy, but her approval was good for the whole band.

"You know I always supported you with your rock-and-roll music, honey," she said, embarrassing me in front of the band, "but I really like this more country kind of sound."

"Thanks, Mama."

"Some of those characters in the Half Breeds were a little sketchy. But these are all nice boys. And very talented!"

"Mama! Boys? We're all grown men."

"You'll always be my little, boy, honey. Now, all you boys come on in the house. I'm frying up three chickens for supper."

Mom charmed the socks off those guys over supper, telling them a lot of embarrassing stories about me growing up. This was actually a big help to me. The boys in the band started to look beyond my rock star image and think of me as a wholesome country boy. After supper, we went back to the barn and ran through our set one last time. We were ready for the audition with Morris the next day.

Even so, I didn't sleep at all Friday night. It wasn't just the showcase for Major Witherspoon. The poker tournament was going to wrap on Saturday, and I knew what that meant. I was worried about it all going as Dan had planned, for if it didn't, my career, and indeed my life, might never be the same.

Saturday was shaping up to be the scariest and most important day of my life. Not only did I have the professional opportunity of a lifetime to cinch with Morris, but I had to patch up things with Dorothy, as well. Without Dorothy, I had realized, the record deal would be meaningless to me.

As I lay in bed that night, I worried about everything that could go wrong the next day. What if Morris saw the tabloid photo? What if the hospitality room scam went wrong? What if Dorothy could not find it in her heart to forgive me? What if, what if, what if . . .

Finally, realizing that I wasn't going to sleep, I sat up in bed and said a quick prayer. "Lord, get me through this." Then I set my mind to doing my part in making everything click when the sun came up. I had told Dorothy that I worked well under pressure. Now I was going to have to prove it.

WE HAD been talking about wrapping up the tournament in Houston for weeks, but in reality, the wrap would happen in the Houston suburb of Pasadena, at Gilley's, that most famous of all honky-tonks. Accordingly, I drove my tour bus to Gilley's Club early Saturday morning to secure the parking spot Dan had told me to occupy outside the dance hall.

Gilley's was a natural choice of locations for the final round of

The World Championship of Texas Hold 'Em Poker. It would hold a few thousand people, and had a great sound system for my band. On top of all that, Dan had worked briefly at Gilley's as a bouncer after he returned from Vietnam. He got along great with the club's co-owner, Sherwood Cryer, which wasn't always easy to do.

About the time I got the bus situated in the parking lot where Dan had told me to put it, I saw Sherwood himself arriving to unlock the doors on his main source of livelihood. He was a hands-on kind of business owner, even to the point of unstopping the toilets himself. He was on-site early to get Gilley's ready for the TV shoot and all its attendant surprises.

"Morning, Mr. Cryer," I said, stepping out of the bus.

He was wearing a coverall jumpsuit and some newfangled running shoes marketed by some upstart company called Nike. "Who the hell are you?" he asked, wheeling on me, his hand reaching into his pocket.

I knew Sherwood had shot more than one man trying to rob his place, so I stopped in my tracks. "It's Ronnie Breed. My band's playing here today."

He narrowed his eyes at me. "I'll be damned. It is you. You're here early."

"Just want to make sure everything's set for the show."

He glared over my shoulder. "Who told you you could park that goddamned bus there?"

"Dan told me to put it here," I said. "He insisted it had to go right here."

"Dan? Well, all right, then, I guess." He turned the key and unlocked the side door to his behemoth dance hall. "You want a beer?"

"It's a little early for me," I said.

"It's what?"

"Sure, I'll have a beer."

We went inside and Sherwood fished one of last night's beers out of the lukewarm water in what had been a trough full of ice and Lone Stars several hours ago. Then he got on the phone and cussed out his soundman for not being there to meet me and get the stage set. He sat down with me to watch me drink my beer.

"I saw that picture of you on that news rag. *The International Incubator,* or whatever they call it."

"Oh, that," I said.

"I've seen some gals pull knives in here before, but never dolled up like those hussies."

"Actually, it was just a rat-tailed comb in the photo," I explained.

"That's not what the story said."

"I know, Mr. Cryer, but those tabloid writers lie."

"Ain't it the goddamned truth?" he agreed. "The damn *Post* and the *Chronicle* both have slandered me up and down since I opened this place."

The two daily newspapers in Houston were hardly tabloids, but I didn't argue that point with Sherwood. Dan arrived about that time, and got a much warmer welcome from Sherwood than I had. Mona showed up soon after Dan, catching Sherwood's eye in her denim shorts, tank top, and flip-flops. I introduced them.

"You look familiar," Sherwood said to Mona.

"She's the girl with the rat-tailed comb," I said.

"I'll be damned. I guess you won the fight."

"I always win my fights!"

Sherwood laughed. "I'll bet you do!"

"Ronnie, I need the key to the bus," she said, turning to me.

"I missed you, too, Mona." I hadn't seen her in almost a week. She had flown off to God-knows-where after Fort Worth.

"Whatever. Give it to me. I need a nap."

I fished the key out of my pocket. "Lock yourself in," I advised her. "The safe is in there."

"I know!" she snarled, snatching the key from my hand and strutting out.

"Cuz, I've got some bad news for you," Dan said after Mona left.

"I hate it when you say that," I groaned.

"I heard it on the radio. Lefty Frizzell kicked the bucket yesterday. I know you were a big fan of his."

"Oh, no," I said, my face dropping to my palms.

"Hey, don't take it so hard, Cuz. He had a good run."

"It's not just Lefty," I lamented. "It's Dorothy. She managed Lefty.

That's how she learned the ropes. She orchestrated his last come-back."

"Oh, great. Wish I hadn't brought it up, now."

Dan went to help Sherwood with some preparations for the TV shoot. I finished my warm beer and thought about Lefty, his life, his death, and how it was going to hit Dorothy.

My soundman showed up, so I spent the next couple of hours setting the stage the way I wanted it for the Truebloods showcase and testing the PA with him. Gradually, the dance hall employees began to show up for work. Some swept and mopped. Others stocked bars with hundreds of cases of beer. One guy dragged in some new foam padding to surround the mechanical bull. (All the employees at Gilley's were instructed to keep a constant look-out in Dumpsters and alleys for large chunks of discarded foam rubber.)

Bartholomew and his TV crew showed up. They parked the pro-duction van beside my bus, so they could run a cable into the bus for the closed-circuit TV in the hospitality room on wheels. The poker tables were unloaded from the equipment truck and put in place. Lights were set up, cameras wheeled into their positions. This was actually going to happen, I thought. I said a silent prayer that everything would go according to plan, and that I could resume my normal life, beginning tomorrow. At least, as normal as life could be for the living legend I aspired to be.

I heard the phone ring behind the bar.

"Mr. Breed!" shouted a bartender in a cowboy hat and a white T-shirt. "Phone call for you. She says she's your manager."

I trotted to the bar and took the receiver. "Thanks, pard. Doro-thy?"

"Morris is fogged in at Heathrow in London." Her Southern voice was all business.

"Oh, no," I groaned. "We're so ready for this showcase."

"There's a chance the weather may clear. Morris is flying the Concorde to New York, and his private pilot is waiting at JFK. He could still make it there by tonight."

"Do you think he really wants to?"

"He's trying hard to get to Houston. Either he really wants to hear you, or he really wants to see me."

"Can't say that I blame him. I mean, in regards to seeing you."

She was silent for a few seconds. "I told him about the Topaz tapes. I told him they sound phenomenal."

"So, you listened to them?"

"Over and over. I cried."

"That bad?"

"No, that good. This album will change popular music, if you can manage not to screw up the live audition."

"We're ready for this, Dorothy. But if Morris doesn't get here today, I'm not sure I can hold on to the players another week. They're all getting offers to go on the road. Even Henry has to go back to his day job if we don't get a contract."

"I've done all I can do, Ronnie. I can't make the fog lift in London any more than I can make it lift from your mysterious life."

"The fog lifts tomorrow," I promised. "One way or another."

"What does that mean?"

"That means tomorrow, no more mystery." I could hear her breathing on the other end of the line. I could almost hear her heartbeat. "Dorothy?"

"I heard you. I just don't know what to believe anymore."

"Dorothy, I heard about Lefty. I'm sorry. I know you cared a lot for him."

"I should have gone to see him," she said in a small voice, as if to herself more so than to me.

"You had no way of knowing when he was going to die, Dorothy. How could you have known?" I heard her suppress a sob.

"I have to catch my flight. I'll see you at Gilley's."

I found myself holding a dead line to my ear, wishing I could embrace her while she cried on my shoulder.

33

A CROWD of several hundred souls filled Gilley's dance hall by noon. Some hoped to get drawn to play poker. Some just wanted to watch. Others were actually there to hear the Truebloods, for I had phoned in some interviews to local radio stations, and Sherwood had been putting posters of me up for weeks. Others just wanted to get drunk and pick a fight at Gilley's on a Saturday. There were local TV news cameras, some prominent radio deejays, and some newspaper entertainment writers buzzing around.

Archie Zeller showed up with Jack Diamond, Luis Sebastian, and Lady Daniela. The four of them had gone out the night before to paint the town, Zeller showing them around the Bayou City. Mona came out of the bus dressed in a little pink jumpsuit, no doubt inspired by Sherwood's attire, and started makeup work on the star poker players. Bartholomew had them sit down for pregame interviews.

When I sat down for makeup, Mona hovered over me silently for a while, powdering my face. "Where's Dorothy?" she finally asked.

"On her way here," I said.

She fluttered her powder brush across my face. It felt nice. "Not that I really care, but I hope that works out for you."

"That's probably the sweetest thing you've ever said to me."

She looked into my eyes ever so briefly. I think she was actually beginning to like me. Then she cackled up at the ceiling. "I'm about as sweet as a turpentine pie, and you know it!" She brushed my hair back out of my face and sprayed a little hairspray on it. "Still . . . it's been nice, Ronnie."

"Yeah," I replied. "I'm actually going to miss you."

"Damn right you will. Now, go over there and act like you're doing an interview with Bartholomew."

The band showed up, so we walked across the dance floor to the stage to get our amps in place and line-check our instruments before our short set.

"Where's Major Witherspoon?" Henry asked.

"On his way," I claimed. "He won't be here for our opening set, but I'm hoping he'll make it for that second set we're doing, just before the TV shoot wraps. That's when we'll showcase the new songs."

"As long as he gets here for the dance tonight," Warren said. "We can play the new songs again."

"No, we really need him to listen in the set before the dance," I answered. "Don't ask me why. I'm just telling you. That's when I need you guys to be at the top of your game, in the showcase set *before* the dance."

"All right, boss," Henry said. "Hell, we're ready whenever."

As we approached the stage, I saw someone whom I took for one of the employees scurrying away from the backstage area, and out a side door. Only, the Gilley's workers typically knew how to dress like authentic "kickers," as the members of local rodeo set were called, and the guy I saw in the shadows looked like some citified foreign dude, maybe from Connecticut or something, trying to pull off a cowboy look without much success.

I didn't think much of it until we got onstage and tried to turn on our amps. Nothing seemed to work. A quick investigation revealed that someone had come along and cut numerous power cords and microphone cords in an apparent act of vandalism or sabotage. I found a pair of heavy-duty wire cutters that had been thrown down backstage.

"What the hell!" Slim shouted, staring into his open guitar case. "Somebody cut my guitar strings!"

I ran for the side door where I had seen the unknown figure escape. Bursting outside to the parking lot, I saw a car speeding off. It looked like a rental. I had a suspect in mind.

"McLeod," I growled to Mojo, who had run out behind me.

"You gotta be kiddin'," he said.

I found Dan and Sherwood and told them what had happened. Amid much creative profanity, Sherwood corralled some tools and some electrical tape, and we all began patching power cords for our amps. The soundman had several spare microphone cords to replace the damaged ones. Slim changed his strings. Sherwood assigned one of his bouncers to guard our stage for the rest of the day.

All this took some time, and put us behind schedule, which I realized was a good thing, for the delay would give Morris more time to arrive. I decided upon a new personal strategy: *stall*. For example, hiding behind some amps as everybody else repaired damage, I secretly used McLeod's discarded wire cutters to cut my own guitar strings, then closed my case.

Later, as the Truebloods prepared for our short set, I opened my case and called upon all my acting skills when I railed:

"The no-good, sorry SOB cut my strings, too!"

"Why didn't you check earlier?" Dan said, looking at his wristwatch.

"I've been a little busy, Dan."

"Well, how long will it take to change them?"

"Not long, but then I've got to let the new strings stretch out. Maybe an hour."

"I'll give you thirty minutes!" he barked. "We've got a time line to follow here!"

In spite of all these distractions, the band sounded fantastic when we finally got to play. The Gilley's crowd hit the dance floor on the first intro. Sherwood had been telling everyone for weeks that there would be a TV shoot going on, so the dancers had dressed for the occasion and were showing off their best moves. This would have been the perfect set for Morris to hear, in the best place—the world's largest dance hall. I hoped he would arrive for the later set we had planned as a showcase.

On our last song of the opening short set, I saw that Dorothy had arrived, for she was watching from the far side of the dance hall. She was actually smiling. Maybe she was over being mad at me.

"Thank you, cowboys and cowgirls, kickers and kickerettes!" I said over the mic after the last song. "What do y'all think about my new band, the Truebloods?"

A great roar of applause, whistles, hoots, and hollers rose from the dance floor.

"We'll play some more songs for you later. Now it's on with the poker tournament! Good luck to all of you!"

Mona drew names for the camera. Contestants were seated at their tables, and we began to play the first round of poker to decide the players for the finals. Of course, I knew who would be in the final round—the usuals: Zeller, Daniela, Luis, Jack, and myself. Dan's cardsharp dealers would see to that. Over the past four weeks, the five high rollers had amassed points according to Dan's system. The higher you finished at any of the four cities we had played, the more points you won. The only high roller who had failed to win at one of the four previous cities was Jack Diamond. This, too, was by design. Dan's secret script had been setting Jack up as an underdog for this day. The script had also established Luis Sebastian as the guy who never, ever bluffed. All of this would play into our plans later today—assuming everything went according to Dan's detailed script.

On my way to my table, I greeted Dorothy. "Thank you for being here. I know you're grieving over Lefty."

She shrugged. "Life is for the living. Lefty knew that as well as anyone."

I nodded, impressed with her toughness. "I've been missing you. You look gorgeous."

"Thank you," she said politely. "You look good yourself. You should spend more time with your mother."

"You're right," I agreed. "Any word from Morris?"

She nodded. "The fog lifted in London. Looks like he's going to make it."

"Thank God," I said. "Has he seen that tabloid cover?"

"Not yet. My sorority sister in London kept him totally distracted."

"I have a request," I said.

"Yes?"

"I can't tell you why, but we need to have Morris here for the short set during the filming break, right before the tournament champion is crowned."

She snarled her lip at me. "Why? You're playing an entire dance tonight. There will be plenty of time then."

"I know this sounds crazy, but you've got to trust me on this. We need to have Morris here for the shorter set. Looks like that'll happen about nine-ish tonight, the way things have been going."

Her eyes were puzzled. "Don't you think it would be better to let Morris go to his hotel, shower, change, enjoy a dinner, rest awhile . . . *then* hear the showcase during the dance?"

"I can't tell you why, but we don't have that luxury. Please don't ask me how I know this, but I sense there's going to be trouble here tonight after the TV shoot wraps, and I don't want to embroil Morris in it if I can help it."

She scowled at me. "Trouble? Oh, of course! Your middle name!"

Now I started backpedaling and throwing out false reasons for my request: "This place can get rowdy on a Saturday night. Morris might not be able to concentrate. It would be more impressive for him to see us in front of the television cameras. Also, somebody might say something to him about the tabloid. My gut feeling is that he needs to be here for the earlier set this evening. Then you can spirit him away for the negotiations."

She seemed a little peeved at my insistent tone, but she saw the serious look of concern in my eye. "I'll do my best to get him here early. If the band showcases as well as you played that first set, the contract is ours. I have to admit, y'all kicked some serious butt with those four songs."

"Thanks. So, are we okay, Dorothy?"

Her eyes drifted off somewhere. "I think we might be able to work together, if that's what you mean."

"I'm talking more about our personal relationship."

"At this point, I'm keeping my options open, Ronnie. I'll be honest with you. Morris told me he wants to have a serious personal discussion with me this weekend. Right now, I just don't know who you are. I . . . I need time."

"I understand," I said. "But tomorrow, when all this is over, I have some things I need to come clean about. I think you'll begin to get to know the real Ronnie Breed, starting tomorrow."

She let a glimmer of softness slip into her guarded glare, and I had to believe I still had a shot.

"No promises," she said, slipping back into her armor.

"Ronnie!" It was Dan's voice. "Get over here, man! It's time to deal!"

I CONTINUED my stalling tactics as I played the amateurs in the first round of the Houston tournament. I studied at length over every bet and made small talk with the players and spectators at every opportunity. By the time the other high rollers had defeated the locals at their tables, I still had two guys sitting in at my game.

Dan came around with his producer's headset on and spoke in my ear: "I know what you're doing. You're stalling so Witherspoon will have time to get here. Wrap this thing up, Cuz. You know what you agreed to do."

In spite of Dan's insistence, I continued my sluggish pace. Then, as I was about to eliminate the last player, I happened to hear the shutter click of a camera. I shaded my eyes with my hat brim and glanced toward the source of the sound. Though the photographer ducked away behind a veil of cigarette smoke, I caught sight of his cross-eyed face. It was Rudolph Richards!

I was in poker mode, so I didn't let on that I had recognized him. Instead, I looked at the TV camera, and said, "Cut!"

As I got up from the table, Dan came running over to me. "What are you doing? You're not the producer!"

"I need a break!" I complained. "I have to go to the men's room." With my eyes, I motioned for Dan to follow me, so he did, still lecturing me about keeping the action moving for the cameras, though he knew something else was up. Inside the men's room, I got the chance to tell him I had spotted Rudolph.

"That son of a bitch," Dan said. "We really don't need our likenesses in the tabloids. Take your time in the men's room. I'll come get you when I figure out what to do."

A couple of minutes later, Dan found me in one of the stalls.

"Here's the plan," he said. "The TV crew is taking a break. You and Mona are going to slip out the side door like you're going to get some hanky-panky on in the parking lot to bait Rudolph into following you. Sherwood and I will be waiting for him outside.

"Hanky-panky?"

"Yeah, like a quickie or something."

"All right," I groaned. "Don't let Sherwood kill him. I don't want accessory to murder added to our list of felonies."

Mona was waiting for me. She obviously knew the plan already, because she took me by the arm with seduction in her eyes and pulled me toward the side door. On the way across the dance floor, she actually grabbed my butt in front of everyone. I looked around, rather embarrassed, and happened to see Dorothy. Her jaw dropped at the scandal of it all.

"Did you have to do that in front of everybody?" I asked Mona as we passed through the door. Once outside, I saw that the sun was sinking on Pasadena, bathing the parking lot in a reddish brown glow as it shone through the big-city smog. I noticed Dan's T-Bird near the door, its trunk open.

"I was baiting the paparazzi guy," Mona explained. "Do you think I like grabbing your ass?"

Now I saw Dan and Sherwood hiding behind the door we had opened.

"Shut the door and keep walking," Dan ordered.

I did as he said, then heard the door open behind me again. By the time I turned around, I saw that Dan had grabbed Rudolph by the collar. With a snakelike motion, Sherwood drew a pistol from his coveralls and clubbed the paparazzo on the back of the head, knocking him unconscious. Dan covered the photographer's mouth with duct tape as Sherwood held his head up out of the gravel. They dragged him to the open trunk of the Thunderbird and threw him in, facedown. Sherwood tied his wrists behind his back with a length of rope and closed the trunk lid on him.

"I noticed this cross-eyed asshole earlier," Sherwood said, "hanging out like a hair in a grilled cheese sandwich. Should have known he was up to something."

Dan picked up the camera Rudolph had dropped and pulled the film out of it. "Problem solved. Go back to work, Ronnie." He threw the camera in the backseat of the T-Bird.

"How long are you going to leave him in there?" I asked.

"That's up to you," Dan replied. "The quicker we get this thing over with, the sooner we can let him out. Now, quit stalling!"

I reentered the dance hall with Mona, who skipped over toward the nearest bar, where Zeller and the other high rollers were waiting. On my way back to my poker table, Dorothy overtook me. "You and Mona going separate ways, huh? You look pretty chummy to me."

"I can explain that," I said.

"Don't bother. I'm not interested in your explanations anymore. I'm going to the airport to pick Morris up. Be grateful that I'm willing to do even that for you."

Dejected, I went back to my table and beat the last local amateur with the next hand provided to me by our dealer. I should have been elated that Morris would soon arrive to hear me showcase my band. Instead, I was crushed that Dorothy hated my guts. I had all but driven her right into Morris's arms. I only hoped I could explain things to her tomorrow.

We took our break for supper. Dan had arranged for a typical Texas barbecue buffet to be catered in to Gilley's. I was too nervous to eat more than a bite, after which Dan pulled me aside. We found Zeller, who was sitting with Mona. They were sitting way too close when we walked up.

"Did you bring your bettin' money?" Dan asked him.

"Damn sure did. It's locked up in the trunk of my car, just outside the Choirboy's bus."

"Archie," I said, "you just called me Choirboy one time too many.

When this thing is over, you and me have a score to settle out in the parking lot."

"Oh, please, Ronnie!" Mona said. "You can't beat up Wildcat."

"The hell I can't," I said. "I'm going to use his head for a mop and his butt for a bootjack!"

"Bring it on, Choirboy!"

Dan laughed. "You two multimillionaires are going to be so happy when this thing is over, you'll be huggin' and kissin' instead of punchin' and kickin'. Remember why we're here. You two have to work together to get rich."

"Yeah, yeah," Zeller said.

"Then we'll settle it later," I promised. "I don't care how rich I get, I'm still going to kick your ass."

"When they put a man on the moon!"

"Uh, hey, genius, they did that six years ago already."

"You believe that crap? You don't know a con when you see one."

I didn't feel the need to reply to that one. Instead, I just looked away, and when I did, I saw Morris Witherspoon enter the dance hall with Dorothy. He looked a bit bedraggled and jet-lagged, but still possessed his swagger. The stage and my band were ready. It was just about showtime for Ronnie Breed.

34

AFTER SUPPER, in the championship round, I lost first, by design. Calling upon my acting experience, I bowed out graciously, leaving Zeller and the other three stars of the tournament still playing. My nerves were on edge, because I knew Zeller would lose next. Then the time would come for Zeller and me to make our final hospitality room bets, followed by my band's audition for Morris. I went to the nearest bar and ordered a beer to settle the butterflies in my stomach.

"Rawn!"

I turned to see Slim rushing up behind me.

"I seen the dude, man."

"What dude?"

"McLeod!"

"Are you sure?"

"Dressed up like some fool cowboy, tryin' to look like these rodeo bums."

"Where?"

Slim tossed his head toward the faraway stage, which was barely visible through the cloud of cigarette smoke hanging in the huge dance hall. I saw a suspicious person lurking nearby. I recognized him by his body language, posture, and his overall sneaky demeanor. The stage was still guarded by the bouncer, but McLeod was looking for an opportunity for more sabotage.

"Watch him," I said. "I'm going to get Dan."

On my way to fetch Dan from the film set, I came up with a plan. My creativity was beginning to kick in amid the stress.

Grabbing Dan, I said, "I need Rudolph's camera, and the key to your trunk."

"What the hell for?"

I briefed Dan on my plan. He approved, somewhat reluctantly, and gave me the key. "His camera's in the backseat."

"This won't take long." I went out the side door to Dan's T-Bird. I heard Rudolph kicking on the inside of the trunk.

Glad to know that he was conscious, I shouted, "Hey, Rudolph!"

The banging inside ceased. I heard his voice trying to yell for mercy through the duct tape.

"Shut up and listen. This is Ronnie Breed. I've got a deal for you. Do you know Joe McLeod?"

More grunting, but this time in the tone of a question.

"Yeah, of the Half Breeds. How would you like to get a shot of him vandalizing my stage in order to sabotage my showcase with Morris Witherspoon?"

He grunted affirmatively.

"I'll let you out and set the shot up for you, but you've got to promise me one thing."

The grunting asked what that thing might be.

"I want a retraction and a correction on that stupid knife-fight photo. It was a rat-tailed comb, and you know it."

I heard the acquiescent grumble through the trunk lid and duct tape.

I opened the trunk and pulled him out. I yanked the tape from his mouth.

"Where's my camera?" He turned so I could untie his wrists.

"Backseat," I said. "But first, I want a handshake. You promise me you'll write the retraction."

"If I get the shot of McLeod, it's a deal." He shook my hand, and rubbed his wrists where the rope had bound him tight. "How's this going to work?" He opened the door of the T-Bird to get his camera from the backseat.

"You peek through the side door and watch the stage. I'm going to call the guard off the stage. Joe's already lurking nearby in a cowboy disguise. When I see him move in to wreak havoc on my stage,

I'm going to flip the stage lights on and send the bouncer to catch him. We'll pull the disguise off him, and you'll get some good shots."

"I like it," he said, loading a fresh roll of film into his Nikon. "Let's do it." He rubbed the back of his head where the pistol butt had smacked him, and headed for the side door.

I reentered the dance hall and motioned to the guard onstage, taking care not to look where I knew Joe was lurking. "Hey, Hoss," I said. "I need your help over here for a minute." As I led the guard away, I told him what was going on. He hid where he could watch the stage and ready himself to pounce on Joe.

I then trotted to the soundman's booth where the stage light controls were also located. By the time I got there and peeked out, I could see the shadowy figure of Joe McLeod, dressed in a ridiculous Roy Rogers shirt and a straw farmer's hat, moving onto the stage. He lifted a ball-peen hammer and was getting ready to smash the condenser tubes out of the back of Slim's amp!

I glanced at the side door and saw Rudolph's long lens and flash unit jutting through from outside. I hit the spotlight just as Joe wielded the hammer. He was blinded and startled to the point that he missed the tube and only smacked the back of the amplifier cabinet. The timing of Rudolph's flash told me he had gotten a great shot of the hammer descending on the amp.

Hoss, the bouncer, rushed in and collared Joe as he tried to escape. Hoss pulled the silly hat off the vandal, exposing rock star Joe McLeod, caught in the act of sabotage. Rudolph was inside on the dance hall floor by now, shooting away with his 35-millimeter Nikon.

"Drag him outside," I said to Hoss, who had Joe in a headlock.

About a hundred spectators broke into applause, having noticed the incident unfold from across the empty dance floor.

Once outside, Hoss released the headlock, but kept Joe pinned against the wall. I looked my former bass player in the eye. He appeared somewhat crazed. He was drunk, and possibly high on something, too. "I could have you arrested," I said.

Joe looked at me fearfully. "I can't go to jail!" he slurred. "I'm too messed up, man!"

I pointed my finger at his face. "I'll make you a onetime good deal, Joe. I'll let you go to your car and sleep it off. I won't press charges as long as you give up your claim to the band name—the Truebloods."

He fumed, but nodded.

"Give me your keys."

He produced a Hertz Rent-a-Car key ring. I took it and gave it to Hoss. "I'll give you twenty-four hours to fax the legal release of the band name to Morris Witherspoon's office. Otherwise, I'm calling the Pasadena Police." I jutted my thumb at Rudolph. "I've got some real good photographic evidence and a lot of witnesses against you."

Poor Joe broke down and started crying.

"Come on," Hoss said. "I'll open your car door for you so you can crash."

Rudolph was grinning. "Thanks for the tip, Ronnie."

"You remember our deal, right?"

"You have my word. I'll make them write the retraction before I agree to sell them the McLeod photos. You realize I don't write that bullshit copy, don't you? Those idiots at *The Inquisitor* just buy my pictures and make up whatever they want to."

"Just see to the retraction. If you do that for me, I'll give you some exclusive backstage shots somewhere down the line. Make an honest photographer out of you." I smiled to soften my language.

He shook my hand. "Deal."

I felt pretty cocky about solving the Rudolph Richards and Joe McLeod problems in one fell swoop. I just hoped my run of luck would carry me through the hospitality room high jinks in the bus, and my upcoming band showcase for Morris Witherspoon. It was all going to come to a head at once, and my nerves were on edge with anticipation.

Stepping back into the dance hall, I saw Zeller at a table with Lady Daniela, so it was clear to me that they had both been knocked out of the tournament. The championship round had come down to Luis and Jack, as planned. The last big bet would happen soon in the bus, and this would all be over.

But first, I had to get Morris to the bus so he could win his money back. I found him and Dorothy at the bar.

"I need to borrow Morris," I said. "Actually, I'd appreciate it if you'd come, too, Dorothy. Morris might need the luck in the hospitality room."

"Do come with me, dear," Morris said to Dorothy.

"Why not," she said irritably.

"Where is the hospitality room?" Morris asked.

"It's in my bus, outside."

He leaned in closer. "Same secret knock?"

"The same."

"I'll just be a moment in the men's room, Dorothy, my dear," Morris said, leaving us there.

"Are you crazy?" she said, glaring at me. "The hospitality room again?"

"Don't worry. I've arranged for him to win his money back, plus a little extra. Call it an investment."

She blew a stray hair away from her cheek out the side of her mouth. "You're making me nervous."

"Don't be. It's all fixed. I also took care of *The International Inquisitor*. They're going to print an apology. Oh, and I got Joe McLeod to relinquish his claim on the band name, the Truebloods, so there will be no legal fees to pursue on that issue. He's going to fax the release to Morris tomorrow."

She glared again at me, dubiously this time. "How did you do all that?"

"Hey, I'm working my butt off to make this contract go through, Dorothy."

"Finally! It may be too late."

"I've got to go tune up," I said. I winked at her and left her standing there. "Have fun in the hospitality room. You might see some familiar faces in there, whether you recognize them or not."

"What does that mean?"

"I'll explain later."

I found the band in the Back Forty, behind the mechanical bull, sipping beers; a couple of them smoking cigarettes. "Let's get ready, boys," I suggested. We went to the stage, checked our equipment, and took our places to wait for the break in the tournament filming.

"I'm going to get Major Witherspoon. It won't be long now."

I left the band, went out the side exit, and gave the secret knock on the bus door. Leisure Suit opened the door and stuck his head out.

"Has he won yet?" I whispered.

"Yeah. Get him out of here." LS opened the door wide for me.

"Would you tell Major Witherspoon the audition is about to start," I said loudly.

"We don't use names here," LS growled. He shut the door in my face.

In a moment, Morris came down the bus steps, all smiles, Dorothy right behind him.

"Ronnie, I had the most amazing run of luck," he said. "I made up for last week's little loss, and then some. The big fellow made me take my winnings out of the pot."

Dorothy looked a little relieved.

"That's wonderful, Morris. Congratulations. Now, would you like to hear a really good band?"

"Indeed, I would," he said with a Clark Gable smirk.

We began to walk back toward the dance hall. "I'd like to ask you a favor," I said.

"I'm sure you wouldn't ask for anything unreasonable."

"If a fight breaks out, I want you to get Dorothy safely out of here."

"A fight?" Dorothy said.

"Why would a fight break out?" Morris asked.

"This *is* Gilley's," I said. "Just promise me you'll look after her if a brawl starts."

"You have my word as a gentleman," he vowed.

"I *can* take care of myself," Dorothy insisted.

I left Morris and Dorothy at the bar, and went to Zeller's table. He was sitting between Mona and Lady Daniela, apparently having the time of his life. "Let's go watch the championship hand," I suggested. "Dan wants us in the audience for the camera shot."

"Where eeze Dan?" Lady Daniela asked in her lilting French accent.

"I believe he's in the production van with Bartholomew, checking the camera angles." I shot a glance at Zeller as I leaned in close and lowered my voice. "Let's go watch Luis and Jack so we'll have an idea of who to bet on in the bus."

"Well, eef I can't be zee champion," Daniela said quietly, "I might as well make some money off zee champion."

"You've got a fifty-fifty shot," I said. "We're down to two players."

As we walked up to the film shoot, we could feel the tension among the spectators. The dealer had apparently just flipped the river. Jack Diamond, who claimed the larger pile of chips, made a wager that amounted to about half Luis's holdings. Luis studied the cards awhile. He drummed his fingers atop his hole cards. He looked up at Jack. Expressionless, Luis went all in, shoving his chips toward the center of the table.

A murmur rippled through the crowd. I remember thinking how outlandish a poker tournament as a spectator sport had seemed to me just a few weeks ago. I was amazed now at how entranced the audience was with this thing. Could a show like this ever really succeed? I shrugged off my speculations. I had other concerns right now.

Lady Daniela leaned across Zeller to say, "Luis always plays zee odds. I've never caught heem bluffing."

"If you're wrong," I answered, "this will be the last hand, and Jack Diamond will be champion. Just in case, I'm going to get my bet in on the bus."

"Cut!" yelled one of the cameramen, who then rushed over to me to whisper in my ear.

I turned to address the crowd.

"Folks, we're going to take a production break here to reset the cameras!"

A collective groan emanated from the audience.

"Aw, come on, let's see them cards!" some cowboy drawled.

I stood on an empty chair to rise up above the spectators. "I know you all want to see this hand revealed. But you've probably noticed that every time we get down to two players, and one of them goes all in, we always take a break to make sure we get set for the next shot, because it could be the last hand of the game, right? We want to have the camera angles right. On top of all that, we're down to the last two players in the championship round, so we're going to make sure everything is perfect."

There was more grousing and even some swearing from the audience.

"If it helps," I said, "I've got a surprise for you. My new band, the Truebloods, is going to play you a few new songs off our upcoming album."

"Big shit!" some redneck said.

"And I'll buy you all a Gilley's beer at the bar!"

A great roar went up around me, and the crowd dispersed for the nearest bartender.

I motioned for Zeller, Lady Daniela, and Mona to head for the hospitality room on wheels. We exited through the side door and angled toward the bus.

"I'm gonna get my cash from my car," Zeller said. He popped the trunk on his Cadillac and pulled out a large Samsonite suitcase.

I gave the secret knock, and LS opened the door for us. He was wearing a shockingly crimson leisure suit this week.

"That's even worse than last week's suit," Zeller said.

LS looked up and down at Zeller's khakis. "Like *you* know something about threads?"

The old lady from the Fort Worth hospitality room was in my bus, sitting at the dinette. "I'll put a hundred on the Brazilian," she squawked. "Luis don't bluff."

"A hundred?" Zeller said derisively.

"That's a hundred thousand, sonny!" she yelled at him. She shoved a wrinkled brown paper grocery bag toward LS, who began removing stacks of cash, which he placed on the scales on my tour bus's galley counter. Laboriously, Old Lady got up. "I'm going out to show myself on the cameras now. I suggest you all do the same if you want an alibi."

LS finished weighing Old Lady's bet, and made a notation on the small notebook he kept in his pocket. He looked at Lady Daniela next. "Ma'am?"

"Theese game eesn't over," she said in her lovely accent. "Luis seemply doesn't bluff. I'll put feefty on Luis." She opened her handbag to dump five ten-thousand-dollar bundles of hundreds on LS's scales.

LS checked the weight, nodded at Daniela, and put her wager away under the counter.

"Gentlemen," she said, glancing at me, then Zeller, "Meese Mona . . . I weel see you beside zee championsheep table when Luis weens theese hand." She flashed her perfect teeth in a confident smile, and left the bus.

LS glared at me next. "Well?"

"I'm thinking."

The phone rang. Dan had run a telephone line out of Sherwood's office window and into my bus, which was the reason he had ordered me to park my bus in this spot, so we would have a telephone line to our hospitality room on wheels. LS lifted the phone receiver and said, "Bus," into the mouthpiece. He then handed it to me.

"Yeah?" I paused to listen. "I told you I was just gonna make one quick bet, Dan! I know the crowd is anxious." I rolled my eyes at Zeller. "I'll be onstage in two minutes." I handed the phone back to LS.

"Well?" he said, slamming it down.

"Nine hundred," I replied.

"Thousand?"

"Of course." I opened a cabinet overhead and pulled out a cardboard beer carton labeled OLD MILWAUKEE, which I placed on the dinette table Old Lady had vacated. I opened it to reveal stacks and stacks of hundred-dollar bills.

"I ain't got time to count this," LS. said. He put the box on the scale to weigh it. "That looks like nine hundred grand, all right. Who you puttin' it on?"

"Hell, I don't know," I said. I took a quarter out of my pocket, flipped it, caught it, smacked it on the back of my left hand, looked at it, and said, "Jack Diamond."

LS shook his head and made a note on the pad he took from his pocket. Now I had given Zeller the information he needed to make his bet. I could hear the gears of greed talking to him inside that thick skull of his: the pocket cameras had told us this really was the last bet of the championship and that Jack Diamond was about to win the crown.

LS tucked his notepad back into his pocket. "You put that kind of money on a coin flip?"

"Sir," I said, "that's chump change to a rock star like me. I'm about to go in there, play a few songs, and land a multimillion-dollar contract for my next album. I can't lose." I backhanded Zeller on the shoulder. "Good luck, Arch. I'll see you in the parking lot later." I hustled on out of the bus.

"I'll be waiting with your ex-girlfriend, Choirboy!"

I heard Mona giggle as the door closed. "Oh, Wildcat!"

I was really looking forward to taking a couple of punches at that windbag, and I knew the time was fast approaching.

35

YOU CANT imagine all the distractions I had going on in my head when I stepped onto that stage: Mona, Zeller, Dorothy, Morris, McLeod, Rudolph, Dan and his scheme . . . But I hadn't lied to Dorothy when I told her that I worked well under pressure. We were about to play eleven three-minute songs for Morris. That had to be the all-absorbing focus of my life right now.

I knew better than to even try to think about the eleven songs at once. The first song was called "No Time to Linger." As I strapped on my guitar under the cool stares of my band members, I thought only about the intro to the tune. The rest would follow.

"Here we go," I said to my bandmates.

There was a local deejay on the stage who had been given the task of introducing us. I nodded at him.

"Ladies and gentlemen . . . ," he began, using Warren's microphone.

I shifted my eyes to Mojo behind the kick drum. I shot him a cocky grin.

". . . KIKK radio and Gilley's Club present . . . the world debut of Ronnie Breed and the Truebloods!"

Mojo clicked the tempo, and with rock star urgency I struck my first chord with the band. Instantly, I felt that my rhythm guitar was magically playing every instrument onstage. The neon beer sign lights blurred and swirled into a paisley whirlwind. No, I was not hallucinating on drugs. I was high on the power of music, the energy of a well-rehearsed band.

I remember thinking: *Screw Morris Witherspoon. He can't do what I'm doing. I was born to wield this power. He's not the only promoter in the business.* And that was just the attitude I needed. I attacked the microphone with my vocals and heard the speakers belt my voice through that cavernous tabernacle of twang.

We rammed that first country rocker down the listeners' throats, took a breath or two as they applauded, and mercilessly piled into song number two—a pounding dance tune that shamed anyone in the building who had failed to learn how to two-step. There was a four-voice harmony part in the chorus that made the eyes of the dancers bulge as they scooted and whirled past the stage. When they heard our vocal blend, their jaws dropped, then sprang back, lifting their mouths into stunned smiles.

We stepped back a notch on the third tune—a belly-rubbing belt-buckle polisher for the dancers called "Let 'Em Dance Around Us." It came off as smooth as honey in the sunshine, with the band singing background oohs and ahhs so precisely that they sounded better than the demos over which we had fretted in the studio.

Four, five, six . . . Our songs just kept shaking the steel girders of that fabled honky-tonk. I saw a beer can at my feet vibrating like a cartoon alarm clock. When my eyes focused beyond it, I now noticed that half the dancers had released their partners to crowd the stage shoulder to shoulder, wide-eyed, trying to gather in our juggernaut of electric vibes. Our ascension was no accident. We had juggled the set list through two days of rehearsals to find this hypnotic sequence of grooves, tones, textures, and tempos. It was working on the crowd even better than we had planned, and carrying the band to unexpected heights of euphoria.

Seven, eight, nine, ten . . . Not one tune missed. We could do no wrong.

"What do you think about the Truebloods?" I yelled, addressing the crowd for the first time since stepping onto the stage. I waited for the lengthy roar of approval to fade. "That's Warren Warren on the fiddle, Henry Campos on bass, Mojo Stevens back there on the drums. And on that amazing blues-rock-country guitar, the great Slim Musselwhite!"

Again, I waited for the listeners to vent their approval. "I'm Ronnie Breed," I said quietly. "Now, folks, we have a special guest in the audience: Major Morris Witherspoon, of Silver Spoon Records."

The spotlight found Morris, who waved to a smattering of applause. Dorothy was beside him, shading her eyes from the glare.

"Morris, I believe you requested a waltz. We've got one for you here, appropriately titled for *The World Championship of Texas Hold 'Em Poker*. It's called 'What Are the Chances.'"

I nodded and the band followed Mojo's tempo into the song. We had argued about this in rehearsal—ending with a slow waltz—but I had insisted, claiming it was Morris's peculiar request to hear the waltz last. In reality, I was playing this song because we knew—we being Dan, Mona, and I, among others—we knew from our research that the only type of dance Archie Zeller could pull off was a slow dance. And, I needed him out here on the floor at this moment for reasons that will soon become obvious.

Morris led Dorothy out onto the wood parquet floor to dance, both of them waltzing beautifully. She looked at me, not sure what to think of me. That was good. I had her off balance again, instead of the other way around. I sang to her as the lyrics fell smoothly into the meter:

What are the chances of you giving me one more chance?
What are the odds that you'd even consider a dance?
I lost a bet with your heart.
I was a fool from the start.
What are the chances of you giving me one more chance?

She smiled at me, as if to say the chances were pretty good. Morris and Dorothy disappeared behind a growing sea of cowboy hats on the dance floor. I looked for Zeller and Mona now, knowing Mona would be leading Zeller into position in front of the stage. The band modulated smoothly to a higher key. . . .

What was I thinking when I placed a bet with your love?
I should have held you as close as a hand in a glove.

As close as a heart to the vest
The hand that I held was the best.
What was I thinking when I placed a bet with your love?

There was a lead instrumental break here, beginning with War-ren's fiddle and wrapping up with Slim's guitar. Then we modulated again, and I repeated the first verse. Mona caught my eye whilst dancing a jerky waltz with Zeller. Her hand was on his back. She signaled to me with a thumbs-up sign, then flashed two fingers. I knew very well what this meant. It meant that Zeller had made his bet in the bus, and he had bet not one, but two million dollars.

What a greedy so-and-so, I thought. He just had to have a bigger slice of the winner-takes-all pie. His thinking was that I had put in only nine hundred grand. If he put in two million, he would win proportionately, taking more than two-thirds of the hospitality room pot. You could see the cocksure look on his face, not only because he had bested me with the pot, but because he really believed that he was in the process of stealing my girlfriend, too. Man, was he in for a surprise.

The song ended. Mona grabbed Zeller by the hip pocket, stood on her tiptoes, and placed her mouth on his right in front of where I stood on the stage. This was it. I racked my guitar.

"Oh, shit," Slim said, knowing what I had to do to save face in this redneck crowd.

"Zeller!" I shouted into the mic. "You no-account so-and-so. She may be on her way out, but she's still my girlfriend."

Mona's kiss had pushed Zeller's cocksucker hat onto the side of his head. He looked at me strangely, charged with greed and lust, lipstick smeared on his mouth. As my spotlight widened to take him in, he raised his right fist, clenched, then deployed his middle finger like a switchblade.

"Screw you, Choirboy!" he said.

The crowd made a collective gasp, followed by an ominous groan.

I dropped from the stage like a paratrooper on D-Day. Mona backed away into the crowd, giving me a wry smile, but I dared not react to her. Instead, I walked up to Zeller and, without a word of warning, re-smeared the lipstick on his shit-eating grin with a left jab followed by a right hook that sent him and his cocksucker hat flying backwards into some witless, drunken cowboys.

The cowboys stumbled domino-like into some hard-bitten rough-necks just off some rig, spilling their beers. From there, the fight spread like the ripples from a hand grenade tossed into a pool of jet fuel. It took only a few seconds for Gilley's to erupt like a refinery blast inside a sealed tank of crude. Men cursed and girls screamed; then the din of the mushrooming brawl transmogrified into the gnashing and howling sounds of hellhounds escaped from the gates of Hades.

I looked back at the stage and saw that a trio of bouncers had jumped between the melee and the Truebloods to protect the band. When I turned back around, I saw that Zeller—who was not ex-actly a stranger to bar fights—had collected himself and was rushing me faster than I had planned. He managed to graze the side of my head with a roundhouse punch, but I fended him off with Marine Corps hand-to-hand tactics that Dan had drilled into me during regular sessions all summer long.

Finding my feet squarely under me, I readied my defenses for his next assault. It was a pathetic, slow-motion attempt to grab my shirt and pound me with a meaty right ham. I was so charged with dislike for the sorry old slant-driller that I believe to this day that I could have crushed his skull with a mean right cross. Instead, I took it easy on him with a trio of jabs, a hook, and an uppercut that knocked him out cold. He fell back onto the stage like a sack of rot-ten spuds, his head landing right between Sherwood Cryer's Nike running shoes.

Sherwood reached for my hand and pulled me out of the pits of hell and up onto the stage. I looked across the barroom brawl and saw Morris using a pool cue to clear his way to the side door with Dorothy in tow. Relief began to bathe me like a total-immersion baptism. It was almost over. I was almost free! The film crew and some of the bouncers were rushing the cameras and poker tables out of the dance hall through the side door.

Standing beside me on the stage, Sherwood elbowed me. "Better roll him over, or he'll choke on his own blood!" the honky-tonk owner shouted over the noise, pointing down at Zeller's bloody face.

I got my boot under Zeller's shoulder and flipped him onto his side.

Sherwood then pulled his .38 autoloader out of the pocket of his jumpsuit and sent three shots into the cedar-paneled walls. Nothing rings louder than a pistol shot in a honky-tonk, but a few brawlers fought on, so Sherwood aimed at a neon beer light and shattered it with a bullet, sending glass and sparks raining down on the last trouble spot.

He grabbed my microphone and said, "Everybody clear out! The police are on the way!"

The evacuation, while not orderly, was swift. Those who could not walk out were dragged out by friends.

Meanwhile, I turned to the band. "Y'all hightail it out the side door. I'll call you all tomorrow to let you know if we have a record deal or not."

Slim shook his head and chuckled. "Well, Rawn, if you don't get the record deal, maybe you could go pro in the ring." He tossed his guitar pick down on the prostrate form of Archie Zeller.

"That was badass, Ronnie," Mojo added.

Warren tucked his fiddle case under his arm. "I hope we didn't scare Major Witherspoon back to Nashville. But if we did . . . hell, who wants a promoter who scares that easy? We'll catch you on the flip-flop."

Henry patted me on the back. "That was a short brawl, Ronnie, but I wouldn't have missed it for the biggest contract in music history. See you tomorrow, win or lose."

When the band and the crowd had cleared out, I found myself alone inside the dance hall with Sherwood Cryer and Archie Zeller. Everyone else was gone. Poker players, film crew—gone. Morris and Dorothy, Dan and Mona—all gone. The drinkers, the dancers, the brawlers, the bouncers—vanished. Even the poker tables and the TV cameras had been loaded out and hauled off somewhere. It had all happened with military precision.

Sherwood fetched a plastic mop bucket full of water.

I stretched out beside Zeller and braced myself for the bucket of water Sherwood poured mostly in Zeller's face, saving enough for me to make it look good.

Zeller gasped, coughed, and sat up. The look of confusion on his face was priceless. When he looked at me, I rubbed the back of my head as if I had been waylaid from behind.

"The cops are on the way!" Sherwood yelled at us, waving his pistol in our faces. "You two bums get the hell out of here, or I'll tell them about your little gambling den on wheels out there!"

Zeller's eyes bulged. Greed became the smelling salts beneath his nose. "My money!" he said. He got up, stumbled, rallied, and trotted toward the side door.

I followed. The bus door was open outside.

"Shit!" Zeller said. Like a junkie scrambling for his fix, he clawed his way onto the bus. I was right behind him. The door to my bunk in the back of the bus was open. The bed covers had been thrown aside. The safe door was open. The safe was empty.

"Where's my money!" Zeller roared.

When he turned on me, he found the crazed look on my face that I had rehearsed in the mirror time and time again, all summer long. "You sorry son of a bitch," I said. I threw open an overhead cabinet door inside my cushy tour bus and pulled out an old Colt revolver I carried around for protection. I pointed the pistol at Zeller's face and stalked toward him for what he must have thought was going to be a point-blank shot.

"What are you doing?" he said, backpedaling until he fell down on his rear and rolled back with his hands and arms shielding his face.

"You were in on it!" I yelled. "You old con man, you were part of this from the start!"

"I swear I wasn't!" he cried. "They got me, too, remember? They took me for two million!"

I cocked the pistol. "I don't believe you! You're a dead man!"

"It wasn't me! I swear! It was Dan! It was Dan! Think about it!"

I had done a few B movies, but this was my finest role. "Think about my bullet slamming into your brain, motherf—"

"No, wait. Where's Mona? Think about it. You said Dan introduced you to Mona. Where the hell is she now?"

"Mona?" I said vacantly, as if I were as woozy and greed-crazed as Zeller himself.

"She was in on it. She played us both for a couple of fools. Where's the TV crew? The other gamblers? They were all in on it. Don't kill me! They got me, too, Breed!"

In the distance I heard a siren. "I'm gonna tell the cops!" I said.

"You can't! I took money from my payroll account. That's a federal offense! Don't tell the cops, Breed! We'll both go to jail."

"Shit!" My eyes shifted crazily, as if looking for an answer. I waved him toward the door. "Get off my bus before I kill you!"

He scrambled past me on all fours like a dog and tumbled down the steps to the gravel parking lot. I started the bus and looked down the gun sights at him one more time. "If I ever find out you were in on this," I said, "I'll send people to kill you. And it won't be a pleasant death, either."

"I ain't in on it, Breed! They got me, too, goddamn-it!"

I shut the door and drove away. In the mirror I could see him trying to run toward his Cadillac, weaving and stumbling as he fled. I pulled out onto the Spencer Highway and checked my speed. There were no lights tailing me. The police car had turned into Gilley's. I took a deep breath or two. One of my favorite Johnny Cash tapes was playing in the dashboard-mounted eight-track player. I grinned. Then, like a prisoner freed from Folsom, I began to laugh.

36

BY NOW you realize that I haven't been completely honest with you in the telling of my tale. I haven't told any outright lies, but I have omitted quite a number of details. My apologies for that, but I figured it would make a better story if you knew only as much as Archie Zeller knew, up until the final act.

Directly, I'll enlighten you on all the details of how and why we did it—how we swindled Archie Zeller out of two million dollars. And I'll explain who "we" were, and why we took such a chance, and what we did with the money. But first, I've got to tell you about the aftermath the next day.

My mother woke me at the farm about 6 A.M. "Ronnie, honey, there's a phone call for you. You better wake up and take this one."

"Is it the police?" I said groggily.

She laughed. "No, it's Dorothy. Come take her call, honey."

"Well, I don't quite believe this," Dorothy said, her voice as cold and hard as steel, "but Morris actually had the time of his life."

"You're kidding."

"He loved the Truebloods showcase. He wants to hear the tapes."

"I'll be there in thirty minutes."

I got dressed and drove my mom's Buick Riviera to the hotel where Morris and Dorothy were staying.

Morris greeted me warmly in the lobby. "My life is now complete!" he gushed. "I've always wanted to fight my way out of a honky-tonk!"

"You picked the biggest honky-tonk in the world to fulfill your ambition," I said, smiling.

"I tend to do things in a big way, Ronnie."

Dorothy was much less giddy. "Let's go," she said. "I'm catching the first flight home as soon as you drop Morris at the studio."

We drove to the studio I had arranged as a listening room for Morris. I sat him down in the air-conditioned control room, mixed a mimosa for him with hand-squeezed orange juice and Dom Pérignon champagne, pressed the play button on the reel-to-reel tape machine, and left. Dorothy had waited in the car.

"Dorothy, I can explain everything," I said as I stepped back into the car.

"I don't want to hear it," she snapped. "I've already negotiated the contract for you, like I promised, but after Morris signs, you'll have to find another manager."

"Dorothy, listen, please. Things are going to really settle down now. It's all over—the poker tournament, the TV pilot, Mona . . . They're all in the past. . . ."

"Ronnie, the day I met you, you gave me some advice that I'm now going to take to heart. You said not to mess with a client who can't stay out of trouble. Your exact words were, and I quote—" She took a deep breath. "—'Don't ever take any crap off a temperamental, prima donna, exhibitionist glory hound who thinks he possesses a voice that is God's own gift to the human ear. He's not worth it.' "

"I said that?"

"Word for word."

"Well, I'm the only exception to that rule."

"Your picture is in the rule book next to that rule! Take me to the airport."

"You've got to let me explain, Dorothy. I can guarantee you that there will be no more surprises."

"Take me to the airport before I start hollering *rape*!"

I started the car and drove, but I did not head for the airport. As we got farther into the countryside, Dorothy became more suspicious.

"I don't see any aircraft in the vicinity, Ronnie," she said angrily. "Where are we going?"

"I want you to meet somebody. Then, if you want, I'll take you to the airport."

I turned into an unpaved ranch entrance flanked by barbed-wire fences and drove through an open gate. At the end of the half-mile-long oyster-shell driveway, I saw a collection of cars and trucks, and a familiar old farmhouse.

"What are we doing here?" she demanded.

I stopped the Buick halfway between the paved road and the farmhouse. "I want to introduce you to my uncle Bubba."

"Why?"

"He was our father figure, for both me and my cousin Dan."

"Dan's your cousin?"

I nodded. "Uncle Bubba pretty much raised us."

"He didn't do a very good job," she said.

"In 1962, my uncle was swindled out of several million dollars of mineral rights—oil royalties. It was a slant-drilling scam. The guy who cheated him out of all that money was Archie Zeller."

This intrigued her. "The ugly cigar-chewer from the poker tournament?"

"The same. Uncle Bubba never told us about the swindle until a few years ago. Then, last year, his heart began to fail. My uncle needs a heart transplant. If he doesn't get it, he'll be dead in a year. But he can't afford it and he won't take charity, from me or anybody else. He's old-school that way. He told Dan and me that he was seriously thinking about hunting down Zeller and shooting him dead for all the misery he had caused people over the years, and we were afraid he was really going to do it. Dan simply came up with a better idea."

Her beautiful eyes narrowed on me. "You're not making this up, are you?"

I shook my head. "Archie Zeller grew up the son of two flimflam artists, before he started the slant-drilling scheme. He was a con man. We conned the con man. We took two million dollars off him yesterday. We did it to save our uncle Bubba, not for ourselves."

She looked dubious. "How much was your cut?"

"Zero. Dan, too. Uncle Bubba is taking what he needs for the heart transplant. We're donating a hundred thousand to the De-Bakey Heart and Vascular Center. The professional con artists are splitting the rest."

She looked me up and down. "And who were these professional con artists?"

"An international team of swindlers Dan recruited."

"How does one recruit such a team?"

"Dan was in prison in Colombia for smuggling guns to the anti-communist freedom fighters. That's where he met Luis Sebastian, the leader of the team. Luis had gotten caught trying to con some corrupt communist officials down there. Luis is the most legendary con artist in all of South America."

"I take it Luis Sebastian is not his real name."

"You catch on quick. You can meet everybody now if you want to. Or perhaps you'd rather I take you to the airport."

She looked over her shoulder, back down the oyster-shell road to the blacktop. She then glanced forward toward the farmhouse. She sighed. "You piece of crap," she said. "You knew I'd be intrigued."

I put the car in gear, but kept my foot on the brake. "I've got to swear you to secrecy about all this."

"You're taking quite a chance doing this."

"There's only one reason I'd take such a chance."

She smirked. "The contract with Morris."

"No, you idiot!" I pounded my palm on the steering wheel. "I'm in love with you, damn-it!"

This clearly shocked her, for her mouth hung open in a most attractive way. Her eyes welled up with tears that she held back. She smiled. "I promise to keep your secret a secret."

I stepped on the gas and drove up to the house. Dorothy followed me up onto the front porch, and I opened the screen door for her.

"Let me handle this, and just play along," I said.

She nodded.

"Hey, Dan!" I yelled.

"Come on back to the kitchen, Cuz!"

Keeping Dorothy behind me, I walked through the living room and peeked into the kitchen. There, I saw stacks of cash on the kitchen table. Luis was doing the counting. Uncle Bubba was sitting at the end of the table with a cup of Sanka, quietly telling a story for the amusement of Dan, Mona, Daniela, Bartholomew, and three cameramen. The Vegas dealers, who were not aware of the confidence scam we had been running, had already been paid their agreed-upon fee.

Uncle Bubba finished his story, causing his listeners to throw their heads back in laughter. I stepped in.

"There he is!" Dan said, spreading his palms to present me to the team.

To my surprise, they all broke into applause. I went in to hug my uncle, who had tears streaming down his face.

"You're a lifesaver, nephew." He gripped me with all the strength he could muster. "I love you."

"Not bad for an amateur!" Mona said.

"I have a surprise for you, Uncle Bubba. There's someone I want you to meet."

A hush fell over the team of con men. I gathered that they didn't like surprises at this point, but I went ahead.

"Dorothy," I called.

She stepped boldly into the doorway, tossing her hair back over her shoulder. She smiled, and her mouth lit up the whole room.

"Amateur is right!" said Bartholomew. "You brought somebody here to see this!"

"It's all right, I've been sworn to secrecy," Dorothy said reassuringly. She came around the kitchen table to offer her hand to Uncle Bubba.

He smiled at her. "Darlin', a handshake just won't do. You give me a hug, now, you hear!" He even got up out of his chair, with my help, to embrace Dorothy.

"You didn't get up for me," I said, feigning a complaint.

"This was a bad idea," Luis said, the cash evidence spread before him.

"Cuz, you should have asked me about this," Dan lectured.

"Dan, I'm qualified to make my own decisions. Now, I would appreciate it if you'd give my guest a more hospitable welcome to our boyhood haunts."

"Well!" he replied. He came around the table. "Welcome, Dorothy." He offered her a hug, which she accepted.

"I don't like this!" Bartholomew sang.

"We'll all be out of the country in an hour anyway," Dan said, looking at his watch.

I knew he was right. There was a chartered jet waiting on a private airstrip not far away.

"She doesn't even know your real names," I said.

"And I don't want to," Dorothy added.

"You've got to prove your complicity," Luis said. "We don't want Interpol hunting us down all over the globe."

"I won't tell," Dorothy promised. "Or rat, or sing, or whatever the term is in your field."

"How can we be sure?" one of the cameramen asked. "She's seen our faces."

"Make her take some of the money," Jack Diamond suggested.

"Oh, shut up!" Mona yelled. "Can't you see? She's not going to get our Ronnie-boy in any trouble. Haven't you noticed her face over the past weeks? She's in love with this amateur! She wouldn't snitch if they tortured her."

They all stared at Dorothy suspiciously.

"Here, I'll prove it," Dorothy said. She turned to me and took my hand. "Ronnie-honey. I'm in love with you. I fell in love with you the moment I met you, and I've only fallen deeper in love with you every second, in spite of this ridiculous summer. How could I not protect a man who would take such a risk to save his dear uncle's life? Ronnie . . . I love you, and I will always love you."

I felt a stupid smile stretch across my face; then Dorothy kissed me, right there in front of everybody. I lost track of time, but when I came back around, the professionals were still looking at Dorothy and me with lingering doubts.

"Okay," Dorothy said to the gathering in the kitchen, "let me put it in terms *y'all* can appreciate." She turned back toward me.

"Ronnie, you know I'd never talk about this day to anyone. It would jeopardize your career, and that would jeopardize *my* career. As your manager, I'm going to get filthy rich, and nothing is going to stand between me and my money!"

"See, I told you she was all right!" Mona said. "I liked you from the get-go, sister! Sorry about the rat-tailed comb."

"No harm done," Dorothy said.

Mona continued: "You know Ronnie and I were just pretending to be boyfriend and girlfriend, don't you? We had separate rooms. We never *did it* or anything."

"Not that it would matter," Dorothy said, stepping closer to me and slipping her hand behind my back. "He's all mine now."

"He's not even my type," Mona continued. "Twenty-four hours from now, I'll be shacked up with some Latin beach bum with tattoos and buns you could bounce a gold ducat off of."

"I just have one question," Dorothy said. "Where are the others?"

"What others?" Dan said, a smirk on his face. "We're all here."

"What about the hospitality room? What about Leisure Suit, and Old Lady?"

Dan affected his Afro-personality. "We don't use names here!" he growled.

"You were LS?" Dorothy said, shocked at the thought.

"With a Sly Stone wig and some movie-grade makeup applied by Mona."

"What about Old Lady?"

Dan pointed at Bartholomew.

"Want some peanuts, sonny?" the erstwhile director cackled.

"Nobody does drag like Bartholomew," Mona said.

Dorothy put her palms on her face and laughed.

"With the help of some disguises, the off-duty cameramen also doubled as high-rolling bettors in the hospitality room," I explained. "That way, they don't have to split the take so many ways."

"Speaking of which," Luis said, standing at the kitchen table. "It's time to collect our earnings. There's an equal stack for everyone."

"Ladies and gentlemen, we got away with it!" Dan announced. "Good thing, too, or we'd all be going to jail for a long, long time—"

The back door to the kitchen flew open and Bruno Marques burst into the room, his large-caliber autoloader leading the way. "FBI! Nobody move!" he ordered in a loud, guttural yell.

Panic almost made my heart burst as Bruno scowled at me over the gun sights. How could this happen? How could we have been so stupid? I was going to jail, and worst of all, I had dragged Dorothy into it.

Then Bruno started laughing. "You ought to see the look on your face!"

Everyone in the room but Dorothy and me burst into guffaws.

"Sorry, Cuz," Dan said. "When I saw you pull up, I couldn't resist. I sent Bruno out the back door so he could jump back in and *surprise* you."

"Damn-it, Dan!" My relief overwhelmed my anger, and I had to chuckle. "You told me Bruno was legit!"

"Legit bullshit," Bruno admitted.

"Hey, I had to get some real emotion out of you in front of Zeller. I wasn't sure I could rely totally on your acting skills. I wanted him to see you worried when Bruno showed up, and I wanted him to see you relieved when we got our FBI stamp of approval."

As the con artists poked fun at me and picked up their pay, the phone rang.

"Now, who could that be?" Uncle Bubba asked.

"It's probably for me," I replied, stepping over to the phone on the kitchen wall. "I gave Morris this number." I grabbed the phone in the middle of the second ring. "Hello, this is Ronnie."

"Ronnie. Morris. I've listened twice. I really don't care when you come to get me. I could listen to these sides for hours. But I want to hammer out a deal today."

"That's the second-best news I've heard all day, Morris." I looked at Dorothy and telegraphed the good news to her with my smile. "Dorothy and I will be there in an hour. We've got to say good-bye to some friends first."

I hung up the phone. The money had been divvied. The swindlers were shaking Uncle Bubba's hand, and heading outside to the vehicles.

"Good luck," Mona said to Dorothy and me.

Luis stepped up to Dan and looked him in the eye. He glanced at Dorothy, and back at Dan. "You trust her?"

"I do," Dan said. "Ronnie trusts her, and I trust him more than anyone in the world, except for Uncle Bubba, here."

Luis smiled. "Good enough for me. Let's go."

There was a stack of cash on the table for Uncle Bubba's transplant. Dorothy shoved it aside and sat by my beloved uncle—my father, for all practical purposes.

"Let's get better acquainted, Uncle Bubba," Dorothy said, pulling a chair up to the table.

"I'm going outside to see Dan off," I said. As I stood beside Dorothy, she slipped her palm into mine and lifted it to her lips to kiss the back of my hand.

37

SO, YOU may be wondering about the poker tournament. Was it real? Well—yes and no. When Dan first conceived the con that would con the con man, he designed it to appeal to the mark, Archie Zeller. Zeller liked poker, and he liked to celebrate his infamy. The televised tournament was the perfect vehicle to draw him in, especially since we convinced him that he could make a lot of money by getting involved.

You remember the back-alley Houston poker game in the empty warehouse where we first hooked Zeller? Remember Ralph, Ramón, and Benny? Those roles were played by Luis, Jack, and Bartholomew. It was Jack Diamond, disguised as the Mexican, Ramón, who pulled the gun on Zeller. Dan had backhanded him against the wall, if you recall. But Dan had pulled his punch, and Jack had bitten down on a capsule full of fake blood to make the whole thing look real. We made it look as if Zeller possibly owed his life to Dan. That was part of the bait we used to hook Zeller.

We used other bait, too: money, Mona, fame, more money. . . .

You see, even before Dan contacted Luis Sebastian to enlist him and his team of con men and con women, he sat down and planned *The World Championship Series of Texas Hold 'Em Poker*, starring Archie Zeller, in detail. Dan had worked some CIA operations where all manner of fake businesses had to be set up, so he had some experience with these things. When Dan got onto a project like this one, he didn't sleep much. He just worked and worked, planned and schemed, hustled and connived.

He wrote contracts, drew up set designs, printed out timetables, designed a logo. Except for the fact that the cameras were not even shooting, it was pretty damn real. The cameramen were really con men. There was no videotape in the cameras. The pocket cams under the championship poker table didn't even function. The video of the poker games that we watched up in the hospitality room had been staged and shot beforehand. It wasn't live at all.

And, speaking of the hospitality room, what about those phone calls I received from Dan, telling me which way to bet? Totally fake. The phone wasn't even hooked up to anything. It was just a prop for me to talk into. Dan wasn't at the other end. He was standing right beside me, in disguise as the hospitality room host known as "Leisure Suit." LS made the fake phone ring by stepping on a hidden switch on the floor.

You may also be wondering why I—as a successful rock star—didn't just give my uncle Bubba the money he needed for his heart transplant. First of all, Uncle Bubba would never have let me do that unless he was in a coma. Secondly, I was broke. I was a creative guy, and a hit songwriter, but I was not managed well before I met Dorothy. I had made some idiotic investments and lost my shirt on a bunch of nonsense. I simply didn't have the money to help Uncle Bubba when his problem was diagnosed. I didn't have ten thousand to invest in the poker tournament. I never owned a lakeside house in Tahoe. My bus fleet in '75 amounted to one bus. I was all but broke.

The only other recourse would have been to sell Uncle Bubba's ranch, plus my mom's place on the bayou, and my aunt's place, but Uncle Bubba wouldn't hear of that, either. Those places had been in the family for generations, and he wouldn't see them sold to fund a high-risk surgical procedure that might not even work.

So, Dan—who was much more creative than I ever was, but in different ways—dreamed up an alternative plan—the poker tournament. Then he contacted Luis, who had escaped from prison by that time and was back in Brazil. Together, the two of them perfected the swindle that is now known as the Hospitality Room Scam, and is still in use by con artists around the world.

About Sherwood Cryer, the co-owner of Gilley's: I have no idea how much he knew about what we were doing. That was between Dan and Sherwood. Dan was Sherwood's favorite bouncer. Sherwood probably just agreed to go along with whatever Dan said to do and didn't ask a whole bunch of questions. Sherwood would do just about anything to sell dance hall tickets.

But—you may be wondering—why would I, with everything I had going for me in the music world, take such a risk? If the thing had gone wrong, I could have gone to prison, right? Probably not. Dan had insisted that if Zeller got wise and blew the whistle on us, he would cop to swindling Zeller and me, both. He would plead guilty to conning his own cousin and take the rap. Dan had been in a couple of prisons abroad. He did not fear an American lockup. He bragged there was no prison that could hold him for more than a couple of years, anyway.

"If it goes bad, I'll do a little time, and escape," he had boasted.

I did not doubt Dan. The risk to me, personally, was rather minimal. I trusted Dan that much. So you can imagine how mortified I was for those few seconds after Bruno Marques burst into Uncle Bubba's house as the con men were splitting up the loot. At that point, I was still convinced that Bruno was indeed a Special Agent for the FBI. He had been listening to our conversation outside the farmhouse, and had caught us all red-handed—including me. The sickening feeling in the pit of my stomach that I felt for those few seconds scared me straighter than a tight guitar string for the rest of my life. Not that I would have ever gotten into any other kind of serious trouble, but I haven't even let a library fine or a parking ticket go unpaid since that day!

As for my career, you know the rest, if you're any kind of music fan at all. We didn't go back into the studio to record our first record for Silver Spoon Records. We didn't have to. Morris loved the raw energy from the demos, and wouldn't let us cut the songs a second time. The album was already in the can. His record label took the Truebloods immediately to the top of the charts, which we continued to visit through the next three decades. And when I say "charts," I mean that in the plural sense. The pop charts, the country charts, the rock charts, the folk charts, the alternative charts—we topped them all.

After his public embarrassment over Rudolph's photos taken at Gilley's, Joe McLeod joined Alcoholics Anonymous and got permanently straight and sober. As I mentioned, he went on to a solid career in the Christian music business. He and I mended fences and have been friendly ever since. He even filled in on a Truebloods tour once, when Henry was in the hospital recovering from an emergency appendectomy.

Archie Zeller? He never made a peep about his loss in the swindle. I think he was afraid of me, of Dan, of Sherwood, of the IRS. He still had a few million to live on the rest of his miserable life. He died alone, twenty-one years after the summer of '75.

I never saw any of the professional con artists again, but I can't help thinking about them—particularly Mona.

Rudolph Richards had the retraction printed in the *Inquisitor,* as he promised. I gave him exclusive rights to photograph my wedding with Dorothy in the spring of '76. Morris walked Dorothy down the aisle. It was the celebrity wedding of the decade. Thirty years, two sons, and five grandchildren later, Dorothy and I are still madly in love. We've had a tiff or two over the years, but nothing that didn't lead to an equally passionate makeup.

Immediately after Uncle Bubba got hold of a small portion of his rightful oil royalties denied to him by Zeller, he got his name placed on the transplant list. A few weeks later, a state trooper was killed when a car struck him on the side of the road. He was handing a warning ticket to a driver when it happened. The officer had signed up to be an organ donor. His heart was strong. He gave my uncle Bubba over seven years of peaceful retirement that he otherwise would not have lived to enjoy.

God bless organ donors.

Dan disappeared for a while, but would come and go unexpectedly, dropping in once a year or so to visit Dorothy and me, or Uncle Bubba. I think he was a spy. He retired to Texas in 2000. I've mentioned his unfortunate but fitting demise on the Padre Island causeway, just a few days after 9/11. But he's not really dead. Dan, too, was an organ donor. His heart still beats in the body of a gentleman who lives in Florida.

Dorothy and I don't talk about *The World Championship Series of Texas Hold 'Em Poker* much, unless we're reminiscing in private. It seems like a dream or a movie or something. For a few months, reporters would ask about the card-game TV pilot I had shot. There had been an unfortunate fire in the editing room, I would say, and most of the tapes had been destroyed. Soon, people just forgot about the whole thing.

A couple of years later, however, I noticed that one of the major networks—I think it was CBS—aired the final round of the World Series of Poker. Did they get the idea from Dan's fake pilot? Who knows? But over the years, poker continued to crop up on television from time to time.

Then, on a winter afternoon at home in our mansion outside Nashville in 2003, Dorothy and I snuggled up on the couch to do some rare channel surfing during an overdue break in our busy lives.

"We almost never go couch potato," she said, pushing the channel button about once per second as she sifted through the insipid offerings of a couple of hundred satellite networks.

"You're much too sweet to be a couch potato, anyway," I said. "You're a sweet potato. You're my little sofa yam, that's what you are." I started nibbling on her neck.

Dorothy even giggled with a drawl. Suddenly, though, she gasped. "Oh, my Gawd!" she said.

I looked at her, then followed her astonished gaze to the huge TV screen on the wall of our living room. There, I saw a pocket cam revealing the hole cards of some poker player in a Vegas showdown!

"Is that hold 'em?" I said.

"It is!" my wife replied. "The dealer just threw down the flop!"

My mind drifted back to that day outside Uncle Bubba's farmhouse. While Dorothy got acquainted with my beloved uncle, I had gone outside to wave good-bye to the con team convoy leaving the ranch, and to give Dan a brotherly hug.

"You know something, Cuz," I said. "That danged hold 'em idea attracted more of a following than I ever expected. You don't think we really could have pitched that show to a network, do you?"

Dan rubbed his chin. "It did look like it was gonna take off there for a while," he agreed. Then he chuckled that old cocksure laugh of his as he jingled his car keys impatiently in his hand. "Nah! Who are we kiddin'? Texas hold 'em on TV? Who'd want to watch *that*?"